BRINK OF DESTRUCTION

Captain Olenowski looked over at Murdock. "We'll know if our ship is there soon. If she is, what's the next step?"

"We can't blow her out of the water and drop all that plutonium just off Majuro. Somehow we have to board her, take down the pirates, and regain control of the ten tons of plutonium."

The captain lifted his brows. "Right now I'm glad that's your job, Commander. Sounds like somebody could get hurt."

"We hope it's only the bad guys who pick up the bullet holes, Captain. We train for this almost every day."

A moment later, a scratchy voice came into the CIC.

"Not sure who I'm talking to. My name is Keanae. I'm on board the *Willowwind*. We're anchored at some small island. And I'm in deep trouble here." Before he could say anything else, they heard two gunshots sound over the radio.

Then the transmission cut off.

SEAL TEAM SEVEN
ATTACK MODE

KEITH DOUGLASS

BERKLEY BOOKS, NEW YORK

Special thanks to Chet Cunningham for his contributions to this book.

This is a work of fiction. Names, characters, places, and incidents either are the product of the author's imagination or are used fictitiously, and any resemblance to actual persons, living or dead, business establishments, events, or locales is entirely coincidental.

SEAL TEAM SEVEN: ATTACK MODE

A Berkley Book / published by arrangement with the author

PRINTING HISTORY
Berkley edition / November 2003

Copyright © 2003 by The Berkley Publishing Group
SEAL TEAM SEVEN logo illustration by Michael Racz.

For information address: The Berkley Publishing Group,
a division of Penguin Group (USA) Inc.,
375 Hudson Street, New York, New York 10014.

ISBN: 0-425-19323-3

BERKLEY®
Berkley Books are published by The Berkley Publishing Group,
a division of Penguin Group (USA) Inc.,
375 Hudson Street, New York, New York 10014.
BERKLEY and the "B'' design
are trademarks belonging to Penguin Group (USA) Inc.

PRINTED IN THE UNITED STATES OF AMERICA

10 9 8 7 6 5 4 3 2 1

Dedicated with humility
To those courageous men and women
In the armed forces
Who have made the ultimate
Sacrifice and have given their lives
To the cause of freedom in the
Fight against terrorism
And all
Of its demented atrocities.

SEAL TEAM SEVEN

THIRD PLATOON*
CORONADO, CALIFORNIA

Rear Admiral (L) Richard Kenner. Commander of All SEALs. Based in Little Creek, Virginia.

Captain Harry L. Arjarack. Commanding Officer of NAVSPECWARGRUP-ONE, in Coronado, California. 51.

Commander Dean Masciareli. Commanding officer of Navy Special Warfare Group One's SEAL Team Seven in Coronado, California. 47, 5' 11", 220 pounds. Annapolis graduate.

Master Chief Petty Officer Gordon MacKenzie. Administrator and head enlisted man of all of SEAL Teams in Coronado. 47, 5' 10", 180 pounds.

Lieutenant Commander Blake Murdock. Platoon Leader, Third Platoon. 32, 6' 2", 210 pounds. Annapolis graduate. Six years in SEALs. Father an important Congressman from Virginia. Murdock has a condo in La Jolla. Owns a car and a motorcycle. Loves to fish. Weapon: Alliant Bull Pup duo 5.56mm & 20mm. Speaks Arabic.

ALPHA SQUAD

Timothy F. Sadler. Senior Chief Petty Officer. Top EM in Third Platoon. Third in command, 32, 6' 2", 220 pounds. Married to Sylvia, no children. Been in the Navy for fifteen years, a SEAL for last eight. Expert fisherman. Plays trumpet in any Dixieland combo he can find. Weapon: Alliant Bull Pup duo 5.56mm & 20mm with explosive round. Good with the men. Speaks German and some Farsi.

*Third Platoon assigned exclusively to the Central Intelligence Agency to perform any needed tasks on a covert basis anywhere in the world. All are top-secret assignments. Goes around Navy chain of command. Direct orders from the CIA and the CNO.

David "Jaybird" Sterling. Machinist Mate First Class. Lead petty officer. 24, 5' 10", 170 pounds. Quick mind, fine tactician. Single. Drinks too much sometimes. Crack shot with all arms. Grew up in Oregon. Helps plan attack operations. Weapon: H & K MP-5SD submachine gun.

Luke "Mountain" Howard. Gunner's Mate Second Class. 28, 6' 4", 250 pounds. Black man. Football at Oregon state. Try-out with Oakland Raiders six years ago. In Navy six years, SEAL for four. Single. Rides a motorcycle. A skiing and wind surfing nut. Squad sniper. Weapon H & K PSG1 7.62 NATO sniper rifle.

Bill Bradford. Quartermaster First Class. 24, 6' 2", 215 pounds. An artist in spare time. Paints oils. He sells his marine paintings. Single. Quiet. Reads a lot. Has two years of college. Platoon radio operator. Carries a SATCOM on most missions. Weapon: Alliant Bull Pup duo 5.56mm & 20mm explosive round. Speaks Italian and some Arabic.

Joe "Ricochet" Lampedusa. Operations Specialist First Class. 21, 5' 11", 175 pounds. Good tracker, quick thinker. Had a year of college. Loves motorcycles. Wants a Hog. Pot smoker on the sly. Picks up plain girls. Platoon scout. Weapon: Colt M-4A1 with grenade launcher, alternate Bull Pup duo 5.56mm & 20mm explosive round.

Kenneth Ching. Quartermaster First Class. 25, 6' even, 180 pounds. Full blooded Chinese. Platoon translator. Speaks Mandarin Chinese, Japanese, Russian, and Spanish. Bicycling nut. Paid $1,200 for off-road bike. Is trying for Officer Candidate School. Weapon: H & K MP-5SD submachine gun.

Vincent "Vinnie" Van Dyke. Electrician's Mate Second Class. 24, 6' 2", 220 pounds. Enlisted out of high school. Played varsity basketball. Wants to be a commercial fisherman after his current hitch. Good with his hands. Squad machine gunner. Weapon: H & K 21-E 7.62 NATO round machine gun. Speaks Dutch, German, and some Arabic.

Bravo Squad

Lieutenant (j.g.) Christopher "Chris" Gardner. Squad Leader Bravo Squad. Second in Command of the platoon. 28, 6' 4", 240 pounds. From Seattle. Four years in SEALs. Hang glider nut. Married to Wanda, a clothing designer. No kids. Annapolis graduate. Father is a Navy rear admiral. Grew up in ten different states. Weapon: Alliant Bull Pup duo 5.56mm & 20mm explosive round. Alternate: H & K G-11 submachine gun.

George "Petard" Canzoneri. Torpedoman's Mate First Class, 27, 5' 11", 190 pounds. Married to Navy wife Phyllis. No kids. Nine years in Navy. Expert on explosives. Nicknamed "Petard" for almost hoisting himself one time. Top pick in platoon for explosives work. Weapon: Alliant Bull Pup duo 5.56mm & 20mm explosive round.

Miguel Fernandez. Gunner's Mate First Class. 26, 6' 1", 180 pounds. Wife, Maria; daughter, Linda, 7, in Coronado. Spends his off time with them. Highly family oriented. He has family in San Diego. Speaks Spanish and Portuguese. Squad sniper. Weapon: H & K PSG1 7.62 NATO sniper rifle.

Omar "Ollie" Rafii. Yeoman Second Class. 24, 6' even, 180 pounds. Saudi Arabian. In U.S. since he was four. Loves horses, has two. Married, two children. Speaks perfect Farsi and Arabic. Expert with all knives. Throws killing knives with deadly accuracy. Weapon: H & K MP-5SD submachine gun.

Derek Prescott. Radioman Second Class. 23, 6' 3". Comes from a small town in Idaho. Expert marksman. On the Navy rifle team before SEALs. Played college football at University of Idaho as a tight end. Is an expert kayak man who does ocean runs when he has a chance. Unmarried. Speaks good Japanese. Weapon: H & K G-11, which fires caseless rounds.

Jack Mahanani. Hospital Corpsman First Class. 25, 6' 4", 240 pounds. Platoon medic. Tahitian/Hawaiian. Expert swimmer. Bench-presses four hundred pounds. Divorced. Top surfer.

Weapon: Alliant Bull Pup duo 5.56mm & 20mm explosive round. Alternate: Colt M-4A1 with grenade launcher.

Wade Claymore. Radioman Second Class. 24, 6' 3", 230 pounds. Unmarried. Played two years of Junior College football. A computer whiz. Can program, repair, and build computers. Shoots pistol competitively. Lives in Coronado. Weapon: Alliant Bull Pup duo with 5.56 & 20mm explosive round.

Paul "Jeff" Jefferson. Engineman Second Class. 23, 6' 1", 200 pounds. Black man. Expert in small arms. Can tear apart most weapons and reassemble, repair, and innovate them. Weapon: Alliant Bull Pup duo 5.56mm & 20mm explosive round.

1

Barry Stillman watched with a cautious and practiced eye
as the last of the one hundred lead tanks protected in
sturdy plank boxes eased toward hold number three. The
crates were extremely heavy for their size and were his
only cargo. Captain Grafton had watched part of the loading, then became bored and went to his cabin, where he
probably had screened another western movie on his video
player. Stillman leaned tanned arms against the rail as
the semitropical breeze ruffled his dark hair. His sun-
weathered face held blue eyes, a nose that had been broken and not quite set straight, and a square jaw that had
taken its share of pounding by bare knuckles. He was
thirty-eight and had been in the Merchant Marine all of
his adult life. Now he was second in command of the
Willowwind, a three-hundred-foot-long freighter with a
double hull and the latest in electronic navigation. She
was small by today's standards and one of the new
breed—fast, dependable, and completely computer operated.

Stillman watched as the last lead tank moved into the
hold. The crates were made of heavy wooden planks, and
the containers inside were cast from solid lead three
inches thick, with a small opening in the top that was
stoppered with a melted-in eight-inch plug of lead. Nothing could possibly get in or out of the lead coffins.

Nothing better. Inside those one hundred tanks was
enough weapons-grade plutonium to make nuclear weap-

ons that could blast all of the major capitals of the earth into radioactive dust. Shipper: the United States Government. Maybe the Nuclear Regulatory Commission, but Stillman wasn't sure. He heard the cost would be five billion dollars by the time the project was finished. This little no-name island was an atoll, with killer coral heads creating a calm blue lagoon. There were only four acres of actual land. The highest point on the atoll was thirty-two feet above the restless Pacific Ocean. There was no food or freshwater source on the atoll.

The speck of land was thirty miles east of Kure Island, the last of the Hawaiian Islands to the west. That atoll of sand and coral was a little over fifteen hundred miles west of the big Island of Hawaii. The Hawaiian chain lay in a crescent and contained a hundred and twenty-four separate islands. They were the tops of a string of volcanic mountains that barely reached the surface. There had been no people on this atoll when the U.S. government moved in six months ago with bulldozers, carpenters, plumbers, engineers, and specialists in one particular field. Their job was to build a plant that would be used to remove the plutonium from hundreds of nuclear warheads, nose cones, and bombs, and package it for transport.

Russia had agreed to do the same thing, but backed down when they found out the cost would seriously damage its fragile economy. The U.S. plunged forward with the task of removing fifty tons of weapons-grade plutonium from decommissioned nuclear devices.

This was the second shipment of ten tons. Stillman had been on this same ship for the first transfer. It went off without a hitch. Eight easy days to San Diego, where the secret cargo was handled with care, unloaded at night, and moved through darkness by unmarked trucks, inland across two states to a highly restricted desert location that nobody would talk about. There, another newly constructed plant put the plutonium through immobilization. The plutonium was mixed with highly radioactive waste, which made the resulting product useless for fueling nuclear weapons.

As the last crate was lowered into the hold, a cable slipped and the heavy box swung dangerously close to a bulkhead. Stillman grabbed the rail, his heat pounding. If that crate shattered and the lead tank fell and ruptured . . . He wiped sudden sweat off his forehead. There was enough of the deadly radioactive plutonium in each of those crates to fry everyone on the ship and the island into crispy critters in seconds. The alert crane operator caught the problem, adjusted for the swing of the crate, and stopped it before it crashed into the bulkhead. Then the operator lowered the dangling box the rest of the way into its place in the hold.

Stillman let his breath out and wiped more sweat off his forehead. The plutonium was over-crated, so the chances of it breaking open were slim. Still he worried. Every man on board worried about it. It was like hauling a jug of nitroglycerine over a bumpy road on a cart with no springs. He vowed that this would be the last trip he made hauling plutonium. He and all the officers and crew were pulling down double pay for the run. The word was out that the next load would be ready in two months and would bring triple regular pay for all hands. Stillman wasn't going to do it again. On this one he'd had five good sailors quit when they found out their hazardous cargo was plutonium. They demanded to be flown back to Honolulu. They were union men, so he had to comply. That put him in a bind since he had to find five replacements who would take the job and get them out here from Honolulu before time to sail.

The union rep in Honolulu said he wasn't happy with the men he had to send, but the bottom of the barrel had been scraped a dozen times lately. The company had flown in the five men. He talked to each of them, and wasn't impressed. Their seamanship experience was far below what he had wanted. Two were from the South Pacific—Majuro Atoll in the Marshall Islands. One was a Filipino, and the other two were brown-skinned and had papers from California, maybe Mexicans. All had the usual U.S. seaman's papers and union cards. A strange lot. But the rep said it was the best he could do. He had four men turn him down when he told them they would be hauling a hazardous cargo. So Stillman was stuck with these guys. Now the crew members had their adjusted assignments for the trip and had settled down. They would be sailing in two hours. In eight days he'd get this devil's brew into San Diego and off loaded, then he was moving to another company.

Something on the horizon caught Stillman's attention and he looked up. A freighter twice as big as the *Willowwind*. What was she doing out here? She was well off the usual shipping lanes. Images of South Pacific pirates flooded his brain and he shook his head. Pirates would be crazy to try to take this cargo. It would take a large ship and they did have a gun locker on board. He'd never seen it opened. He shook his head. Pirates worked the South Pacific, not way up here in the middle. Forget the pirates.

Jeffers, an able bodied seaman and one of the twenty-four men on the ship, came up to the rail.

"Mr. Stillman. Cap'n wants to see you, sir."

"Thanks, Jeffers. We should be buttoning up and getting ready to cast off. Check out the hold covers."

"Aye, aye."

Stillman did not like the captain. He was gruff, sloppy, and drank too much. Some day that could cost him his captain's ticket. Eugene Grafton was from the old school—get by with as little trouble, and as little work as was absolutely required. If past performances were holding true, the captain would be in his cups an hour before they set sail. The term "set sail" always troubled Stillman. On the old three masters they actually did spread out their sails and set them in place when they were ready to leave, so the wind would catch in them and power them out of port. Now the meaning had become lost in valves and drive shafts and computerized navigation.

He knocked on the captain's cabin hatch, then opened it and looked in.

"You called for me, Captain Grafton?"

"Aye, I did. Come in and relax. I hear the last of them blasted lead tanks is safely on board and secured below."

"Yes, sir. Last one just went down. Will we still be sailing at eighteen hundred?"

"Aye, just before dusk, get us out of here. Then eight more days of nightmares and we'll be free again."

Stillman nodded. "Captain, I hear they turned down our request for a military guard to sail with us."

"They did. No cause—waste of manpower, etcetera, etcetera, they said. I asked them for a squad of Marines."

"I keep thinking about those seagoing South Pacific pirates."

"Worry wart," Captain Grafton said. He downed the last of the liquid in his glass. He had four videocassettes in his lap. The Captain was fifty-eight and said he would retire in a year and go back to Oregon. Grafton stood only five feet six, and had put on fifty pounds over the years to add to his beefy frame.

"Stillman, did I tell you I picked out the farm I want to buy in Oregon? Just five miles upcoast from Tillamook. Eighty acres of good bottomland ideal for pasturing my milk cows. I'm going to start with a herd of forty."

"That will keep you busy, Captain."

"Oh, I'll have help." He paused, burped, and shook his head. "Well, Mr. Stillman, you better get this craft underway. Stand by to set sail there, Chief Mate. Look alive now."

Stillman saluted and hurried out of the room. Another quarter of the bottle and two John Wayne westerns and the captain would be blotto for the rest of the afternoon and all night.

Four minutes before 1800 they cast off the last lines and the three-hundred-foot freighter eased away from the newly constructed floating pier that allowed the *Willowwind* to come close enough to the atoll to onload the cargo. Chief Mate Stillman watched closely as the big ship edged away from the fragile wooden dock. Then they

were clear. He checked the computerized navigation set-
tings, confirmed that they would be making the required
southeasterly course, and turned control of the big vessel
over to Wayne Ludlow, the second mate from San Mateo,
California.

"Last trip for me, too, man," Ludlow said. "Just thinking what's in them crates makes me want to heave. You
realize how many nuke bombs some wild-eyed country
like Iraq could make with this load?"

"Yeah, true. But the fucking Iraqi navy hasn't been
reported in the Pacific yet, so I think we're safe. See you
in the morning."

Stillman smiled as he went to his cabin. Ludlow had a
wild imagination, but he was a good sailor. He had control
of the big ship until the morning watch came on at 0600.
Stillman had been looking forward all day to a new movie
he had had sent in from Honolulu. He'd ordered six cas-
settes and got all of them. All war movies and action
flicks. He'd ration himself to two a day, then start re-
peating his favorites.

By 2300 he was dozing through parts of *First Blood*.
He turned off the tape and considered taking a shower.
No, tomorrow. He'd make one courtesy call to the bridge
to chat with Ludlow, then turn in. It had been a long and
draining day.

Stillman had just passed the captain's cabin hatch when
he heard a loud sound. A shot? He hesitated, then knocked
on the hatch and, as usual, opened it a foot and looked
inside.

"Captain?"

A second later a face loomed in front of the chief
mate. Stillman recognized him as Jomo Shigahara, an
able-bodied.

"Yes, Chief Mate Stillman, I was just about to come
looking for you. Come in, come in, the captain asked me
to call you."

Stillman frowned, opened the door farther, and could
see into the second half of the cabin and the captain's
bed.

"Shigahara, I don't understand. What are you doing in the captain's cabin? Did I hear a gunshot?"

"A gunshot? I didn't hear one. The Cap asked me to bring him up some rum from the kitchen."

"Rum? Didn't know the captain drank rum."

"You know the Cap, he drinks anything. You better talk to him." Shigahara motioned toward the bed.

"Yes." Stillman stepped into the cabin and walked over to the bed, where the captain lay on his back. It wasn't until the last moment that he saw the small hole in the near side of the captain's head and the spray of blood and skull fragments on the pillow and the bulkhead on the other side. Too late Stillman cried out and started to turn. He sensed movement behind him, then something hit him hard on his head and he dropped to his knees. The second blow sent him sprawling on his stomach toward the captain's bed, and the dark furies closed in around him and finally covered him. He could see nothing more.

Jomo Shigahara grunted as the chief mate fell. Usually one whack with his .45 pistol was enough to knock out a man. He must be slipping. He nodded at a man on the far side of the room. "Tie his hands and feet together and make sure he can't get free. Then we follow our plan. You five guys from Honolulu really set us up. Next we get the crew quarters and then the bridge."

The other man nodded. His name was Matsuma, one of the Polynesian men in the group of five flown in as replacements. "The one guy on the bridge we've got to watch for is the lookout. The guy on tonight usually wanders around the ship."

"Yeah, he's Pokey. No trouble from him. This time of night the rest of the crewmen should be in their bunks. The other officers might be a worry. We got the captain and chief mate. That leaves the second mate, Ludlow, the engineering officer, and the radio officer. We'll get them last."

"Jomo, looks like this might work. When you told me to get four reliable men with papers in Honolulu, I wondered if we could pull it off. Damn, looks like we gonna do it."

"We are. I don't plan nothing this much and not get the job done. So we take down the crew quarters next. Could be ten hostile crewmen. Two will be on the bridge. We'll see if any of them want to make some extra money. Some huge extra money."

"Let's do it."

They left the captain's cabin and moved down to the weather deck and forward to the crew quarters. Down one deck they came to the crew cabins. The first hatch was open a foot. Shigahara rammed it open and jolted inside with the .45 pistol pointing into the room. Three men lay on bunks, two reading and one with earphones on.

"What the hell?" the first seaman said, looking up.

"Just hold your hands out and don't ask questions," Shigahara snapped. Matsuma went behind the gun, leaned in, and strapped plastic riot cuffs around the man's wrists.

"What the fuck is going on?" the man with the earphones asked, pulling off the headset. Shigahara slapped the side of the heavy .45 down across the man's head, slamming him back into his bunk. The sailor shook his head.

"Shigahara, you bastard. Why you hitting me?" The sailor snarled in fury, kicked out of the bunk, and charged Shigahara, who stood only four feet away. The report from the .45 firing twice blasted into the small steel-walled cabin, sounding like 155mm howitzers going off. Both heavy slugs caught the seaman in the chest and drove him backward. Everyone in the cabin went temporarily deaf as the echoing gunshot sound boiled through the room, crashing from one steel bulkhead to the others.

Shigahara pointed at the third man, and Matsuma reached out and bound his wrists. Shigahara leaped out of the cabin door and eyed the other hatches down the companionway. The one nearest him opened and a man pushed his head out. The gunman's hearing came back slowly.

"I hear a shot, man?" the sailor asked. Shigahara heard

something but didn't know what the man said. "Huh? What?"

"Thought I heard a shot."

Now his hearing was good enough that he understood. Shigahara held the .45 behind his back. "You're having nightmares again, Ewing. Anybody else in there with you?"

"Yeah, Shig. What the hell's going on?"

Shigahara brought the .45 around and pushed Ewing back into the cabin. "I'm taking over this stinking bucket. Anybody here want to help me? You help, you get fifty thousand dollars when we're done."

"Fifty grand?" a new voice said. Shigahara looked at the three other men in the cabin.

Ewing shook his head. "No way. I'd be the guy they hung. I'll pass. Are you shooting people? What's the middle ground? I won't help you, but I don't want to get shot."

"You get a vacation in the locked dayroom for the rest of the trip. You guys with Ewing?" The other three nodded.

It took them a half hour to get the rest of the crew collared and marched into the dayroom. It had two Ping-Pong tables, two TV sets, and a rack of movie videos. One man had volunteered to come with the hijackers. The ten others stood close together watching.

"Where do we sleep?" Ewing asked.

"On the floor. I'll be back to get the two cooks to start work at three A.M. Is that about right, Pete?"

One man looked up. He was six feet four and more than 250 pounds. He was the head cook. "Our usual start time is oh-two-thirty," Pete said.

"Good enough. I want to eat well on this trip. You'll be cooking for twenty-two so far, not twenty-four. Any questions?"

"Usual mess times?"

"Right."

"We bring food in here for the men?" Pete asked.

"My men will bring in the food." Shigahara looked

around. "I have no fight with any of you. Just stay out of my way and you'll live to sail again."

He stared hard at each man there, then went outside with his six men. They pushed a steel rod through the handles of the double doors, locking the sailors in the recreation room. Shigahara looked at the new recruit—Keanae, a Hawaiian who had been a loudmouth and a troublemaker on the first trip. "You know we're taking over the ship and rerouting her?"

"Hell yes, I heard."

"You're all right with that?"

"Hell yes. I don't owe them fuckers nothing."

Shigahara smiled. "Good. Stay with us, do what you're told, and you'll get a big payday. Now, let's get up the bridge and see what the second mate has to say. Remember, no matter what I tell him, we need him and the radio officer alive to help us run this ship."

They attacked with two armed men through hatches on both sides of the bridge. Shigahara pushed open the port hatch and saw the three men, one at the console.

"Lift your hands, fuckers, or I'll blow your heads off," the Japanese-American shouted. The three men looked at him and, with scowls that showed disbelief, lifted their hands.

"Shigahara, what in hell are you doing?" Ludlow asked. "This is piracy. The captain can have you hung."

"Not likely. Now, my conditions. I'm taking over this vessel. You will obey me to the letter. You will do precisely what I instruct you to do. Ludlow, you will act as navigator and captain, and you will see that all ship's functions are carried out. If you don't, I'll blow your brains out. Clear?"

"It's the damn plutonium, isn't it? I told the government we should have a squad of Marines on board."

"Did I make myself clear, Second Mate Ludlow?"

"Perfectly. Where's the captain?"

"He and Mr. Stillman are in the captain's cabin. Now, for the specifics. Matsuma here will give you a new course. You will enter it into the computer and make all needed changes. You will increase speed to fourteen knots from eleven. You will do that now. Matsuma will check your every move."

Matsuma went to the second mate and gave him a piece of paper with the new course. As soon as Ludlow read it, he looked up in astonishment.

"You're kidding. This means we'll be heading for the middle of the South Pacific. How much fuel do you think we have on board?"

"We have plenty to make a five-thousand-mile trip, Ludlow. Now make the course change."

Ludlow scowled, punched the change into the computer, and watched the numbers come up.

"Course change is entered, Captain."

"Well, I got promoted. Thank you. Do you need three men on the bridge?"

"Absolutely."

"Then two of my men will replace these two. Matsuma will monitor everything."

"Why, Shigahara?" Ludlow asked.

"Not your worry. Remember, all of my men are armed. We don't need you to run this ship, Mr. Ludlow. So don't even try to do anything brave or we'll shoot you down before you get started. My man will be on the radio, so don't think you can get any help there. I know about the required messages via satellite, so don't worry about that. Any questions?"

"It's the plutonium?"

"Of course. Now, you're on duty until oh-six-hundred. I'll see that you're replaced. Oh, and about that little thirty-eight revolver you keep in your locker, under your extra uniforms. We have it now and the shells. A nice little weapon. Be careful, Mr. Ludlow, and you will live."

Shigahara felt the ship change directions as it began its turn from southeast to southwest. They had a long run ahead, but the faster speed would help. He turned toward the bridge hatch when one of his men ran inside, his face flushed, eyes wild.

"Shig, we've got trouble. That guy who volunteered to join us, that Hawaiian, Keanae. He just took the weapon away from one of our men and shot him, then he vanished. I don't know where the hell Keanae is."

2

NAVSPECWARGRUP-ONE
Coronado, California

Lieutenant Commander Blake Murdock stared at the strange-looking vehicle parked on the Silver Strand that ran between Coronado and Imperial Beach. This was one of their prime training areas for the four teams of SEALs based in Coronado. Today Murdock had his Third Platoon, SEAL Team Seven, working out with the Turtle. It was a new experimental craft that his SEALs had helped design. It was to be used specifically as an amphibious landing craft that could move his men from any body of water onto shore and then miles inland if needed, with the armor protection needed to withstand small arms fire. They'd had it for months but hadn't had time to really get familiar with it.

"Officially this is the combat entry/attack vehicle, CEAV," Murdock told the assembled SEALs. "It can be hoisted aboard a destroyer or almost any ship, then launched ten or twelve miles away from the target and run us into a specific beach or waterway, where it swims to shore and rolls up on dry land."

"Looks like it's got flat tires," Jaybird said.

"Yeah, half-flat and twice as wide as a car's tires," Murdock said. "Lets them roll right through soft sand and mud and still charge along at fifty-five miles per hour on a good road."

The SEALs began crawling over the rig. It had a bow, hull, and closed bow that ended with a slanted steel panel that extended up two feet, where the windshield should be. There were four view slots in it.

"Must be sixteen feet long," Howard said. "Didn't we see this before with a fifty-caliber on it?"

Murdock looked at a spec sheet. "She has a fifty topside just behind the driver. She's unsinkable. Fill her with water and she'll still float and function. She has Cadloy steel armor plate over all that protects her from anything up to 7.62 rifle fire. The wheels gyro down when she hits the sand and give you a two-foot obstacle clearance when she's on land."

"Twice as big as a Rubber Duck," Canzoneri said. "What about her speed in the water?"

"Does twelve knots and is relatively quiet, with a Cummins V-504 diesel engine that kicks out two hundred and two horsepower."

"I still don't see no fifty-caliber," Howard said.

Murdock scanned the spec sheet again. "Yeah, the fifty raises hydraulically when you want to shoot, which gives the gunner a three-hundred-sixty-degree field of fire."

"Damn near a whole circle," Jaybird said. Somebody threw a rock at him.

"How do you switch her from water to land?" Senior Chief Sadler asked.

"Don't have to," Murdock said. "It's all automatic. She has sensors on the wheels. As soon as they hit sand or mud, the computer signals the drive shaft, which switches in half a second from prop to wheels and you're off and driving.

"Now for some more data about her. She rides low in the water to give radar men fits. Has only eighteen inches of freeboard. The let-down sides button up tight on top to make her waterproof for rough water. Inside she has bench seats along the sides and a swivel chair for the driver up front. The dashboard looks more like a car than a boat, with the usual readouts for overheating, low oil, generating, and a fuel gauge. Automatic transmission."

"So we gonna get to work out with her or is this just a beauty contest?" Bill Bradford asked.

"Oh, we're working out. We have all morning. I want each of you to drive this Turtle out through the surf and back in. Every man has to be able to operate this vehicle. We'll be here until all of you can make it purr like a kitten. Any questions?" There were none. "This is another piece of our equipment. It's like our weapons and gear. We get the best results from them with repeated and quality training. So let's get at it. Senior Chief, load up Alpha Squad and take them out for a run. She has a steering wheel and brakes. Go."

Alpha Squad piled into the Turtle. Murdock showed Sadler how to start the engine and work the gears. It even had a reverse and two speeds forward. Then he stepped out.

"Go out a half mile, turn around. Alpha Squad, you bail out and swim back. Senior Chief drives in alone. I don't want to see even a face mask until you're within fifty feet of the beach. Then come in on the breakers and play dead driftwood logs washed up by the waves until the beach is cleared by your scouts. Go."

Murdock watched the Turtle work out through the wet sand, then the foam from the waves, and at last take a three-foot breaker head-on and dive through it. Quickly the Turtle was beyond the surfline and turning. The rig was too large to fit inside the Navy's choppers, but could be airlifted by heavy choppers from one ship to another. So far the SEALs hadn't put the little craft into operation. It would hold just eight men, so they would need two of them for a platoon mission. Murdock had had word this week that a second one should arrive in Coronado within a day or two. Good enough reason for a hard workout on the rig to be sure they could handle it if the need arose.

Murdock watched the Turtle head for shore, then he turned to Bravo Squad. "JG, take your squad down to the Kill House. Put everyone through twice, then come back for your turn on the Turtle. I want scores recorded and brought to me."

"Aye, aye, Commander, we're moving." JG "Chris" Gardner made two hand signals and his squad fell in a line of ducks. He led them at a six-minutes-to-the-mile-pace run a quarter of a mile down the beach, toward the navy radio antennas. The Kill House had been dug into the sand at the far end of the strand. Most of it was underground, with bullet-absorbing walls and overheads that wouldn't let any stray rounds escape. The Kill House had four rooms, each set up with furniture and pop-up targets of bad guys and good guys. It was all computer-controlled with fifty thousand combination targets that were always changing. It was a live firing range for·all weapons except the 20mm. Murdock had been running his men through the Kill House once a day for the past two weeks. It was one of the best ways to keep them sharp and ready for anything.

Murdock heard a beeping and looked around. Then he swore softly, dug into his shirt pocket, and took out an inch-and-a-half-square plastic beeper. He had argued against using one, but the boss, Commander Masciareli, had insisted that every platoon leader in Team Seven have a beeper and a cell phone, and they would be in use whenever the men were on or off duty in the Coronado area.

Murdock took out the beeper and looked at the window. A phone number showed. It was Master Chief Mac-Kenzie's number at the Quarter Deck. Murdock fought against it a moment, then shrugged and took a cell phone from his pocket and turned it on. He dialed the number.

"Quarter Deck, Johnson here, sir."

"Master Chief MacKenzie please," Murdock said.

A moment later the familiar Scottish brogue came marching over the airwaves.

"Well, you are available, Commander, lad . . . sir," MacKenzie said. "Wondering if you knew that a cell phone has to be switched to the on position before it works? Did you know that now, lad?"

"I've heard something about it, Master Chief."

"Good idea to keep it turned on; otherwise it's not much good."

"You must have something important to say, Master

Chief. Or is it just that the fishing is good off the kelp beds?"

"Fishing is good, aye. But there is one item. Sorry to break up your training routine, Commander, but your team commander himself wishes a word with you and JG Gardner. He said immediately, so I'd say that's as soon as you can get your bodies up this direction."

"The JG is currently at the Kill House, but he'll be returning in about ten and we'll choggie our way up to the Quarter Deck."

"Aye, lad. I'll tell him you're on your way."

Fifteen minutes later, Murdock and the JG stepped out of the Turtle and walked over to the Quarter Deck. From there it was a short distance to the Team Seven commander's office. Murdock knocked, and the two officers entered when they heard a growl from behind the door.

"Good you're here. Gardner, are you dripping?"

"No, sir. Just sweating."

"Good. At least he went through channels this time. We have a small problem in the Pacific Ocean. Somewhere out there. Finding it is going to be a problem. It seems that we have a three-hundred-foot merchant freighter missing."

"Missing, sir?" JG asked.

"That's right, Lieutenant. She was supposed to dock here in San Diego two days ago and has not shown up. Her satellite transmissions were on schedule, and she reported every night for the eight days of the trip. Each time her position was consistent with her eleven-knot speed working toward the mainland. She isn't here. The CIA and the Nuclear Regulatory Commission are up to their armpits in deep shit."

"Nuclear, sir?" Murdock asked.

"More than nuclear. Ten tons of pure plutonium packed in lead transfer tanks. The whole damn ship with the plutonium is missing, and we don't have a clue where she might be."

"Where did she sail from?" Gardner asked.

"That we know. A little atoll fifteen hundred miles almost due west of Honolulu. Draw a circle from there for ten days of travel at eleven knots and the ship should be in that circle somewhere."

"Damn big circle," Murdock said. "Say she makes eleven knots for twenty-four, that's two hundred and sixty-four nautical miles. Ten days of that and she could be two thousand, six hundred and forty miles from that atoll. That's a lot of ocean to search."

"That's what they're doing," Masciareli said. "I understand they have repositioned two satellites to scan the area so they can log in and chart every ship of that size or larger. The Navy had a carrier group at Pearl, and it pulled out six hours ago and headed to the southwest. That's where the brains think the hijackers may be headed. They could try to get lost down there in that maze of South Pacific islands."

"So we're on standby?" Murdock asked.

"Your platoon is on a six-hour travel alert. It could take them three or four days to find the ship. When they think they're getting close, we'll ship you to Pearl and then probably to the carrier, whichever one they sent down there."

"Is Don Stroh involved?" Murdock asked.

"Yes, he's your control and he'll be on base before ten hundred today. He'll be going with you whenever you leave."

"He opens a lot of doors for us," Murdock said.

"We'll get our travel gear ready and tell the men to stay within arm's reach of a phone when they're off duty," JG Gardner said. "They say anything about special weapons or equipment?"

"Not yet. I'm suggesting they fly your Turtle over to Pearl and have it nearby in case you need it on some of those atolls and islands out there," Masciareli said. "I talked with the CNO this morning and he's authorized the transfer of the Turtle by air to Pearl. We have it, we might as well get some good out of it."

"Agreed," Murdock said. "We'll get her dried out and ready to fly. When does she leave?"

"Tomorrow at ten hundred from North Island."

"We better alert the men and get putting some travel packs together. Is there anything else, Commander?"

"I'll keep you informed. Oh, be sure to keep your cell phones turned on when you're not in the water."

"Yes, sir," both men said, then turned and walked out of the office. Gardner went to bring the SEALs back to the platoon area. Murdock went to his office to start getting gear lists made out for the expected trip. He found Don Stroh sitting in his chair waiting for him.

"Commander, I've decided I don't want to trade places with you. The damn chair isn't right, and then if I sat here, somebody would want to shoot at me sooner or later. How's it going, big, tough SEAL?"

"Around and around, Stroh. I hear you're going with us this time, so I'm getting a set of combat gear all ready for you. What weapon do you want, a submachine gun?"

"Hey, hold on there, Petruchio. I'm support, not backup. I don't like getting shot at. What do you think of this new job?"

"Sounds impossible. How can you find the ship?"

"Satellites and AWACS for starters. Then we've contacted every island in the South Pacific with a radio or telephone, telling them about the hijacking, and they are watching. We've also put out a million-dollar reward for whoever finds the ship. All of the big ports are covered like a security blanket. Now we concentrate on the little islands that are populated. We have a chance. But it could take a couple of days."

"We'll be ready."

"Murdock, your guys can be ready in a couple of hours. That's why I've arranged for an afternoon fishing trip out of Seaforth. We shove off at twelve-thirty. I've got six reservations and I hear the yellows are just jumping in the boat out there."

Murdock chuckled. "Big international crisis, enough

weapons-grade plutonium out there to blast apart half the world, and you want to go fishing?"

"Just trying to relax some of the men before a big combat mission, my strategy. Always works. Besides, I checked. The half-day boats are bagging up to two yellowtail per pole. Sure, they are small, maybe eight to ten pounds, but hey, that's a good fight."

Murdock shook his head. "You are off the scale, Stroh. You must know they won't be calling us for at least two days." Murdock shrugged. "Hell yes, let's go. Your expense money. We should leave the JG here to mind the troops. Pick your men."

"Timmy Sadler, Jaybird, Lam, and Fernandez. Make a good crew and I can outfish the lot of you."

"That we'll see, Stroh. We rent tackle, right?"

"Right. We'll be on a special recon mission, classified, in case anybody asks. I'll square it with the master chief. Have your troops in undercover civilian clothes. Oh, be sure to bring your cell phone and beeper."

"What happens if we get our six-hour call?"

"No problem. I've got connections. A Coast Guard cutter will zap out there at twenty knots and pull us back to the dock."

Two hours later, the fishing on the *New Seaforth* had picked up. Don Stroh hooked the first yellow but didn't keep his line tight enough and the big fish threw the hook.

"I'll get the next one," he boomed.

Jaybird, Murdock, and Sadler all hooked up as a school of the young yellowtail came through. Murdock and Sadler boated their catches, both about eight-pounders. Jaybird's broke the line.

"Drag's too damn tight," Jaybird yelled. A crewman stepped up and checked the drag, loosened it a bit and handed the pole back to Jaybird.

The half-day fishing boat had settled in at a favorite spot about a mile offshore from the Children's Pool at La Jolla. She hadn't moved for an hour. Don Stroh finally hooked up again on a live anchovy bait and yelled when he thought he had color.

"No color yet," the crewman said. "Pump your pole up slowly, then wind like crazy as you ease the tip of the pole down. Less strain on the line that way."

"Easy for you to say," Stroh growled. He kept pumping and after a five-minute struggle and moving halfway around the eighty-foot-long fishing boat, he had the yellow up showing color. The crewman made one swipe at it with the gaff and lifted the big yellow on deck.

"Biggest one I've seen so far," the deckhand said. "Has to go at least twelve pounds." Stroh promptly carried his prize around and showed it to the rest of the SEALs.

The bite petered out about 1630 and the captain called for the fishermen to bring in their lines. Time to go home. The SEALs gathered just below the bait tank on the stern and compared notes.

All had two yellowtail except Stroh with his one.

"But mine is the biggest," he shouted. "Just wait until I win the jackpot. Must be fifty bucks in there."

As the crewmen looked through the sacks, they lifted out the heaviest fish and checked them against another big fish on a balance rod, with hooks on both ends and supported in the center. The heaviest fish pulled down and lifted the lighter fish up.

"Okay, that's it," the crewman said. "Sack twenty-four wins the jackpot. Who has sack twenty-four?"

"Hooooooo ha!" Stroh bellowed and charged up with his ticket half that showed his number twenty-four written in marker pen. He turned to the SEALs. "Hey there, guys. Just who the hell is the best fisherman now?"

They all clapped him on the back and asked for a loan. They watched as the crewmen quickly filleted out the yellowtail and a few rockfish and put the boneless meat in plastic bags along with the gunnysack half-ticket.

Murdock used his cell phone and called Chris Gardner.

"Hey, buddy, how is the training?"

"Murdock? Went fine. Master chief says you owe him one."

"True. Hey, fish fry at my place tonight at seven. Invite all the guys and find out how many can make it. I want you there for sure. Also invite the master chief. He won't come, but invite him anyway."

"Will do, Cap."

"Hey, I like these cell phones. Can come in handy. See you later."

Eighteen SEALs, wives, and girlfriends had a great time at the fish fry. Murdock had called Ardith, and she had everything but the fish ready when they arrived home at 1830. To the surprise of everyone, Master Chief Petty Officer Gordon MacKenzie came and Murdock decided the old salt had a good time.

He shook his head when Murdock asked. "So far, lad, there's been no results from the search in the South Pacific. My hunch is that you'll fly out sometime tomorrow afternoon on your way to Pearl Harbor."

3

San Diego, California

After the day's training sessions were over, Kenneth Ching didn't go to the fish fry. Instead he drove his two-year-old Mazda across the bridge to San Diego and down to the small area that was all that could claim to be called Chinatown. He cruised through the area twice, looking closely at the vegetable stands, at the various shops and stores. He was trying to soak up some of his heritage. Sometimes he regretted that he hadn't gone into business with his father in San Francisco. He would have been on his way to being a rich man by now. But the Navy had claimed first rights on his soul.

He turned uptown and parked near a large Chinese restaurant, the Friendly Dragon, on the refurbished Fifth Avenue section called the Gas Lamp Quarter. Several blocks along the street had been upgraded, with new firms, flashy restaurants and cafes. It was now a major tourist attraction.

Ching studied the outside of the building for a few minutes. Mostly non-Chinese were going in, evidently for dinner. He walked through the doors and old China hit him with an emotional surge that he hadn't anticipated. The décor, the staff dressed in authentic Chinese costumes, the paper lanterns, the low singsong music of a China he had never known but had heard so much about when he was growing up—Kenneth Ching stood there a moment drinking in the atmosphere, and didn't notice the slender Chinese girl who spoke to him.

"Uh-oh, what?"

She smiled. "You seemed a thousand miles away. I asked if you came for dinner or cocktails?"

"Oh, yes, excuse me. I was taken by the décor. I haven't been here before." She watched him, then lifted her brows.

"Oh, I'm here to see Mr. Kwan Tung."

"Yes, our illustrious owner. He's in his private dining room this time of day. Did he ask you to come?"

"Yes, we had a six o'clock appointment."

"So, your name, please." He told her.

She smiled and motioned for him to follow, and led him through the dining room with dozens of tables to a side panel of rice paper that slid back. Inside, a hallway stretched out in front of them. She stopped at the second door, also made of a wood frame with the fragile rice paper as the covering. She knocked, then opened the door and bowed low.

Ken Ching looked into the room done entirely in old China décor. He saw dragons and paintings of oriental vistas, and a large bronze Buddha sat on a delicately carved dark wood table. To one side two men rested on cushions around a low table.

The girl spoke quickly in Mandarin. Ching understood it. She was announcing him. She nodded, bowed again, stepped back, and motioned him inside, then she closed the panel. He watched the older of the two men both in ceremonial Chinese robes.

"Ah, yes, Kenneth Ching, son of my great and good friend Ching Gschu of San Francisco. Welcome. Pardon me for not getting up, but my old bones do not like to move even when I order them to. Please sit down." He waved to a spot across the intricately carved table that Ching thought must be teak or perhaps mahogany.

"Honored Grandfather, I come to visit you and bring greetings from my venerable father." Ken remembered some of the etiquette of the older Chinese. He had no idea why his father had insisted that he come visit this rich restaurant owner. He had intentionally made no contact with the Chinese community in town for the three years he had been stationed in the San Diego area. He moved over and sat on the heavily brocaded silk pillow. Glasses of rice wine rested on the table, and Ken saw that there was one in front of the place he sat. He nodded at the older of the two Chinese and sipped the wine. Strong and good the way he remembered. The younger Chinese man said a few soft words to the man beside him, then rose, bowed, and left the room past a sliding panel.

"Now, we will talk, we will eat, we will have good wine, and we will remember the old days when I, too, was in San Francisco." He looked at Ching's glass. "Drink, my friend's son. Drink the good wine from China and we will dream that we are walking the green fields and the majestic mountains of our homeland."

A panel opened and two girls came in who Ching guessed were about seventeen. Both were topless. They began performing one of the ancient dances from China that Ken barely remembered. They were poised, expressionless, and graceful as butterflies. The music came up and the dance grew faster, and one girl embraced the other as the music came to a jolting climax. Both girls froze in their embrace, then hurried off the small stage and out of the room.

"A little entertainment," Tung said. "My mind remembers many pleasant times that my body can no longer perform. It is comforting. Tell me about your work with the U.S. Navy. Your father tells me you are a SEAL. I understand it is the most dangerous job in the armed forces today."

"Yes, Honored Grandfather, it is dangerous, but we are highly trained and specialists in the work we do."

"Friends of mine tell me that the SEALs kill people, men the government does not want to go on living."

Chin hesitated. They had been instructed repeatedly how to field questions such as this one. He frowned, then looked the old Chinese in the eye. "Officially there is no assassination in the U.S. operations," Ching said.

"Yes, but unofficially?"

"That's something I can't comment on, Honored Grandfather."

"Inscrutable, I like that. Now it is time to eat and drink. I hope you like Peking duck. We have a chef who is one of the best in the world at cooking it."

Another panel opened and two women brought in trays filled with covered dishes. They set five plates in front of each man, then added cups of green tea and bowed as they backed out of the room.

"Yes, food, one of my many weaknesses," Tung said. "Enjoy. Take off the covers and enjoy. If you want more or something else, we can serve you any dish you wish."

"Oh, no, this is fine. Much fancier than the food we get in the mess hall." He uncovered the dishes. They included three kinds of vegetables, two kinds of meat from the Peking duck, and sauces and biscuits made of rice flour. They ate.

Partway through the meal, Tung looked up at his young visitor. "Your father never did tell me why you chose not to go into business with him. Your two brothers have, and they are well respected and leaders in the Chinese community in San Francisco. They are also both well off and soon will be wealthy. Both are younger than you. Why did you not stay with your father's businesses?"

Ching finished a bite of the delicious duck, then smiled. He'd known he would be asked the question and was ready. "I have no talent or feel for the business world. I'd go broke in a year. The Navy is where I feel I can contribute to our nation's security. I love the work I do."

"You kill people."

Ching shifted on the cushion. He looked at the ancient Chinese and wondered how old he was, ninety, ninety-five? Slowly, Ching nodded. "Yes, but only the bad people and only when it is necessary."

A gleam of satisfaction came from the ancient eyes. "Ah yes, now we have it. 'But only the bad people.' " The old Chinese laughed, and it echoed around the room.

When the meal was over, the two serving girls brought in delicate desserts for each. Ching ate his not knowing for sure what it was. Part ice cream, part flaked chocolate, part whipped cream and something else he couldn't tie down. The whole thing was carefully layered into a crisp pastry shell that tasted of cinnamon and nutmeg.

There was no talking for a time. Then the host looked up.

"Kenneth Ching, your father has decided it is time that you quit the Navy and come to function with your own people, and live and work here in Chinatown. You will be given an opportunity to hold a position that will interest you and at which you will be well compensated. Your enlistment is up next month. Your father has commissioned me to counsel you, and to make a place for you in my organization. I hope that you still listen to the commands of your father and that you will show proper respect for his wishes and for mine as well."

Kenneth Ching stared at the old man. He knew of the power and influence the ancient Chinese man had. He had heard of the way the Tung family operated in San Diego. Even so, he could not do what this man, and perhaps his father, had asked.

Slowly he shook his head. "Honored Grandfather. I am Chinese, and I have great respect for my father and his wishes, but he does not control my life. I'm sorry, but I can't accept your gracious offer of employment."

"You would defy your father's wishes?"

"My father has not told me what his wishes are. No disrespect to you, but this is something he should have told me himself. He can afford to fly to San Diego."

Tung gave a curt gesture with his right hand. Two panels behind him opened and three of the largest Chinese Ching had ever seen walked in and stood behind Tung. All wore black jeans and black T-shirts. Ching estimated that they must each weigh over three hundred pounds and stand six feet six inches tall.

"Honored Grandfather, are you trying to scare me, to intimidate me into working for you?"

"I have said nothing of the sort, young Kenneth. You

are not yet mature, not yet capable of deciding your own life's path. You need counseling."

"These are your counselors? This goon squad is going to reason with me?"

"These men are my bodyguards, to see that no harm comes to these old bones."

"Yeah, sure they are, and I'm a millionaire twice over." Ching shifted his legs and lifted to his feet. Two of the huge men moved around the table and one stood on each side of him six feet away.

"Kenneth Ching. The San Diego Chinese Cultural Society wishes you to join our ranks, to help us with our large number of community services to our people. There are no Chinese in San Diego who are on welfare. There are no Chinese who are homeless or street people. We serve an honorable and noble purpose."

"I'm sure that you do. But there are several sidelines the tong also performs. For example I know that your tong controls all Chinese gambling in the city, that you have a strong and protected prostitution ring. The most disgusting of all is the protection racket that your goons run bleeding every Chinese merchant who has the guts to open a store in this town."

Tung scowled and spat out Mandarin Chinese words quickly, but Ching understood them.

"So now you tell your muscle men not to let me leave. Your Mandarin holds no secrets from me. I will leave. I do not take this type of pressure lightly. Remember this, old man Chinese. If I take a blow, I will repay it tenfold. If I happen to stumble and break a bone, I will repay the man who did it fiftyfold. If these dolts don't understand English, you better tell them right now."

Kenneth Ching saw each of the men at his sides start to move toward him. He sprang backward to the only solid-looking wall in the room. On a table lay an ancient Chinese fighting long sword, two feet of tempered steel. He picked it up. The two-inch-wide blade was surprisingly heavy, but well balanced. He held it a moment. The thug nearest him stopped.

"That sword is a priceless artifact from the Ming Dynasty," Tung said. "If it is harmed in any way . . ."

"Blood won't harm it; let your men here demonstrate that. You are right. I can't take out three of them, but surely two will go down before I do. Take your choice." The old Chinese remained silent.

A half a step at a time, watching the three bodyguards, Ching edged toward the panel he had entered the room by. The guards didn't move. Ching made it to the door, slid it open, and kept the sword as he ran down the corridor. He was halfway down when he glanced backward. There was no pursuit. He grinned. Then, before he could stop or dodge it, from an open panel a heavy chair flew out directly in his path and only a foot away. He crashed into it, the sword flew ahead of him a dozen feet, and he tried to stay on his feet but stumbled, felt the blow of the arm of the chair into his belly, and crumpled on the floor hurting all over.

When he tried to sit up, a heavy boot pressed down on his stomach, pinning him to the floor. Ching looked up at one of the goons who had been in the private dining room.

"Move your fucking foot," Ching bellowed with all the air he had left in his lungs. Surprisingly the boot moved, only to return a fraction of a second later, kicking him in the side just above his kidney.

"Bastard," Ching shrilled. He rolled over, and got to his knees when the boot came again, jolting into his stomach, lifting him off the floor, and dumping him near the chair. He had to get off the floor or he was dead. He surged toward the chair, grabbed it, picked it up, and swung it with all his strength. He didn't even know if anyone was behind him. The big man had moved in again and Ching's sudden surge caught him by surprise. The heavy chair legs caught the man in the side and slammed him against the side of the corridor, through a rice paper panel, and out of sight. Ching dropped the chair and ran down the hallway, hunting the restaurant.

Before he got there, a smaller man blocked his path. He held a thin fighting knife six inches long, waving it

back and forth in front of him. Ching never hesitated. He
ran full speed at the man, jumped, and thrust out both feet
at the waving knife and the man behind it. The tough sole
of his black Navy shoe caught the knife almost at the
point and spun it out of the man's hand, and his feet
continued on to strike the Chinese in the chest, jolting
him backward into the hall and leaving him gasping for
breath.

Ching jumped over him, only to find two more men at
the end of the hall. To Ching's surprise, one of them
spoke.

"Mr. Ching, we hope there will be no more violence.
We have been asked to escort you through the kitchen
and to the street. If you will follow us, please." They
turned and walked down the hall to the door, then turned
away from the restaurant section. Ching bolted the other
way and was almost into the serving section of the eatery,
when a heavy blow hit the back of his neck and he felt
his whole body turn to jelly as he sank to the floor, fighting to maintain consciousness.

He felt someone pick him up and carry him. Then the
coolness of the evening air hit him and he knew he was
outside. Probably in the alley. He was getting back more
of his senses, but he kept his arms and legs limp so they
would think he had passed out. One man tried to stand
him up. He collapsed. Another man lifted him; then,
through slitted eyes, he saw one of the huge goons swinging his fist. He was directly in front of Ching. The SEAL's
legs stiffened and he kicked his right foot upward, slamming it into the big man's crotch, driving higher, smashing penis and testicles against pelvic bones and bringing
a bellow of agony and protest before the man slumped to
the alley holding his crotch with both hands.

Ching twisted and came free of the man who held him,
but a third man blasted a hard fist into his left kidney and
Ching knew he was going to vomit. He slumped to his
knees. He couldn't stop the kick that came to his right
kidney; then he was on the ground trying to pull his legs
up into a fetal position. He wrapped his arms over his

head to protect it and waited for the next kick.

It didn't come. He thought he heard scuffing as shoes and boots moved up the alley. A door closed. He tried to open his eyes, but they refused.

It took Kenneth Ching ten minutes before he could sit up. He had vomited twice and the bile taste in his mouth almost made him gag. When he sat up at last, he looked around. It was an alley, with back doors of several businesses. There were no cars or trucks, only some garbage cans and one streetlight halfway down. Ching gulped in air to try to stabilize his system. He'd never been beaten up so severely. A few barroom blasts but nothing like this.

More than an hour passed before Ching could get to his feet. He crawled over to a garbage can, held on to it, and slowly lifted up to his feet. His kidneys still drilled pain into his system. The goons knew what they were doing.

By the time he made it to the end of the three-hundred-foot alley, he could walk almost normally. Where did he leave his car? He checked his pocket and found his car keys where they should be. His Mazda was west of the restaurant. How far? He couldn't remember. On the way up the sidewalk he checked every car he came to. He looked farther up the street and saw the restaurant sign. His car had to be this side of it. His was the tenth up the block. He nearly fell down getting the key in the lock, then he swung the door and eased into the driver's seat.

At once he smelled something all too familiar. It was the coppery odor of fresh human blood. His eyes snapped wide open and he looked in the backseat. There lay a woman with blood all over her throat and chest. She was half-nude, and without checking Ching knew she was dead. How in hell? Tung did it, the bastard. The cops were supposed to catch him red-handed. The bastard.

No time to figure it out. He heard sirens in the distance. Police or ambulance? He didn't know. Tung could have dumped the body in the backseat and called the cops. What the hell, Ching had to get out of there. He started the engine and eased away from the curb; then, driving

cautiously and obeying every traffic law and sign, he
worked his way away from downtown and along Market
Street until he was near Fortieth Street. There he parked
near a vacant lot, shut off the engine, and killed the lights.
He sat there breathing deeply and trying to control his
heart rate. He was feeling a little better. His kidneys still
pained him, but he could live with it. Tung wanted him
down and out. The bastard! Ching looked around and saw
no one. Nobody on the street. No stores around. Old
buildings, and a vacant area, four or five lots. He opened
the door and stood there watching the whole area. Two
men up the street going the other way. No houses or businesses nearby. He took a deep breath and opened the back
door. He grabbed the Chinese girl by her bare feet, tugged
her out of the backseat, and lay her on the parking lot.
No blood on his hands at least. He looked around again.
Closed the car door. He couldn't see a single soul. No
lights came on. He got back in his car and drove away
sedately. With luck no one had seen him dump the body.
With luck, no one had spotted his car or his license plate.

Must be blood all over the backseat. He'd have to
worry about that later. An anonymous tip to the cops
could put them crawling all over his car. That damn Tung
probably got his license plate to give to the cops. There
might be an APB out on it right now. Once they found
the car, he was dead. The DNA in the blood all over the
backseat would be a perfect match with the murdered
girl's and he'd be in prison for life.

He drove slowly toward Coronado. What could he do
with the car? Tung must know where he lived, or could
find out easily enough. He couldn't park at his condo. No
way. Put it in a storage area somewhere? Change the license plates? He wasn't used to trying to dodge the cops.

He parked on the San Diego side of the Coronado Bay
Bridge and tried to figure it out. First, he'd dump the rear
seats somewhere they wouldn't be found for a while. A
canyon out in East County. He could drag them off the
road and throw them down a canyon. Both of them, the
seat and the backrest. Then he'd use his flashlight and

check for blood. Depended how much seeped between the seats. Hell no, that wouldn't work. Must be blood on the rear carpet and on the door frame. The cops had equipment now that could reveal blood you thought had been scrubbed off. That wouldn't work.

Then he had it. Burn up the evidence. Get out in the country, siphon out most of the gas, and spread it all over the car, then light it off and run like hell. Should burn up and get rid of all the blood. He'd report the car stolen and then they'd find it and check the motor number and tie it to him and he could collect his insurance. No more blood. Maybe. Best idea he'd had. He had to disguise himself and hitchhike back to town. What time was it? Only 2005. Good. He stopped at a gas station and filled the tank, then bought a two-gallon can and filled that. The clerk didn't really notice.

He drove out Highway 94 and headed out past Casa De Oro and on to Campo Road. He found an ideal spot on a side road just past Rancho San Diego. It was a lane that led off the highway and into a little canyon. He drove in until he couldn't see the lights of cars on the road, then stopped and opened the gas tank and sloshed the two gallons of gas on the backseat and the front seat. He lifted the hood and opened all four doors. Then he lit a matchbook and threw it into the car from twenty feet. The whoosh of the gasoline fumes almost reached out and touched him, but not quite. The seats and the inside of the car burned like a torch, and he turned and walked away, not using the road. He was a half mile down the highway, heading back toward town, when he heard the gas tank explode.

The fifteenth car going past stopped. Two teenage boys.

"Hey, man, we used to hitch all the time. What happened?"

"Ran out of gas back a ways. Long damn walk."

"Say that again. Hey. You want to drive? Both of us had a few beers, you know. Okay, we had two six packs." The kid giggled and edged over the center line into the wrong lane, then came back.

"Yeah, I better drive," Ching said. The kid stopped at the side of the road and Ching slid into the driver's seat. He didn't ask them where they wanted to go. Within ten minutes both young men were sleeping.

He drove to within three blocks of his house in Coronado, parked on a side street, and put the car keys in the kid's pocket, then slid out of the seat and left the two of them sleeping. Tomorrow they wouldn't have the slightest idea how they got to Coronado, and for damn sure they wouldn't remember picking him up.

Ching walked the three blocks to his condo. His body was working on half throttle. His kidneys still ached from the blows. He just hoped there wouldn't be a run on the O course tomorrow. A half a block from his place he stopped in some shadows and watched his corner condo. No lights on inside. No unusual activity in the parking lot. He knew most of the cars that parked there. None seemed out of place. He moved up and did another recon. It looked clean. He came out of the bushes and walked the last stretch to his condo and up the stairs. Nobody in the hall. He unlocked the door and pushed it open, standing against the wall. No shots came. Ching reached inside and turned on the lights. Nobody home. Good.

He called Jaybird and asked him to pick him up in the morning.

"That Mazda give out on you?"

"Hell no, went downtown and somebody stole it. I been walking and taxi hopping ever since. Just got home. Now I've got to put in a police report for a stolen car. Hear you can do it by phone."

"True. See you tomorrow."

Ching hung up and then dialed information for the right cop phone number to report a stolen car. He wasn't used to lying, but this time he had to. Just thinking about Tung Kwan was enough to make him lie like a pro. After the police report, he had to figure out how to do a huge payback to that old Chinese man who ran the local tong. Now, there would be an exercise in caution, with a lot of planning and a payback that would shake up the whole damn San Diego tong.

4

Mid Pacific Ocean
On board the *Willowwind*

That first day of the hijacking, there had been a struggle
by Keanae to get a gun away from the hijacker Benton.
The revolver had gone off and Benton took a round in
his heart. Keanae knew he couldn't cover it up, so he
changed his plans again. This time he would hide out on
the ship. The hijackers didn't know this vessel; they'd
never find him. His big job now was to get to the radio
and try to notify someone of which direction the freighter
was heading. First he had to be sure of the course.

Keanae didn't expect that it would take him four days
to get the course settled and the plan worked out. Now
he had it. It was a southwest course and that meant the
Marshalls. If his calculations were right, they would hit
the farthest north islet and atoll first. That was Sibylla. He
had memorized half the names and locations of islands in
the South Pacific.

Fifteen hundred miles southwest of the tiny atoll she had
sailed from, the *Willowwind* anchored in shallow water
off Sibylla Island, the northernmost of the Marshalls and
more than five hundred and twenty miles northwest of
Majuro Atoll, the capital and commercial center of the
widely scattered thirty-four atolls that make up the Marshall Island nation. It was a little after three A.M., and the
ship's navigator and his radar had brought them into the
island perfectly.

Jomo Shigahara sat in the captain's chair on the bridge

and stared through the moonlight at the small native village on the tiny island. It was two hours to dawn. The
takeover of the big ship had not gone well over the past
six days. This was the start of day seven. First there had
been the problem of Keanae, the double-crossing Hawaiian who had volunteered to join then, then shot dead one
of his conspirators and vanished into the bowels of the
freighter.

Shigahara and his hijackers didn't know this ship well
enough to find him. He had bedeviled the five of them,
raided the kitchen for food, and even broke open the arms
locker and took two pistols and a rifle. He was a constant
threat.

A select few of the crew members Shigahara needed to
help him run the big ship had caused him all sorts of
problems. At night when Matsuma wasn't watching, the
helmsman twice had angled the ship well off the given
course and had caused a two-day delay in arriving at this
given point of land. It was far enough away from everything that he felt comparatively safe here. He was sure
that the U.S. government had sent out screaming notices
to every port in the Pacific warning them about the
Willowwind and her cargo. They were covered as far as
her name went. One of his men had a knack for painting,
and he had been let down over the bow to repaint the
name. The old name had been painted out on both sides
of the hull, using the same color as on the hull. The new
name, the *Challenge*, was in the correct size and style of
the previous.

Shigahara left the chair and went to the front windows
and stared at the small island and its neighboring atoll.
He'd known things would be primitive, but he had no idea
they would be this basic out here in the South Pacific.
This island was not his primary destination. That would
come by radio, but so far he had heard nothing on the
satellite reading set.

Chief Mate Stillman had given him the most trouble.
At least twice he had turned off the engines and let the
ship coast to a complete stop. It took them a half day to

get underway again. He at last had to lock the chief mate in his cabin and cut his food to one meal a day. The outside hatch to the cabin was secured with a special hasp and padlock, for which only Shigahara had a key.

Matsuma was on the helm now, and the ship was safe at anchor on the lee of this small island. No boats had come out to investigate them. Shigahara wasn't even sure there were many people on the small bit of land that could not be more than two hundred feet wide and a thousand feet long, with a heavy growth of trees, vines, and bushes. A dozen small buildings nestled around a tiny harbor with a rickety looking pier. Smoke came from one of the shacks, but he saw no people. But then, why would they be up at this time of night?

Shigahara paced the bridge for two hours, unable to sleep, even to catch a nap. He was pumped up about his operation. When this went through, he'd be a rich man. Filthy rich. He'd be able to go anywhere he wanted to, do anything . . . The Japanese man looked at his watch again. It was five o'clock. He went to the radio room for the second time that early morning. There were two hijackers on guard and one asleep. He asked the operator if there had been any messages.

"Not a one, Shig. Want me to try to contact them again?"

"Yes. It's almost five o'clock. Maybe somebody is awake out there by now."

The call went out. "Conquest, this is Wanderer, seeking your call. Have arrived at Point Alpha, looking for more instructions." They waited. After five minutes the call went out again. It was in voice and in the clear, with no way to encrypt it.

Two minutes passed, then the speaker rumbled.

"Yes, Wanderer, we've been waiting for your call." The voice was soft and slightly accented, and Shigahara didn't recognize it. "You are to proceed at once to Point B and meet with our representative there for the first delivery."

"Will you be at Point B?"

"No. You are to deliver one package there and move

on at once to Point C. You'll get directions to Point C
when the first delivery is made and you're ready to sail.
Timing will now be critical. You should sail before noon
today."

"Understood. Business is business. We'll contact you
again right after the delivery at Point B."

"Fine. Goodbye."

Jomo Shigahara smiled. It was happening. Yes, his
dream was coming true. He would be a rich man before
this cruise was over. He had just taken another giant step.
He had grown up in Sendai, Japan, the second son of a
businessman. He had gone to the university, and his father
assumed he would enter the family business, as his older
brother had, but he did not. His father refused to speak to
him for two years.

He had drifted from one dead-end job to another. For
a while he had been a tutor at the university, helping with
English. Then he worked for an importer for a while. All
the time he had been attending one strange group meeting
after another, at last landing with a cell that believed in
world domination by the Muslim faith and those who cel-
ebrated it. He soon became a leader in the group, but
yearned for more. He traveled in the Near East and
learned to speak Arabic and Farsi to go with his almost
perfect English. It was in Lebanon that he had been contacted by his current employers. After six months of in-
tense training, he had led two bombing raids into Israel.
Both were successful and he returned with all of his men.
He was given a new assignment. Because of his fluent
English, he was sent to Hawaii to watch for the progress
of the United States' decommissioning of nuclear weapons.

He didn't know if his employers were from Iran or Iraq;
it didn't matter to him. The man gave him fifty thousand
dollars and he flew to Hawaii and began monitoring the
progress of the removal of plutonium from the warheads
and bombs. It was not a secret operation. The only secret
was the date the first shipload would be sent to the United
States to be processed to make it useless for making weap-

ons. He studied the seaman's manual, worked on board several local ships, and soon found a counterfeiter where he could obtain his seaman's card and U.S. Merchant Marine papers so he could work on Merchant Marine vessels.

He learned that any shipping from one U.S. port to another U.S. port had to have a U.S. flagship do the hauling. When time was nearing for the first shipment, he found out which ship would do it, and applied through the union for a job on her. When the sailors found out she would be hauling hazardous cargo, several crewmen quit the ship. He hired on. He had made the first run from the tiny atoll to San Diego more than three months ago, and then back to Hawaii, where the ship sat at anchor, waiting for the next run. That gave him plenty of time to recruit five more men to train and get on board. The word of double pay for the trip spread through the *Willowwind*'s crew quickly, and senior union members had first choice.

That had been a huge problem. Shigahara solved it by convincing five of the men who had already signed on that it would be too hazardous—that they would be hauling ten tons of plutonium. He scared off five men, who quit the ship once it sailed to the atoll. His five men had signed up on a waiting list for the *Willowwind*'s run, in case there were any last-minute openings. All five were hired and rushed on board one day before sailing from the atoll.

He grinned as he walked back to the bridge. He would give the engineering officer notice that they should make preparations to get underway. They would move as soon as the engines and machinery was warmed up and ready to go. He knew that this could take several hours. He was in no rush, not now. Point B was the Rongrik Atoll two hundred and ten miles slightly southwest. He'd have Matsuma plot in the headings and put them into the computer for the new route. At twelve knots they could make the trip in a little over seventeen hours. He checked his watch. Slightly after five-thirty A.M. Seventeen hours would put them near the atoll sometime during the night. Yes. He smiled again as he thought what he would do with the five million U.S. dollars the Arabs had promised him. He could do almost anything he wanted to.

Shigahara called Inbrook, the engineering officer, in his cabin. The man was sleepy and hard to understand.

"Inbrook, we need to get underway by noon. Will that make any problems for you?"

"Of course not. I'll report in at oh-six-hundred as usual and check all of the equipment. There should be no cause for delay."

"See that there isn't, Mr. Inbrook."

Shigahara called the kitchen to have an early breakfast sent up. He always had sent up a breakfast steak, a three-egg omelet, orange juice, coffee, a six-stack of pancakes, and a bowl of mixed fruit. Then he ate whatever part of it interested him at the moment.

The phone rang on the bridge at two minutes past six A.M. The helmsman waved the handset at Shigahara.

"Yes?"

"Mr. Shigahara, I'm afraid it won't be possible to get underway. Well, it might be by noon."

"What do you mean, Inbrook?"

"This morning I have been checking my equipment as I always do, daily, and I noticed a problem with my main engineering computer. Something isn't working. I don't know if the computer crashed or if it's just a hiccup or what."

"I thought the computers on the bridge ran the ship," Shigahara said.

"They do, but my engineering computer is a slave to your computer. Your big one tells my smaller one what to do, and it does it. Only now when I tell my computer to give me readouts, for example, it suddenly shuts down and tells me I have done an illegal operation and the system must shut down. I don't understand it. I've had my top computer expert on the ship down here since five-forty-five trying to figure it out. Until he does, we're dead in the water."

"Inbrook, if you've sabotaged your equipment, you'll be shot and thrown overboard."

"No, sir, I wouldn't do that. This is my baby. I would never harm any of the gears or bolts or any piece of equipment down here. We're working as quickly as we can to get the computer up to speed."

"If my computer tells your computer to start the engines and bring them gradually up to fifty percent power, what would happen?"

"I'm not sure, Captain. Punch in the order and I'll let you know."

"Done." He talked to Matsuma. "Let's test the engines. Give the order on the computer to start the engines and bring them up to fifty percent power."

"Right, Captain," Matsuma said. "Starting engines, and moving to fifty percent power. The orders are in, sir."

Jomo picked up the phone to Engineering. "Well, Inbrook, what happened? The orders went in to start the engines."

"My computer came on, took the order, then at once the red flags came up telling me I had done an illegal operation, and it shut down."

"You mean we can't move? We're stranded here until you can fix the damn computer?"

"I'm afraid so, Mr. Shigahara. My man is working as quickly as he can. Ken Schafer says he has about twenty possible solutions and he's been at it now since five-forty-five. I'd hope he can have the problem fixed by noon, or three P.M. at the latest."

"Inbrook, you listen to me. I'm coming down to Engineering. If you don't have that computer fixed by noon, I'm going to shoot you in your right knee. For every hour the computer won't work, I'll shoot you in another non-fatal spot. You better tell your expert to rush it."

Mike Keanae had fixed up little nests for himself in four parts of the big ship, all in out-of-the-way places the crew never visited and where Shigahara and his goons wouldn't think to look. One was in the Engineering Department, in back of some storage areas. Just now he had heard most

of the talk with Shigahara that Mr. Inbrook had put on
his desk speaker.

Keanae grinned. He had put a minor virus program into
the computer last night that shut down the slave computer
when sent any order. It might be a day or two before the
computer man on board thought to check for a virus. Anything now to delay the movement of the big ship. He had
his orders. He could have put in the computer virus at any
time, but he wanted the ship to be in an easily identified
spot. Now the Navy wouldn't have any trouble finding
the *Willowwind* or the *Challenge,* as she was now named.
Wouldn't if he could find a way to get word to somebody.
He wanted to bring a SATCOM, but his control said not
a chance. He'd be discovered quickly. Not even a satellite
cell phone. So he had to figure out how to get to the ship's
radio. Lately Shigahara had been posting three of his men
on the radio every nighttime minute. The hijackers didn't
come off the radio watch until daylight.

Keanae thought of all the handy little gadgets that the
Company had that he'd used in the past. Several would
have been perfect. Now he had to figure out how to get
into the radio room and use the radio on an international
hailing frequency, hoping to contact someone who would
talk to the U.S. Navy, and then get out of there without
arousing any suspicion. As a last resort he'd have to barge
in, knock out the hijacker guarding the radio, send his
messages, and then leave. Or he could kill the hijacker
and cut down the odds. He'd thought of doing that, re-
ducing the number of bad guys. He wouldn't have any
trouble taking out one every night for two or three nights,
until they really got paranoid. Trouble was, Shigahara
might kill one of the Merchant Marine crewmen for every
hijacker Keanae threw over the side. Might be worthwhile
to do one and see if Shigahara was serious.

Twice Keanae had been through Shigahara's seabag
and his belongings. He had found nothing written down
that would indicate there was a hijacking in progress, let
alone the final destination. At least he knew where they

were now. This far northern island of the Marshall group was the closest to Hawaii.

He checked over the time they had been on the ocean. Going into the seventh day since leaving Hawaii. Those course changes by one of the crew had helped stretch out the cruise. The chief mate shutting down the engines twice had also aided the cause.

Keanae had no hideout close to the radio room. It should have been a nighttime move, say about three A.M., when the man would be tired and maybe dozing. It should have been done last night. He would get through on the radio to somebody. He could call the port master in Majuro Atoll if he could not contact anyone else. They must have an alert by the U.S. Navy by this time, about the missing ship. He patted the big .45 automatic in his waistband that he'd borrowed from the ship's arms locker. At least he had the loyalty of the crew members. Three times now he had picked the padlock and taken baskets of food to Chief Mate Stillman. It had been quick and easy. He'd seen several members of the crew who had been working on assigned jobs outside the dayroom. They had grinned and waved silently at him and given him a thumbs-up.

He shifted his position behind the boxes and stores in Engineering. He had to get up to the radio room. No way around it, he'd have to do the takedown on the radio now.

The ship's public address system came on, with Shigahara's slightly accented voice. "You men all know we have a murderer on board. The seaman who calls himself Keanae shot down one of our crew in cold blood a week ago. He's been hiding on board ever since. He's becoming a nuisance. I am offering a reward of twenty-five thousand dollars for any of you men on board who can catch or kill Keanae. Dead or alive, he's worth twenty-five thousand dollars. You men in the regular crew, don't let petty loyalties stand in your way. Help us root out this murderer and hold him for justice back in Honolulu, and at the same time pick up twenty-five thousand good U.S. one-dollar bills. Watch for him, then shoot him or call for help. We need to find this killer before he kills again."

5

Lieutenant Commander Blake Murdock settled down in his bunk in the four-man cabin in officer country and tried to relax. They had just landed on board the carrier after a hectic flight from San Diego to Hickam Field in Hawaii, then by COD to the *Vinson,* which was somewhere south and west of the Hawaiian Islands. Lieutenant (j.g.) Christopher Gardner lay in the bunk above him. The only other man in the transient officer cabin was an ensign awaiting assignment to the crew.

It was nearly 0400. So far nobody knew where the hijacked freighter was. Murdock couldn't sleep. He lifted up and pulled on his cammies and his boots.

"So where are we?" Gardner asked.

"Not close enough to anything yet," Murdock said. "This is the eleventh day of the hijacking. The carrier has been steaming toward the southwest for almost a full day. Which means we've covered about eight hundred miles. The Pacific is one hell of a big ocean. Over five thousand miles from San Diego to Tokyo."

"I hear the satellite's doing a great job of identifying freighters," Gardner said.

"They better. There's over six million square miles of Pacific Ocean out there just in this corner."

Murdock headed for the hatch. "I'm going to the CIC. Maybe the Combat Information Center will have some data on just where we are. JG, come daylight, I want you to get down with the men and see if they need anything.

We could be out of here on an hour's notice. We need all bags packed, ammo bags full, and all equipment double-checked. We're all on standby. We might reclassify that after I check with the CIC."

"Yes, sir, right away," Gardner said, rolling over in his bunk. "Got my wrist alarm set."

Five minutes later, Murdock stepped into the CIC and nodded at the CAG, the commander, air group, head man of all aircraft on board the carrier. He was an ex–F-14 pilot with an aviator's style and still some of the old bravado. His name was Janos Olenowski. At forty-eight years he was on the top of his game and on the fast track to making admiral. He was a head shorter than Murdock, a little heavy, and always grouchy without a cup of coffee in his right fist.

"Captain, guess you couldn't sleep either."

"Never can times like this. Coffee runs my engine, Murdock. Here's our latest. We've got two of our Hawk-eyes working two-hundred-mile swaths out, as far ahead of us as their fuel supply will last. They're in shifts working twenty-four. They can fly ahead of us two hundred miles and then scan out another hundred. With this big an ocean it doesn't seem like much. But we're making progress.

"Our F-14s have buzzed eighteen freighters so far and found that none of them match the configuration of the *Willowwind*. We're still heading for the Marshall Islands unless we find some reason to change. Out last GPS puts us still about seven hundred miles from the capital of the Marshalls, Majuro Atoll."

"Still too far to send out a stripped down F-14 on a recon?"

"Right. They max out at five hundred seventy-six miles for combat radius. We strip off all the missiles, we could push one to six hundred fifty miles coming home on fumes."

Murdock pondered it. "Is there an airport on Majuro where an F-14 could land on a one-way trip?"

Captain Olenowski grinned. "Been thinking about that.

There's an airport there, but we're not sure how long the runway is. I've got some radio men working on that question right now. Yes, that would be an option. Have to wait for first light to watch for any freighters in the flight path. Should happen in about an hour, they tell me."

"You've got two Seahawks stripped and ready to take our sixteen men?"

"We have. Radius there is about three hundred seventy miles. They will be ready by daylight." Captain Ole-nowski shook his head and stared hard at Murdock. "You and your men are the point of our spear on this one. We can't sink the ship; we don't have the men to attack her from small boats. So it's up to your SEALs. It isn't often that I talk directly with the CNO. The chief of naval operations told me yesterday that this task force is yours. Whatever you and your men need, you get. Ammo, food, bunks, aircraft. You ask, you get. Must be a good feeling for you."

"Yes, sir. But it also feels like I'm pulling rank on you. My only concern is that we get what we need to accomplish the mission, that's the bottom line. When do you estimate that we'll be in a position to take a run with the Sixties to check out any freighters that look like suspects in or around the islands?"

"We're coming in from the northeast, which puts us a hundred miles east of the farthest north atoll, called Si-bylla. It's five hundred miles from the capital atoll. It'll be west of our course, so we'll stay on line for the capital. That's the best bet for a big ship to land."

"Thanks, Captain. I'll hang out here and watch developments if it's all right with you?"

"Be my guest. How about some coffee?"

Down in the compartment the Navy had assigned the SEALs, Kenneth Ching was having trouble sleeping, too. He still hurt over half his body. The officers hadn't noticed anything wrong with him. Thank God. Senior Chief Petty Officer Sadler had noticed it right off that first day after his beating, when he reported across the Quarter

Deck. The senior chief must have seen the careful way he moved, not making any sudden direction changes, not talking as much as usual. The senior chief had nailed him at his locker.

"Ching, I can tell you're hurting, and if it's none of my business, you just keep your yap shut. But if you're not ready to go do the whole O course right now, then you and me have something to talk about."

Ching looked up at the senior chief, his face serious and a bit grim, but he didn't say a word.

"All right then, you're fit for duty. Don't think we have anything too serious set up for today anyway."

That afternoon they had flown out of North Island and he had time to get his system functioning again. He'd kill the next man who kicked him in the kidney.

Now, two days later, the hurt was half-gone, but the nagging anger, the fury at what Kwan Tung had done to him, burned brightly. There would be a payback. Kwan might not understand that, but he would. There would be a serious strike at the heart of the tong that would make them leave him alone. If he did it right, his hit at them would make the tong steer clear of him whenever they saw him. He had to decide exactly what that payback would be, and how he would administer it.

It was 0450 in the CIC that same morning when Murdock came back from the head. The unshaven CAG had stayed the course, checking the instruments, the readouts, and the screens.

Captain Olenowski nodded and looked over at Murdock. "All right, we're getting closer. My men tell me we're a little less than six hundred fifty miles from the Majuro. Two of our F-14s have been stripped down of all offensive weapons and ammo, and everything that wasn't nailed down. They can make a six-hundred-fifty-radius flight and we'll be cutting down the distance every hour. Be near dawn in thirty, and we'll put our two birds up heading for Majuro. If they don't find anything promising there, they'll check out eight or nine of the smaller atolls on the way back."

"Sounds good. We guessed at the Marshalls. At even two hundred eighty miles a day, the *Willowwind* has had time to get well beyond them by now, but I hope she hasn't. It's been eleven full days since the hijacking. That would be about twenty-nine hundred miles the ship could have traveled. She could be heading west and be halfway to China."

"That would make our search tougher."

Thirty-two minutes later, Murdock watched the two Tomcats take off from the forward hydraulic rams. The sleek birds climbed into the sky and turned, heading southwest, their afterburners painting two red flames in the near darkness. At over fifteen hundred miles per hour, the Tomcats would need only twenty minutes to be over the capital of the Marshalls. Cruising the atoll wouldn't take long. Murdock had no idea what kind of port facilities they had there. The coral heads might require a big ship to anchor well off and use small boats to go ashore.

In the lead F-14, Lieutenant Ralph J. Kleen settled into the seat and checked his wingman, "Rusty" Clover. They were in a loose formation heading for a speck of coral about six hundred and fifty miles away. Kleen had memorized the configuration of the freighter they hunted. She wasn't exactly a standard brand. She had one large on-board crane amidships and an unusual house just in back of that. It gave her a slightly out-of-balance appearance. She was three hundred feet and had *Willowwind* painted on both sides of her bow.

"Home Base, this is Skycap Fourteen."

"Home Base, go."

"We're coming up on eighteen thousand and leveling off. Speed just at fifteen forty and steady. I show time to objective as seventeen minutes and twenty seconds."

"Roger that, Skycap Fourteen. Start your verbal report of what you see at minus three."

"Will do, Home Base."

Captain Olenowski looked over at Murdock. "We'll know if our ship is there soon. If she is, what is the next step?"

"We can't blow her out of the water and drop all that plutonium into the ocean just off Majuro. Somehow we have to board her, take down the pirates, and regain control of the ten tons of plutonium."

The captain lifted his brows. "Right now I'm glad that's your job, Commander. Sounds like somebody could get hurt."

"We hope it's only the bad guys who pick up the bullet holes, Captain. We train for this almost every day."

"I saw an odd-looking rig below deck this morning. Is that yours?"

"Must be our Turtle. Yes, sir. It's ours. It's a small amphibian that lets us swim up to an island or landmass, roll out of the water, and motor inland to an objective. She's well armored and has a fifty-caliber on a mount over the driver."

"Thought you'd go in by Sixties."

"We usually do, when noise isn't a factor. The Turtle will be used more for silent missions and sneaking in and out."

A few minutes later the radio came on.

"Skycap Fourteen calling Home Base."

"Go Fourteen."

"We're about five out. It's almost full light. We're picking up three or four small atolls on our right. We're down to a thousand feet, and there doesn't seem to be much development on any of the coral humps, and no freighters anchored. Now we have the big one coming up. String bean of land with a beautiful lagoon in the middle. Yes, she has an airport but not a lot of roll-out room. Docks, where are the docks?"

"Skycap, there might be only offshore anchoring."

"Right, I see a tanker and two merchantmen. Right, small boats moving from each of them to a pier with warehouses behind. Figures. The two merchantmen are too large to be our baby. The whole island down there can't be more than thirty miles long. Two sections. No more freighters. Sorry. Our boy isn't here at the capital."

"Skycap, check once more, then start your return on a heading slightly northwest. You should be able to look over ten more atolls up there. Some you saw when you came in. The last one should be about five hundred miles from Majuro. Check them all out, then we'll give you a new heading to come home."

"Roger that, Home Base. We're turning now and flying generally northwest, following the chain of atolls up that direction. Looks like slim pickings so far. Oh, we saw one freighter on our trip down. We checked it out, but it was far too large and had the wrong configuration. Skycap out and moving northwest."

"So, if the ship isn't in the Marshalls, where is she?" Murdock asked.

"There are thirty-four of those little chunks of sand and coral out there in the Marshalls. We'll have to check all of them. They're scattered all over the Pacific."

"But if the ship isn't here, where did it go?"

The captain shook his head. "Hell, the South Pacific is a monstrous place. Huge, with all sorts of chains of islands. Just to the west is the Federated States of Micronesia. It includes the Caroline Islands and a total of six hundred spots of land and atolls. If that ship gets in there, we're in deep shit."

"So first we check out all the other Marshalls," Murdock said. "Don't we have some people on Kwajalein?"

"Missile base, tracking I'd guess. Yeah, when we get inside the Marshalls, we'll send a dozen planes out to check every atoll in the area. They're spread out almost eight hundred miles from one side to the other and from top to bottom. Take us a while."

"Now what can we do?" Murdock asked.

"Now, Commander, we wait. That's the hardest part of this job. I was used to kicking a Fourteen around at twenty-five miles a minute. Now I sit here and wait for somebody else to have all the fun."

He grinned, and Murdock knew he was only partly serious. But the SEALs knew something about waiting, as well.

"Skycap looking for Home Base."

"Go, Skycap."

"Captain, we've covered nine atolls so far, and nothing larger than a twenty-foot power boat at any of them. Moving on up to the most northern one. Be there in about ten minutes. We're doing a high fly-over at fifteen so if there is anything on any of these specks of dust out here, they won't even know we were up here."

"Good idea, Skycap. Tell us soonest. Home Base out."

Murdock looked around the CIC and nodded. "Yeah, Captain, I know, now we sit and wait again."

Five minutes later one of the crewmen came into the CIC.

"Captain, sir. Communications has some civilian on the international hailing frequency. Says he wants to talk to the U.S. Navy or the missile base on Kwajalein."

"Patch him through here, Petty Officer. Put it on the speaker."

A moment later a scratchy voice came into the CIC.

"Not sure who I'm talking to. My name is Keanae. I'm on board the *Willowwind*. I know Don Stroh. A lot of people know about this ship. We're now anchored at some small island. My guess is one of the northern Marshalls, probably Sibylla Island. And I'm in deep trouble here." Before he could say anything else, they heard two gunshots sound over the radio, then the transmission cut off.

6
_____

Willowwind
Sibylla Atoll, Marshall Islands

Keanae dropped the microphone when the bullet dug into his right shoulder. The second shot missed him. He spun around toward the door of the radio room, grabbed a heavy notebook off the counter, and threw it at the gunman, who still stood in the open hatch. The notebook absorbed the next shot, then slammed into the terrorist's chest. The blow surprised and hurt the gunman, who almost dropped his handgun.

In the three seconds that the man hesitated before he brought up the weapon for another shot, Keanae jolted forward three steps and tackled him around the waist, driving him backward against the bulkhead. His skull crashed into the hard metal. The shooter dropped the weapon and slid down the bulkhead, unconscious.

Keanae knew the three shots would bring other crewmen on the run, other hijackers. He scooped up the revolver, darted down the companionway to a ladder, vanished down a deck, and then rushed to his nearest hideout. This one was in the kitchen, and with the total cooperation of the three cooks. No hijacker ever came into the kitchen. In the canned goods and dry good storage compartment, he had moved cases of canned goods and boxes of Corn Flakes and fashioned a concealed area large enough to lie down in. At least in this spot he didn't have to worry about food or drink. He let out a sigh and tried to relax. He had contacted someone; he wasn't quite sure who. It sounded like military, which would be either the

Navy or the men at the missile listening site. Either one would do. Now he had to wait and see what developed.

He had intended to hit the radio room at three A.M. But Shigahara must have been worried about the radio and its potential to hurt him. He had shut down the radio and put three men in the room. One could be sleeping, but two had to be awake and alert and armed at all times from midnight to six A.M. Keanae thought of a diversion, maybe a small fire in one of the cabins, but he gave up on that one. He didn't want to endanger the crew, and a fire on a ship like this might take off and nobody could stop it.

That meant he had to chance a daylight hit. Two of the hijackers went off duty at six A.M. and he moved in. He had opened the hatch silently. The man was at the console, his back to the door. He should have shot him with his silenced .45. Instead he threw two empty tin cans from the kitchen to the man's left. The hijacker whirled that way and gave Keanae time to surge into the room and club him with the automatic. He went down and out. Keanae wasted a few seconds binding his hands and feet, then turned on the radio and began sending out his calls on the international hailing frequency. The tenth time he made the call he had a contact. They asked him to identify himself, and he had just got his message through and his location when the hatch must have been opened silently and a hijacker opened fire.

"Hey, Keanae, you okay?" a friendly voice came from beyond the stacked foodstuffs. "Thought I saw some blood on your shoulder when you came blasting through here. And there's a bunch of blood spots on the floor. You come out of there and I'll do some first aid."

In the surge to get away, Keanae had forgotten about his shoulder. He'd been shot before. Now that he knew he had been hit, the shoulder began to throb with pain. "Yeah, let me move some Corn Flakes. You know what you're doing?"

"I'm the ship's emergency medic," the second cook said. His name was Wally Torrance. He was five-eight and forty pounds overweight and didn't give a damn.

"Hey, Keanae, you never did tell us who you really are. After watching you work as a seaman for those six days in port, it was obvious you weren't no swabby. You got to be CIA or maybe FBI."

"Afraid I can't say, Torrance. Get this shoulder patched up so I can have a nap. I don't like being shot. You have a dozen or so ibuprofen?" He took four of the pills, then watched the medic at work.

"We still anchored right off this little island?" Keanae asked.

"Oh, hell yes. If we got underway you'd feel it. From what I hear topside, we're just sitting here and waiting. I don't know what for. How the hell these guys gonna break down them lead tanks of plutonium to sell them? Won't they get fried into crispy critters by that hellishly powerful radioactivity?"

"They'll probably try to sell it in the two hundred-pound lots."

"Yeah? What's the going price for plutonium?"

"Whatever the seller asks and can get from the terrorists."

"We're talking twenty, thirty million a lead bottle here?" Torrance asked.

"Sounds like a low-ball price to me, but just depends how much the terrorist nation needs the plut."

"You call it plut? Goddamn, then you got to be a CIA spook."

"Whatever, Torrance. Did the fucking bullet come out of me, or is it still inside?"

"We got an entrance hole and we ain't got no exit hole, so you're about five ounces of lead heavier than you were."

"How long do I have to get it out before it kills me?"

"Five days if you want to live long enough see your grandchildren." Torrance put a final wrap on the bandage and fastened it with plastic tape. "Best I can do, CIA man. At least you won't bleed on the Corn Flakes."

"Thanks, and remember, I'm just a lowly swabby."

"Yeah, sure. Hell, I won't tell nobody."

On the bridge, Shigahara shouted into the phone. "What do you mean two of our men are on the floor of the radio room unconscious?"

"Out like a light. Sanchez has a big scrape across his forehead like he got pistol-whipped. His hands and feet are tied. Socha has a nasty bump on the back of his head. He ain't moving. He could be hurt bad."

"Lucas, you take over the radio room. Lock the door and don't let anyone but me inside. Put Sanchez into the hall and slap him until he wakes up. Watch Socha to see if he comes out of it."

"Aye, aye, Captain, sir."

Shigahara growled into the set and pushed the button for Engineering. Somebody grabbed it on the first ring.

"Inbrook, why aren't we moving?"

"The computer. We just got it figured out. Rather Ken Schafer figured it out. It was simple. Somebody put a new program into the works. Every time my computer was given an order to perform some function, any kind, even coming up with the internet, the program told the computer that an illegal act had been performed and shut it down."

"A virus?"

"Not really, but kind of."

"So you take that program out and we're moving?"

"Not quite. Schafer says he needs to write a new program that will cancel out the bad one. Take him about three hours. He also told me that if you want him to do it, the charge is ten thousand dollars. He says he don't work for free."

"What? I should have him shot."

"Then we'd never get away from this island."

"That little sonofabitch. I remember him. Too smart for his own good. Nothing else I can do. Yeah, tell him we have a deal. You come up to the bridge and I'll give you five thousand. He gets the other five when we're moving."

"He figured you'd go for it. I'll be right up. Oh, he's been working on the new program for an hour. Figures another hour and he'll have it. Maybe we can get under way in two hours."

On board the *Carl Vinson* CVN 70

"Skycap calling Home Base."

"Go, Skycap."

"We've got a positive on a freighter at the Sibylla Island. It's up here at five hundred. You better put a nursemaid in the air. We're not going to make it back to the ship without a drink of juice. We've stayed at fifteen and made a positive ID on the type of freighter. Same onboard crane amidships and that crazy looking house just in back of the crane. She's at anchor and I don't think anyone on board knows that we're up here. Want us to fly CAP on her or head home for drink about halfway?"

"No CAP, we don't want him to get lucky. Come back for some fuel and then set down. We're changing course for that island. The helm tells me we're only three hundred miles due east of there. Good work. Come home."

"What's next?" Murdock asked.

"We'll switch one of our Hawkeyes to circle the area up at least twenty thousand, and keep us informed about her position. If she moves, we'll know it. What's next for you and the SEALs?"

Murdock looked at his watch. "Hey, it's oh-six-thirty-two. I almost missed breakfast. Then we get the SEAL heads together and figure out the best way to take down this ship."

7

After morning chow, the SEALs gathered in their quarters and began kicking around ideas.

"We know these hijackers went on board as seamen, so they probably don't have any long guns or machine guns," Senior Chief Sadler said. "Might be a pistol for each of them, so maybe the best way would be to rope down from a chopper to the deck."

"No way," Jaybird said. "They went to all the trouble and planning to get on board, my bet is that they sneaked on board at least five or six Ingrams or maybe taken-apart Uzis. Roping down is just too risky. We'd be perfect targets. Besides, by now they must have found the ship's gun locker. Don't most freighters carry a few rifles on board?" Nobody knew.

Murdock doodled on a pad of paper. He wrote "rope down" then crossed it out.

"Then we go in with Rubber Ducks and climb up the side," Lam said. "That freighter can't have a rail more than forty feet off the water."

"Done that before," Canzoneri said. "Maybe they'll have a pair of men on watch with rifles. We'll be damn easy targets."

"How about having the Tomcats blast the whole damn thing with twenty millimeters and then we rope down," Bradford said. "I like going down better than up."

"It's anchored now; what if it starts to move?" Murdock asked.

"No difference," Mahanani said. "We can do any of our plans with it making twelve knots or anchored."

"Let's use the Turtle," Jefferson said. "Hey, that's what we got her for. She's quiet. We do a silent approach and up the side, take out any deck watch with silenced shots, and we're halfway home."

"We can only move eight men in the Turtle," Lam said. "For this one we need all of us."

"How big is the deck?" Omar Rafii asked. "We could drop in six men in chutes, have them secure the deck and then bring in the rest of the men by Rubber Duck."

Murdock kept making his list and circling or crossing off items as they went.

"JG, what do you think?" he asked.

Chris Gardner frowned and rubbed his face. "We don't have a lot of options. We need to take her down as quickly as possible, before she knows we're on to her. Has to be a night mission, at first dark I'd guess, maybe twenty hundred. I'd use the Rubber Ducks and go in with one boat on each side and go up in a coordinated move."

"No jumpers to secure the deck?" Murdock asked.

"That's a small target, at night, and we don't know about the winds down here. Too dangerous for the benefits."

Murdock looked at his men. The brightest ones had spoken up. He stood from the bunk he'd been sitting on. "Jaybird, Senior Chief, JG, we'll have a meet with the CAG and some of his people and see their reaction. First we'll have to get within ten miles of her to use the Ducks. I'll see when we can have a meeting."

Murdock found the closest phone and contacted the CAG. Captain Olenowski reported that the freighter was still anchored and the Hawkeye was watching her.

"When can we set up a meeting? We need a plan to use to go in and grab the freighter."

"Make it in an hour, in a room just off the CIC."

"Be four of us. We're looking to hit the freighter an hour after first dark."

"Sooner the better. We don't know what she's doing there or when she might move."

The meeting went quickly. Murdock outlined the plan

to use the choppers to take them within ten miles of the freighter. "Then we'd go the rest of the way by the IBS. You do have a pair of IBS craft in your fleet, don't you?"

"I'll check," a captain who wasn't introduced said. "We usually have a dozen. After you get to her, you go up the sides and take down the pirates?"

"Yes, sir. We've done this type of attack more than a dozen times under fire. We've only had to back down once, when they saw us coming and sprayed us with machine-gun fire."

"You don't expect any heavy weapons on this boat?" the CAG asked.

"No, sir. It would have been hard to get them on board in Honolulu or on the atoll."

"So you'll need two Sixties stripped down, one for each squad," Captain Olenowski said.

"Yes, sir," Gardner said. "The distance should be no problem. The Sixties have plenty of range."

"We'll get to her well before dark," the CAG said. "We'll stand off twenty miles and be ready to give any assistance."

"Might be a good idea to have a pair of Tomcats with a full load of twenty-millimeter rounds flying CAP, just in case we need them," Murdock suggested.

"You've got them," Captain Olenowski said. "Let's set up the takeoff time. Your men need any supplies, ammo, weapons?"

"We're combat loaded at the moment. Depending on the action here, we'll be looking for some ammo later."

"Take off at twenty-two hundred, Commander?"

"Fine. We'll be ready."

On board the *Willowwind*

Jomo Shigahara scowled at the engineering officer. "You mean he hasn't got it fixed yet? You said it would be an hour and that was three hours ago."

"The program Schafer put in nearly worked, but the virus was worse than he figured. He says another hour and he should have it."

"If he doesn't, I'm going to cut off the little finger on
his right hand. You tell the bastard that. Also, if it isn't
done in an hour, he doesn't get the other five thousand
dollars. Go tell him."

Shigahara watched the engineering officer leave the
bridge. So far this was not going the way he had hoped
it would. He turned as one of his men came up. He'd
been on the radio.

"Message just came in, Captain," Socha said.

"Better be good news."

"You'll like it," Socha said and handed him a sheet of
paper. Shigahara read it and grinned.

"Yes, good news. Get that middle hatch open and warm
up the crane. We're back in business. Glad you recovered,
Socha."

They watched from the big ship as men at the far side
of the lagoon took camouflage off a boat. She was a sixty-
footer and looked fast to Shigahara. The men backed her
out of the small concealed dock and worked her gently
out through the coral heads in a channel that couldn't have
been more than thirty feet wide.

The boat came alongside and hailed them. The crew
put down a rope ladder and a man swung off the small
boat, grabbed the ladder between swells, and climbed on
board. The visitor was short and tough looking. A Micronesian with soft brown skin, black hair, and piercing dark
eyes. He wore shorts and no shirt.

"You were supposed to be gone from here. You're not,
so the plans have been changed. We'll take one package
now. Get it over the side and into our boat. I'll have a
briefcase roped up as soon as the package is on board."

"You know how heavy this package is?"

"I've heard. Two hundred pounds of plutonium inside
a lead tank that weighs over a thousand pounds. Yes, my
boat can handle it. A crane also will move it at the destination."

The two men watched the onboard crane move the
hatch covers, then lower its cables into the hold. A few
moments later the hooks had been attached to the rings

on the sturdy box surrounding the plutonium.

One of Shigahara's men ran the crane. He was an expert. They didn't want the package dropped into the ocean or dumped on deck and the lead tank smashed open. Shigahara felt sweat beading his forehead as the large wooden crate came out of the hold, swung over the side, and began to descend into the ship bobbing on the waves below. Two men on the ship guided the box into a cushion of Styrofoam that flattened as the full weight came on it. They had a moment when the case almost tilted the wrong way, then it swung into place on the open deck of the ship and was quickly lashed down with cables and heavy ropes.

Shigahara had one of his men let down a quarter-inch line and below one man tied the rope to a briefcase and signaled. The deckhand pulled up the briefcase and gave it to Shigahara.

"Look inside," the native man said. "No misunderstandings, no problems. There it is—three million in cash, all one-hundred-dollar bills. As soon as we are safely away from the island, we'll radio that we have made the transfer and your people will receive the electronic transfer of twelve million dollars. Agreed?"

The short man held out his hand. Shigahara shook it and watched the native ease over the rail and go down the rope ladder like it was a walk in the park. At the bottom he waited for the swell to bring the boat within two feet of the side of the freighter, then he dropped three feet to the deck and let go of the rope ladder. At once the boat turned and worked its way past the big ship and around the coral. It didn't return to the small lagoon, rather it headed away from it. From here it could go anywhere. Shigahara guessed that this one would go to Majuro. The airport there was large enough to land a transport needed to lift the heavy package into the air. Shigahara touched the hundred-dollar bills, then grabbed a handful. This was his first partial payment. He was a fucking millionaire. A huge smile flooded over his face and he closed the briefcase and hurried back to the bridge.

He had to find a good hiding place for it. He was certain that any one of his four fellow hijackers would kill him for the money if he thought he could get away from the boat and back to civilization. Shigahara wouldn't give them the chance.

On board the *Carl Vinson CVN 70*
Captain Olenowski took the message from the Hawkeye and closed his eyes for a minute. Then he called Murdock.

"Better come down to CIC right away. We've had a breakout. A small boat has just taken a package off the *Willowwind* and is heading south, the Hawkeye tells us. Might be going to Majuro. Bring Don Stroh with you. We've got new problems."

Murdock and Jaybird came into the CIC four minutes later. Don Stroh wasn't in his cabin, but two sailors tracked him down and he came in puffing.

"I'm getting too old for all this fun," he said. "I hear we have a breakout of one of the packages?"

"We can't be sure, but the small boat was alongside the freighter for about twenty minutes," the CAG said. "The Hawkeye said their radar showed something being off-loaded. Now the boat is moving south, heading in the direction of Majuro."

"Where there is a large-sized airport with planes big enough to hoist one of those lead bottles into the air," Murdock said.

"Stop him," Stroh said.

"We can't shoot him out of the water," Olenowski said. "That would dump the plutonium into the ocean and could cause a horrendous dead zone."

"Shoot the twenty-millimeter in front of him and order him to stop," Stroh said.

"If he has the plutonium, the man in the boat knows that we won't sink him, so a bluff over his bow wouldn't stop him," Murdock said.

"Why not shoot off his rudder with those twenty-millimeter rounds?" Stroh asked.

"Possible, but at nine hundred miles an hour there's no

guarantee of pinpoint accuracy from the Tomcat's guns," the CAG said. "We might end up sinking him. Not an option."

"Send out a chopper and four of us will rope down on his deck and take over the boat," Jaybird said. "We can spray the cabin with MP-5 automatic fire on our way down and not endanger the cargo."

The CAG looked at Murdock, who nodded. "We can do it. Leave two men in the chopper door to give covering fire as we go down. Swing us on board and we drop off the ropes and take over."

The CAG looked at a paper. "He's making eighteen knots. Take him a long time to get to Majuro, over five hundred miles away."

"I've been checking with the office," Stroh said. "Twenty-five of these atolls in the Marshalls have air-fields. Don't know how big any of them are. Most of them are probably for small private planes. What's the closest atoll to the one he left?"

The CAG looked at one of his men at the maps.

"That would be Bikar, sir. She's about a hundred and eighty miles southeast from Sibylla."

The Navy captain looked at Murdock, then at Stroh. "Sounds like the best plan. We'll send two Sixties. You can have cover-fire men in one, your ropers in the other. We have some two-inch line which should be like the ones that you use."

"Sounds like they should work," Murdock said. "Let's get mounted up. We should be taking off in the birds in thirty minutes."

"I'll get somebody to find the ropes and give them to you at the choppers," the CAG said.

Murdock and Jaybird trotted back to the compartment. On the way Jaybird asked the question. "Who's on the ropes?"

"You, me, Bradford, and Ching. Put our snipers in the other bird—Claymore, Canzoneri, and Fernandez—all shooting out one door as the bird circles the boat."

● ● ●

Twenty minutes later the SEALs were on board the two choppers waiting on the flight deck. The heavy ropes had been found and one end was wired tightly to the top of each of the chopper door posts. They were fifty feet long and neatly coiled so they could be kicked out at a moment's notice.

The four SEALs on the ropes all had H & K MP-5 submachine guns strapped on their backs with plastic tubing. One yank and they'd be ready to use. The four SEALs had heavy gloves designed to act as brakes as the men slid down the heavy rope.

Stroh walked back and forth in front of the birds, like an expectant father. Captain Olenowski came out and talked to Murdock.

"We've got a go from the Task Force commander and from Stroh's boss for this operation. Then we worry about the freighter. Good luck out there, and bring everybody back."

"What do we do with the ship and cargo when we have it secured?"

"You signal the chopper you have control and we'll send out a heavy lift bird to pick up the package and move it into our radiation proof vaults. Go."

Murdock stepped into the SH-60 Seahawk and waved at the crewman he was ready to take off.

Jaybird wrote on a pad of paper and gave it to Murdock.

"We're about a hundred miles from the boat. Take us about thirty minutes to get there at two-oh-seven mph."

Murdock nodded. He checked out the open door and saw the twin SH-60 fifty yards to their right.

Murdock went up to talk to the pilot.

"When we get to the boat, the other bird will circle it and our men there will use covering fire on the cabin and pilot house. Then we move in. Come in straight for the stern. As soon as you're over the stern, slow down and match his speed. Then edge forward twenty feet and we'll kick out the ropes and go down. When we have the boat secured we'll signal you by holding a weapon over our heads with both hands. Then you call the CAG and tell him we have control."

Murdock realized he'd been shouting to make himself heard. The pilot grinned, nodded, and gave Murdock a thumbs-up.

In the other chopper, Claymore, Canzoneri, and Fernandez checked their guns. Fernandez had his H & K PSG sniper rifle. The other two had MP-5s for spraying the boat with 9mm lead.

"What if we don't see anybody?" Canzoneri asked.

"We spray where they should be," Claymore said. "Fernandez will put some 7.62 hot lead through the cabin and pilot house. We'll get their attention and keep their heads down. Then we pull off and watch for trouble as our guys go down. Fernandez will get the call then if anybody shows up shooting at our guys."

They waited.

Twenty-nine minutes after takeoff, Fernandez yelled. "Hey, I've got the boat. It's blue and has a big square crate on the rear deck. Takes up half the boat."

Fernandez used his Motorola personal radio. "Hey, Cap, looks like we're here. Do we have a definite confirm on the ID on the boat?"

"Fernandez, we see the crate. I give a firm ID on the target. Move in."

Fernandez waved at the crewman, who told the pilot to drop down to a hundred feet and circle the fast-moving boat. He did.

Fernandez fired first when they were coming into position. He put three rounds through the small pilothouse at the front of the craft and saw splinters fly. Then they were in a tight circle fifty yards from the craft and all three men opened up with their weapons, all firing out the same side door.

"Don't see no fuckers," Claymore yelled. They sprayed the small cabin forward and the pilothouse and then stopped. A moment later a head popped out of the cabin door and looked at the birds. Claymore hosed a dozen rounds at the spot, but the man had already jerked his head back. They waited but saw no more men on the boat. Canzoneri waved at the crewman, who told the pilot to ease away.

The other chopper wheeled into position behind the boat's wake. Murdock and Jaybird stood in the doors, heavy gloves on, one foot poised beside the coil of rope. The Sixty edged closer to the boat. Murdock saw no one on deck. Another minute passed and the Sixty was in position over the stern.

"Now," Murdock called. The two men kicked the heavy coils of rope out, and they unrolled as they fell, the end barely off the boat's deck. At once the two SEALS grabbed the heavy rope and began sliding down. Heat pounded through the gloves into hands, stinging them. Before the first two were halfway down, Bradford and Ching grabbed the heavy ropes and began their slide. The first two SEALs hit the boat's deck and raced forward around the plutonium crate, toward the small pilothouse and the cabin.

Murdock slid to a stop just outside the cabin. He discarded the heavy gloves and edged around and took a quick look inside, then jerked back. Two rounds from what he thought was a pistol sounded, and bullets flew through the opening. Ching skidded to a stop on the other side of the cabin door. Murdock pushed the MP-5 around the hatch and fired three three-round bursts, hosing down the inside. He waited ten seconds. There was no sound inside. Ching pulled out a flashbang grenade and waved it at Murdock. The commander nodded. Ching threw in the flashbang. Both SEALs covered their ears with their hands. The moment the shrieking pulses of sound finished and the blinding strobes of light ended, Ching charged into the cabin. He found two men, one dead with three bullet holes in his chest, and a second writhing on the floor, holding his hands over his ears. He had only a shoulder wound. Murdock tied his hands and feet with plastic strips, then the two SEALs went outside.

"Clear cabin," he called in his Motorola.

"We have us some trouble up in the little pilothouse,"

Jaybird said. "Two of them in there behind some kind of protection. A frag or a flashbang?"

"Use the flash; the protection might save them from the frag. Go."

Bradford pulled a flashbang from his vest and looked at Jaybird. Both nodded. They had discarded the heavy gloves the moment they hit the deck. Now Bradford jerked the safety pin out of the grenade and flipped it inside the pilothouse. It went off with the usual blinding, ear-bending results. Bradford and Jaybird charged into the pilothouse and found the two men, both with automatic rifles, lying behind a steel tabletop. Both were groaning and holding their ears.

Two minutes later they had three prisoners and one dead man. The boat's engine had been throttled back to five knots to keep it from rolling in the swells. Next they checked the engine compartment and what had once been a hold to freeze fish. There were no men hiding in either spot. Murdock looked at Ching. "Anywhere else on this tub anyone could hide?" They both grinned at the same time, ran up toward the bow, and kicked open the head. No one was hiding there either. Murdock used his Motorola.

"Fernandez, you read?"

"Read you, Cap."

"Tell your pilot to advise the CAG we have command of the boat and the package."

"Will do."

The SEALs checked out the heavy crating around the plutonium. It was two-inch-thick pine. Their bullets wouldn't go halfway through it.

"Cap, Fernandez," the Motorolas chirped.

"Go."

"The CAG reports to our pilot that he has a destroyer that was riding herd on this flank that is now pounding its way to this spot at top speed. What's that about thirty-five knots?"

"More like twenty-nine on a good day."

"CAG says one chopper should stand by CAP for you

until the destroyer gets here and gives this boat a tow. Then we won't risk dropping the package into the drink."

"That's a roger, Fernandez. You staying?"

"Right. The other bird has already flown the coop."

"Fernandez, we'll check out this tub and see if they wrote anything down about the final destination of the plut."

"Roger that."

Murdock and Jaybird went over the papers in the pilot-house and found nothing that even hinted at where the package might be headed. Nor did they find any clue about where the boat itself was going.

Bradford and Ching worked every piece of paper they found in the cabin but found nothing about the destination of the boat or of the plutonium package. Then the radios came on.

"Cap, this is Fernandez. Just got word from the CAG. He says the *Willowwind* is moving. It hoisted anchor and moved out about ten minutes ago. Nothing to indicate they know that we're near them. Oh, that first radio message we got from the freighter on the international hailing frequency—the talker said he knew Don Stroh. The CAG hadn't told the spook about it until an hour ago. Stroh reacted strongly and got on his SATCOM. Turns out the CIA has a man on board the plutonium-packing freighter. He must be the one who sent the message. So we need to be careful about keeping him alive when we attack."

8

Murdock and his three men rode the sixty-foot boat behind the tow of the destroyer. Even before the destroyer arrived, the wind had picked up and the sea turned choppy. Then the storm clouds moved in from the west, and ten minutes later a drenching squall dropped sheets of rain on the boat.

The SEALs took cover in the cabin. "Not a chance we can go after that freighter tonight," Murdock said. "Not unless this storm blows over and out of here before midnight."

"Looks like it's settled in for a two day blow," Jaybird said. "You guys forgot I'm a weatherman, too."

"Any idea where the freighter is headed?" Ching asked.

"When they called, they weren't sure," Murdock said. "There are a couple of atolls within two hundred miles. It could be going for any of them. I'd bet on one with a good-sized airport."

"So we're thinking here that the air escape is the best for those packages of plutonium," Bradford said. "If they get them in the air, it's gonna be damn tough to track them."

"Yeah, especially if they fly out with four or five of them at the same time," Jaybird said.

"Is anybody checking those airfields?" Ching asked.

Murdock shook his head. "Not yet. As soon as we get off this bobbing cork, we'll talk to the CAG. Right now I just hope that the seas don't get so rough that the destroyer has to cut us loose."

Two hours later, the destroyer came close enough to

the carrier that they sent over a chopper to pick the men off the sixty-foot boat with winches. When the SEALs and the dead man and his three hijackers were all on the carrier, Murdock went to talk to the CAG and the carrier captain.

"The last heading we had on the *Willowwind* showed that she was sailing for Bikar Atoll. That's about a hundred and eighty miles from where she was at the first atoll. That's a big guess. There is a string of six or eight more atolls moving on southeast. He could be looking for any one of them."

"Which has the largest airport?" Murdock asked.

"I don't know," the CAG said. "I'll get in touch with the people on Majuro and find out. Yes, they might try to get a plane that would take out one or two of the boxes. Wouldn't take a huge plane to do that. What did you figure those crates weigh?"

"From twelve to fifteen hundred pounds. Most of the weight is in the lead bottle."

"What about a helicopter airlift?" Captain Walton asked. He was the top man on the carrier.

"Sir, wouldn't take a big chopper to lift one of those packages off the deck of the freighter," Murdock said. "Majuro would be the best place to find one for the job. Right now they're outside most of those choppers' radius range."

The CAG rubbed his right knee. An old wound still gave him some trouble now and then. "How far are we from that second atoll, Bikar?" He looked at one of his aides in the small room, and he left at once. "What I'm thinking is we could send a pair of Tomcats out there and see if it has an airstrip and any air facilities."

"How much runway does a Tomcat need to land?" Murdock asked.

"I almost always landed on the deck," the CAG said. "Don't know for sure, half mile, three quarters—whatever it is it's got to be a hell of a lot more than these tiny little atolls would have. These are commuter and small commercial planes. Two hundred yards and some of them crates are in the air."

"We probably couldn't see much in a fly-over," Captain Walton said. "Our last weather report from our Hawkeye says this storm is a large one, could last for two days at least. It isn't moving quickly the way some of them do."

"That means the hijackers get another two days free rein?" Murdock asked.

"Absolutely not," the CAG said. "We're on the radio with Majuro and they are cooperating. They understand the seriousness of the situation. They don't want that plutonium dumped inside their waters. They have alerted all of the major islands and atolls to be on the watch for the ship and for any suspicious cargo that tries to land from smaller ships."

"Captain, I thought the Hawkeye could look through clouds for spotting aircraft. Can't it do the same thing to track a ship on the water?"

"Depends on how heavy the rain is. The clouds we can get through with no trouble, but it's the density of the raindrops and their size that give us fits. On any radar going into a cloud, most of it is absorbed and doesn't get reflected. That which does can give us a generalized pattern, but it may or may not be enough to locate a ship on the water below."

"Say the storm is in waves or squalls with clear patterns in between. Then the Hawkeye could do its work on the ocean and try to find the ship?"

"Right and that's what we're hoping for."

A petty officer brought in some papers for the CAG. He glanced at them. "All right, we are about a hundred and seventy miles from that next atoll, Bikar. Our last spotting of the freighter had it on a heading that would put it right on the atoll. The storm might nudge them off course and will certainly slow them down. But at even ten knots, it could be at the island in seventeen hours."

Murdock stood and began pacing the small compartment. He shook his head and almost said something once, then changed his mind and went on walking. His mind was a jumble of plans and drawbacks and problems. The damn weather.

"Captain, can you get in voice contact with the manager of the airfield on Bikar?"

"We've been trying. Evidently it's a part-time job and we don't get any response. We obtained his call letters from the capitol in Majuro."

"Captain, we need somebody on that atoll, to check the airport and the dock if they have one. In this weather it might be impossible to parachute in. Could a Sixty find the atoll in this wall-to-wall rain?"

"Find it and drop you off?"

"What I was thinking. We'd need radios that would reach your CIC."

"Radios would be no problem. The Seahawk might. We could go up to thirteen thousand feet and get over the storm, but then you'd have to come down through it to find the atoll. The radius range would be okay. Finding the damn atoll in all that ocean is the tricky part."

"What's the visibility outside right now, Captain?"

The CAG looked at one of his aides.

"Sir, we're at zero-zero sometimes; now and then we get a quarter of a mile. We have no scheduled flight operations for the duration of the storm."

"So we'd have to hit it within a quarter of a mile or we wouldn't find it at all," Murdock said. "You have any pilots that good with a chopper that they can hit the eye of a needle?"

"I hope so, but I'm not sure I'd let anyone try it."

Murdock scowled and stared at the bulkhead. "Does your latest weather map show any clear spaces between the squalls? Like valleys between the peaks?"

The CAG looked at another officer at the table.

"Yes, sir. The squalls are about twenty miles wide, and moving to the east at about fifteen knots. About every hour and a quarter we should have a fairly clear space. There will still be some high clouds and remnants of the preceding storm, but visibility should be ten to fifteen miles.

"Good," Murdock said. "Now, how big is this window? How wide is that clear valley?"

The same officer spoke. "We never know for sure. Depends how fast the weather cell immediately behind is traveling. If it's moving at, say, twenty knots, it's overtaking the first one and cuts down on the length of time for the clear spell. If it's moving at half the speed of the one ahead of it, the window is open longer."

"That would be my suggestion, gentlemen: that we find that window, move in with two Sixties loaded with our sixteen SEALs, with firm radio communications, and that we drop in on that atoll. We have twelve hours to find a suitable window. In that time the storm may let up, go around us, or die out."

"At ten thousand feet the Seahawk can do about two hundred miles per hour. Say we're a hundred and fifty miles from the atoll by then, take you less than an hour to get there. Would the bird stay on the ground with you?"

"Preferably. We've been stranded in some strange spots without any transport."

"Depending on your mission on the atoll, we could bring you back in the next window or wait," the CAG said.

"If we get there early, there will be a wait. What time is it?"

"Almost sixteen hundred, sir," one of the officers at the table said.

The CAG shook his head. "I can't send you out in the dark, even in a good open window. The weather is too unpredictable. It could close in suddenly and you'd be in danger of not being able to find the atoll or get back to the ship. It'll have to be within an hour, or in the morning first light."

"Agreed," Murdock said. "How does the weather look in the next hour?"

The weather officer frowned. "We're about in the middle of a big cell that won't be pushed past us for another two hours."

"Then it's daylight and we hope for better weather or

we find a valley we can wade over there in. How fast are we going now?"

The captain looked at another officer. "Sir, last reading was thirteen knots. The seas are getting large out there."

"So, by dawn we should be nearly on top of the atoll," Murdock said. "That might change our plans. Be damn nice to know if the freighter had stopped there and then moved on. It should come to the atoll two or three hours before we get there. A furious lot can happen in three hours with these hijackers."

On board the *Willowwind*

Keanae knew too late that he should have done it right then. Jomo Shigahara himself had come down to the galley to bitch about the quality of the food. He was less than fifteen feet from where Keanae hid behind the corn-flakes and cases of canned goods in the storage locker. The door was open. It would have been simple to nail the bastard with two shots from his .45. Now it would be harder.

Since that time the heavy weather had hit and the freighter was struggling to make ten knots. The chief mate had been let out of his cabin arrest and willingly complied with Shigahara's orders to keep the ship from going down, and to get it back on the course that had been set. Chief Mate Barry Stillman had told Wally the second cook that the ship was heading for Bikar Atoll.

"Nice little spot. Has water and lots of trees. Small community there, with lots of fishermen. They even have a clinic and a real doctor. That's where you should jump ship. How are you at swimming?"

Keanae grinned. "Not too fucking good with this shot-up shoulder, but I could make it a half mile or so."

"If we stop there, and I bet you a thousand we will, we'll anchor on the lee of the atoll and go in by that whale boat on the aft deck. Motor and everything. We won't be more than two hundred yards offshore."

"Maybe it'll all be over before then," Keanae said. "Where does the captain take his dinner?"

"In his cabin . . ." Wally stopped. "You thinking of doing something drastic?"

"Yep, should have done it before. Without the head of this snake, the whole damn thing dies."

"He always carries that little automatic. A thirty-eight I think it is, or a nine-millimeter. Say he has seventeen rounds. Your forty-five only has eight, right?"

"Seven in the magazine and one in the chamber. I won't need that many. Who takes the man's food up to him?"

Wally laughed. "Hell, I think that you're going to do it."

"Wally, tell me exactly how the food gets there. Do you knock and say dinner? Or just knock and wait for him to open the hatch? Is there any set procedure he'll be looking for? I'll have a cap on and pulled down when the hatch opens."

"Nothing special. I've taken it up a half dozen times. Just knock on the hatch and when he yells, you yell, 'Dinner, Captain,' and he should open up."

"How long?"

"His tray will be ready in about twenty minutes. He likes to eat promptly at eighteen hundred."

"You say eighteen hundred? You were Navy?"

"Twenty-one years and accepting my retirement checks."

"I'll be ready."

Keanae went behind the stores and put on different clothes. He wore khaki shorts, as most of the men did, and a blue shirt with the tails out. On his head he had bill cap touting the New York Yankees. He pulled it down and put on a pair of light-colored sunglasses. Then he figured that was too much and left the sunglasses with his other gear behind a case of pickles.

He felt dizzy for just a moment as he picked up the tray. That damn lead slug in his shoulder was starting to affect him. The tray was heavier than he'd imagined. Wally said there were always three entrees on the tray. He had the .45 stuffed in his belt under the shirt, which was just long enough to cover it. He wasn't sure how he would do it, but it would get done. He'd have to play it as it fell. Keanae walked the familiar corridors and up the ladders to Officer Country and knocked on the captain's hatch.

"Yeah?" A voice barely came through the heavy steel.

"Captain's dinner is here," Keanae bellowed so Shigahara could hear him.

The man inside said something that Keanae couldn't understand, and then the hatch opened outward a crack. Keanae nudged it toward him with the fingers on his right hand, then pulled it open. He stepped just inside the hatch and held out the tray.

"Put it on the table, idiot," Shigahara snapped.

Keanae took it a dozen feet to the table bolted to the wall, then turned, the .45 already out. The CIA man was surprised to see that the hijacker had his own weapon out and pointing in Keanae's general direction. Keanae fired twice as fast as he could. The first round caught Shigahara in the chest and slammed him backward in his chair. The second round was higher from the surge upward of the weapon's recoil. The second round hit Jomo Shigahara just above his nose, tore off half of his scalp, and pulverized massive amounts of his brain centers.

Keanae hadn't heard the smaller gun fire, but he felt the round jolt into his right thigh and nearly knock him down. He stayed on his feet and felt the dizziness come back. For a moment he looked at the hijacker where he had flopped backward in the soft chair. The hijacking was over. Now if he could just get up to the bridge.

It took him fifteen minutes moving along the familiar corridors and ladders, until he pushed open the bridge hatch, then yelled at the chief mate and fell forward on his face.

When Keanae came back to consciousness five minutes later he still held the .45 clamped in his hand, but his finger wasn't on the trigger. They had lifted him into a chair and somebody had bound up his leg wound. Chief Mate Stillman hovered over him.

"About time you came back to see us. I had a man

check the captain's cabin. Nice shooting. Now what the hell are we supposed to do?"

Keanae shook his head to try to clear it. He was on the bridge. Yes, and with Chief Mate Stillman. Slowly his eyes focused and he took a deep breath. His leg hurt and his shoulder seemed to be on fire.

"What should we do now?"

"Storm still on?"

"Right, looks like a big one. We'll make Bikar atoll before morning."

"Radio the Navy. Tell them where we are. We'll wait for them at Bikar to reclaim the U.S. property and get this tub on its way back to San Diego."

Chief Stillman looked away. He shook his head. "Keanae, I'm sorry to say that we can't call in the Navy. This afternoon Shigahara went into the communications room and shot holes in every piece of radio equipment down there. We can't transmit to anyone, nor can we receive. We're deaf right now to the outside world."

It took Keanae a while to absorb what the chief mate had told him. He blinked, then tried to sit up straighter, but when he put pressure on his left arm, he let out a groan.

"You said we don't have any radio?"

"None at all. He must have been expecting to change ships or something at Bikar."

"Okay. When we get to Bikar we can use their radio. The Navy can't be far behind us." He pushed up with his right hand. Yes, He felt better now. Shigahara was dead. Now for the other four. "Round up the other hijackers. Tell them Shig wants to see them right away on the bridge. We'll take them down and then be ready for the Navy with no shots fired."

Ten minutes later two of the hijackers had reported to the bridge and were promptly disarmed, tied hand and foot, and pushed into a corner. The third one tried to get his gun out, but the chief mate slugged him with a right-hand fist that jolted him to the deck. The last hijacker was not to be found.

Keanae felt better. "Watch for that last one. Socha is his name. He's got a handgun. Now, how much longer until we get to Bikar?"

It was seven hours more before their radar poked a hole in the rain and fog and they had a bearing on the atoll.

"I've been here before," Keanae said. "It's one of the good-sized atolls, with trees and springs for freshwater, and an actual hill almost a hundred feet high. The volcano was more active here. There's also an airport. They might have extended the runway since I was here, but not long enough for commercial jets to land. Maybe a thousand people here. One tourist hotel, lots of beaches and the lagoon, and lots of vicious coral heads. I've still got scars to prove it.

"Come in on the lee side and we should be able to anchor within a hundred yards of the reef," Keanae said. They edged up to the speck of coral. The rain slacked off for a moment, and the small atoll came in clearly. Lights showed in buildings. The lagoon looked quiet and serene. Before they crept up to an anchor spot, they heard a series of submachine gunshots from the atoll. Lights flared through the misty rain and a bullhorn blasted over the whining of the wind.

"About time you got here. I'm sending out a boat for the three million, Jomo, and, you little Jap sonofabitch, you better have it intact or your head is on a platter. After I get the cash in my hot little hands, we'll decide how many of those packages we send out by air while the damn storm is still on. Get some lights over the side so we can see where the fuck we're driving this little motor boat."

9

Bikar Atoll, Marshall Islands

Keanae stood on the rail of the *Willowwind,* stunned by the bullhorn announcement from the atoll. He reacted at once.

"Okay, there are some more hijackers coming out to the ship. We've got four pistols and the rifle from the arms locker. We find volunteers and stand them off. They can't get up the side if we don't lower a ladder. Chief Mate, you have a pistol. Get two more men. I have a pistol and the rifle, looks like an old deer-hunting rifle."

"It belonged to the captain," Stillman said just before he left to talk to the crew, which had been let out of the dayroom the moment they had control of the ship. He came back soon with three men.

"Both ex-military. We each have thirty rounds. What's our strategy?"

"We don't say a word. We let them get close to the ship, then each man fires one round at them. We probably won't hit anybody, but all we need to do is discourage them. As a last choice, we pull up anchor and move out into the ocean. The rain has stopped for a moment. Here they come."

The powerboat negotiated a narrow channel out from the lagoon in the dark. Only an experienced man on the tiller could make the night passage. Then it sped the one hundred yards toward the freighter.

Keanae had told the men with the guns what to do and to fire only on his command. The motor launch came closer. "When I call fire, we all shoot one round, understood?" The men said they did. They were spaced five yards apart along the rail amidships. Keanae watched the boat come through the murky darkness. It had running lights. When they were twenty feet from the side of the ship, he called out sharply.

"Fire."

Five rounds thundered into the chilly night. The man driving the motorboat cut the engine. The same voice blasted on the bullhorn.

"What the hell's the matter with you, Shigahara? You trying to get away with that three million? You know better. Now, cut the shit, and drop a ladder."

"One more round," Keanae shouted and the men fired. This time a scream of pain came from someone in the boat. It surged ahead until it scraped against the side of the ship. Now the sailors would have to lean out over the rail to hit the small craft.

"Bastard, Shigahara. You think we didn't plan for something like this? Hell, we did. We've got two big military-type limpet mines attached to your hull a foot underwater. I hit a radio signal and both of them will blast a hole ten feet wide in your hull and you'll go down in ten minutes. You want that?"

"Shigahara is dead. He won't be helping you."

A shot blasted into the night air, and one of the seamen at the rail screamed and fell backward, clutching at his chest. Keanae knew in a second it had to be the fifth hijacker, the one they couldn't find on board.

He turned and fired three shots from his pistol in the direction the shot had to have come from. He reloaded quickly.

The bullhorn voice came again. "Sounds like some of my men are still up there working for me, whoever you are. You don't have a prayer. I give the word, we have marksmen with night scopes on shore who will clean all of you off that rail. You want to die here in the fucking rain?"

Keanae leaned out and fired five times with his pistol

at the small boat below. Another scream filtered through the darkness.

A submachine gun rattled off a dozen shots from the boat below, and Keanae lunged back to get out of the spray of lead and paint chips where the hot rounds drilled past him. The burst of automatic gunfire must have been the signal. High-powered rifles from shore cracked, and heavy lead bullets whined off the steel sides and rails of the ship. The four men there dove to the deck and rolled away from the rail, searching for something solid to hide behind. Keanae figured twenty shots from shore, then a second burst from the sub gun below ended the sniping.

"Now you see how it is," the bullhorn brayed. "We're at a standoff. You can't leave; we can't get up there. We blow up the fucking boat, it'll be lots harder to salvage the crates in your number two hold. You could just give up. Hell, tell you what I'll do. I'll meet your payroll, double it for rich man, and fly you all to Majuro, where you can get a flight back to Honolulu. What could be more fair? You hear me? Who the hell's in charge up there?"

"That would be me," Keanae bellowed. "Who the hell are you?"

"Just a businessman trying to earn a living."

Keanae thought he heard something, a scraping, but he wasn't sure. He concentrated on listening to the sound of the bullhorn.

"So how about it? I haven't heard you turn down my offer yet. How about a vote of the people? Ask your crewmen if they want to get killed trying to keep us off, or if they want a free ride back to Hawaii."

"Not their decision, it's mine," Keanae shouted. He listened again—more scraping. What the hell?

Before he could lift up to investigate, two men came over the scuppers and under the rail with small Ingram-type submachine guns blasting. One of the sailors who had used a pistol took four slugs in the chest and went down without a word. Another one tried to run for better protection behind the big crane, and he fell with slugs in both legs.

Keanae saw the men with funny goggles on. Then he knew—night vision glasses. He kept low, then lifted up and fired three times at the closest boarder, who still had the magnetic kneepads on. Two of the slugs caught him in the side and he pitched over and didn't move.

In the faint light from a ship's bulb, Keanae saw a third man lift over the rail and rattle off more shots. A small quiet period followed and Chief Mate Stillman shouted.

"Cease fire. Stop the shooting. We give up. I don't want any more of my men killed in this stupid fight."

"Smart man," one of the machine gunners shouted. "You sailors with guns, toss them out. Should be three of you left. Do it now." Keanae figured the talker was hiding behind one of the steel boxes bolted to the deck. Keanae was outgunned. He hadn't even tried to fire the rifle. He waited a moment, picked his spot. He had to get back to his hiding place and choose his time again to strike. In a sudden rush he jolted across the deck and dove toward part of the hatch cover that hadn't been reinstalled.

Two sub guns chattered, and Keanae felt a blow to his right leg as he hit the deck and rolled behind the protection. He dropped the revolver when he rolled.

"We have wounded," Stillman shouted. "Is there a doctor on the atoll who can treat them?"

"There is," the bullhorn voice said. "You talk that last man into surrendering and you have a deal."

"What happens to my ship?"

"That's not part of the deal. Who are you?"

"I'm Chief Mate Stillman, in command. Shigahara butchered our captain."

"Sounds like Shiggy. Talk to your man."

While the two talked, Keanae had been moving. He was more at home with silent movement in the woods or jungle, but here it worked as well. He had a four-foot open space he had to cross. Even in the darkness there were shafts of light stabbing into the area from the ship's normal lights, one of them streaking across his route. He moved across it with slow, agonizing inches, worming ahead and pausing and worming ahead. Any quick movement will attract a watcher. Before Stillman and the bullhorn finished talking, Keanae was on the far side and had cover and concealment. Then he moved swiftly down a ladder, past the crew quarters, and toward the first hold, where he had a hideout. The last surge brought a gush of dizziness to him, and he slowed, then lowered his head until the feeling passed, and hurried on to the hold, down the ladder, and to the small space he had built behind old cardboard cartons and assorted rubble from the last regular shipment. He eased in behind his camouflage and let his heart stop racing. Then he looked at his leg. The slug had gone all the way through. He took off his shirt, pulled off his T-shirt, and tore it up for bandages. Then he bound both the entry and exit wounds as tight as he could stand. At least he wouldn't bleed to death. He had another thirty hours, maybe, to get that slug out of his shoulder. He hadn't felt it during the heat of the battle and the escape, but now it throbbed. He dug into his pocket and took out the plastic bottle of ibuprofen the cook had given him. Four would do. He gulped them down without the help of water. Keanae felt safe here. The problem was, he was also blind and deaf to what was going on. When they stopped looking for him, he would slip up a deck and see if he could find out what the men from the island were doing.

On deck, Chief Mate Stillman had his crew assembled. He had let down a rope ladder and six men had come on board. Two were obviously Arabs, with full black beards and swarthy skin. The others were locals, undoubtedly paid well for this bit of piracy. One of the bearded ones was the leader.

He stared at Stillman in the faint light of the ship's floods.

"Two of your sailors are dead, one wounded—I know there were five men firing from the rail. Another man came in with his empty revolver. What about the fifth man?"

"He's another crewman in the group over there," Stillman said. "Why should I point him out? We're all here."

"You're shorthanded."

"Shigahara was responsible for that. I think he enjoyed killing people."

The Arab laughed. "Yes, yes, that does sound like my little Japanese buddy. Now, where is the three million dollars?"

"He didn't tell me. It was delivered to his cabin, the captain's cabin. Your guess where he hid it is as good as mine."

The three tied-up hijackers and the missing one were greeted by the Arabs like teammates. The Arab leader frowned, then lifted heavy brows.

"What the hell, you're probably right about the fifth shooter. Now we have work to do."

A larger boat had worked out of the entrance to the lagoon and came alongside in the darkness. It was about eighty feet long, Stillman figured. The rain came down again and the hijack leader cursed in Arabic.

The hatch cover had been lifted off the second hold, and the crane now dropped its big hooks into the depths, where crewmen rigged them on the lifting rings on both sides of a crate of plutonium. They moved three of the crates off the ship and into the eighty-foot boat below. It pulled away in the darkness and maneuvered at a cat's crawl through the entrance to the lagoon and then up to the dock. There a crane on wheels lifted the crates off the boat to the dock. Bright floodlights outlined the progress as the men on the merchantman watched. Soon the big boat was back beside the freighter. Six men came up the rope ladder with sea bags. They reported to the bearded Arab, who welcomed them and had one of the regular crew show them to quarters. Then three more plutonium crates were eased into the boat bouncing below on the choppy sea.

One of the bearded Arabs left the ship then, along with

the three machine gunners and four other men who had helped in the off-loading. This time the boat stopped only briefly at the lagoon dock. In the bright lights, Stillman could see eight men get off the boat; then it pushed off and went back out the channel, turned south and headed into the angry Pacific Ocean.

Stillman knew they still had a chance to save the rest of the cargo and the ship. The limpet mines must have been a bluff. Keanae had slipped away and was back in one of his several hiding spots. He had told the chief mate about some of them. The one in the kitchen had been inspired, complete with food, drink, and companionship. Stillman had no idea where the CIA agent was now. The Arab man came up to Stillman as the hatch covers were eased into place and battened down.

"Chief Mate Stillman, you will make ready to get underway. We'll be leaving within fifteen minutes. I'd suggest you get your crew cracking. You might have noticed that we added seven men to your crew. That means we now have ten men on board. All of our seamen are competent in their craft, and are all loyal to me. Each man has two weapons, so instruct your crew to do exactly as they are told at all times by my men. Now get us underway."

"In this weather?"

"Yes. Beautiful, isn't it? I couldn't have ordered a better storm, or one at a better time. It's made to order for the rest of our little operation here. As you're moving the ship, Kassir here will be watching you. He's a qualified pilot and first mate, so be sure you are exact in following his orders. He'll give you the heading and speed and see that you stay with it. Oh, you have no operating radio, so we have brought two on board with us. Now, move."

Behind the ship, on the atoll, a heavy truck had pulled up to the dock. Two of the large crates were loaded on board with the crane, and it sped away into the night. It followed a narrow road near the coast of the island and past a small hill to the southern half, which was nearly flat and had

been bulldozed and rolled down until the coral had been
packed so tightly with the sand and soil that it made a
nearly concrete-like surface. The landing strip was only
eight hundred yards long, and there were definite restric-
tions on how big a plane could be landed there.

The runway was unlighted. Sitting at the extreme north
end of the hard surface was a Spartica aircraft. None of
the men at the small field had ever seen one before. They
were told it had been used in South America for decades
as a rugged and highly reliable short-hop transport plane
for heavy loads. Its loading hatch was over eight feet
square. The truck pulled up near the plane and waited.
Five minutes later, coming out of the misty rain, the rolling crane eased up to the truck and positioned itself, put
down its outrigger braces and hooked up to one of the
crates.

Loading it was tricky. They had to lift it near the hatch,
then slowly lower it onto a dolly that eased it backward
into the plane inches at a time. More dollies were positioned under it as the crane let it down gently. Then it
was safe on the dollies and rolled back in the plane, and
the second crate came and was offloaded the same way.

The pilot and engineer came back and checked the load.
They measured and had the crew move the boxes forward
four feet each before they were tied down.

Two minutes later, through the darkness and the continuing spatter of raindrops, the stubby winged plane's
two wing-mounted turboprop engines roared into life. The
pilot checked his engines a moment. Then he gunned
them, stormed down the short runway, and lifted his
wheels off the ground with only thirty feet to spare. The
craft turned and headed due west. The pilot, an Italian,
settled into his job. He was using the name of Pasquale
for this trip. Just the one name. He had a long flight ahead
of him. He had put on added fuel tanks in Majuro and
had enough gas to fly for three thousand miles before
stopping. That excited him. Then, too, there was the
promised bonus of fifty thousand dollars when he delivered the two crates. He had no idea what was in them,

but it must be highly valuable. For a brief moment he thought of changing his course and vanishing among the hundreds of islands in Micronesia. He might be able to sell the goods for millions. The men who hired him were Arabs, and he wondered what the valuable cargo was. But he had dismissed the idea. His copilot would never go along with the idea. He would have to kill the man. He shrugged. No way was he going to kill his own brother.

10

The South Pacific
On board the *Carl Vinson CVN 70*
At dawn the carrier task force was only twenty miles off Bikar Atoll. A valley in the series of heavy weather cells provided a clear view of the small island, and both the Hawkeye and a pair of F-14s reported that there was no freighter anchored off the island.

"I don't like it," Murdock said. "She could have been there for three or four hours. I want to go in with our two Sixties and check out the locals. Can we take off in fifteen minutes?"

The CAG said the two Sixties were still at standby. Murdock hustled his men into the birds and they launched thirteen minutes later. On the short hop to the atoll Murdock checked with Communications. Yes, they had been given approval by the powers in Majuro to land on any of the atolls they thought might be involved in the hijacking.

The two birds came into the small island from the north and landed on the airfield just south of the small settlement. A pickup truck hustled out to where they dropped out of the choppers. A tanned Caucasian about forty-five, with Navy wings pinned to his flight jacket met them with a big grin.

"Be damned—a real live SH-60. Didn't think I'd ever see another one of them long as I lived. Name's Quartermier. Welcome to Bikar."

Murdock shook his hand. "Commander Murdock, sir.

We're looking for a hijacked freighter that was headed this way. Did it stop here?"

"Sure as hell did. And two planeloads of men. They came in two days ago and took over the island. Had nasty little Ingram submachine guns, and we didn't argue."

"Somebody met the freighter here?"

"Yep. Had a little fire fight to get on board, then some of them guys went up the sides of that freighter with magnetic shoes and gloves or something, went over the side and sprayed all sorts of fire from their Ingrams."

"So they had to capture the ship?"

"Yep, these two Arab guys . . ."

Murdock held up his hand. "You say there were two Arabs?"

"Damn straight. Full beards, talked strange, the whole thing, with the Ingrams and knives. I mean we're pretty laid-back folks around here. These guys were nasty."

"What did they do with the freighter?"

"Took out a ship they brought in here, an eighty-footer, the harbor guys told me. Went out to the freighter and off-loaded six of them big crates. Two they brought out here and loaded them on a plane. Crazy little crate called the Spartica. Built in Spain, I understand. Sturdy, short haul, but he had extra fuel tanks."

Murdock's face turned grim. His eyes half closed. "When did it take off?"

"Let's see, about an hour, maybe an hour and a half ago. In the fucking rain and maybe a half hour before dawn. Headed east, almost due east."

Murdock hurried inside the chopper and used the radio. He reported the aircraft and its heading. A job for the Hawkeyes. He came back. The SEALs stood around waiting.

"You guys are Navy, aren't you?" Quartermier asked.

"Yes, sir, Navy SEALs," Senior Chief Sadler said.

"Be damned. You guys look like commandos."

Murdock came back. "What happened to the other four crates they unloaded?"

"Them? They kept them in that eighty-footer. Her name

was the *Albatross,* out of Majuro. I know the boat. Wasn't the usual crew handling her. Had to use one of our locals to get in and out of the channel. Then they let him off and some others and the ship headed south, maybe southwest."

"Any other planes involved?"

"Yep. Four of them flew in here in a four-place Piper Cub. It made two or three trips from Majuro. Lots of traffic for my little strip here."

"I see your wings. You were Navy air?"

"Damn right, twenty-six years. Wound up in the F-14s."

"Let me talk to the carrier again." Murdock vanished into the chopper and used the radio to report the ship heading southwest out of Bikar.

He came back and motioned for the SEALs to board the choppers.

"Mr. Quartermier, any idea what was in the heavy crates?"

"Not a clue, and nobody talked about it. Damned tight-lipped bunch of men. Didn't like the two Arabs." He frowned. "Something illegal going on here?"

"Absolutely. So the men who attacked the freighter had control of her when she left?"

"Right, and they put six or eight more men on her. Looked like sailors from what I saw of them. They flew them in from Majuro."

Murdock thanked the ex-pilot and ran for the lead bird. It took off at once and headed southwest. Murdock went back to the radio in the cockpit.

"Yes, sir, that's what the ex–Navy pilot said. An eighty-footer with four crates on board. We're heading that way to see if we can find her. Two hours at fourteen knots shouldn't be hard to find. How long will this good weather hold?"

"My weather expert tells me the worst of it is over. From now on we should have only occasional showers, fast-moving ones. I'll send a destroyer at flank in that direction. Let me know if you find the boat."

"We'll find it. We have plenty of fuel. When we find it, we're going to engage. One of our choppers has rope-down capability. We'll use that after our first attack."

"Roger that, Commander, and good hunting."

Murdock gave the mike back to the pilot.

"He shouldn't be more than thirty to forty miles away from the atoll," the pilot said. His name was Paulson and he was from Minneapolis.

"When we find him, there's going to be some shooting. You ever been shot at before, Lieutenant?"

"No, sir. I guess it's my turn. You just tell me where you want me to go, and I'll put you there."

Murdock went back and watched out the open doors, looking for the boat. They were at four thousand feet for a longer view, but after ten minutes and thirty-four miles, they hadn't found the boat.

"The Hawkeyes must be scanning this area," Paulson said. "Let me check with Home Base." After the transmission, he had his crew chief call Murdock up.

"The Hawkeye found the boat. Only one in the area. They gave me some coordinates. We'll be there in four minutes. They changed course and headed more to the south."

"Thanks, Paulson. We're ready." Murdock used his Motorola and told all the SEALs in both choppers that the ship was coming up. "Gardner, you'll go in first and use your long guns on it, then sweep in for the short guns. When you have them beaten down, we'll go in and rope down. You ride shotgun for us. If you see any fire during the roping, use your snipers to silence them."

"That's a roger, Cap. Subguns and snipers. Take it easy down there. These guys are playing for big stakes. It could have been over a billion dollars in sales."

"We'll watch out front; you cover our backs."

"There she is," Jaybird yelled. The SEALs looked out the left-hand door. The boat was making good time in the still choppy sea with six-foot swells.

"Bouncing around like a cork," Lam said. "We going to rope down on that?"

"Piece of cake," Howard said.

"Save me the frosting," Jaybird chirped.

"Long guns on the door," Gardner said on the Motorola. "Tell the pilot to circle her at two hundred yards. That should out-range their Ingrams. Put a dozen rounds into her pilothouse and take out any men you see. Let's do it."

The Sixty came in fast, then slowed as it established a circle pattern, with its left door facing the target. As soon as they were in the pattern, Canzoneri and Prescott drilled the ship with a dozen shots. Then on the other chopper Murdock took his Bull Pup and put a contact 20mm round into the pilothouse. The ship slowed. Gardner's chopper moved into a fifty-yard circle and the MP-5s sprayed the small boat with two hundred rounds.

"Let's go down," Murdock told the crew chief. The chopper came in on the stern of the boat that was barely making headway through the seas. Murdock was thirty feet above the deck. He saw one man lift up and fire at the chopper, then take four rounds from the other chopper, flop on the deck, and not move again.

The bird hovered over the stern, then crept forward ten feet, and Murdock and Jaybird kicked out the ropes. The SEALS had put on their special gloves, and they slid down the ropes with the gloves doing the braking. All eight men made it to the deck in record time, and the chopper pulled away.

Murdock was first on deck. He came down face to face with the dead man and his Ingram. He darted ahead toward the pilothouse. An Ingram chattered for a moment, but the six rounds went over Murdock's head. He sent a three-round burst from the Bull Pup's 5.56 into the pilothouse doorway and then flattened against the bulkhead just outside. "Anybody in there who wants to stay alive, sing out," Murdock bellowed. Nobody answered. Murdock pulled a fragger grenade off his webbing and jerked out the safety pin. He let the handle fly, counted to two, and then tossed the bomb into the pilothouse. The thun-

dering explosion rocked the ship for a moment. Then all
was quiet.

Jaybird and Tim Sadler took the cabin as planned. Jaybird skidded to a stop outside the steps that led down. He
risked a quick look and jerked back. Six rounds from a
stuttering Ingram blasted past his head, barely missing
him. Sadler threw in a stun grenade, and as soon as it
stopped flashing and sounding off, he and Jaybird charged
inside.

They found two men on couches, holding their ears and
their eyes tightly shut. Jaybird bound their hands behind
their backs with riot cuffs and went back on deck. "Cabin
clear," he called on his Motorola.

Murdock darted around the hatch on the pilothouse as
soon as the shrapnel quit flying. He found two men, one
draped over the wheel, dead where he lay. A second man
had blood all over his face and neck. One arm had been
blown off. He glared at Murdock through half-open eyes.

"I die for Allah," he shouted.

"Like hell, you sonofabitch. You die for the almighty
dollar. Don't flatter yourself."

The Arab man, with full black beard and hard eyes,
stabbed a glance at Murdock filled with hatred. Then he
gasped once, and shook over his whole body. He tried to
lift his good arm and the Ingram came up partway. Murdock aimed his Bull Pup, but before the man could lift
his weapon high enough, his eyes fluttered and his
breathing stopped. His head turned slowly to the left, his
unsighted eyes wide open, now staring at his dead hijacker
buddy.

"Pilothouse clear," Murdock radioed.

Luke Howard slid around the back of the first heavy
crate and looked where he thought he saw movement. He
pushed his head out and jolted it back. An Ingram
slammed hot lead past him. He reached around with his
MP-5 and kicked out six rounds, then paused. He heard
a moan. He looked again, and this time he saw a man
sprawled next to the second heavy crate, an Ingram in his
hands, but pointing down.

"Drop it and stay alive," Howard shouted. He came around the crate slowly, his MP-5 trained on the man. The bearded man screamed, pulled up the Ingram, and fired before he had it trained on Howard. Howard fired a three-round burst, but not before the Ingram had tracked to him and put three rounds into his right leg. He saw his own rounds hit the hijacker in the throat and head and jolt him over backward. He sprawled against the plutonium crate and remained deadly quiet.

"I'm hit," Howard said on the Motorola.

"Is the boat clear?" Murdock asked on the net.

"Clear port side," Bradford said.

"Clear starboard," Ching said.

"Clear in the engine room and the fish hold," Van Dyke said.

"Ship clear," Murdock said. "Jaybird, see what you can do for Howard."

Murdock reported to JG Gardner on the Motorola that they had secured the ship, had two prisoners and four dead hijackers. Gardner had his pilot relay the message to the carrier.

Two hours later a destroyer charged up to their position and circled them. A small boat launched over the fantail and came alongside. A chief coxswain called out.

"Commander, my skipper gives you his greetings and asks you and your men and prisoners to come aboard. You'll be flown back to the carrier by our Sixty."

A half hour later, Murdock and his men were back on the carrier. He, the JG, Jaybird, and Lam met with the CAG, the carrier's boss Captain Walton, and Don Stroh.

"No good news about that plane that got away," Captain Olenowski, the CAG, told them. "It had a three-hour head start on us, which could put it about seven to eight hundred miles out there somewhere."

"We have any resources in that area?" Murdock asked.

"Not that I know of. I have a man checking now. That's out in the middle of Micronesia, the Carolines, lots of places a plane could set down."

Jaybird shook his head. "Sir, I don't think that bird is going to light until he runs out of fuel. We've seen Arabs. That plane has to be headed for the Arab world. Which means almost due east. What major landmass is first up, the Philippines?"

Stroh stood and walked around the table in the conference room. "Yeah, makes sense, Captain. This has been well planned out, all the contingencies figured in. Plans and alternates and backup all the way. I'd say the plane is heading for the Philippines then on east. What do we have in that area?"

"Guam," JG Gardner said. "Lots of assets on Guam. Must be an AWACS there."

The CAG looked up, his eyes flashing. "From here Guam is about fifteen hundred miles. We could put up a group of AWACS to watch for that plane."

"If we find it, we can't just shoot it down," Murdock said. "We need the plutonium back. What we can do is track it to its first fueling stop and hope it's a friendly country where we can confiscate the plane and arrest the pilots."

"We could do it in the Philippines," Stroh said. "They owe us for helping them get rid of their guerrillas."

Murdock looked at Stroh. "Talk to your people and have them brief the Philippines." He turned to the carrier commander. "Captain, can you alert Guam to get some AWACS up and watch for that plane?"

"We have any description?"

"A stubby wing prop jet called a Spartica, made in Spain," Murdock said.

"Should be enough. I'll make some radio contacts. I'll have to go through COMPAC."

Stroh shook his head. "Not on this one, Captain. You had orders from the CNO. You can do anything out here you and Murdock need done."

The captain smiled. "Yeah, I guess you're right. My boss will razz me about it, but it'll be worth it. Let me get on it."

The captain stood. Everyone else in the room jolted to

attention as the captain left the conference room. When the door closed, they sat down.

"Now the good news," the CAG said. "We have the *Willowwind*. She's about fifty miles ahead of us and heading directly for Utrik Atoll. The ship is about thirty miles from Utrik. We have two planes in the air checking out the atoll. We don't know how big it is or what facilities they have. We should know in about ten minutes."

"If we take her down now, it would save any more island hopping for her where she could dump out more of the plut," Murdock said.

"Not a good idea to rope down on her in the daylight," Lam said. "We'd be fat fish in a shooting barrel. They must have all the weapons on board that they want, maybe even some machine guns. Certainly sub guns and Kalashnikovs."

"If they have any rocket-propelled grenades, our choppers would be sitting ducks," the CAG said.

"But if we wait until dark, the ship will have had seven or eight hours at the atoll," Murdock said. "They could unload half the crates."

"She's a U.S. flagship," Captain Olenowski said. "I can send in three F-18s and strafe her with twenty-millimeter, and order her to go dead in the water well off the atoll. We'll use the international hailing frequency and demand that she stop and prepare to be boarded."

The SEALs nodded.

Stroh lifted his brows. "Sounds good to me."

A seaman came in with a sheet of paper and handed it to the CAG. "Here's a report from our observation run on Utrik Atoll. She's larger than the last one, has a runway that could accommodate an F-14, and there are three turboprop-type transports waiting on the hard-surface runway. The lagoon has a good channel through the coral and a fair-sized dock, but only ships under forty feet are at the docks right now."

Murdock stood. "Captain, I'd say that report is all the more reason we have to stop that freighter in mid-ocean. If it gets to the atoll and can unload again, we're going to have four planes to track instead of one."

11

On the carrier deck, Murdock watched the two F-18s blast off and then hurried to the CIC. The CAG talked with the lead pilot.

"Hunter One, let me know when you get the ship in sight, then just after you buzz her. Both of you get down to no more than fifty feet over her stack."

"Be a pleasure, CAG."

"Hunter One, you guys buzz her and then I'll try to contact her by radio."

"That's a roger, Home Base."

"How long?" Murdock asked.

"Three or four minutes if the ship is where she's supposed to be."

"Those Eighteens move right along."

"Depending on the altitude, around twenty-six miles a minute," the CAG said. "They are a joy to fly. Damn, sometimes . . ." He looked at Murdock and grinned. "An old pilot's dream."

"Home Base, this is Hunter One. We have the ship in sight. The configuration fits. When we do the fly-over, I'll check the deck to find the loading crane. The outline is as called out."

"Roger, Hunter."

"Dropping down on the deck, here we go."

There was a moment of dead airtime. "Yes, Home Base. I'd say this is the right freighter. Some asshole from the deck fired at me. I saw the muzzle flashes."

"Good. Hold there, Hunter." The CAG took a mike and pushed the talk button.

"Freighter *Willowwind,* this is the U.S. Navy. We have just done a courtesy fly-over. Your vessel is in violation of U.S. laws and we are authorized to seize it. Cut your forward speed to five knots immediately and answer me on this hailing frequency."

The CAG let the button up and waited. There was no reply. He waited two minutes by his watch.

"*Willowwind,* I repeat, cut your forward speed to five knots and answer on the hailing frequency."

This time the speaker spoke. "Don't know what you're talking about, U.S. Navy. Your planes just maneuvered dangerously close to us and we're filing a criminal complaint. This is the *Challenge* out of Singapore. Keep your planes away from my ship."

"*Willowwind,* you have three minutes to cut your speed or you will be fired upon. Do you understand, three minutes? Cut your speed to five knots at once."

"I'm filing a criminal action complaint against you in the World Court and the International Maritime Congress. Keep your planes away from my ship."

The CAG picked up a different mike. "Hunter, that was piped through to you. You heard. Make a run, both of you, and fire ten rounds each over his bow. Do it now."

"Wilco, Home Base, making approach now from two miles. Lining up thirty yards off his bow, firing ten rounds now."

Twenty seconds later: "Hunter One has fired."

A few seconds later another transmission: "Hunter Two has fired across his bow."

The CAG took the hailing frequency mike. "Now you've been warned. You have five minutes to cut your power and bring the *Willowwind* down to five knots forward. Otherwise you will be seriously damaged by twenty-millimeter rounds from the two planes you have seen. Five minutes."

"Idiots. I refuse to talk with you anymore. This is the *Challenge* out of Singapore, not that other name. We will be filing complaints and lawsuits as soon as we dock."

"Before you sign off, you should know that we have

intercepted your two surface boats and have captured them and the four crates of plutonium that they carried. Your plane, the Spartica that flew out of Bikar Atoll, was shot down over the Caroline Islands. You're out of options. Give it up now."

There was no response on the hailing frequency this time.

"Shot down?" Murdock asked.

"He can't have any contact with it. A little juice."

"They won't slow down," Murdock said.

"Correct, but we'll give them the five minutes."

"Then what?"

"Then we fire twenty rounds into the bow of the ship."

"If that doesn't stop them?"

"Then our Eighteens will be instructed to fire fifty rounds each into the bridge, which will destroy her ability to navigate, and she'll go dead in the water."

"I hope it doesn't come to that," Murdock said.

"The men have a cargo worth maybe a billion dollars on the open market. They will do everything they can to keep control of it. We have to figure out what else they might try."

"Their options are grinding down to damn few."

The CAG looked at his wristwatch. "That's two minutes and counting on my stopwatch." He scowled and rubbed his face with one hand. "I'm wondering about my two men up there. Neither of those pilots has ever fired a shot at a live target before. What are they thinking?"

"Captain, probably about the same thing you were thinking when you were in the same situation, several years ago. Not that much changes."

"True, Murdock, so damn true. Mine was a boatload of Viet Cong working up a river. They fired at me first, at least. What a day. I never want to go through that again. That first time you know for certain that you're going to kill a group of men. . . . damn."

"This is Hunter One, how is your stopwatch doing, Captain Home Base?"

"Four-twenty-eight and counting. You might as well

get into your attack mode and line up. One pass each, make it about thirty rounds each. You have guns free in twenty seconds. Keep your rounds all in ten percent of the bow section."

"That's a roger, CAG. Lining up and making a run."

All the men in the CIC waited and listened. The tracking scope showed the *Willowwind* moving along at the same fourteen knots.

"Hunter One and Two reporting. Firing runs are completed. Standing by for additional orders."

The hailing frequency speaker came on.

"U.S. Navy, it's time you need some facts. You have hit our ship with gunfire and killed six sailors from the original crew. You can disable or sink us, I'm sure. But before you consider that, hear this. We have certain packages on board. If we encounter any more threats or any more Navy presence near our ship, we will drop overboard four of the packages. Each is fitted with two pounds of C-5 explosive. The timer detonators on them are pressure rigged, so when they hit a hundred-foot depth, the pressure will set off the C-5, resulting in a huge blast and the destruction of the lead shielding and the escape of the material. As you know, this will turn this section of the South Pacific into a dead zone for five million years.

"This is not a bluff. We have nothing to lose by contaminating this section of the ocean. The fault will be on your head, and the people of Micronesia will forever hate you. So stand down. Recall your planes and leave us alone, or we will drop the packages. We will do this in the open ocean, or at any of the atolls we stop at. Remember the words, Dead Zone."

Murdock looked at Captain Olenowski. "The bastards will do it. They can drop them all over the Pacific and still have plenty to sell. Somebody said there are a hundred of the crates on board?"

"There were. We now have four of them in our nuclear storage area." The CAG rubbed his face again and shut his eyes. He didn't open them. "Recall the two Eighteens," he told an officer. "Their mission is over. We've got to come up with some other plan." He opened his eyes and watched Murdock. "They tell me you're an idea man. I hope to God you get some good ones for this little problem that we have. A meeting in the conference room in twenty minutes. Bring all of your brain-power men with you."

Twenty minutes later in the conference room, Murdock, Gardner, Sadler, Jaybird, Lam, and Canzoneri sat around the table. Also on board were six Navy officers and Captain Olenowski. The CAG brought them up to date.

"We've pulled our planes back from the freighter, but have her under electronic watch. She is just now anchoring off the small atoll Utrik. It's a little after twelve hundred. Meaning we have a lot of daylight left. What are our options?"

"Sir, I suggest we go in with Eighteens and knock out those three air transports on the landing strip," Jaybird said. "It's a calculated risk that they are there solely for the purpose of moving the plutonium. What else would require three transports that size on this atoll? If we're wrong, we compensate the owners."

"Won't they drop plutonium in the sea?" the CAG asked.

"Not a chance, Captain," Jaybird said. "That's a bluff. These terrorists wouldn't have sophisticated pressure detonators like that. They are extremely hard to get. Almost no call for them. They might make a drop, but the packages won't explode."

"Petty Officer, can you guarantee that?" the CAG asked.

"No, sir. But it's the most logical conclusion."

"If we take out the three transports, we cut down the chances they get away with more of the plutonium for the open market," Murdock said. "I'd vote with Jaybird on this one."

"What about the other plane?" Senior Chief Sadler asked.

The CAG looked at one of his papers. "We have had

contact with it since it passed to the south of Guam. It
headed for the Philippines and there the AWACS lost it
in a jumble of air traffic. Authorities at all air facilities in
the Philippines have been alerted for the plane and have
agreed to hold it for us and to place the pilots under arrest."

"If they find it. Captain," JG Gardner said, "say you're
flying that plane. What refueling spot would you pick?
Certainly not a big city airport. I'd go to the smallest dirt
strip I could find with a gas pump."

The CAG nodded. "So we may not have him yet. We'll
keep working at it. Now for this one. I agree on the three
transports. We can't wait until dark, we go in now and
blast them with twenty-millimeter cannon. Damage them
enough so they can't fly, but don't totally destroy them."

"You could ask the pilots to try to shoot their tails off,"
Lam said.

The CAC wrote out an order and gave it to a petty
officer behind him, who vanished out the door.

"Okay, consider the three birds plucked and in the ket-
tle. Now what can we do?"

"There's another way we can put the freighter dead in
the water," Murdock said. "While she's anchored, we can
blow her screws off. She probably has two."

"I like it," Jaybird said. "We go by Sixty within ten
miles of the island, then dump out our Rubber Duck and
motor in to a spot a half mile off the atoll. Leave one
man with a Motorola in the Rubber Duck, and the rest of
the squad goes in underwater to the freighter. We hang
on the charges with five-minute timers and swim away."

The CAG looked at Murdock.

"That certainly would strand them at the atoll," Murdock said. "We can do it with one chopper and one squad.
The JG will take in his men. A simple, quiet in and out."

"What about the plutonium dumping?" the CAG asked.

"We've already blown that one with crippling the transport planes," Sadler said. "If they drop it, they drop it.
We're calling their bluff again."

A seaman brought the captain a sheet of paper. He read

it and looked up. "Two F-18s have just launched. They are heading for the atoll with guns free to knock out those three transport aircraft. We should have some results in about five minutes."

In the air over the carrier *Vinson,* the two F-18s hooked up in a loose formation and headed for Utrik Atoll.

"Home Base, this is Kilroy One and Two heading for the target."

"That's a roger, Kilroy One, your guns are free for the three transport planes on the airstrip, but not the freighter. Confirm."

"Roger, the three aircraft on the airfield, but not the freighter. Kilroy Two, you copy, little buddy?"

"Copy, One. You take the lead, I'll follow in and clean up."

"Roger that. Shouldn't be long now."

"I've got some clouds low and hazy at one o'clock low."

"Should be it, Two. Give us another minute."

A minute later the radio speakers came on again.

"Home Base, have acquired visual on target atoll, we'll make one low-level pass to scare any civilians away from the craft, then do our strafing run."

The pilot could see the atoll clearly now and the runway at the south end. At the north part of the runway near some buildings he spotted the three aircraft, twin-engine transports. He had been at two thousand feet and now slanted down and slammed over the aircraft at two hundred feet. He made a turn to the right and came around and lined up with the target again. This time his thumb was on the 20mm firing button. He put his sights on the tails of the planes and dove in. He fired from four hundred yards, angling as sharply as he could for more rounds on targets. He could see the tail section of the first plane disintegrate as he slashed overhead, pulling out of his angled attack at less than a hundred feet over the water on the far side of the narrow atoll.

Behind him Kilroy Two slanted down and fired twenty

rounds at the second and third planes. After the run, both planes made a right turn again and came back to look at the targets. All three were out of action. Two had their whole tail sections blown off. The third one had the rudder flopped over and serious damage on the rest of the tail assembly.

"Home Base, this is Kilroy One."

"Go, Kilroy One."

"Mission completed, three birds lost their tails. We're coming home."

"Well done, Kilroy One and Two."

In the conference room the CAG received a note. "The three planes have been knocked out of action. Now we'll see if the terrorists make good on their threat and drop the plutonium."

"The sooner we hit her screws the better," Murdock said.

"I can have a Sixty stripped and ready for your squad in ten minutes," the CAG said. "We have acquired four IBS for your use. One will be loaded on the Sixty ready to go."

Lieutenant (j.g.) Gardner stood up. "With the captain's permission, I better get my squad ready and on the flight deck."

"Permission granted, Lieutenant."

Gardner and Canzoneri left the room. Captain Olenowski looked at the men around the table. "Now we wait and see what the real warriors do, and how the terrorists react."

Gardner and Canzoneri rushed back to the SEALs compartment and spread the news. Bravo Squad got its gear ready, put on wet suits, and hoisted the usual combat vests and short weapons.

"Two screws," Gardner said. "We'll wire on three one-quarter pounders on each screw just to make sure. Bring timer/detonators. I want Canzoneri to carry the three quarter chunks of C-5. Prescott you carry three timer/detonators. Fernandez, you tote the other three quarter-pounders, and your timer/detonator man is Rafii. Everyone know his assignment? Four on the screws, the other four of us on watch and security. Let's choggie."

Murdock watched Bravo Squad come on deck. He had already checked the bird and the inflatable Rubber Duck. The engine had a full tank of gas; all was ready. Gardner put his men in the bird, then turned and popped a salute to Murdock, who was so surprised he almost forgot to return the salute. Then the door closed and Gardner saw his men sitting down on the bare floor of the SH-60.

"I understand we're only twenty miles from the atoll. We'll fly in to the ten-mile mark to insure total surprise. That's going to take us about four minutes in the air. This pilot will take us down to ten feet over the swells, where we push out the Duck. We've done it a dozen times. Mahanani, you'll be custodian of the Duck while we're gone. When we're done, we'll swim back on the same course we went in on. When we're a half mile out, we'll use our Motorolas so you can find us. Any questions?"

"There'll be a drift," Mahanani said. "I'll use a floating flare and try to judge the direction. If I can't find you I'll call in the chopper to figure out where you are. Should be a piece of cake."

"One minute to drop," the crewman said.

"We'll go out the back as usual," Gardner said. "No fuckups."

The rear hatch swung up, showing the sky and the blue water below them. When the bird settled down to ten feet, the chopper crewman yelled, "Go, go," and they pushed out the Rubber Duck and jumped off behind it.

There was a current. It took them five minutes to get all eight men into the IBS. Then Mahanani started the engine, turned to the right azimuth, and powered the little boat toward the atoll. The chop was gone from the water. Mahanani figured they could make eighteen knots. That meant about thirty minutes to move the ten miles toward the atoll—if he figured this current right. He edged the angle of the boat more to starboard to compensate for the drift. Now he hoped that he could find that speck of sand in the damn big South Pacific.

12

"We've been motoring for twenty minutes," Prescott said. "Where's the fucking atoll?"

"We're still too far out," Mahanani said.

"In San Diego we can see land from five miles," Claymore said.

"Only here there aren't two thousand foot mountains behind this little atoll, and no forty-story buildings near the beach the way there are in San Diego," Mahanani said. "Give me another ten minutes."

Nine minutes later on Mahanani's stopwatch, he saw a small pile of clouds twenty degrees to port. He angled that way and two minutes later he saw it. "There it is, you disbelievers. That damn little coral atoll must not be more than twenty feet off the waves. We'll motor in another quarter, then you're on your own. We're still about a mile out. Swim will be good for you."

When Mahanani stopped the boat, JG Gardner had his course plotted and they dropped over the side and went down fifteen feet. He used the compass board and checked his men. Four sets with buddy lines. They swam toward shore. Gardner counted strokes, and when he figured they had done a half mile, he told the men on his underwater Motorola that he and Claymore were going topside to check. He barely broke the surface of a swell with his face. He was in a trough and saw nothing but sky and water. He waited for the trough to develop into a swell and at the top he looked again. Yes, there it is, a quarter of a mile and three degrees to the right. He went back down and told the men where they were, and they moved forward. The big freighter sat on this side of the atoll, making the approach easier.

They came up amidships on the freighter, and the four sappers went to the stern. The other three men hovered out twenty yards, watching upward and to the sides for any enemy swimmers or boats.

Fernandez took the port screw and was surprised again how big the propellers were. He made doubly sure the big screw wasn't turning, then swam up to it and unwrapped the wire and the three packages of plastique explosive in quarter-pound chunks. They reminded him of quarter pounds of butter at the supermarket.

He wrapped the wire around the end of the drive shaft just behind the propeller and forced the plastic explosive against the hub of the propeller. When he was finished, he held out his hand, and Rafii handed him two timer/detonators, which he pushed into the soft plastic explosive. Fernandez used the Motorola.

"I'm ready here on the port blade. Setting the two timers for ten minutes, agreed?"

Canzoneri came on the net. "Hold up, I'm not quite done. Damned wire hung up on me. There. Now I have it, all snugged in tight. We don't want to have to come back for seconds. I'm inserting two timers into the C-5. They are set for ten minutes each. Ready to activate?"

"I'm ready," Canzoneri said. "We'll activate on your count of three."

"One, two, three."

Both men pushed in the activating levers, and all four stroked away from the ship. The men guarding them also headed away. They would swim out the same way they came in, and after a quarter of a mile, they would surface and get together for the rest of the swim out to the mile marker.

Mahanani had followed the conversation. He punched up his stopwatch and scanned the water ahead of him for any sign of the swimmers. There wouldn't be any, but he looked just the same. He had drifted about ten degrees to port and now started to adjust, but as he thought about it, he realized that the swimmers would also have a port drift. He waited.

At nine minutes he figured he'd see some heads pop out of the water to escape the concussion that would push through the ocean in all directions when the blasts went off underwater. There would be a lot of dead fish floating into shore tomorrow.

He thought he saw a small splash a hundred yards out, but then it dropped into a trough and he lost it.

"Four, three, two, one," he counted down to ten minutes. Ten seconds later he felt the concussion as the sea trembled. At the stern of the freighter a geyser of water shot fifty feet into the air and the heavy cracking roar of the sound came out with the water. Was there one blast or two? Or did they come right on top of each other? He wasn't sure. The men closer to the blasts would be able to tell.

The heads he thought he had seen were gone, nothing but the placid Pacific settling down into its beautiful routine of swell and trough and swell.

In the water, the JG came to the surface with Claymore. He did a three-sixty but couldn't see the Rubber Duck. "Mahanani, where the hell are you?" the JG asked on the radio.

"I'm here. Where are you? Nice shooting. Did I hear one blast or two?"

"Two almost at the same time. We're on the same course we went in on. Where are you?"

"You drifted about five degrees to port. I drifted, too. Do a stand tall and I'll check you out."

Both Claymore and the JG surged upward and scissors kicked to get as far out of the water as possible.

"Missed you," Mahanani said. "Why don't all seven of you do the same thing? I'll check another quadrant."

This time the seven SEALs lifted as high out of the water as they could and slapped the water with their hands as they came down.

"Gotcha!" Mahanani shouted. "You're about fifty yards short and to the west. Stay there. I'll come pick you up."

Five minutes later all eight of the SEALs lay in the rubber boat. They didn't move, watching for any developments they could see on shore. A small boat gunned out a channel in the coral and motored to the freighter. They saw two copper-skinned men dive into the water.

"Checking out our work," Canzoneri said.

"Let's get out of here, as quietly as possible," the JG said. "Five knots will be just fine."

When they were three miles off the freighter, the JG took the carrier radio, about a foot long and three inches square. He turned it on and hit the send button.

"Home Base, this is Waterwings."

"Waterwings, go."

"Ready to come home. We saw two blasts, so if we know what we're doing, the freighter should be screwless. Send us a chopper with a rope ladder. We're a little west of where he dropped us. A current is working. We're about three miles off the freighter, but we don't care now if they hear the bird or not, right?"

"Right, Waterwings. A bird is lifting off now. Should be at your position in about twelve minutes."

"Should we shred the Rubber Duck when we leave it?"

"Right. Dismount the motor and drop it overboard, then shred all the air pockets you can reach. See you in about thirty."

"Gun the motor up to give us fifteen knots so we can meet that Sixty partway there," the JG said.

"Think we got both of the screws?" Canzoneri asked Fernandez.

"Hell, I nailed mine. If you got yours, it's a clean sweep."

"Yeah, we got them," Canzoneri said. He leaned back and closed his eyes, but held on as the little Zodiac craft bounded along over the swells north and east toward the carrier.

It was almost dark by the time the Sixty picked up Bravo Squad and hauled it back to the carrier. The men changed and had chow. In the CIC Murdock listened to Gardner tell the CAG about the mission.

"So, looks like we got both screws. Which means that tub is stranded for some time. Where in this neighborhood are those hijackers going to get new screws?"

"This is boat country," Murdock said. "Half the economy is in boats. My money is on Majuro. Marine repair. CAG, do you have someone monitoring radio frequencies from that ship to Majuro?"

The CAG nodded at Murdock and Gardner. "Yeah, we been scanning all the bands they might use. Twenty minutes after your boys blew his screws off, the hijacker was on the air to Majuro talking to a marine salvage and repair outfit. They have two used screws that will work. Might be a little small and cut down his speed, but the *Willowwind* can get operational again."

"Only if that repair boat gets here," Murdock said.

"The repair guy got talked into a night run. It's two hundred and eighty-five miles on our charts from Utrik to Majuro. The repairman said his ship can only do twelve knots. Take him almost twenty-four hours to get here."

"So we have some time to stop him," Murdock said. "What I'm wondering is why did the ship anchor here at Utrik? Is this another contact point?"

"We've talked with the mayor of Utrik by radio. He says he's seen some newcomers around lately. The three transport planes landing there were a surprise. He asked us why we shot them up. I told him. I scared the hell out of him when he heard about the plutonium. He has two men in his entire police force. He'll cooperate in any way he can."

"At least they didn't take over this atoll," Murdock said. "I still wonder why they stopped here."

Gardner shook his head and looked up. "It's got to be small boats. This is coming down to a crapshoot. They know they can't keep the freighter all the way to Iran, so they use whatever they can to spread as many of the packages as they can, hoping that several of them will get through and they can use them or sell them."

"This is boat country," Murdock said. "There must be a thousand seagoing boats in and around the atolls. How many forty-footers or larger are in the lagoon right now?"

Captain Olenowski talked to one of his men. "Our latest report from the Hawkeye shows that what could be four boats that size or larger were in the lagoon. They haven't checked that lately."

"Any way that we can watch the freighter tonight to see if it's off-loading any of the crates?" Gardner asked.

"We could put three men on the atoll, across the lagoon from the ship," Murdock said. "Send them in with a twenty-power scope. They'd have to have lots of lights on to do a night loading."

The CAG scowled. "They could be off-loading right now. We don't have anybody flying CAP on them. Let me check with the Hawkeye."

"Can they track a boat as small as a forty-foot?" Murdock asked.

"They like larger targets but I think they can do it." He waved at one of the men, who handed him a microphone.

"This is Home Base calling Skyhigh One."

"Skyhigh here."

"Can you track a forty-foot oceangoing boat?"

"Sometimes, depending on conditions. That's a small item for us to follow."

"Has there been any activity of that sort around Utrik in the past few hours?"

"Affirmative. We have three tracks moving away from the atoll. Two just before dusk, and one since."

"Any idea of their size?"

"One looks like a hundred-footer, the other two probably eighty feet."

"Stay on them. We need to know exactly where they go and if they hit any other atolls."

"Wilco. We're on it. You want updates?"

"If they land at any other atolls, we want to know immediately."

"That's a roger, Home Base."

"Those boats could be innocent civilians on legitimate commercial runs," Gardner said.

"True," Murdock said. "Captain, can you contact the mayor again and ask him if the freighter has off-loaded anything today?"

Olenowski said he could and talked to the mayor on the radio.

"Oh, yes, this ship, the *Challenge* unloaded large crates into at least three boats I know about. The boats came in a few days ago waiting for the ship."

Murdock scowled. "They must have the plutonium packages. Those boats could scatter those packages all over the South Pacific. We've got to take her down tonight. We'll do it by roping down the way we did before. First we hose down the whole damn deck with fire from our sixteen guns out of two Sixty choppers. Then one squad goes down as the other guards and shoots at any opposition. Then the other squad comes down and we take over the damn ship and stop this proliferation."

Don Stroh had walked up a few minutes before, and he looked grim, but he nodded. "Yes, I agree. It's time to put a stop to this hijacking, and to find out if my man on board is still alive."

"When, Commander?" the CAG asked.

"We'll need a half hour to get suited up and on deck. We'd like two Sixties without their torpedoes."

"You've got it, Commander. Let's go take down that damn freighter, then we can worry about those three boats that could have some of the plutonium crates on board."

13

It was thirty-two minutes before the two SH-60 Seahawks lifted off the carrier *Vinson* at 2142. All sixteen SEALs were fit for duty. Howard's three rounds in his right leg had been in and out and had missed the bones. He limped a little bit, but he said there wasn't a chance he'd miss the take-down. Murdock made sure everyone had full loads of ammo.

On the short ride to the freighter he gave final instructions on the Motorola. Both choppers had been fitted with two of the two-inch-thick ropes to drop out the side doors. "Bravo, you take everything forward of the house about amidships. Alpha will take it from the front of the house and the crane to the stern. We'll use the twenty-millimeter for those who have contact rounds for the air attack. We want to wash this baby clean on the deck. Don't target the bridge. After our first barrage, Alpha will go in and rope down on the stern section. Bravo will cover us and take out any opposition with small rounds, no twenties. When we're down, we'll cover Bravo roping down on the forward deck. Let's do it."

Murdock looked out the open side door, and he could see the running lights of the freighter. They wouldn't burn for long. The two birds split up and each zeroed in on its section of the target.

Alpha Squad fired out the left-hand door as the bird circled the stern, careful not to get too close to the other circling bird.

Murdock fired his 20mm at a set of lights near the stern, and when he fired, the rest of his squad blazed away out the door. Three men lay on the chopper deck, the rest fired over their heads. Sadler saw a man run toward the house from a hatch near the stern. He led him and dropped him in the middle of a 20mm round, which also slammed shrapnel forward into two lights and some hatch covers.

After one circle Murdock yelled into the radio. "Cease fire. We've got their heads down. Chopper, move up on the stern deck. Get us down to thirty feet and we'll go out."

The pilot had been rigged with one of the spare Motorolas.

"That's a roger, Commander, Moving in on the stern. Now about fifty feet wet, coming in to dry feet in about ten. Okay, we're now hovering about twenty feet over the deck and twenty feet from the stern."

"Go," Murdock shouted to Jaybird, who kicked his rope coil out and let it fall to the deck. Murdock did the same. At once they reached out, grabbed the rope, wrapped their legs around it, and slid down, using the heavy gloves as brakes.

Murdock hit the deck first. He had ordered his men not to use the twenties once they were on deck. He saw movement ahead, near the big crane, and he slammed a six-round burst at the movement. It stopped. The SEALs had their assignments. Murdock and Jaybird would advance up the deck to the house amidships and go up the ladders, with the bridge as their target. The bridge was four stories above the main deck. They charged into a hatch and up a ladder on the port side, then cleared two small rooms. They had started up the next ladder when a handgun popped three times above them. Hot lead ricocheted off steel and flew past them. They glued themselves against the steel bulkheads and looked up the ladder.

They could see no one. Murdock grabbed a fragger and pulled the safety pin. He'd angle the bomb up the steps so it would hit on the landing and roll against the bulkhead. He let it cook two seconds after the arming handle flipped off, then tossed it underhand. He and Jaybird jolted down the steps and felt the concussion as the bomb went off. Hot shrapnel from the grenade peppered the stairwell, but none reached the SEALs.

They both surged up the ladder when the whining chards of steel stopped singing. On the landing they found a man with a handgun. He had taken dozens of pieces of the grenade in his torso and was dead.

Jaybird pointed up the next ladder. They went up silently, found no one on the landing, and checked two dark rooms. Officer country but nobody at home.

The last ladder was shorter, ending in a steel hatch that Murdock knew could be battened down from the inside. He tried the twist handle and found it free, unlocked. Both SEALs paused at the hatch, then Murdock nodded, twisted the handle, and slammed the hatch inside. They both jolted into the room, which had bright lights. Three men stood next to the front windows peering down at the deck.

They were not armed. One man threw up his hands. The other two cheered. "About damn time somebody came and rescued us," one of the seamen said.

The other one laughed. "Don't believe that sonofabitch. He's one of the hijackers. He's got a pistol in his pocket; he's just too chickenshit to use it." The man snarled at the other seaman, spun, and drew a pistol. Jaybird tracked him and drilled his chest with three rounds from his MP-5 before the gunman could get off a shot.

"Never draw against an aimed weapon, pardner," Jaybird said in his best Western drawl. The shots in the closed bridge made hearing hard for a minute or more. Jaybird was the only one who knew what he had said. Murdock leaped forward and smashed to the floor the man who'd had his hands up. There he searched him, then bound his wrists behind his back with riot cuffs and put another set on his ankles.

"Where are the rest of the hijackers?" Murdock asked.

The seaman slumped in a chair near the wheel. He shook his head. "Man, them things are loud. What kind of a weapon is that?"

Jaybird told him. "Where are the others?"

"I heard some of the hijackers talking. The head man here, a guy named Taliva, told them he had expected the Navy would attack him and take down the ship before now. Late this afternoon he went to the airport. He said he had three planes there, and he would use one of them to get away."

"How many of them left on board?" Murdock asked.

"Four or five. He told them to hold the ship as long as they could. Promised them each a hundred thousand U.S. dollars."

"The regular crew?" Jaybird asked.

"Most of us are locked in the dayroom forward. Man, you guys really shot up the place. You commandos?"

"Navy SEALs," Jaybird said.

"Not the Navy I used to know. Damn."

"Can you show us where the other hijackers might be?"

"I saw one of them go into the captain's cabin. He was drunk as a turtle and wanted to sleep it off."

"Show us," Murdock said.

They left the two men on the floor and followed the seaman down one level and to the rear, where they found the hatch partly open. Murdock kicked it inward and Jaybird charged in. A man lay fully clothed on the big captain's bed. When he'd slept off his drunk, he'd find himself tied hand and foot.

"How many boats loaded the crates on this afternoon?" Murdock asked the seaman.

"Four of them that I know of. One was going to the planes, the other three headed out to sea."

"Any idea where the last three went?"

"All headed east and south. Of course, they could change directions anytime out there. It's a big ocean."

"We're finding that out," Jaybird said. They headed back to the deck to find the rest of the SEALs.

When Gardner and his squad hit the forward deck, they had only one gunman shooting at them. They flattened out and took any cover they could find.

"Anybody see his gun flash?" Gardner asked.

"Thought I saw some muzzle show down around that

first hatch cover," Jefferson said. "That's closest to me. I'll take a look." Jefferson sprinted from his cover to another spot nearer the hatch and dove behind a large coil of rope. There was no firing. He checked the area, spotted a large wooden box that could have come from the hatch, and jolted forward toward it. This time he took fire—three three-round bursts from a sub gun. He screeched and rolled behind the box.

"Jeff, you hit?" Gardner asked.

"Just a scratch. I'll edge around this box. He's exposed, so he runs or gets blasted. I'm moving now." A moment later Jefferson pounded six rounds at the dark lump he saw halfway down the long hatch cover, in the blackness. Nothing happened for an extended five seconds. Then a scream came and the sub gun chattered again, only this time it was aimed straight at the night sky as the man stood, stumbled toward Jefferson two steps, then collapsed and sprawled forward. The submachine gun chattered out of his hands on the steel deck.

"He's down," Jefferson said. "Where the hell is that medic?"

"I'm coming," Mahanani said on the net. "Stay put, I know where you are."

"The rest of us, let's flush forward to the bow, then we'll clear it to the house. Remember there are civilians on board. Don't shoot up the regular crew."

"Where are they?" Prescott asked on the radio.

"Probably locked up and safe somewhere below decks," Gardner said.

The SEALs moved cautiously, using what little cover they could find working to the bow. There was nobody else there. They turned back toward the middle of the ship and were within twenty yards of the house when a rifle cracked. The SEALs hit the deck.

"Where?" Fernandez asked.

"Near the second hold, closest one to the bridge house," Canzoneri said. "I saw him fire and drop. I think he's behind the hatch cover. It's open. Could be where they loaded out the plut."

The SEALs moved up cautiously. Only then did Gardner remember the night vision goggles he wore. He pulled them down and scanned the area, lifting past the first hatch cover. Beyond the gaping hole of the second hold, he spotted a jumble of what had to be wooden boxes, but not the plut ones. He caught a sudden movement as a head jolted upward and scanned the area, then dropped down.

"Anybody close to those wooden crates on the port side of the hatch cover?" Gardner asked.

"I'm about twenty," Rafii said.

"I just saw him. He's behind those wooden boxes. Can you drop a fragger in there?"

"That's a roger, JG. One fragger coming up. It could bounce so take damn good cover."

"Cook it two seconds," the JG said.

Rafii took a grenade off his combat vest and pulled the ring that held in the safety pin. He judged the distance again, then let the arming handle fly off. He waited two seconds, then lofted the grenade underhanded toward the boxes that were backed up against the bulkhead. The hand bomb cleared the first box, hit the steel bulkhead, and bounced inside the jumble of crates. It exploded after its 4.2-second fuse train hit the main charge.

"Go," the JG said. Rafii came off his knees and jolted forward, his MP-5 on full auto as he sprinted the twenty feet to the boxes. One had tipped over from the force of the grenade. He pushed it aside. Behind it were two more boxes. Rafii swung his weapon's muzzle at both, then stood beside them. He pulled out his minilight, held it away from his body, and shone the beam into the murky darkness. He spotted a hand that was not attached to an arm.

A scream shrilled through the night from the wooden boxes.

"Come out with one hand up, and we might save your worthless hide," Rafii barked.

One box moved. Another edged aside. A figure came into the beam of light. His left hand held an Ingram sub gun. It was aimed at Rafii. The SEAL's weapon fired a dozen shots, blasting into the hijacker and throwing him backward, slamming him against the bulkhead. The hijacker's head slumped to one side, and he slowly slid down the steel plate until he sat on the deck, the Ingram still dangling from his left hand.

Rafii shone the light on the man once more. "Clear forward," he said.

"The forward deck is clear," the JG reported. "Should we check out the forward cabin areas?"

"That's a roger," Murdock said. "A seaman here says the crew is locked in a dayroom forward."

"We're moving."

Just beyond the third hold they found a hatch that opened on a ladder that went down one flight. Claymore and Fernandez led the squad. They cleared four cabins with four bunks each, then found a pair of double doors with an outside lock on them.

JG Gardner came up and nodded. "Rafii, can you do this one?"

Rafii looked at the hasp and lock. He shook his head, waved the others back, and shot it off the hasp with three rounds from his sub gun.

They heard yelling from inside. A moment later the doors slammed open and fifteen men came charging out.

"Don't shoot," one bellowed. "We're the good guys. From all the shooting topside, we figured you must be the Marines."

"Not a chance," Canzoneri said. "We're SEALs and we just saved your asses. Any more lockdowns around here?"

"We're it," the tall man said. "You leave us anything to use to sail this tub out of here?"

"You get new screws and you should be in business," Gardner said. "Any idea where any more of the hijackers might be hiding?"

"Several," one of the crewmen said. "We also have a CIA man on board who's shot up. Hope to hell you can take a slug out of his shoulder. It's overdue."

"Where is he?"

"Hiding from the hijackers," the man said. "I'm Pete

and I cook on this tub. I'll show you where Keanae is.
Hope you have a medic."

It took the SEALs an hour to comb through the rest of
the ship. They found only one more hijacker, hiding in
the laundry room under some dirty sheets. Mahanani
treated Jefferson's scratch.

"Just a scratch, huh, Jeff?" the medic said.

"Yeah."

"Two slugs in your shoulder is a damn scratch?"

"Hell, one went on through."

Murdock got on his carrier radio and asked the ship to
call the head man on the atoll and see if they had a doctor
who could come out for two patients. They did and said
he'd be there within twenty minutes.

"Turn on some lights in that hold and get a count on
how many crates of plut are still there," Don Stroh said.
"We need to know how many we're trying to track down.
Right now I want to talk to a man named Keanae."

They put Keanae on the radio.

"Don Stroh here."

"What the hell you doing out here in the glorious South
Pacific?"

"Trying to save your worthless ass. What happened to
your SATCOM radio?"

"At the last minute they wouldn't let me bring it. Said
it would blow my cover."

"How bad is the shoulder?"

"Got a doctor on the way. I figured I'd be dead by now.
Must be this new kind of bullet the bad guys were using."

"We've got two choppers on the way to you now. Have
you in sick bay here within a half hour. You hang in
there."

Out of the original crew of twenty-four, there were
eighteen left. Murdock talked with the ranking officer,
Chief Mate Stillman.

"They shot the captain when they took over, then one
after another our men were shot down in cold blood. We
didn't give them any cause. They dumped the bodies

overboard. I hear we have new screws coming from Majuro. We could be ready to get underway in two days."

"You'll need some fuel. Majuro can help you there. I'd bet you'll have new orders to get you back to San Diego."

"God, I hope so. Oh, we'll need some kind of portable radio. Shigahara shot up our whole setup. I know for sure that this is my last run on one of these plut carriers. I've had enough."

The team came up from the second hold. Jaybird gave the report. "Quite a hole in the crates down there, Commander. Near as we can tell there are twenty of them missing. We count eighty crates in that second hold."

"I know where ten of them are," Murdock said. "Eight we captured and are on the carrier. Two more are on that plane headed east. We've got our work lined up for us to find those others, and before they get too far away. There could be ten bottles of plut on those three small boats that left here this afternoon. We have to nail them fast before they get where they're going, and damn well before they tie up with any more aircraft. If that happens, there's no way in hell that we can contain them."

14

The island doctor came on board ten minutes after Murdock made the call. He shook his head at the wounds on Jefferson and Keanae.

"That slug should have come out of there two days ago, young man," the doctor said. "You're lucky you're alive." The doctor was in his fifties and had retired to the island from Majuro. His usual day was spent sitting in the sun, playing with two grandchildren and fishing in the lagoon. He was overweight, bald, and wore a full beard. There was a sly twinkle in his eye. Murdock decided he was a native of one of the islands, ethnically a Micronesian.

"I hear you've got a load of pure plutonium 239 on board," the medic said. "That's weapons grade. Worth a few billion dollars on the terrorist open market. Glad I'm not forty anymore or I might have made a try for some." He watched Murdock, whom he had met when he first boarded. "Commander, you know about that fourth boat, don't you?"

"The crew said there was one loaded."

"It's still down by the airport. Near a little break in the reef. I heard they saw the planes shot up and they rammed the boat right up on the sand. Tore the bottom out of her but they got her beached. Amazing what a backhoe can lift, let alone bury in just a few minutes."

Murdock stared hard at the doctor. "Yep. Figured you might want to take a look. Use my boat down at the ladder there."

Murdock pointed at four SEALs, and they grabbed fresh rounds from other SEALs to fill up their ammo quota and ran for the rope ladder over the side of the freighter.

"These assholes think they can bury the stuff and come back and get it when we've forgotten all about it?" Jaybird asked.

Murdock's face was grim. "Don't know, but that sure sounds like it could be their plan. Two men, the doctor said? We get to shore, grab a car, and roar down to that airstrip. Can't be more than a mile or two away."

Lam took over the ten-foot powerboat and gunned the engine, then took them into the lagoon through the wide channel. Somebody had done some good dynamite work on the opening, Murdock decided. They hit the dock and a man came down to meet them. He squinted at them in the dim lights on the dock.

"Steal the doc's boat?" he asked. He was a native, with smooth brown skin and dark hair. He was grinning.

"Doc said we could find a car here. We need to get down to the airport fast."

"Me do that," the man said. "Pickup, Ford pickup, you bet."

In back of the dock's small building stood a four-year-old pickup. The SEALs jumped in and the man headed down the atoll.

"Drive without your lights on," Murdock said. "We'd like to surprise these guys."

"Me Manjili," he said "I can do that. Do everything for the doc and the mayor. You know we got mayor here?"

"Good," Murdock said. He had the front-seat spot and watched the Witch's Wild Ride–type driving that Manjili did. He would do great in New York City traffic. "How far to the airport?"

"Mile and one quarter, near enough," Manjili said. "You have guns. Them other guys with the boats had guns."

"We're the good guys," Murdock said. "United States Navy."

"Navy, good. We like U.S. Navy."

The pickup wound down the narrow road, swung

around a line of trees, and they were at the airport. The first thing Murdock saw were the three shot-up twin-engine transports. They looked like they could have hauled twenty of the plutonium crates each. Not now.

"Where did the boat beach itself?" Murdock asked.

"Dumb shits, wreck good boat," Manjili said.

"Down other end runway."

They drove that way, and Murdock asked the man to stop when he could see the end of the hard-surfaced strip. Brush and trees shielded the beach from their location.

"We'll go on foot from here," he told the driver. The five SEALs spread out ten yards apart as they ran for the line of brush and trees. Murdock was in the middle, with Lam and Jaybird on his left and Canzoneri and Rafii on his right. He had grabbed the four men closest to him as he hurried off the ship.

Lam ran out front as usual, scouting. He worked silently through the trees and brush. They all had their radios on. Lam bellied down the last five yards and looked out from behind two trees. Thirty yards ahead and half that much to the south he saw a brightly lighted area with a backhoe working at digging a hole in the sandy, coral-spotted soil.

"Got them, Cap. Two men and one on the backhoe. The hoe man looks like a local; the other two are not. One has a beard; the other's clean. Can't hear what they're saying."

The rest of the SEALs moved up. Murdock saw the three crates of plutonium stacked neatly to one side, in the splash of the set-up floodlight. The arm of the backhoe vanished into the hole and came up with the bucket filled with sand and dripping water. "I want the bearded one alive," Murdock said.

"I've got the other one," Jaybird said.

"Don't shoot at the backhoe man," Murdock warned. "I'll shoot the bearded guy's legs out from under him. Jaybird, sight in. We'll go on three."

"Ready," Jaybird said.

"Ready here. One, two, three." Both men fired, then

they were all on their feet charging forward, all weapons pointing at the three men in the light around the backhoe. Jaybird's three rounds had all caught the clean-shaven man in the chest and drove him backward into the pile of dirt from the hole.

Murdock's bearded target took at least two rounds in his legs, and he fell to one side, swearing in Arabic. He grabbed an Ingram submachine gun and swung it around at the SEALs. All five of them fired when the man brought up the sub gun. Before he could shoot, three rounds hit him in the chest and neck and he went down, dead before he sprawled on the dirt.

The man on the backhoe stood in the seat and held up both hands.

"I'm just working man, you betcha," he said. He was slender, brown-skinned, and wore a San Diego Padres baseball cap. The SEALs continued their charge to the hole, checked both men, and then waved the operator down.

"Did they pay you to bring down the crates and dig the hole?" Murdock asked.

"Oh yes, pay in advance. My rule with strangers. You strangers, too?"

"No, we're friends," Murdock said. "Do you know what's inside those crates?"

"No, man. Just do what they pay me to do. Not a lot of work on island."

Rafii and Canzoneri searched the two bodies. The bearded one had a small leather bag on a long strap slung over his shoulder. Canzoneri opened the flap on the bag and looked inside.

"Goooooooood dammmmmmmn. We're fucking pirates and we just found the buried treasure." He jerked the strap off the dead Arab's shoulder and took the bag to Murdock.

"Check this out, Cap," Canzoneri said.

The others crowded around. Murdock lifted out a stack of bills. He riffled through it. "All hundreds. Looks like these boys were well financed. How much did these two pay you to get the crates off the boat and dig the hole?" Murdock asked the local man.

"Two hundred dollar. They argued, but I said I get backhoe all salt wet and have to oil everything and dry and cause sombitch bunch trouble. They pay."

"Fair enough. I'll give you another two hundred to fill in that hole, and then carry those crates one at a time back to the dock and load them on a boat. Can you do that?"

"Can do, mister boss man. Yeah, can do."

"Get to it." Murdock scowled. It was getting late. Those three boats had been on the open sea for two or three hours by now, maybe more. His watch showed it was just after midnight.

Murdock touched his Motorola. "Gardner, do you copy?"

"Loud and clear, Cap. You find the boat?"

"We did and three crates of your favorite breakfast cereal. We're moving them back to the dock. Take us about an hour, I'd figure, we'll make three trips. See if you can get us a boat at the dock big enough to bring the crates out to the freighter for loading."

"Can do. I'll let you know what I find."

Lam ran back through the trees and found the pickup truck driver in the brush.

"Damn good show," he said. "You maybe want ride back to town?"

"We do and we have two more silent passengers for you," Lam said. "You'll have to get your chief of police to check them out. They might have identification and they might not. Can you drive down near the backhoe?"

Two hours later they had dropped off the two dead men at the small office of the atoll's police department. Murdock had taken off the bodies the only identification they had, which he figured was false. The policeman was a local, with a shaved head and the softest eyes Murdock had ever seen. He smiled when he saw the two dead men.

"Been hoping somebody would dispatch these guys. Absolute assholes. Demanded whatever they wanted. Oh, they paid, but they treated us like shit. Yeah, they'll never be missed. No problem. We'll bury them and send a note about a couple of dead men dropped off a freighter going by." He grinned again. "Don't suppose they have any I.D. on them?"

"None to speak of," Murdock said. He handed the chief a hundred-dollar bill. "Here's burial money. Save the county the cost."

The chief took the cash and smiled. "You men have a good journey, wherever you're going."

The SEALs kept the bag of cash, after paying the back-hoe man his two hundred.

"We gonna split up the finders keepers money?" Jay-bird asked.

"Sure, we are," Canzoneri said. "Didn't I hear a story about you guys had five hundred thousand fucking dollars in a duffel bag dragging it over half the world? You didn't keep that."

"This is still in the bank wrappers," Murdock said. "A hundred bills to a stack. That's ten thousand dollars. There are fifteen wraps of bills in that bag, which translates out to a hundred and fifty thousand smackaroos. We can dream about keeping it, but that's about as close as we come."

"Don Stroh will grab it as soon as we hit the ship," Jaybird said. "You watch and see."

They stood by as the backhoe man eased the three crates into a sixty-foot fishing boat that had a wide rear deck. They tied them down, and the boat wallowed a little as it eased out of the lagoon and through the surf to the big freighter. Murdock and his crew followed in the doctor's boat.

The doctor was on the bridge, talking navigation with the chief mate. Murdock waited a respectable time and then spoke to the doctor. "Did my two men get patched up, Doctor?"

"Yep. I did a little temporary work on them, and then a big bird landed with a pair of Navy doctors and the prettiest nurse I've seen in years. They checked over your two men and that CIA guy and hustled them on board the chopper and flew them back to the carrier, where they have a whole damn hospital."

He shook the dregs out of his pipe and sucked on it a couple of times. "Course I guess you'd need a whole damn hospital with five thousand people on board. I can't hardly believe that. A ship big enough for five thousand people to live on it. I hear it's got a gym, a store, a post office, probably even a boxing ring. Five thousand people. Been a long, long time since I've even seen that many people. Course there are over thirty thousand in Majuro, but that's a whole island over there. Too many people— why I left."

Murdock's second call was on Don Stroh, who hadn't gone back with the doctors. He found Murdock before Murdock found him.

"I hear you're a rich man," Stroh said.

"Only until I see you and get an official U.S. CIA receipt."

"A receipt? We don't give no damn receipts."

"You will on this one. I want it in writing off a computer printout from your CIA office, and I want everything all legal and straight so I don't get my ass in a wringer."

"No, the expression is 'tit in a wringer.'"

"That either."

"Can I at least look at it?"

"Sure, you betcha, as my local friends say." He tossed the leather bag to Stroh, who caught it and leaned against the rail.

He opened it and laughed. "Holy shit, look at that." He stared at Murdock. "Is it real?"

"You're the government spy, not me."

Stroh took one bill off a stack and held it up to the light. He grinned. "Yep, there are all those lines and doodads just where they are supposed to be. Can't fake that. Real, all right. A hundred and fifty thousand?"

"If all the stacks have a hundred bills. They might have spent some off one of them. I spent two to the guy who brought in the plut. I figured he earned it. Then another hundred for burial expenses with the local cops."

"Yeah, right. Okay. As soon as we get back to the carrier, we'll have the ship's payroll department count the loot for us, and they will certify it and then I'll give you a receipt for it, and get an email from my boss, and eventually I'll turn it over to him."

"I don't want to get a statement of charges for a hundred and fifty thousand from the Navy," Murdock said.

"You won't. Now, what about those three other boats? Where are they and what do we know about them?"

"We'll have to wait and talk to the CAG about that. When is the next chopper due on this milk run?"

"I can have one here in fifteen minutes."

"Good. Call him, and I'll get my platoon ready. Where have they been landing, on the aft deck?"

"Right."

It was a little more than an hour later that Murdock put his combat vest and his Bull Pup in the locker in his four-man compartment and went to see the CAG.

"We found all three and have been shadowing them with choppers out as far as we can. The Hawkeye put us on them. If the choppers get outdistanced, we'll use F-18s to track them. Looks like two of them are heading southwest down the chain of islands and atolls toward Majuro."

They went to a blown-up map of the Marshall Islands on a screen in the CIC. It showed the northern islands.

"Here we are south of Utrik. From here to Ailuk Atoll it's only about sixty miles. The boat heading for that one is making no more than ten knots and wallowing a little. Our chopper pilots say it looks like she's overloaded and sluggish. She's been gone from here now we figure for about five hours and could have a landfall in another hour. Or they might already have landed on that first atoll."

"We can't shoot it up," Murdock said. "We might sink her. We're still short seven crates of plutonium 239. Each of those three tubs could be hauling part or all of them."

"We can get there in twenty minutes if we decide that," Captain Olenowski said. He rubbed his face and scowled.

"Can your boys be ready in twenty minutes to take your Sixties down to that atoll and see if that boat has landed there?"

"First we need some chow—box lunches, whatever. Two per man. Then we resupply our ammo and get out of here. The other two boats going on longer cruises?"

"Looks that way. This close atoll is the hot problem."

Murdock used his Motorola. He found that the signal carried well on board the big ship.

"SEALs, get your vests filled up with normal ammo loads. We'll be heading out in about twenty. Box lunches on board. We've got another port of call sixty miles south."

"What about the cash?" Jaybird asked.

"I'm asking Captain Olenowski to stand in as our proxy on the count. I think we can trust him."

The CAG grinned.

"Get your asses moving, SEALs. We now have eighteen minutes to takeoff."

"Another night problem?" Lam asked.

"It's sure as hell night; I hope it won't be a problem," Murdock said.

15

Murdock and his thirteen SEALs arrived at Ailuk Atoll twenty-one minutes after takeoff. It was 0135. The island was a dark blob in the sea, except for lights round the boat dock. This atoll had a wide and long lagoon and two docks, both full of forty- to sixty-footers.

The lead chopper, with Murdock, circled the docks from three hundred feet.

"How do we know the bad guys?" Jaybird asked on the radio.

"Usually they are the ones shooting at us," Murdock said.

They saw a man run out of one boat to the dock, shield his eyes from the dock lights, and look into the sky. Another man came out from a second boat. He carried something in both hands. Murdock put his NVG on him and yelled at the pilot.

"He's got an RPG. Get out of here." The pilot had his Motorola, and the chopper took a sudden turn to the left and dropped fifty feet, then slammed the other direction in a maneuver to outguess the rocket-propelled grenade shooter below. The man fired, but the rocket, trailing a plume of gray smoke, slanted through the air thirty yards from the bird and detonated in the lagoon.

Well out of RPG range, Murdock told his sniper to put six rounds into the second boat from the end. That was the one the RPG man had come from.

"Now, get us set down somewhere close to the dock," Murdock told the pilot.

"A play field, right behind what could be a school," the

pilot said. "Maybe two hundred yards from the dock."

"Go," Murdock said, and the pilot swung that way. The second bird trailed him.

As soon as the wheels touched down, the SEALs jumped out of the chopper and charged across the softball diamond to the street, beyond heading for the dock.

"Lam, get out front. I want to know if the men on the boat are going to fight or run." Lam darted ahead in the darkness, past a store and across a street and then past one more store to where he could see the second boat on the dock.

The rest of the SEALs moved up cautiously, spreading out along the street, pausing in the deep shadows of the last three buildings so they could see the boats.

"No movement on board that boat," Lam reported. "No lights on inside. I don't hear anything. I'm moving up. Cover me if they start shooting."

Lam scurried from the side of the building to an old car across the street and slid in behind it. Now he was just across a ten-foot wooden pier from the boat. He listened, heard some movement. One man, maybe two. Lam lay behind a fifty-five-gallon steel barrel. He stood, edged around it and without a sound crossed the planks to the edge of the dock, right beside the sixty-foot boat, and listened. Yes, sounds, movement inside. Then he heard what he figured had to be boots going up steps. Someone was coming out. He charged back behind the barrel and waited. A hand pushed back a canvas drape and a shadowed face looked out of the cabin. The man paused, then he pushed the drape aside and stepped onto the deck, went across to the gap in the rail, then down the portable steps placed next to the boat.

The man looked dark. Murdock could see in the faint dock lights that he had a beard. He wore dark clothes and a watch cap. After checking both ways along the dock, he ran lightly across the planks and up the street that led back into the tiny town.

"I'm on a runner," Lam whispered on the Motorola. "I think the boat is empty. Somebody check it out. Figure we should know where this guy is going. He is probably the guy who shot the RPG at us. He may be forting up and getting with his friends."

"Roger that, Lam," Murdock said. "Fernandez, check out the boat, and be careful. Try to tease anybody on board to come out."

Lam faded from one dark building to the next. Then he was out of structures. The man jogged ahead down the hard-packed coral road. He was moving south. This side of the atoll was less than a quarter of a mile wide, with the large lagoon to the right and then the string of outer coral reefs protecting the lagoon beyond that. It would be a pretty spot if he had time to look at it, Lam figured. The man ahead stopped and turned, looking behind him. Lam caught his move and was flat on the ground by the time the man stared to his rear. Lam let the man get a little farther ahead, just so he could spot the runner in the night darkness.

They passed a grove of trees and brush, then a barren strip that looked to be mostly coral or maybe some type of volcanic rock. Just beyond the rocky place Lam came to an airstrip. It was much smaller than the others he had seen on the atolls. This one was not more than a third of a mile long. Small planes only could land here. He saw two tied down near a T-hangar, and one more to the side.

The runner kept up his jogging along the road, past the airport and beyond another group of trees. Here the land surged upward to the highest point on the atoll. Lam figured it might be fifty feet high. Then the runner vanished. He stepped into a copse of trees and then he was gone. Lam pulled back twenty yards and nestled into some trees and brush, from which he could see the area where the jogger had vanished.

"Cap, I lost him."

"Lost him on a postage-stamp island this size?"

"True, Cap. I'm south of the airstrip. Just light planes can land here, on a short runway. Then beyond that are more trees and a small hill maybe fifty feet high. He just vanished at the edge of the trees. I don't know where he went. I'm hidden in a spot where I can see the area. We might have to wait for daylight."

"If we have time. We checked out the boat. No one on board, and no crates of plut. If we had a Geiger we could check to see if the plut had been there. That stuff is so strong it has to give off some rads. You hold there. I'm going to find the mayor of this island."

Murdock found one boat with some lights on. He pounded on the side until a sleepy-eyed woman came to the cabin door and poked her head out.

"What the hell do you want? It's almost three o'clock in the morning."

"Sorry, ma'am. I'm new in town. What can you tell me about that second boat on the dock down there?"

"Nothing. Look, come back in the morning. I'll probably never get to sleep again. Who the hell are you, anyway?"

"I'm a United States Navy SEAL, ma'am."

"Damn, you say. Hey, don't shoot me. That second boat. Came in about three hours ago. Had a truck and a fancy backhoe that lifted something damn heavy off the deck and drove it away. Near as I remember they did that six or seven times. The truck wasn't gone long, so they didn't go far." She giggled. "Hell, not far to go any direction on this fucking tiny island."

"Thank you, ma'am. Can you tell me where the mayor lives? The head government man in town."

"You call this a town? You must not get out much. Oh, hell yes, I can tell you. See that small building over there with the flag flying? That's the post office. Two houses down the street is the mayor of the whole fucking island." She yawned. "That do it? I'm going back to bed."

From inside the boat Murdock heard a man's wild laugh. "Better hurry up, woman. I can't maintain this thing forever."

She giggled and closed the door.

Murdock chuckled and took Jaybird with him and ran across the dock and up the street to the mayor's house. There were no lights on. He knocked a half dozen times and at last a light flashed through an upstairs window. It opened.

"Who the hell is down there and what the hell do you want?" The voice came raspy and angry.

"Commander Blake Murdock, Mr. Mayor, U.S. Navy. I have some important business that can't wait for daylight. I need to talk to you about a tremendous threat to your whole atoll."

"You shitting me, mister? Ain't no U.S. Navy on this rock."

"Didn't you hear the two helicopters land about a half hour ago? That was us. I really need to talk to you. There is a huge problem we need to help you solve."

"You serious, son? Get me out of a cool bed just to come yammer away with you?"

"Exceedingly serious, sir. It concerns radioactivity."

"Radio. . . ." The raspy voice cut off. "Be down in about a minute. Let me get my pants on."

Two minutes later the mayor let the two SEALs into his front room. He stared at their weapons.

"Hope there won't be any gunfire. We don't allow many guns on the atoll. Vote of the people. Now, you say radioactivity?" The mayor was short and thin, with wispy gray hair, a potbelly, and arms that were corded with muscle. His eyes were clear, blue, and full of questions.

"Yes, sir, radioactivity. Have you had any strangers coming to your atoll in the past few days or weeks?"

"Not lately. But about three months ago we had a batch of them. One gent came and talked to me and showed me a badge and a bunch of official stationery and papers and such. Said he had a secret mission here on the atoll, and wanted to set up a small lab on our little hill, down on the southern end. He paid a permit fee of ten thousand dollars and I said go ahead.

"For the next month they worked down there. Bulldozers and drag lines and concrete mixers and the whole thing. Brought in all their own workers, and when they was done, everybody but about ten men up and shipped out on the transport that brought in all of the equipment and materials."

"He didn't say which government agency?"

"He said not to tell anybody and I promised I wouldn't."

"So what have they been doing since then?"

"Not a lot. Said they were waiting for a shipment."

"A shipment of what?"

"He wouldn't say and made me promise not to ask."

"How many men there now?"

"Four of them left by boat one day. We have a kind of irregular ferry service between the atolls. They headed for Majuro."

"Mr. Mayor. We've been tracking some hijackers who grabbed a whole freighter and sailed her this way."

"Whole damn freighter. Must have had something valuable on board."

"She did. On the open market the goods were worth about ten billion dollars."

"Now, that is a bunch. What was it?"

"It was, and still is, plutonium 239, one of the most dangerous radioactive substances known to man."

"Plutonium? Isn't that the stuff they use to make nuclear bombs?"

"Yes, sir. One of the boats at your dock brought several large crates to your atoll today, probably came after dark. Did you see them?"

"No, stayed in mostly. Heard the truck going back and forth. Know the sound of that project truck down there south of the airstrip." The mayor stopped. "Hey, you trying to tell me that them government agents dug themselves a hole in my atoll and now it has a bunch of that plutonium 239 inside it?"

"Yes, sir, Mr. Mayor. That's what I'm saying. The plutonium is sealed in three-inch-thick lead jars, so it can't get out. What is curious to me is why these hijackers go to the trouble to build an underground complex."

"That's easy. I did see them moving the crates. Huge things and dastardly heavy. Leaf springs in that truck were flat and the tires were squished down soft. Big lots like that would be hard to sell to terrorists. They need a place where they can safely open the lead containers and break the plutonium down into smaller lead bottles so they can easily transport and sell it."

"That is what we have decided. We can't let them do that. I have fourteen men here all heavily armed, all experienced in this type of warfare. Our job is to stop them and recover the plutonium. The Navy has had permission from Majuro to land on any of the Marshalls and take what action is needed."

"So why do you need me?"

"Courtesy call, Mr. Mayor. And to get an idea what we have down there at the end of the airstrip. Were you ever in that underground bunker?"

"Nope. I asked; they said no. I didn't have clearance."

"Figures. We're going to be moving that way. Are there any residences or businesses down there?"

"Just Miwah at the airport. Yell at him and he'll grab his bike and get up out of your way in a rush."

"Thanks. You can explain to the people what's going on. Oh, if you have a cop or two, could they block off the far end of the air strip so nobody from town can get down there?"

"Yeah, be glad to." The mayor hesitated. "You be damn sure that none of that plutonium gets spilled on my atoll."

"We'll try our best, Mr. Mayor."

Murdock and Jaybird left the house and jogged back to where the SEALs waited on the dock. "Let's go for a hike," Murdock said. "We're going to play spelunkers and investigate an underground cave complete with your own radiation bath."

16

The thirteen SEALs met on the road just south of the small village, and Murdock told them what he had found out about the lab.

"So we can't go in blasting with our twenties," Murdock said. "We don't know what stage of breaking down the plut they are in. The only reason to build a secure complex like this is to divide the jugs of plut into smaller lead jugs so they can sell them easier. The two hundred pounds of plut could go for a hundred million. If they can break it down into protected twenty-pound jugs, they could still charge fifteen million each and make more money."

"So, how can we dig them out?" JG Gardner asked.

"Very carefully," Jaybird said.

Lam came in on the net. "This has to be the front door where I'm watching. It's concealed. So there must be a back door, too. They know that we're here. They had to hear the choppers come in, and one of them shot at us."

"We can't do an awful lot until daylight," Murdock said. "Lam, you have NVGs with you?"

"Negative."

"I'll send Jaybird down with mine. You keep that area under watch and try to figure out where the door is. We'll go to the sides and back of the hill and try to determine where some other entrances must be. How did they get those heavy crates in? Not through the place you are, right? Too many trees?"

"Yeah, Cap. You're right. So look for a side door with

a cleared ramp where the truck could ease up to it and a crane could lift out the package."

"I like the way you think, Lampedusa," Murdock said. "JG, take your squad down the road to what you figure should be the far end of the bunker. We don't know how big it is, but let's say it's not more than a hundred feet long. Check with Lam on the way by and then find some cover down there and we'll wait for daylight.

"Alpha will cover the front and try to find that truck entrance. Let's move. We have about two hours to daylight, or maybe three. No handy newscaster is going to tell us when sunrise is down here in the South Pacific."

Both Howard and Jefferson were in the carrier's hospital, so that left each squad with seven men. Murdock accepted that and sent the JG on his way.

Gardner put his men five yards apart and led out to find Lam. They told him they were coming and he met them on the road. They talked with Lam then moved on along the trail. They quickly passed what looked like a drive that ended abruptly against the jungle growth of the hill. Farther along they passed two new-looking Ford pickup trucks. The JG kept going to what he figured should be the end of the bunker. He was maybe two hundred feet from Lam. He reported in to Murdock and told him about the suddenly stopping road and the pickups.

Murdock had waited for Gardner to get Bravo well down the road before he took his squad. It was more of a trail than a road here past the airport, but he could tell even in the darkness that it had been used a lot. It had crushed coral spread on it, but grass and weeds had grown up between the twin tire tracks. Murdock passed where he figured Lam was. He clicked his mike twice and Lam came on.

"Yeah, Cap, you're about twenty feet up trail from where I figure the entrance is. With all the concrete and lead shielding they must have in there, the place must be as soundproof as a Beatles recording studio."

"Agree. We'll check out the trail here for a truck entrance. Should be easy to find."

Murdock and Jaybird led the way. The moon fought off a series of scudding clouds left over from the storm days before. They were rushing toward a low-pressure area far to the west across the Pacific.

The twin tracks led down farther than Murdock figured and at last turned right and stopped at a wall of jungle growth. Murdock put his men down in the brush near the trail, and he and Jaybird moved forward a slow step at a time, testing the area, trying to find anything that would indicate a building.

All they found was the sudden end of the truck tracks at a wall of growth. They touched the growing brush and small trees and Jaybird chuckled softly.

"Bastards," he whispered into his mike. "Try to move some of that growth. It doesn't budge. It's fastened to a real wall. It's living camouflage, so there must be boxes of dirt below the wall where the damn plants and trees take root and grow. Then somehow they lift or swing the wall and the greenery to the side. That's what I call hiding something damn well."

"Back," Murdock said. He and Jaybird retraced their steps to the trail, which they now found also continued straight ahead for another fifty feet. There sat two Ford 350 pickups, both with oversize tires and extra leaf springs that lifted the bodies a foot higher than usual.

"Rigged to take a damn heavy load," Murdock whispered to Jaybird.

They went back where the rest of the squad had settled down near the front of the bunker.

"Sadler. There's a wall up there with living camouflage of trees and vines. That's your target. Jaybird and I will back up Lam at the front door. We'll move slowly and see what happens when the sun comes up. Do they live in, eat out, or just stay in there and work now that they have something to work on? We'll find out as soon as we can. JG. What have you found back there?"

"Not a hell of a lot, Cap. We went fifty yards beyond those two Ford pickups, but we ran out of hill. We're moving back to within about twenty yards of the trucks and finding cover and concealment. Something will pop come daylight."

"Yeah, we hope," Murdock said. "If they don't come out, we'll have to use twenties on the doors we can find and blast them down. Hope they didn't use reinforced concrete slabs for their doors."

Five minutes later he and Jaybird contacted Lam and settled down in concealed positions. It was still dark.

"One man on each spot on guard duty. The rest of you can sack out. Keep your ears on. Ten four."

"Ten four?" Jaybird whispered. "Cap, you got to stop watching those old cop shows on TV."

After that it was quiet.

Murdock took the guard duty on the front door, but he didn't think that Lam would do any snoozing. He brought up the NVGs he had borrowed back from Lam and concentrated on the area Lam had pointed out where he saw the man vanish. Had to be a door there somewhere.

If they were discovered, what good would it do them to try to break down the tanks of plut? Maybe they weren't sure who it was they had shot at. Maybe. Sure, and maybe they were complete idiots. They had to know the Navy was on the island. Did they think they could outgun the whole fucking U.S. Navy? Or did they have some other pipeline?

Murdock thought about it until his head began to hurt. Now he realized just how much he appreciated and relied on the input from those men around him. Third Platoon was a team in more than one sense.

More than two hours later, Murdock was getting tired. He moved again, this time going prone and propping the goggles up with his hands and his elbows into the soft mulch under the trees and vines. He heard something. A squeak? A hinge moving? Then into the ghostly green of the NVGs a man stepped out of the trees and stood there. He had a cigarette cupped in his hand and now took a long pull and inhaled the smoke, then blew it out.

No smoking inside? Murdock wanted to take him out, but he didn't have a silenced weapon. "Lam, Lam, wake up," he whispered on the Motorola. "Lam, do you have a silenced gun? We've got a man outside the door."

"Uh, what the hell? Skipper?"

"Do you have a silenced weapon? We've got a man outside the entrance."

"Yeah, silent, but you've got the goggles. I can't see him up there."

"Jaybird?"

"Can't help you, Cap. Take him out with one of the 5.56s. They'll never hear it inside that tomb."

Murdock sighted in with his Bull Pup, making sure he was on 5.56. Just as the man turned to leave, Murdock pulled the trigger on a three-round burst. The three shots from the rifle sounded to Murdock like 105 field artillery rounds going off in the pristine pure South Pacific air and the total silence of the night. Murdock watched as the man slammed backward. At least two rounds hit him, Murdock figured.

"Lam, you're closest," Murdock said.

The SEAL leader saw Lam lift out of his hiding spot and rush to the fallen man. He bent over him a moment, then hoisted him on his shoulders and walked quickly to the road and down it toward the village.

"Jaybird, stay," Murdock said, lifting up and running to catch up with Lam. They put the man down in the brush twenty feet from the road.

"Dead as a turkey on Thanksgiving morning," Lam said. They went through the pockets of the civilian clothes he wore: a billfold with five hundred dollars in it, two bank credit cards from London, some old clippings, and a U.S. Maritime Seaman's card.

He had a full beard and black hair.

"Could be an Arab," Lam said.

"Probably. He'll be missed." Murdock used the Motorola. "Anybody awake. We took out one of them who came outside to smoke. That means they may be working inside and not allowing smoking there. We have one less to deal with when we get inside."

"People inside probably didn't hear the shots," Gardner

said. "If that place is made of concrete and lead, it's totally insulated from outside sound."

"Even if it is built like a tomb, it has to have air vents," Murdock said. "Unless they purify and reoxygenate the air through some kind of rebreathers. Not likely."

"So let's find them," Gardner said. "Canzoneri and Prescott, go up the side of the hill from the back and start hunting for the vents. They'll be cleverly camouflaged. Should be on the very top of the little ridge."

"Right. Lam and Jaybird, get up to the top on this end and do a search. Go."

"When we find one?" Jaybird asked.

"Give a call on the net and I'll come and look it over with you. Be great if we could pour five gallons of gasoline down each one and then drop in a WP. But that would leave this atoll with a continuing problem of several hundred pounds of deadly plutonium 239 splattered over half the land and the lagoon, and we really don't want to do that. The easy way won't work this time."

"So what's the hard way?" Lam asked.

"That we're going to have to find out minute by minute as we try to dig those bastards out of there without dumping that plut all over the landscape. If that happens, we'll be the first victims, dead in about a half hour."

"That shit don't mess around, does it?" Jaybird said. The two scouts were halfway up the side of the forty-foot hill when Jaybird called.

"Might want to look at this, Cap," he said on the net. "I think I've got one."

Murdock left his post and hurried up the direction he had seen Jaybird go through the goggles. He found him a short time later. Jaybird sat beside what looked like a tree stump. Only it wasn't. It was slabs of wood fastened around a three-inch black iron standpipe. Every house in the States with a bathroom has one poking through the roof. Lam put both hands over the pipe covering it. He grinned in the darkness.

"Suction, pulled my hand hard against the top. It's an

intake pipe. This is how they get fresh air into the place."
The Motorola picked up what they said and everyone on
the net knew.

Less than a minute later, Canzoneri sounded off. "I've
got a second one, Cap. Looks like an intake vent."

Within a half hour they had the area covered and had
located three intake vents and three exhaust tubes. The
exhaust type was made of foot-diameter sheet metal tubes
that came three feet out of the dirt of the hillside and had
been camouflaged with green paint and covered with
growing vines and small brush.

"Who has those folded plastic emergency water carrying sacks?" Murdock asked. They were designed to haul
water in desert situations, but folded into a three-inch
square less than a half inch thick. He had seven responses
on the net.

Murdock took one of the plastic sacks from his combat
vest and unfolded it. The plastic was tough—yes it would
work. "All right, I want one of these sacks on each of the
vents. Use as many thicknesses as you can to cover the
top of the large and small vents, down at least six inches.
Then use good old green tape and tape the plastic on tight,
so nothing can get in or out. Let's do it now."

Murdock folded the heavy plastic again and put it over
the intake pipe, then quickly brought it down around the
sides. Both he and Lam held the plastic in place, and
Jaybird put on three wraps of the tape. The plastic on top
sucked down a half inch as the pumps below tried to bring
in more air. The plastic fluttered, then held solid. No fresh
air would get down this intake pipe.

"When the sacks are all on and secure, we go back to
our first stakeouts. Somebody is going to be coming out
of there within ten or fifteen minutes. Let's move."

Murdock, Lam, and Jaybird ran down the side of the
hill, through the brush and to their dark hideout spots near
the front of the bunker.

"Has to work, man," Jaybird said. "They can't get in
fresh air and can't get rid of the old stuff. Yeah, fifteen
minutes sounds about right."

• • •

It took twenty minutes, then two men came running out
the front door through a fringe of brush and into the open.
Lam was less than twenty feet from them. He cut both
down with silenced rounds, and they jolted backward and
sprawled in the green growth, never to move again.

"We've had two come out in front," Murdock said on
the net.

Five minutes passed, then Sadler came on the radio.

"The wall at the road is starting to move. It's going like
a snail with foot problems, sliding to the left. If they want
fresh air inside they have to leave both doors open."

"Take out any men who show themselves," Murdock
said.

"Nobody coming out," Sadler said. "Behind the door is
a blank wall maybe eight to ten feet away. Looks like it's
all concrete."

"Don't risk any shots inside until we know more than
we do now," Murdock said.

They waited ten minutes. Nothing happened.

Murdock eased up from behind his cover tree. "Who
has tear gas grenades?" he said on the radio. There were
two responses.

"Down the intake air vent?" Omar Rafii asked.

"No, they could have filters on the intake. One man to
the rear door. Climb up the side of the hill and get a good
throw to punch the grenade into the bunker as far as possible. Who?"

"Rafii on the rear truck door," he said.

"Sadler. I'll come around to the front. Wait for me Rafii, we'll hit them both at the same time."

The front door was still in shadows and darkness. The
faint fracturing of the black sky showed dimly in the east.
It would be dawn in ten minutes.

"Let's move it before we lose the dark," Murdock said.

Rafii scrambled up the side of the hill and crawled to
the top of the opening. He hung over it, looking into the
bunker. "I can see inside," he said. "Two of the big crates

of plut. No people. I can get the tear gas in about thirty feet."

"Wait," Murdock said.

Sadler had ghosted up through the darkness and picked up Lam, who showed him where the door was. It was a regular-looking wooden door, now hanging open, giving out a faint glow of lights. A drape of heavy cloth hung two feet in back, blocking off the light and the interior. Jaybird found a long stick, pushed up near the side of the door, and rammed the stick into the drape, then pushed it to one side.

Sadler grinned and pulled the pin on the grenade. "I'm ready, Rafii, how about you?"

"Go," Rafii said. They both threw their tear gas grenades into the bunker and retreated into the fading darkness.

Murdock heard the small popping sound as the small charge blew the fragile tear gas cover off the cylinder and the gas spewed out into the bunker. He heard a cry of anger, then a weapon fired and three slugs whispered out the front door. The SEALs were all behind solid cover and none were hit.

They waited. No one came out either door.

Murdock scowled. "All right, men, they could have gas masks in there to counter any gasses from the plut. Whatever they have, it worked for them. I need some suggestions here, team. Just what the hell should we do next? It's going to be daylight in another five minutes."

17

"Hold your positions, but let's get some input," Murdock said.

"I have some movement," Gardner said from the rear. "Two men just charged out a hidden door and scrambled into the Ford pickups. No good shots at them yet. You want the pickups stopped or the men down?"

"Get the men. Don't use the twenties. The island can use two new pickups."

Murdock heard firing from the rear of the hill.

"One man down, one pickup is moving," Gardner said. "Can't get a shot at him. Take out the tires, somebody."

Murdock heard the high-pitched snarl of an Ingram submachine gun on full auto, followed by fifteen or twenty shots from larger bore weapons.

"Truck is down and stopped," Gardner said. "The man is holding up his hands. Could we use one who can talk?"

"Yes, keep him healthy. Rafii, you check him out. He could be an Arab. Go."

"We have to go inside and dig out the rest of them," Fernandez said.

"We've accounted for five," Bradford said. "How many can there be in there?"

"However many there are, they will be in solid defensive positions," Mahanani said. "All that lead and concrete. No way we can storm in there and not take fifty percent casualties."

"Why not use a WP on each end?" Claymore asked. "With all that concrete and lead in there, can't be much that will burn. We storm in right after the WP has splattered and pick up the pieces."

"You ever smelled a good strong WP smoke in a contained area?" Sadler said. "It's murder."

"Let it air out a little," Claymore said.

"Let's stop right there," Murdock said. "The WP might be the answer. We can move slowly, use one on the front, let it air out a little, and then move in and see what we can see. We're blind out here. If you haven't noticed, it's daylight. So be sure you have cover out there. Gardner?"

"Yeah, let's try the WP. Only one at each end. Nothing is going to burn that I can see inside this big door. Those timbers Rafii saw on the plut crates might smoke some, but they won't flame up. That WP splash will go right through them and won't faze the lead."

"Rafii, anything from our newfound friend?" Murdock asked.

"Not much. He's an Arab, from Yemen. Tried to knife me when he thought I wasn't looking. Poor guy suffered a broken arm. He's talking more now. He claims there are twenty men still inside. With a little more persuasion he'll cut that down. He said they have already put plut from two crates into twenty lead boxes that hold twenty pounds of plut each. That may be true."

"Keep working on him," Murdock said. "Keep him alive if possible. I'm sure the CIA will want to reason with him later. Gardner, take your men up around that rear truck door and put one WP in as far as you can. We'll do it together. Ching, how does your arm feel?"

"A hundred percent, Cap. I get to lob in the WP?"

"You guessed it. Get up to the door. Jaybird, use your stick again on that drape. Both you throwers, tell me when you're ready."

"Ready front," Ching said.

Prescott called from the rear on his radio. "Ready rear."

"Do it," Murdock said. He watched Ching hold the WP smoke grenade and then pull the pin and throw it sidearm under the curtain where Jaybird held it up inside the bunker.

"Front door WP inside," Ching said.

"Rear WP about ready to go off inside," Prescott said.

The powder charge in a WP grenade is larger than that in a tear gas grenade, and Murdock heard the explosion deep in the bunker. Then another one farther away.

He punched his wrist stopwatch button and waited. Within a minute, white smoke seeped past the drape, then billowed out faster. The men near the door faded away into the brush and found solid protection behind larger trees now that it was daylight.

They waited ten minutes. The smoke came out in volume, then slowed and at last faded to wisps. Nobody came out.

"Bradford, get up to that front door and rip down that drape, but don't get yourself shot."

Bradford made the run and flattened against the side of the bunker, then reached around with Jaybird's stick and pulled out the end of the drape. He grabbed it with both hands and lunged away, using all of his two hundred and fifteen pounds. The heavy cloth held for a moment, then ripped off and sent Bradford sprawling on the ground. He did a shoulder roll, came to his feet and raced back to a fallen log, then dove behind it.

There was no gunfire out the door.

Murdock gave it another three minutes. "Lam and Ching, on me. We get to the side of the bunker, then we go in one at a time diving. Doesn't look like room for right or left. I'm first, then Lam, then Ching. Inside we'll see what we have to do."

They sprinted for the green of the hidden bunker, and all made it. Murdock peered around the side of the door at ground level. There were no lights on inside. He took out his large flashlight and motioned to the other two to do the same. Then he sucked in a deep breath, came into a squat position with his boots firmly on the ground, and jolted forward into the bunker, hitting on his right shoulder and rolling, his Bull Pup cradled in his arms flat against his chest.

He stopped his roll on his belly and turned on the flash-

light. The beam probed through remains of the WP. He
saw nothing at first, then crawled forward and heard the
other two men come in behind him, and their lights joined
his. They were in a room ten feet square, the floor half-
covered with what looked like lead boxes a foot square
and half that deep. None had covers. The room was all
concrete, with a ceiling seven feet off the floor. To the
left ahead Murdock saw an opening more than four feet
wide. He came to his feet, darted ahead to the side of the
opening, and shone his light into the void of smoke and
darkness.

The next room was twice the size of the first. The
planking from one of the two-hundred-pound crates of
plutonium lay scattered on the floor. Another crate had
been emptied and stood against the far wall. There was
no sign of the two two-hundred-pound lead containers of
plutonium 239. Against the other wall sat a small forklift
truck. The three SEALs surged ahead to the forklift and
looked past it into the next room, through another four-
foot-wide opening.

Inside was another room twenty feet wide and that
deep. Across the far end stood a lead-shielded wall. A
man sat on one of two tall stools next to the lead barrier.
He didn't move. Murdock shone his light on the man. His
hands were gripping mechanical devices that evidently extended through the lead shielding. Directly in front of him
was a large video screen that showed mechanical hands
poised over one of the two-hundred-pound lead containers
of plutonium.

"Be damned, video," Lam said. "I wondered how they
could do it and not get fried into crispy critters."

Murdock held up his hand for quiet.

"Sir, you at the video. You're under arrest. Don't try
anything violent. You must give yourself up."

Slowly the man turned on the stool. His shirt had been
burned off his chest and great third-degree burns dug into
his flesh. His face held only one eye; the rest of it was
churned into a froth of blood and charred flesh. His hair
had burned entirely away. His one eye stared at Murdock

a moment, then he turned more and fell off the stool, his face striking the concrete floor first, leaving a bloody smear as he gave one long sigh, letting all the breath of life gush out of his lungs. Then his bowels voided.

Murdock stepped over the corpse and studied the video screen. It had come through the WP undamaged. He moved the mechanical hands and the camera followed them. He could see two of the large lead vats in the enclosed room that was entirely shielded by lead blankets, inside and out.

"We got here in time," Murdock said. "Another six hours and they would have divided that plut into those small lead boxes and it could have been on its way to fifty ports throughout the world."

He used the radio. "We're in, found one man dead. Gardner, how are you doing?"

There was a faint whisper and then static, but no voice came through.

"Too much lead shielding," Jaybird said. "It will stop most radio transmissions. Remember that lead blanket we used in London on that live nuke?"

Murdock nodded and pointed toward another four-foot-wide opening. They had to be that big to get the forklift through, he decided. The next room held a small kitchen and beyond that sleeping quarters. The next opening led to a day room, and then they heard friendly voices ahead.

"Gardner, is that you?" Murdock bellowed.

"Yep. We found two more varmints in this rat hole. Both of them dead. The WP got them."

They met, and Murdock gave the men a guided tour past the lead-shielded room and the mechanical hands, then they hurried out through the front and assembled. The prisoner was wrist tied and they started their march back to the village. Before they had gone twenty yards, a rifle shot blasted into the stillness.

Sadler, bringing up the rear of the line, grunted and pitched forward on his chest on the crushed coral road. At the sound of the shot, the SEALs scattered, rushing into the woods beside the road. The prisoner went with them, evidently not willing to trust the shooter to miss him.

Sadler remained in the road. Claymore was nearest to him. He charged out of the protection of the trees, scooped up the two-hundred-twenty-pound senior chief like he was a sack of marshmallows and ran with him to the woods. Three shots tracked him, but all missed.

Lam had moved to the rear of the group still in the woods. "My meat," he said on the radio.

"Fernandez, go with Lam, find that bastard out there, and don't bring him back alive," Murdock said.

Mahanani with his first aid kit was already kneeling in front of Sadler. He ripped open the senior chief's bloody cammy and found the chest wound.

"Damnit!" Mahanani shouted. "It's an exit wound, Cap. Sadler got shot in the back by a good-sized round and it came out his chest just under his clavicle. I can get the bleeding stopped, but you better get that chopper down here fast. The pilot still have a Motorola?"

Murdock touched his mike and called the chopper. He had his Motorola turned on.

"Chopper Sixty on the atoll. Hope to God you're still there."

"Yes, Murdock. I'm here waiting for your call."

"Good. We have a casualty. Hit bad. Lift off and come down south. There's a white crushed coral road that goes past the little airstrip. Keep coming another five hundred yards and you'll find us. Get here as fast as you can, and alert the carrier to have a trauma team on the flight deck when you land. Move it. Now."

"That's a roger, Murdock. Warming up and lifting off."

Murdock went into the fringe of trees next to the coral road and waited. He heard the bird coming a few minutes later and went into the middle of the road to flag it down.

Lam and Fernandez jogged the first fifty yards past the bunker, staying in the trees.

"He had to be on top of the bunker to get a shot at us,"

Lam said. "Highest point on the whole damn atoll. Where would he go from there?"

They had been moving with little noise; now they slowed and made no sounds whatsoever as they walked slowly toward the center of the hill covering the bunker. They were well to the side, away from the road. Lam held up his hand and both stopped and listened. Nothing. They were in sight of the hill now and moved slowly from one covering tree to the next. Lam used the radio, whispering.

"I'll fire at the top of the hill and dive behind cover. You watch for any return fire and blast him."

Lam fired and dove behind a fallen tree. His rounds peppered the top of the hill. There was no response. Lam held up his hand again for silence. Fernandez shook his head. Lam nodded. "Yeah, I've got some movement well ahead. Like he's trying to circle us and get back to the village. Not that much room here to get around us. We stay together." Lam gave the forward motion with his hand, and they moved to their right, edging away from the bunker and toward the widest part of the island, which was less than a quarter of a mile here.

They moved cautiously, from cover to cover, then waited in one place for five minutes, listening. Fernandez shook his head. Lam nodded. "Yep, he's coming toward us. Out maybe a hundred yards. Not being careful, like he's in a hurry to get somewhere."

"Maybe more of them in the village," Canzoneri said on the net.

"Cap, you copy us?" Lam asked.

"Roger. Heard about some more might be in the village. Let this one come past you and tail him wherever he's going. We'll be staked out in the village to net him in if he's just running. We moved the senior chief out by chopper. He should be near the carrier by now."

"Will tail him. Roger."

In their jungle cammies and floppy hats, Canzoneri and Lam blended in well with the green of the growth around them. Lam nodded again that he heard something and pointed to their right. They were still a hundred yards

inside the shore of the lagoon. Both men had sturdy trees
to hide behind and settled down to wait for the terrorist
to come to them.

It took him another five minutes. He moved with more
caution now. Lam spotted him first. The man wore khaki
pants and shirt and no hat on his black hair. He had a full
black beard and glasses. He lifted up from behind a fallen
log and studied the area ahead of him. Lam eased fully
behind his tree. The Arab stood then and jogged through
an open space and into a thicket of brush and small trees.
Lam let him go. He gave him a two-minute lead, then he
stood and waved at Fernandez and they followed.

The Arab never looked to his rear. He studied the area
ahead continually, sometimes pausing a minute or two
between movements.

Back at the road into the village, Murdock held up the
march as Rafii questioned the prisoner. He spoke to him
in Arabic and the words came quickly on both sides. Rafii
stared hard at the young Arab, then took out a knife from
his pocket and snapped open its four-inch blade with a
flick of his hand. The gleaming steel knife was Rafii's
favorite shaving tool. He placed the side of the steel
against the Arab's neck.

"I can kill you with one quick swipe of my pet here,
you know that?" Rafii spoke in Arabic and the other man
responded in the same language.

"Every man dies. Some die for the glory of Allah."

"You lie. I am a Moslem, too. Allah does not condone
killing or terrorism or any violence. Your leaders have
betrayed you. They are using you for their own ends."

"You lie. If I die I will be a glorious martyr for Allah."

"If you insist." Rafii moved the blade and made a slice
down the man's cheek, four inches long and deep enough
to bring a gush of blood running down his cheek and
dripping on his legs where he knelt in the grass. His hands
were still tied behind him.

"Bastard," the Arab shouted.

"Pain is the mother of all heroes," Rafii said. "Or have
you forgotten that part? You will suffer much pain in the

next half hour, then you may die. Tell me if there are any of your group still in the village."

The Arab shook his head, and some of his blood splattered on Rafii. "I will be an honored martyr for Allah."

Murdock had watched the interrogation. He touched Rafii on the shoulder. "Do what you have to do, but don't kill him. The CIA will want to roast his bones in their oven."

Murdock then moved the rest of the platoon down the road past the airstrip, to where a police car blocked the road. He called on the Motorola to the second SH-60 chopper that had brought them in.

"Chopper two, do you read me?"

"Loud and clear. Go."

"Contact the carrier on your radio and tell them we have a small problem. It's what could be a live radioactive chamber with two large jugs of plut that may be uncorked. Have them send in their top radiation experts to evaluate and see who and what needs to be sent here to reclaim the plut. We also have two crates not opened. Get a reply for me."

"Will do, Murdock."

Before the platoon made it to the edge of the village, Murdock's Motorola spoke.

"Murdock, have some messages for you from the carrier."

"I'm all ears."

"First, the head man on the nuke power plant on board is coming in on a Sixty with five of his top men and equipment and testing gear. They'll take charge of the plut. Next, they want to know when you'll wrap up your work here. Third is a note that they have tracked the other three small ships that may have plut on them. They are heading for different atolls but none have reached one yet. Keeping them under surveillance."

"Roger, Sixty. We're still tracking one of the terrorists. There may be more in the village. We have one prisoner. Tell Don Stroh. He's still alive but beat up some. Will let you know how much more time we need."

The chopper responded and Murdock took his men into the village. He could see it better now that it was light. There were about twenty houses, five or six small stores, a post office, and two good-sized warehouses near the dock. Small boats would have to bring in any freight or goods from large ships that stopped by. He hit the net.

"I'm wondering if the terrs had an in-village house? Did they have a place to rest up and relax while waiting for the arrival of their goods?"

"We could ask the mayor again," Jaybird said.

"We could do a house-to-house," Bradford said.

"Let's check at the restaurant down there," Claymore said. "Any men even in this place would eat out most of the time."

Murdock sent Claymore to the small cafe and Jaybird to find the mayor. The rest of them went over to the Sixty and waited.

Rafii slapped the Arab terrorist gently on the cheek, splattering the slow stream of blood.

"You disappoint me. What did you say your name was?"

"Didn't."

"Attitude, you have an attitude, even though I can kill you with one quick swipe of my blade. Should I cut off your trigger finger? Would that help your memory? Or just cut off your cock and let you bleed to death. I could stop you bleeding to death and let you live with half a prick, knowing you'll never fuck another woman as long as you live. Yeah, that sounds better." He moved toward the man's crotch with his knife. The Arab tipped over, smashing into the ground away from Rafii.

"No, no, wait. I don't know much. No more with the knife. I came here with the construction crew. This is my part in the whole operation. I don't know anything about anything else. Just here. We were to get in four big bottles of plutonium. Our job to break it down into twenty-pound lead boxes, seal them, and ship them out as regular cargo."

"That's it? Who's behind it? Who paid you the cash to do this job? Where were the finished boxes of twenty pounds supposed to be shipped to?"

"We were to be told that by email when we were ready to ship."

"How many more men in town?"

"Town? It's just a village. I had twenty men to start. The boat that left the plut took four men away. Seventeen of us left."

"We killed seven inside. Where are the other nine?"

"Who knows?"

Rafii kicked the terrorist in the side, on his left kidney. The man on the ground howled in agony and doubled up with his knees to his chest to fight the nausea and pain.

Rafii used his Motorola. "Cap, Rafii here."

"Go, Rafii."

"This asshole says there are nine more men in town. I don't believe him but that's his line."

"Bring him up to the village. We need him alive. He has to be able to talk to the CIA. Don Stroh is going to have some work to do after all."

Claymore pushed open the screen door on the cafe and went inside. He kept his weapon slung over his shoulder, with the muzzle down. Most civilians were afraid of guns. The eatery was a small affair, with six booths and a counter. A woman with a wipe rag paused in her work on the counter and looked up with a big grin.

"Well now, we do get to see some of the Navy boys. I hear you're SEALs and here to help us get rid of those sombitches who dropped in on us about three months ago."

"Yes, ma'am. I wondered about them. They eat in here?"

"Eat like sows in heat." She grinned, and it lit up her shy face with a friendly glow. She was in her thirties, tanned, blond, and probably wishing she could lose fifteen to twenty pounds. She pointed at his Bull Pup. "That thing loaded?"

"Yes, ma'am. Can't very well do much good with an unloaded rifle."

She nodded. "What can I do for you? Breakfast?"

"No, ma'am. Wondering about the strangers who came. How many of them are still here?"

"Well, let's see. I'll get you a cup of coffee while I figure it out. Were about forty of them for the construction. We did a great business then. After it finished, they were down to about fifteen. Somebody said that five of them left on the boat that dropped off those big packages last night."

"So, maybe ten of them left?"

"If my arithmetic is any good. Here, coffee. Never knew a sailor to turn down a cup of joe."

Claymore sipped it, then gulped two big swallows. "Yeah, ma'am, that's good coffee. So, about ten of them. I better talk to my boss." He turned to leave, then looked back. "Oh, pardon me. I thank you kindly for the coffee."

She grinned, stretching so her pink uniform pressed tightly against her full breasts. "More than welcome. You just come back and see me anytime."

Claymore hurried out the door and used his radio. "Lady at the cafe says there could be only ten of them left on the atoll," Claymore said without calling in first.

"Roger that, Claymore. We've got a nine count on them, which could leave only one missing, if her count is right. On the other hand could be six or eight more. Now all we have to do is find the fuckers who must be playing hide and seek."

Just as he said it, a rifle snarled from nearby and a heavy slug skidded off the concrete-hard coral street and whined off into the lagoon.

18

The sound of the rifle shot came from the left, back toward the cafe and the post office. The SEALs dove for cover that would protect them from that direction. One more shot blasted into the morning stillness but missed the target. This time Murdock saw the muzzle flash from an upstairs window on the only two-story building in town.

"It's from the post office," Murdock said into the Motorola. "Who has cover to get to the side of that building?"

"Yeah, I can make it," Mahanani said. "First that old sedan down about ten, then the pickup and I should be free. Kick a couple of rounds into that window up there, Cap, and I'm off and running."

Murdock sent a three-round burst of 5.56 into the open window. He saw Mahanani leap up and race for the sedan, then the pickup. No more shots came from the window.

"I'll look for a back door," Mahanani said on the radio as he ran. The medic carried his usual Bull Pup. He peered around the end of the pickup at the second-story window. The guy had no shot at him from that angle. Mahanani stood and sprinted for the side of the post office thirty yards away. Once there he took some deep breaths and worked his way to the back and peered round it. Yeah, he could see a back door. Before he could move, a man came out the door. Mahanani put a three-round burst of 5.56 into the air.

"Hold it right there. Don't move or you're a dead man."

The figure turned slowly and pushed both hands into the air. Mahanani saw that the man was in his sixties or seventies, had no weapon, and must belong there.

Mahanani ran up to him. "Sorry about that. Didn't mean to scare you. Our platoon was shot at from this building. How do I get to the second floor?"

"No sweat, young fellah. My building. Stairway just inside. Didn't hear nobody upstairs. Mostly empty, yeah, sure enough."

"Thanks. Anybody else up there?"

"No, mostly empty. Storage."

"Stay out of the place for a while. I'm going in." Mahanani edged up to the door and looked inside. "You get that, Cap?"

"Heard. Take it easy. Might be more than one. You want some backup?"

"Nope. I'm cool. Moving inside." He stepped through the door and flattened against the side wall. The steps were to his right. He listened. He'd learned that much from Lam. Nothing. He eased up the first three steps, staying near the wall to cut down on any squeaks. Both the fourth and fifth steps creaked as he put his weight on them. He stopped, the muzzle of the Pup centered on the doorway at the top of the stairs.

He could hear no movement above him. He turned off the Motorola so it wouldn't give him away with an incoming call, then eased on up to the landing. The door there was closed. He checked the knob. Unlocked. Mahanani turned the knob and edged the door out an inch, then went to the floor beside the wall and nudged the panel open another inch so he could peer around the door-jamb into the room.

Dust, a pile of old newspapers and magazines, a dozen boxes. Not a sound from inside the twenty-foot square room.

"You've got five seconds to come out with your hands up; otherwise I throw in two grenades and your ass is blown up with a hundred chunks of hot shrapnel making you into one fucking bloody pincushion. Your choice, asshole."

There was no reaction. Mahanani shrugged, pulled a

flash-bang grenade off his vest, and worked out the safety pin. He held down the arming spoon, decided where to throw the nonlethal grenade, and pitched it into the room underhanded. Then he closed the door and put both hands over his ears.

He was on his feet when the last blast of sound receded inside the room. He pushed open the door and charged inside. He checked the parts of the dimly lit room that he could see. Nothing—certainly no terrorist. He checked behind the boxes. Nobody. Then he saw something near the window. He moved up cautiously, not quite sure what the object was. He saw the rifle first, an AK-47 that had fallen to one side. Then he could make out the body. He stepped closer and saw the crumpled figure with a bullet hole in his forehead and half of his skull blasted off in back.

There was no one else in the room.

Mahanani turned on his Motorola. "Relax, Cap. Nice shooting. The only terr up here caught one of your rounds in his forehead. He must have been looking out the window at exactly the wrong time. I'm coming down with his AK-47."

"That's a roger, Mahanani. Have you seen Lam?"

"Negative."

"That's 'cause we're not to the village yet," Lam said on the net. "Our boy is hightailing it in your direction. We're letting him run. He should be showing up there in about ten. You could put a net around this side of the buildings and take him as he comes in."

"Good idea, Lam. We're on it." Murdock moved his men to backyards and doorways facing the jungle to the south of the village. They were ready within five minutes and settled down out of sight to wait for their quarry.

"Like the beaters chasing a lion into a trap where the hunters can shoot it," Jaybird said.

"Not a lion, dumb-dumb," Canzoneri said. "More likely a wild pig or maybe a lonesome water buffalo."

"Whatever," Jaybird said.

They waited.

Gardner picked up the terrorist first. "I've got somebody in jeans and a T-shirt coming along the edge of the lagoon," he said. "Yes, he has a rifle. Could be our boy."

"I can confirm on the clothes," Lam said. "Guy we're following has a rifle and is wearing jeans and a white shirt."

"Let's take him alive if possible," Murdock said. "Don Stroh will love it. Does this runner look like an Arab?"

"Black hair and a beard, so it's a chance," Gardner said. "I can get to the next building, and if he keeps on course I should be able to surprise him at about six feet. I'm moving."

"Oh yeah, he looks like an Arab," Prescott said. "He's on the same course, near the lagoon. There's some kind of a garden down there and then some brush and a building next to that warehouse. He'll come between the warehouse and another building, maybe a store."

Gardner slid past the house he had been crouching near and sprinted for the next building. He worked around the side of it, out of sight of the terrorist. Then he peered around the corner and saw the man still coming. He was on course. When he passed the big warehouse, he would be within a dozen feet of the store Gardner hid behind. Gardner made sure his Bull Pup was on the 5.56 barrel, then slid off the safety and waited.

He chanced one more look around the wall. Yes. The man was twenty feet away and coming toward him. At the last minute the terrorist changed direction and sprinted for the store that hid Gardner. The JG saw the move. It would bring the man within three feet of where Gardner waited. He reversed the weapon and held the barrel of the Bull Pub. He could hear the man's feet hitting the crushed coral. He had to time it just right. He waited, holding his breath.

Now. Gardner stepped out and swung the Bull Pub like a club. The terrorist ran right into it. The stock hit the man in the chest and right arm, stopping him and driving him back a step.

Gardner leaped forward and slammed his fist into the terrorist's jaw, jolting him backward. He stumbled, dropped his rifle, and fell. A moment later the Bull Pup's 20mm muzzle pushed down and hovered an inch from the terrorist's eyes.

"Don't even think about moving or you're dead," Gardner said.

The dark-faced man swore in Arabic and his face twisted in hatred, but that was all he could do.

"Come pick up the garbage," Gardner said. "I've got one bag full, down and wishing he was dead. Stroh should have a field day."

Twenty minutes later the two prisoners were sitting in an SH-60 waiting to go out to the carrier. The bird had just brought in the radiation experts from the nuclear division of the carrier. Murdock had borrowed a pickup and taken them and their equipment down to the bunker. Another party of six sailors had arrived in another chopper to arrange for a local boat to ferry the plutonium crates out to the carrier. The big ship had steamed closer to the atoll and now cruised slowly five miles to the north.

Murdock watched the radiation testers do their work in the bunker. There were only traces of radiation in the bunker itself. They put a probe into the sealed room and found radiation levels much higher, but not lethal.

"Neither of the lead containers of plutonium has been opened, so there is no big problem," Commander Whitfield told Murdock. He was the officer in charge of the nuclear propulsion unit on the carrier. "We can breach this lead wall, go inside in radiation-proof suits, and put added protection around the lead containers. Then we'll crate them up and get them back to the ship and put them in our sealed radiation safe room. Routine work for my men."

"I'll leave it in your hands, Commander. I think it's time I got my men and our two prisoners back to the ship. Have you heard anything about the other two boats with the stolen plut on board?"

"Only that they're still at sea and are being monitored closely."

Murdock thanked him and jogged back to the choppers.

"Let's load up and get out of here. Do we have two birds that can fly?"

They did. In fifteen minutes they had boarded, taken off, and landed on the carrier. Don Stroh met them.

"We've got some meat for your grinder," Murdock said when he saw Stroh. "Not sure what they know, but I bet you'll find out. If you're keeping score, we left eight dead on the atoll and brought you two. Most of this bunch were Arab-looking men in their twenties."

Stroh looked at the two prisoners with hands tied behind their backs, and one with blood all over his face. "Yes, you did well on this one, Commander. We'll see that both of these gentlemen have the proper welcome into the Company."

"Where are the other two boats?"

"Not sure. I've left that up to the CAG and the captain. They have tabs on them at the CIC."

Murdock thanked him, sent the SEALs back to their quarters, and he and Gardner went to sick bay to check on the three wounded men. Howard had one leg in a cast and kept swearing at anyone within sight.

"How can I get with the program with all that damn plaster on my leg? Just a little nick on the bone and the doctor went ballistic. Hell, I walked in here on it. No reason I can't get back to duty."

"Sailor, you'll do what the doctor tells you to do, and you'll keep your mouth shut for the next twenty-four," Murdock said. He scowled at the SEAL. "Yeah, it's tough being out of action. I've been there a time or two. Just ride with it, and we'll get you back in the loop. Rest up and read some skiing and windsurfing magazines. I'm sure there are some around."

Howard closed his eyes and shook his head. "Yes, sir, Commander sir," he said. Then he grinned. "Hell, Cap, it's tough as shit week in here. But I guess if I got to, I got to."

Murdock slapped his shoulder and turned to Jefferson,

who was in the next bed. His right shoulder was bandaged but there was no cast.

"Hey, Cap, you come to spring me, right? Kick in the bail money and I'll get out of this hoosegow."

"Don't you wish, Jefferson. You've got a month's pass. Your shoulder is all cut up and you'll need probably two months on rehab to get back to fighting trim. That's why you get the big bucks, right?"

"Oh, hell yes, Cap. Huge money." He shook his head. "Ke-rist, but I was hoping. You nail some of them bastards?"

Murdock told them about the operation on the atoll.

"You took it to them fuckers. Damn straight." Jefferson paused. "I hear the senior chief took a round in the back. How's he doing?"

"Don't know. We haven't found him yet. I'll stop back and let you know how he is."

They found Sadler. He was in intensive care and getting oxygen and a close watch. A nurse brought his doctor. The medic checked the chart and then turned to the two men still in their dirty cammies.

"Your senior chief has had a dangerous wound. The bullet went in his back and all the way out his upper chest. It broke one rib but didn't push it into any vital organs. The round did clip the top of his lung, and it collapsed before we got him to the carrier. We fixed that, but there's also more damage up in that area. There was quite a bit of internal bleeding, but we think we have that located and stopped. He's on antibiotics and oxygen and an IV. He had two pints of blood and a three-hour operation. We think we have found all the problems. He's still groggy from the anesthesia. He will be able to talk to you in about four hours."

"He'll make it, right, Doc?" Gardner asked.

"Oh yes. He's a tough one. Vital signs are all good and he's stabilized. If nothing else goes wrong, he should be up and around in two weeks."

Murdock thanked the doctor and nurses, and they left, heading for the CIC.

"Now back to work," Murdock said.

The CIC was its usual busy self. Captain Olenowski, the CAG, was on a stool watching a display screen. He turned when the two SEALs came in.

"We're still watching the other two boats. One of them went right past Ailuk Atoll and headed for the next one down the chain. He's about thirty miles from Wotje Atoll, and we don't know anything about that speck of coral."

"Sir, where is the second boat?" Gardner asked.

"That one is heading due east and straight for Rongrik Atoll. That landfall is a hundred and sixty miles from us here at Utrik. We think the boat is having some trouble. It seems to be speeding up and slowing down. The average speed has dropped to about six knots and we think that one, too, is overloaded. Right now she's only halfway to that atoll."

"So what's our next move?" Murdock asked.

The CAG rubbed his hand over his face and stared at the screen. "We have two crews at this atoll now, recovering the plutonium in there. The two crated ones are now on a sixty-foot boat bringing them out to us. We'll hoist them over the side. The other two will take longer, about an hour more to get them crated and protected and hauled out here. Then we have a decision. Do we go to Wotje or to Rongrik?"

"Sir, a suggestion."

"That's why the CNO asked you to come, Murdock. Shoot."

"The SH-60 moves a little over two hundred miles an hour. Three point four five miles a minute. We can beat both boats to their respective atolls. Put a squad of SEALs in each chopper and rattle them out there. We meet them if they land, and take them out and recover the plut."

The CAG looked hard at Murdock. "You're down to thirteen men. That's six and seven to a squad. How about we send a squad of Marine Recon with each of your squads? Beef up your firepower."

Murdock glanced at Gardner. He lifted his brows. "Fine

with me, Captain," the platoon leader said. "I'd prefer all enlisted in the squads."

"Yes, sir," Gardner said. "Eight more men would be a help. That is eight to a squad?"

"If you want eight, you get eight," the CAG said. "This way we don't have to wait to clear the plutonium here. The Sixties have plenty of range to get to the atolls and return. Let's do it. I'll get the Marines on the line."

"We need to do some ammo fill and equipment check," Murdock said. "It's now about oh-eight-thirty. If our SEALs could have some chow, we'll be ready to hit the flight deck at oh-nine-thirty."

"I'll phone the mess that you'll be there in thirty. I want each squad to have a radio you can use to contact us directly. I know you have a SATCOM, but this will be quicker. Bring them to you on deck. Good hunting, men."

The two SEALs saluted smartly and hurried back to their compartment.

Promptly at 0920, Murdock and his SEALs came up to the flight deck and back to chopper country. The two squads of cammy-clad Marines were already there. One man stepped forward. He wore no rank on his uniform.

"Sir, Sergeant First Vuylsteke reporting with some Marines. Hear we're going hunting."

"True, Sergeant. I've seen you Recon guys work. Pleased to have you along. Out here we have no rank. Every man supports every other man. I know you all can swim, but we probably won't be getting wet. What kind of firepower do you have?"

Murdock checked it out. Each squad had an M-60 light machine gun, two sniper rifles, three H&K MP-5s, and three Colt M-4A1s.

"Sir, we have double ammo, six grenades each, and the Colts have six forty-millimeter grenades for their tubes." He stared at Murdock's weapon. "Sir, is that really a twenty-mike-mike rifle? Shoulder fired?"

"It is. You'll get them in 2005 or 2006." He handed

the weapon to the Marine. The others gathered around
looking at it.

"You can use it for air bursts off its laser sighting up
to a thousand yards?" the sergeant asked.

"Can and do. Every foot soldier will soon have an artillery piece of his own. It's going to change the way we
do ground fighting."

The crew chief signaled.

"Time to load up. Sergeant, bring your squad in the
first bird with me. We have six extra Motorola radios.
Three for each of your squads. You keep one. It's instant
communication among the squad. Let's load."

There was little talk during the flight. The first bird was
heading for Rongrik.

"Take us about forty-seven minutes to get there," Jaybird shouted to Murdock. He nodded. Murdock showed
the sergeant how to rig the Motorola, and he set up two
of his squad the same way.

"Net check," Murdock said on the radio. His five men
checked in, then the three Marines called in.

"Vuylsteke, how do you read?"

"Good, sir. Even in here. Outside it will be great."

"We have about forty-seven minutes for the flight. Relax while you can. We don't know what we're going to
find out on that atoll. And when you talk to me, I'm either
Murdock or Cap. Okay?"

"Yes s—Right, Cap. I can do that."

Twenty minutes later the crew chief brought Murdock up
to the pilot. "We're running into a heavy squall. Rain and
lightning. I'm going to have to detour around it. Don't
know how big it is. Could cause us all sorts of problems.
We're looking at at least another twenty to thirty minutes
of flying time. I'll keep you informed."

19

The South Pacific
Near Rongrik Atoll
The helicopter edged around the worst of the furious
clouds and lightning strikes but was still punished and
battered by the raging winds. Murdock had checked his
stopwatch, and after twenty minutes of buffeting around,
he went back to the pilot.

"We should be out of the storm in five minutes, the eye
in the sky tells me. He's given me a new heading to get
to Rongrik. The only change is we'll be about a half hour
behind our original ETA."

Murdock groaned. "That puts us on the atoll about ten
minutes behind the guys in the boat. Can we contact anyone on the atoll by radio?"

"Not sure, Commander. I'll call the CIC and see if they
can give us any kind of a frequency. There's a chance."

"How long until we land?"

"I'd say about twenty minutes. If we don't hit another
squall."

Murdock watched out the cabin windows as the rain
faded and the clouds scudded away to reveal the blue
Pacific Ocean and a blue sky.

"More like it," Murdock said.

The pilot grinned. "We're ten minutes away now and
should be sighting the speck of coral soon." The pilot
looked at a pad of notes. "Oh, Commander, CIC called
the weather station out here on Rongrik. They had the
right frequency, but couldn't raise anyone. Somebody else
on the circuit responded and said that the Rongrik weath-

erman had been ill for a month now, so he wasn't using
the radio or giving any reports. Sorry."

"We're going in blind again," Murdock said. "We
should be getting used to it."

He went back to the men and told them what was coming.

"There's a chance that the small boat beat us to the
atoll. If so, we find where it's docked and start tracking
the men and the plut. Shouldn't be hard. Might not be
more than a few dozen people on this atoll. Strangers will
stick out like a hockey stick in a lunch box."

"How can they hide the plut on a tiny little atoll like
this one probably is?" Bradford asked.

"It all depends on the situation and terrain," Murdock
said. Half the SEALs and the Marines joined in the rec-
itation of the old military truism. "It does depend. We
recon and see what's there, then ask a bunch of questions.
We fan out and work the buildings if we don't get any
answers. We find them, or we draw fire from the bad
guys.

"Now, if the boat had problems getting through the
storm, it might not even be in the lagoon yet. Let's hope
we can meet it when it tries to dock. We should know
that in a fly-over of the village."

Murdock was hoarse from shouting his words to get
them heard over the roar and clatter of the chopper. He
went back to the cabin and watched.

Twelve minutes later they spotted the atoll, with a large
lagoon inside coral reefs, a small plane landing strip with
two T-hangars, and a minuscule dock next to a clutter of
a dozen buildings that must be the downtown and suburb
housing all mixed up in one place.

They did a fly-over of the dock and Murdock swore.
"Looks like a fifty- or sixty-footer down there tied up,"
he said. "Wonder how long she's been there. I didn't see
any crates lashed to the deck. Set us down as near to the
village as you can."

It was a combination baseball field and soccer field fifty
yards behind the main group of buildings. The SEALs and

Marines jumped out of the chopper, formed into a column of ducks, and took off for the dock at a swift jog. Murdock and Lam led them out. They passed a half dozen curious people who called and waved.

Murdock took them to the dock and went up to a short, fat Polynesian, who grinned and held out his hand.

"Damned in the morning, the U.S. Navy has landed. I saw the markings on the chopper. Nice-looking bird. Wish I had one. You looking at the boat over there?"

"I am," Murdock said. He took the man's hand and pumped it. "Lieutenant Commander Murdock, U.S. Navy SEALs. How long has this craft been docked?"

"Maybe an hour," the man spit out the shell of some seed and nodded. "Yes indeed, I would say it's been about an hour. Two men met them. Seen the two strangers around here for a month or so. Kept to themselves. Claimed they were hunting souvenirs from the old Jap tunnels they had on this chunk of coral. Oh yeah, big battle fought here during World War II."

"Did they off-load two big crates from the boat?"

"Damn me, but you know it already. Yep. Two big crates. The two strangers who been living here brought down the only forklift on the atoll and carried the crates away. Don't know where they took them. None of my business, right? My guess is that they went north along the main part of the atoll. Widest up there, and the Japs had it laced with tunnels and gun emplacements and hundreds of machine guns, so I've been told."

"North?" Murdock asked. "They made two trips with the forklift?"

"Oh yeah. Them crates was heavy as sin."

"Thanks," the SEAL leader said. He turned his men around, and they quick-timed past several buildings and out a thin coral-topped road up the north prong of the fishhook-shaped atoll.

"He say how many men came on the boat?" Ken Ching asked on the Motorola.

"I didn't ask."

Lam jogged along beside Murdock. He looked over and

frowned. "These guys going to try to break down the crates into smaller boxes?"

"Doubt it. They would need another safe room. Doesn't sound like they built one here. Maybe just a storage spot until they can sell the goods."

"They must know that the Navy is hot on their tails. Did they think they could get lost down here in the South Pacific?"

"Been done before. Only back then they didn't have the eyes in the sky to scan the whole bloody ocean."

Murdock checked the ground. It was a typical atoll, nothing here more than fifteen, maybe twenty feet off the surfline. The finger of the atoll was a quarter of a mile wide, six hundred yards at the most. Lots of room for tunnels, bunkers, and gun emplacements. There was some scrub growth here, but no jungle, no trees, mostly a few clumps of brush and some vines.

A rifle shot cracked into the gentle breeze and the constant sound of the waves breaking on the ocean side of the atoll, away from the lagoon. The men dove for the ground.

"Anybody see a muzzle flash?" Murdock asked on the net.

"Yeah, I caught it," one of the Marines said. "About one o'clock, just past that bunch of brush."

"Hold fire," Murdock said. He sighted in on the brush fifty yards away and fired the Bull Pup. The round hit the brush and detonated, stripping most of the leaves off the slender stalks of brush and showing a concrete entranceway behind them. He fired again, putting the next round inside the opening. It detonated quickly and a billow of smoke came out the doorway.

"I want a line of skirmishers, twenty yards apart. Move it now," Murdock bellowed into the radio. The men lifted off the dirt and coral and sprinted to form the line of fourteen men across the spit of land. They covered more than half of the center of the atoll but not to the sides, which showed beach sand.

"We're looking for any opening, and anything that

moves," Murdock said in his mike. "Marines, tell your people without radios. Let's move out, slow and steady. Probe every spot of brush and weeds, every lump of coral. When we find something, everyone stops in line."

The men moved forward at a slow walk, weapons pointing ahead and ready to fire. Twenty yards ahead, Bradford came on the net. "Cap, I've got a vent pipe, three-inch black iron."

"Must be dozens of them along here," Murdock said. "Drop a live grenade down it and move ahead."

"Oh yeah. Just like in the *Dirty Dozen* movie."

They didn't hear the grenade go off. The line moved forward slowly. They were still thirty yards from the entranceway Murdock had fired into, when another call came.

"Cap, I've got a rat hole here," Lam said. "Looks like the opening to a tunnel, maybe three feet wide on top. Goes down at an angle."

"Throw in a WP and we'll see if we can flush anybody out."

"Roger that, Cap. One WP going down." Nobody came out of the tunnel.

The line moved again, and Murdock angled over to come up on the concrete entrance. It was old construction. It showed only two feet above the ground, dropped down two feet, then steps went down with a five-foot overhead. Jaybird came up and checked it out.

"Want me to go down there, Cap?"

"Not yet. Put a WP down and see if anything happens. They must be somewhere else. There's got to be a larger opening somewhere around here if they moved those crates inside. What are they, six foot square?"

"At least, Cap," Jaybird said.

Twenty yards farther up the finger of the atoll they found a dozen air vents.

Lam came over to Murdock. "Cap, we've got to find the tire tracks. That forklift would make serious depressions in this loose coral and sand with that heavy a load. I had a few tracks back a ways, but I lost them. I need to

work ahead along this trail of a road and see where the
forklift left the harder surface."

"Go," Murdock said. "Take a Marine with you for
backup."

Lam saw Marine Sergeant Vuylsteke point to one of
his men and then at Lam, and the two of them jogged
ahead down the hard-packed coral road. It lasted for another fifty yards, then showed signs of breaking up, with
twenty or thirty yards of open sand and loose coral.

"Oh yeah," Lam said at the first sandy spot. "Got him—
three tracks, going and coming. He's on up here somewhere, Cap. I've got about a half mile of this atoll left
before we get wet again."

"Go," Murdock said. He scanned the atoll ahead. No
peaks or valleys, almost flat, a gradual slope up to the
twenty-foot ridge in the right quarter. No place to hide,
except underground. They had to have a large bunker door
to get that plutonium crate inside. Where in hell was it?

Ahead to the right, just past the small ridge, an automatic weapon pounded off ten rounds. The SEALs and
Marines hit the dirt and returned fire.

"Cap, I've got a Marine down," Marine Sergeant Vuylsteke said. "He took two of those slugs in his chest. He's
in a bad way."

"Our medic isn't with us, Sergeant. Do the best you
can."

Ahead, Lam and the Marine, called Willy, heard the
automatic fire and hit the dirt, then got up and sprinted
for the next sandy area of the old road.

"More tracks, Cap. We're on his trail."

"Roger that, Lam. Let's move the line again, skirmishers. Return fire if we get shot at. Move out."

Lam and Willy had just sprinted thirty yards forward
to another stretch of sandy coral. Lam went down on one
knee and Willy followed. Lam pointed. The tracks had
dug in six inches as the rig moved off the old road into
the loose sand. Then the tracks stopped. Lam could see
where the forklift evidently had been backed up and
turned, and had gone back to the road.

"Right there, somewhere," Lam whispered to Willy. "But where the hell is the damn door?" Lam looked over the area again, viewing it a small section at a time. Then, just past the midway point he spotted something different. The sand and coral here had a smattering of brush around it, but now he noticed that one part of the brush formed a perfectly straight line. The tracks went almost to that spot and stopped.

Lam reported on the net what he had found.

"Hold there, Lam. I'm coming up with plenty of C-5."

Lam studied the area again. Lots of loose sand and coral. No signs of recent construction. A slight depression and a bank about two feet high just in back of the straight line of inch-thick brush that went six feet high. Lam had to know. He went to all fours and, with his weapon tied over his back, crawled forward fifteen feet to the edge of the straight line of brush. He scooped sand and coral away from the edge of the brush.

Nothing.

He scraped lower, then higher, then lower again, until he was at the bottom of the two-foot mini bank. He pawed at the loose material, moving it sideways, not toward him. He had dug a trench a foot wide and six inches deep at the base of the bank when he felt something unusual. He checked it out with ultimate caution. Yes, what he had expected. He held a thin wire, stretched taut from one side of the brush to the other. A trip wire. If he had been pulling the material forward, he would have set it off. Some kind of antipersonnel mine, maybe a pair of Claymore mines with their two hundred pellets aimed at the center of the wall of brush. He eased back and checked the brush on both sides. Nowhere could he see any antipersonnel mines.

Murdock jogged up to the site and waved Lam back. The scout reported what he had found.

"It must be the main entrance or the truck entrance," Murdock said. "With tunnels this extensive, the Japs would have had to haul hundreds of truckloads of material out here for construction and supplies. What's your suggestion?"

"A half pound of C-5 at both corners and one in the center, with five-minute timers, and we get the hell back fifty yards," Lam said. Murdock nodded. Lam took out four blocks of the C-5. Murdock pulled two from his vest and they crawled forward. When they both had the C-5 planted where they thought the door had to be, Lam waved and they pushed in the timers preset for five minutes. Then they crawled back and took Willy and jogged back fifty yards.

"A minute left," Murdock said. He warned the men on the net there would be a big bang or two. "It's us, the good guys," Lam said. They had positioned themselves so they could see the suspected large door. Murdock counted down the last few seconds.

"And five elephants, four elephants, three elephants . . ." Before he finished to one, two cracking, roaring blasts shook the atoll. As soon as the wave of sound and surge of hot air slammed past them, the three men came to their feet and ran for the site. Where the wall of brush had been there now was a gaping hole eight feet wide and nearly that high. The sand and coral in front of the door had been blasted away like it had been swept clean, revealing a concrete pad that led to a loading dock six feet wide. Beyond that they could see a cave that had been carved downward into the coral. It had been concrete lined and now held a layer of dust, sand, and coral from the blast. Smoke and dust still eddied slowly out of the tunnel.

"This one we investigate," Murdock said. He used the mike. "I need Alpha Squad and all the attached Marines up here to the blast site on the double. We're going exploring."

Three minutes later the rest of Alpha and the Marines ran up and stared at the cave entrance. Sergeant Vuylsteke motioned Murdock to the side. "I lost Parsons. Looks like one of the slugs caught his lung, the other one his heart. He was gone in minutes."

"Sorry. We'll take him back with us. You up to this next mission?"

"Yes, sir."

"How did they move those big crates of plut down that incline?" Lam asked.

"Maybe they had a forklift inside," Murdock said. He counted heads, then motioned to Lam to lead the way. "Let's take a look and see what we have down there." Before Lam could take a step onto the concrete loading dock, a submachine gun chattered from inside the cave and a dozen angry sounding bullets slashed through the air around the men.

"Oh, damn, I'm hit," one of the SEALs growled.

20

The SEALs and Marines jolted to the sides of the tunnel mouth. Murdock and Jaybird each sent a 20mm round into the cave and heard both explode.

"Who's hit?" Jaybird shouted.

"Over here," Ching called. "Bastard got me in the leg. Never been hit in the fucking leg before."

Jaybird sprinted across the cave opening and skidded down beside Ching.

"You're a magnet for hot lead, Ching. Right leg, up high. In and out?"

"Hell, you're the damn expert." Ching groaned. "Yeah, I think so. Hurts like a goddamn red hot poker in my thigh."

"Known to happen. Let's move over here a little more out of the line of fire and I'll get you patched up."

Murdock checked on Ching, then bellied down looking into the cave. "We have to go in," he told Sergeant Vuylsteke, who he had called up. "You've got six men left and I've got four."

"That twenty really makes a bang."

"Yeah, but we probably shouldn't have shot. Hope we didn't rupture one of those plut jugs. Then we'll all be in really deep shit."

"So how do we go in?" the Marine asked.

"Slow and careful. Lam, you hold it here; I'm going to go down and take a look. We have the EAR with us?"

"Negative, Cap. Didn't figure we'd need it."

"Okay, I'm over the side. When I give the word on the

Motorola, come down in pairs. Can't commit everybody at once. Got it, Lam?"

"Right, Skipper."

Murdock nodded and crawled over the lip of the vegetation onto the concrete platform and then slid down the loading ramp and into the cave. There was no gunfire. He held the Bull Pup in front of him and came up to a crawl. He could see nothing at first. The light from the entrance faded and he came up to a crouch and moved forward. So far no trip wires, no Arabs, no plut. The tunnel was at least eight feet high and that wide. Ahead he could see light and soon caught sight of a bare bulb hanging from the top of the tunnel. He figured he'd come about forty yards. "Send in four men, Lam. You come and give the con to Sergeant Vuylsteke."

Murdock moved forward. He was walking now, taking slow steps, watching everything he could see and evaluating it. Even so he tripped on something and looked down. A body. He used his penlight on the face. An Arab. He had jagged wounds over his face, neck, and chest. The twenty had nailed him. Probably the same man who fired out the entrance. He still clutched an automatic rifle.

Twenty feet ahead, Murdock stopped. The tunnel split, with both the branches equal size. They took off at a forty-five-degree angle. Murdock waited for Lam. He came shortly with Van Dyke and Bradford.

"Six guys down each tunnel," Lam said. "My suggestion, Skipper."

"Yeah, I agree. We can't use the twenties—a near miss or a direct hit would blow up those lead plut bottles. They came in that fake door out there, so they have to be down here somewhere."

"Slow and go."

They called the other men up. They had left Ching outside with his shot-up leg.

"We use the Motorolas as long as we can," Murdock said. "Depends on how good the reception will be down in these tunnels. Lam, you've got the con on the other

tunnel. Take the sergeant with you and split up the men.
Let's move it."

Twenty yards down the right-hand tunnel, Murdock
found three drifts branching off. They checked out each
one. All were too small to hold the plutonium, but men
could be hidden there. Two men checked each tunnel. One
of them came to a dead end where there were old boxes
of ammo and some rusted-out rifles. The other two opened
to the surface behind screens of brush, with setups for
machine-gun positions. Both were unoccupied.

They gathered back at the main tunnel and moved on.
Now they found new tunnels working up to the surface
every twenty feet. One went right, the next left, as they
alternated. Each one had to be checked. In one of them
Murdock found a Japanese diary. It was battered and
dusty but in remarkably good shape. He stuffed it in his
combat vest and continued the trek.

Ahead the tunnel curved. It was still big enough for the
plut crate to get through. Murdock edged around the curve
and checked out the way ahead. There were still light
bulbs every forty feet, giving off an eerie glow and long
shadows. He peered through the murky light and spotted
sandbags ahead and what he figured had to be a machine-
gun position. He couldn't see any men. Jaybird edged up
beside Murdock.

"For real?" he asked.

"Looks like it. Send in a dozen rounds from your 5.56,
and if anyone returns fire, I'll use the twenty. They
wouldn't have the plut out there in the tunnel."

Jaybird sprayed the sandbags with twelve rounds. An
immediate return fire lashed out, with three ten-round
bursts from the machine gun. None of the rounds hit the
SEALs or Marines who had dropped to the floor, and most
were around the corner.

Murdock triggered a twenty round, and through the
scope he saw the sandbags disintegrate, the MG smash
backward, and the gunner flop to the left laced with steel
shards of shrapnel. The sound of the 20mm round exploding in the closed tunnel was like hearing it in a small

room. Murdock and Jaybird and the men behind them
were stunned at the magnitude of the sound and shook
their heads realizing that they couldn't hear a thing.

"I'll go check it out," Jaybird said and pointed ahead.
Even before Murdock nodded, the wiry machinist mate
scrambled to his feet and sprinted toward the machine-
gun nest. He had his Bull Pup up on 5.56 and set for
three-round bursts. At first the smoke and dust from the
twenty clouded the area, but it blew away down the tunnel
the other way. Jaybird saw motion to the left side, behind
the sandbags, he pivoted the Pup that direction, and
slammed six rounds into a man who had lifted a rifle.
Again the sound of the exploding rounds was magnified
a dozen times in the tunnel, and Jaybird's hearing went
out again. He jumped over the sandbags still stacked and
kicked the rifle away from the dead Arab. The machine
gunner was ten feet down the tunnel and greeting Allah
in his heaven.

"Two down and out," Jaybird said into his mike, not
knowing if anyone could hear him. "Move up," he said a
moment later, and heard a faint response on the earpiece.
The reception was good at that distance; his ears just
weren't working right yet. He looked around in the faint
light. The bulb over the machine gun had been blown out
by the twenty. Jaybird used his flashlight and found two
wooden doors leading off the tunnel almost behind the
MG. He went toward them, but decided to wait. He could
see nothing down the tunnel but felt air moving in that
direction. There was another opening down that way. He
figured they were still moving north, away from the village. Pretty soon they would run into billions of gallons
of Pacific Ocean saltwater.

Murdock jogged up and found Jaybird. Their ears were
clearing.

"So?" Murdock asked.

"Doors," Jaybird said, pointing at them with his flashlight beam. Both were too small for the heavy crates to
get through. They looked like they had been put on recently. New hinges showed that the doors opened out-

ward. The rest of the squad ran up, and Murdock pointed to Vinnie Van Dyke and a Marine. "Put a fragger through that next door down there. Be careful."

Jaybird and Murdock went along the side of the cave to the closest door. They crouched on the doorknob side. Jaybird pulled out a fragger and Murdock nodded. He looked at Jaybird, made a turning motion with his hand, and then pointed at himself. Jaybird grinned.

Murdock reached out and grabbed the doorknob. As he turned it, six rounds of hot lead ripped through the thin door and thudded against the far wall. Murdock jerked the door open a foot, Jaybird let the grenade cook for two seconds after the arming spoon flipped off, then he threw the bomb through the open door and Murdock slammed it closed. Two point four seconds later the grenade went off and the door bulged outward a moment, then blasted off its hinges into the main tunnel, smoke and dust billowing out behind it. Both Murdock and Jaybird charged into the room as the shrapnel stopped flying. They used their flashlights and searched the room in seconds.

"Clear right," Murdock said. "One adult male with black beard and hair who is now history."

"Clear left," Jaybird said. "No bodies, but what's left of one computer with screen and keyboard." They saw the remains of a desk, a filing cabinet, and two desk lamps.

"We'll be back and search this place for any paper that might show us who these guys are and where they were going."

A blast shocked the area close by and Murdock looked out of the first room and saw the second door blowing off its hinges down the tunnel. Vinnie and the Marine charged into the room.

"Clear in the second room," Van Dyke said on the Motorola. "Looks like sleeping quarters for four. Nobody home."

They met in the tunnel.

"The roof is sloping down," Van Dyke said. "They

won't be able to get that big crate through here much farther."

"Van Dyke, take the point," Murdock said. "Move it slow and let us know of any side tunnels."

"Roger that," Van Dyke said. He had his Bull Pup set on 5.56 and his flashlight aimed straight ahead but held at arm's length. The next light bulb was thirty feet down the tube.

A few minutes later, Van Dyke came on. "I have two tunnels, one each side, like the other ones we've seen, but these look different." Murdock ran up to the point and checked out the pair.

"Larger," he said. "Like maybe they had artillery up above." He went up one and Van Dyke took the other one. Murdock saw that the tunnel sloped up quickly, and was still double the width of the other drifts they had explored. Moments later he came to the surface. It was a well-camouflaged concrete pad and had a rusted-out five-inch Japanese coast artillery gun still bolted into the concrete. He reversed his route and found that Van Dyke had discovered the same thing on his side.

They had started moving forward again when they heard a single shot, and thirty yards down the tunnel the next light bulb went out as a bullet hit it.

"Down," Murdock shouted, and the men dropped to the ground. He and Van Dyke, in front of the others, pumped a dozen rounds each down the tunnel. They heard nothing but the ricocheting slugs as they bounced off the coral walls.

"Jaybird, how far have we come in the tunnels?"

"Maybe two hundred yards, Skipper. We're still a hell of a long way from the end of the atoll."

"What I was afraid of. Where are they taking that plut?"

"Protecting it until they can ship it out," Jaybird said.

"So we find it. Let's move. Flashlights, everyone. Jaybird and I'll clear the path with a dozen rounds forward each, then we move at double time. Now, Jaybird."

The Bull Pups chattered off the twelve rounds each, and the SEALs and Marines charged forward.

"What if they took the plut down the other main tunnel?" Jaybird asked.

"Then Lam and the other guys will find it," Murdock said. He slowed and then stopped. "Wet ahead," he said. "Looks like the tunnel has a leak, or we're down to sea level and it's high tide."

"Can't be more than a foot or two deep," Jaybird said. "Otherwise the Japs couldn't have used it."

"Water ahead," Murdock said on the net. "We'll go at a walk. Shouldn't get deep."

Lights showed ahead, the single bulbs dangling from the top of the cave barely eight feet up now. The sides of the tunnel pinched in.

"Bet the Japs dug this coral out by hand and carried it out on little trucks," Van Dyke said. "One hell of a lot of work."

The water came up to their knees, then lowered as they walked ahead. They had just hit dry land on the other side when Murdock called a halt. "I can hear noise ahead. Anybody copy?"

"Oh yeah," Jaybird said. "That's a little one-cylinder diesel engine. Hear how it whacks on every stroke? Got to be a set up for a generator. That's how they get lights in here."

They slowed their advance then, turned out flashlights, and worked through the semidarkness using only the faint lights in the tunnel every thirty feet. The tunnel curved ahead and Jaybird leaned around it to see what was up there. He edged back.

"You better take a look, Cap. I'd say we found the plut, or at least one of the crates full. Then, there's a complication."

Murdock bellied up to the bend in the tunnel and looked around at ground level. Ahead in a glare of lights he could see one of the crates with the heavy lead bottle of plutonium 239 still inside. In front of it stood about twenty people, all were civilians—men, women, and children. Two women carried babies in their arms.

A bullhorn blared into the stillness.

"U.S. Navy, we know you're out there. We know what you want. You can see the advantage that we have. In front of this crate of goods you want so badly are twenty-three residents of the village of Rongrik. Yes, and two babies. There is no room for bargaining. We hold all the chips. You will turn your men around and you will leave the main tunnel by the two artillery emplacements just in back of you. You have five minutes to clear this tunnel. If you do not, one of the villagers will be shot for every five minutes you linger. To prove that we are serious, we will execute the first villager now."

Murdock settled in with his Bull Pup on single-shot 5.56 and centered his sights on the slight, dark bearded man at the side of the tunnel. He held a pistol in his hand and now brought it down to point it at the head of a civilian kneeling in front of him. Murdock refined his sight, squeezed the trigger, and the Bull Pup blasted a round down the tunnel.

21

Lam and his six Marine buddies moved down the left-hand branch of the main tunnel under the bleak exterior of Rongrik Atoll. He figured that the terrs had taken the right-hand branch. When people had a chance, most took the right lane, the right line in the supermarket, the right lane for the border crossing, right-handed everything. Figured, since most people were right handed.

He studied the sand that had filtered down from the sides of the tunnel over the past fifty years. Yes, now he remembered. He had seen something before he hadn't been able to figure. Now he realized that he had spotted tracks to the right-hand tunnel that could only be from the forklift. So he and his buddies were on a blind trail that held nothing of value.

He told Sergeant Vuylsteke and the rest of the Marine squad. "So we'll move ahead quicker than usual. We'll check out any drifts or side tunnels that might be hiding some of the terrorists, and we'll try to check out this branch fast."

"Can you use your twenty to clear the tunnel as we go?" Vuylsteke asked.

"I can't be positive they didn't bring one of the crates of plut up in here, then one in the other tunnel. I don't think so, but I'm not going to risk polluting the whole atoll in case I'm wrong. Let's choggie."

They jogged between drifts, checked out the avenues to the surface quickly, and hurried on. They came to no more surface tunnels, and less than twenty minutes after they started, they were nearing the end of the tunnel.

"Getting smaller," Lam said. "No chance they could get the forklift in here with the plut crate." Lam grinned and fired a 20mm round down the tunnel. When it exploded thirty yards away, it sent back a shock wave and sound storm that battered the men's ears. For a minute they couldn't hear a thing.

Lam waved them forward, and they had come almost to a curve in the tunnel ahead when a submachine gun chattered six rounds at them. They hit the floor of the tunnel but not before one of the Marines took a round.

"Caught one in the shoulder, Sergeant," the Marine said. They stopped and, using his first aid kit, Vuylsteke tied up the wound to stop it bleeding. As he did, Lam took off running for the bend in the tunnel. When he came to it, he went to the floor and edged up so he could see around the wall. Ahead there were a dozen light bulbs, turning the murky tunnel into a daylight scene. Lam lifted his brows. He figured there were thirty to forty lead boxes like those they had seen before, eighteen inches square and about ten inches deep. He saw what had to be lead blankets, and two or three sets of radiation-proof suits. They were going to break down the larger units of plut. Somehow they had got the gear in the wrong tunnel. Lam grinned. Or maybe nobody told them how large the plut crates were going to be. They were too large to come down this tunnel, so they must have taken them down the other one, and all of this gear and boxes and tops and blankets would have to be moved to the right-hand tunnel.

He checked carefully, but couldn't see any people around. Who had fired the shot? He watched and waited, sectoring the area time and again. Vuylsteke crowded up behind him. Lam gave him a quick rundown on the situation.

"Use the twenty," Vuylsteke said. "Only this time I'm going to cover up my ears after I put in earplugs."

Lam considered it. "At least the round will tear up the radiation suits and maybe flush out the shooter, who has to be up there somewhere."

They both put in earplugs and Lam fired one round at

the radiation suits. After this round they weren't quite so deaf. When the dust and smoke cleared, Lam saw the three radiation suits tattered and shredded. Then, to his surprise, one of the lead blankets was thrown to the side and a small man with a submachine gun darted across the tunnel and into a drift.

"Let's get him," Lam said and came up running. Vuylsteke was right behind him. They worked through the lead components and braced on either side of the side tunnel. Lam jumped into the tunnel, angled his Bull Pup upward on 5.56, and fired three rounds. Then he charged up the tunnel that climbed swiftly. There was no return fire. Lam had guessed right. It took only a few seconds to get to the top of the tunnel. Another machine-gun setup. Lam poked his head up and jerked it down. Three slugs hit the concrete platform, and some sang overhead, missing it by inches.

Lam took a quick look and this time saw a figure running toward the village. Lam got up his Bull Pup and fired a dozen rounds, but they missed. He switched to the twenty and led the man three steps before he fired. The round hit a step behind the running figure. The blast and the shrapnel from the 20mm round caught the runner and drove him forward a dozen feet before he sprawled in the dirt and coral and didn't move.

Vuylsteke came up behind Lam. "Nice shooting, kid."

"Yeah, with the twenty it's like throwing a grenade three hundred yards and hitting what you aim at." He nodded to himself. "Let's get back downstairs there and see what we can find. Like a customer list, or a timetable. Anything in writing."

Before he left, Lam tried the Motorola. He had a quick answer.

"Yes, Lam, read you. We've got a situation here. We found the plut but there are twenty some hostages. The terrs are threatening to shoot one every five minutes we stay underground."

Lam told Murdock what they had found. "We're going back down to check everything. May be some more men there, or something in writing. If we can help, give me a call. Lam out."

Down below, Lam and the Marines found little that was useful. A list of the material there, lead boxes, radiation suits, tools they would use for the transfer of the plut. But nowhere could they find a list of potential customers. They did find the body of one more terr. He had over two thousand dollars in hundred-dollar bills in his pants pockets, but no identification of any kind. He was dark, with black hair and a black mustache, but no beard.

"One more Arab," Lam said. They were at the far end of the tunnel. "Let's go topside and see if we can locate a rat hole near where Murdock is. Bring that two thousand. We'll give it to the people who live here."

Back in Murdock's right-hand tunnel, he watched through the scope as the round he fired caught the terrorist gunman in the side under his right arm, which held the raised pistol. The round lanced through the man's ribs, collapsed his right lung, then plunged into his heart, killing him before he could pull the trigger. He slammed to the side, the pistol falling from his hand.

The bullhorn vanished behind the hostages. A moment later another amplified voice came down the tunnel.

"Bastards! You have killed our leader, Khatib, but we are as many as the grains of sand in the desert. Now I will have the honor of killing one of these infidels for every five minutes you remain in the tunnel. Go quickly— we have much work to get done. The mother and her baby will be the first ones killed. So move now, U.S. Navy."

"Not that easy, you sad-assed terrorist," Murdock said. "Your radiation suits have been shredded, your plut boxes blown up. You have nowhere to go with the large bottle of plutonium. It is your turn to give yourself up and live. Already we have killed five of your men. You will be next."

"You are bluffing. I have played American poker. I went to school at Illinois University. I call your bluff." A pistol shot shattered the tunnel's shrouded stillness. The woman in the front row holding a baby slammed forward with a round to the side of her head. She collapsed on the tunnel floor, and the squalling baby rolled away from her.

Murdock bit his lip. There was no target. He could see nothing but the villagers. None of them moved. They were so frightened they might have been paralyzed.

When the sound of the shot faded down the reverberating tunnel, the bullhorn voice came again.

"I don't hear you leaving, U.S. Navy. You now have less than four minutes to move your men down to the side tunnel to the surface. The woman's baby will be next to die."

"No," Murdock said. "Your mission here is finished. There is no way that you can break down the large bottle of plutonium into smaller sizes. I'll give you safe passage out of the atoll, for you and any of your men still alive. I'll trade your safe passage for the lives of the villagers in front of you. Otherwise it's a standoff. All of the villagers die, and you and your men die. Wouldn't it be better to lose on this battle and live to fight another day? You can't win this one. You've lost it already. Why not cut your losses, get out of the game while you still have a few chips to play again another time, another place."

"Safe passage to where?"

"We'll give you the boat you came here in. Refuel it and stock it with water and food and you're on your way."

"To where? We don't know this part of the Pacific Ocean."

"We'll give you maps and charts. It's your only way out."

"There are three of us here. We'll have to talk it over."

"You have five minutes to decide if you want to live or die."

Murdock pulled back around the corner of the tunnel and leaned against the wall. He took two huge breaths and let them out slowly.

"Nice work, Skipper," Jaybird said.

"If it works."

"He has no choice. He dies if he stays there." Jaybird

grinned. "Hey, we really aren't going to let three of them get away, are we?"

"I told him safe passage off the island. I didn't say anything about getting blasted by an F-18 once he gets out to sea."

"Oh yeah," Jaybird said. "I figured there must be an angle. Will he think of it?"

"Let's hope not, Jaybird. Let's fucking hope not."

Murdock checked his watch but it didn't take five minutes. Barely half of the allotted time was up when the bullhorn voice came again.

"Two conditions, U.S. Navy. I get to keep my pistol, and I get to take three of these civilians with me as shields until we can get on the boat."

"Agreed, but if you attempt to harm any of the civilians you're being shielded by, we will cut you down like the killers you are."

"Yes. Now, first, send half your men to the surface via the tunnel just behind you. There are more tunnels ahead to the left. We, the six of us, will use them. Be sure that your men hold any fire as we leave the opening above, or the three civilians will be shot immediately."

"My men know the orders." He pointed at Jaybird, Bradford, and a Marine, and they scurried for the surfacing tunnel behind them. "My men are gone. You may move out as well."

Five minutes later Murdock and his men were on the surface. They met Lam and the Marines and watched as the last of the three terrorists came out of the tunnel mouth, near another machine-gun position. They walked in lockstep, with the civilian men behind them.

The bullhorn voice came again. "U.S. Navy. Can you radio ahead and tell them to fuel the boat and stock it with food and water?"

"No, I have no people there. We do it after we arrive."

"Very well, we are moving."

It took the sorry little procession ten minutes to walk the half mile back to the village. The former hostages had surged out of the machine-gun emplacement opening seconds after the terrorists and run toward their homes.

Murdock's men formed a U around the terrorists. Now he could see that all three had pistols. He let it pass. They wouldn't try shooting anyone. It would be suicide. Suicide by SEALs.

At the boat, the terrs insisted on taking the shields with them on board and keeping them there until the boat was refueled, provisioned, and ready to sail. Murdock had his men surround the pier side of the boat with weapons ready. The fuelling went well, with the terrs paying for it in U.S. $100 bills. Then boxes of food and water were brought on board. Fifteen minutes after arriving at the boat, the leader declared they were ready to go. They put their pistols at the heads of the three hostages.

"We will drop them off just past the entrance to the lagoon," the leader said. "All are locals and good swimmers. They will come to no harm. Now you must honor your promise for safe passage."

"You give me your word that the three hostages will be dropped off just past the entrance?" Murdock bellowed.

"I do."

The engine started; they cast off the lines, and the boat began a slow trip toward the narrow channel through the coral heads of the lagoon.

"They gonna get away?" Jaybird blurted. "That one asshole killed that woman in cold blood."

"Doubt if they get far," Murdock said. "Remember, we still have the F-18s, and the chopper pilots can put us in touch with the CIC on the carrier."

They watched the sixty-foot boat work its way to the entrance and then out into the Pacific.

"Drop them off," Jaybird commanded.

Instead the three Rongrik men were pushed to the deck and the boat surged ahead on full throttle.

"Damnit," Murdock shouted. "Now we do have a problem. Not a chance I'll sic the F-18s onto that boat, not with three civilian hostages on board. Let's get to the chopper and talk with the boss back on the carrier."

22

Murdock sent Jaybird to talk to the mayor of the village and tell him that more Navy people would be coming, to dismantle and remove the packages that were brought in by the terrorists. He said anyone who suffered damages could apply to the U.S. Navy for recovery. Jaybird told them that the Navy would take care of the dead bodies and see that everything was back to normal as soon as possible. Murdock gave the sheriff the two thousand dollars Lam had found. He said it should go to the family of the woman who was killed.

Murdock jogged to the chopper, which remained where they had left it. The pilot put him through to the CIC.

"Murdock here. We've negated the threat to the atoll, and the two crates of plutonium, untampered with, are waiting for retrieval by your radiation experts."

"Good news, Murdock," Don Stroh said. "Any problems?"

"Yes. Three of the terrs got away on the boat they arrived on. The trouble is they have three male hostages from the atoll, so we can't just blast them out of the water."

"That is a small hiccup in the deal. Any ideas?"

"Suggest that you tail them with a destroyer until it gets dark. Then five of us SEALs will drop out of the destroyer's chopper three miles ahead of the boat, wait for it, grab it in the darkness, take down the three terrs, and bring home the three hostages."

"Sounds good here. The CAG says it works for him. The three hostages might want to keep the boat and sail it back to the atoll, so try not to damage it."

"Good idea, Stroh. When did you get so smart?"

"I try not to let it show. The CAG here is working on sending in some radiation experts and a boat to bring back the plutonium. You say it's still in the original crate?"

"That's a roger. Two crates. They'll need a forklift from the island to bring the crates out of an old Japanese tunnel about a half mile long."

"There's one on the atoll?"

"Right."

"Why don't you and your Marines come on home?"

"We'll want medics on the flight deck. We have one Marine KIA and two wounded men, neither serious. We'll wrap it here and move into the sky."

They landed on the carrier ten minutes after taking off. The carrier had moved within five miles of the atoll, and they spent most of their time getting clearance to land. A Marine guard met them and took charge of the KIA Marine. Then the wounded Marine and Ching were taken down to the hospital. Murdock sent Jaybird to bring back a report on Ching, and then he headed directly to the combat information center. Stroh and Captain Olenowski were waiting for him.

"Murdock, good job." The captain held out his hand and Murdock took it.

"Thank you, sir. The Marines came in handy. Sorry that one of their men caught those two slugs."

"We're in a dangerous profession, Commander. I just sent in two heavy lift choppers to bring out the two crates of plutonium. There are three radiation specialists on each bird to take care of the goods. It will be in our secure radiation-proof compartment soon."

"About this boat," Don Stroh said. "Too bad you let them get away with the hostages."

"It was either that or they would have slaughtered twenty-three civilians on the atoll. As it was they killed one woman."

"It's over and done with, Commander. I've spoken with

the carrier's captain. He says he can send a destroyer after the small boat. A Hawkeye will keep us informed of its position and at first dark you'll start chasing them. What can they do, maybe twelve knots?"

"Good guess, Stroh."

"The destroyer has on board an SH-60, which will come to the carrier, pick you up, and take you over to the DDG-61, the *Rampage,* an Admiral Burke–class ship. It will have an uninflated IBS you'll use to approach the small boat."

Murdock grinned. "Damn, Stroh, you've been working. You're not used to this kind of detail. What happened?"

Stroh laughed. "I'm up for review. Besides I can catch more fish of any type than you can."

The CAG frowned and stared at Stroh.

"Oh, Captain, a small continuing contest between the commander here and me. He thinks he's a hotshot ocean fisherman. We go fishing off the kelp bed outside of La Jolla when I can get to San Diego."

"Captain, we might want to go a little later at night, when some of the terrs will be sleeping and the man on the wheel not in the best of condition. Be an easier take-down."

"No problem. You have enough men?"

"Love to have three more, but we can do it with five."

"Pickup?" the CAG asked.

"We'll take a GPS to give your chopper pilot an exact location after the takeover. Then we'll do a rope ladder pickup out of the water beside the boat."

"A rope ladder pickup at night, Commander?"

"Done it many times, Captain. That's why we get the big bucks."

They all chuckled.

"What about Gardner's boat?" Murdock asked.

"Our Hawkeye tells us that the boat has problems. Weather or engine, we're not sure. But it's moving toward Wotje Atoll at no more than five knots. Gardner should be there well before the boat is."

"Good, maybe he'll have an easy time of it. Right now

I think I better make a sick bay call. Half my squad is down there goofing off."

"When will you want to push off for the destroyer?" the CAG asked.

"Let's say twenty-two hundred. Then about an hour to catch the boat and go around it. Meet them about midnight."

"You've got it, Commander. So you won't want any Marines on this one?"

"No, sir. Five of us is plenty."

In sick bay, Murdock checked in with the doctors on Ching.

"He took one round to his right leg," a white-coated doctor said, reading off a chart. "The slug grazed the bone but didn't break it. A basic in and out, Ching told me. Tore up the muscle quite a bit. He'll need some therapy on the leg and won't be ready for any regular SEAL duty for about two months."

"Two months?" Ching shouted. "I can't be out of action that long. They'll give my spot to some rookie."

Murdock stepped to the bed and grabbed Ching's hand. "Yeah, probably should replace your shot-up hide, but I won't. You just do what the doctor and the nurses tell you. We're going for a swim tonight."

Murdock told Ching about the final chapter on the Rongrik mission.

"Slit their throats and drop them into the Pacific for shark food," Ching said. "That bastard really shot that woman?"

Murdock waved and checked on his other men. Sadler was in the worst condition. The slug had gone in his back and out his chest, but not all of it. His condition was still called "guarded." Howard, with three rounds in his right leg, was chipper and ready to get back to work.

"A whole damn month, the medics tell me," he blustered. "Hey, we'll see what my buddies back at San Diego's Balboa Hospital have to say."

Jefferson was in the next bed, reading a paperback book. He scowled at Howard. "I never knew this guy talked so much. I can't get him to shut up so I can read."

Murdock caught his hand and grinned.

"Yeah, the medics told me a month, but they're blowing smoke. They don't know how quick I mend and how hard I can train. I'd say three weeks tops."

Murdock went back to the quarters his SEALs had been given and told the men the schedule. Next they went to a special chow and then hit their bunks.

"It's a mandatory six-hour sleep period," he told them. "We don't want you guys falling asleep on the job tonight."

They flew off the carrier deck promptly at 2200 and dropped onto the chopper pad on the end of the *Rampage* destroyer at 2210. Their pilot was Lieutenant Roscoe Utts. He was lean and tall and young. Murdock almost hated him.

"Commander. Good to be with you. Hear you guys do some amazing things. I've never done a night pickup with a rope ladder out the back door."

"Just hold her steady at about ten feet and we do the rest, Lieutenant. Utts, an interesting name."

"Yeah, I get that a lot. My mother said it was old English but she wasn't sure. We're going to take off about twenty-three hundred?"

"Depending where the target boat is and how long it will take us to find it."

"They'll give me the coordinates and a heading, and we won't miss it by more than fifty yards."

"But we need to miss it by two miles," Murdock said. "We go around it and into their heading a mile in front of them."

"Let him come to you. Yeah. Good idea."

They took off at 2316, and Jaybird figured it would take them twenty-two minutes to catch, pass, and get positioned a mile ahead of the boat. It took them twenty-four minutes. Then they inflated the IBS, positioned it at the rear ramp, and pushed it out when the chopper came down within fifteen feet of the blue-black Pacific Ocean. Murdock and his four men ran out the rear ramp after the boat and caught it before it floated out of sight. There was no moon. A few stars sprinkled the clear sky. Low clouds scudded past in the distance.

Murdock surfaced and kicked fifteen feet ahead to the boat. He heaved on board and found Lam, Jaybird, and Bradford already there. Splashing to the rear produced Vinnie Van Dyke, and they pulled him in. Jaybird checked the engine, cleared it, and got it started. It purred like a tabby cat. "Figure we should have him in about twenty minutes," Jaybird said. "Unless there are some unfriendly surface currents or sudden windstorms."

"Or if he suddenly changes course and heads for another atoll," Van Dyke said.

They sat there trying to dry out a little. They wore their cammies over their wet suits, not sure how long they might be in the water. Weapons choice had favored the short guns. They all carried the MP-5 with sound suppressor.

"That boat has a diving platform off the stern," Jaybird said. "I noticed it when they were fueling it. An easy boarding spot. Now if the guy at the wheel just doesn't check out the back, we'll be in clover."

"Why would he check?" Bradford asked. "He'll have trouble enough staying awake this late at night and trying to stay on course. Didn't look like any of those three were what you'd call experienced sailors."

They were quiet then. Jaybird had out his 6×40 field glasses, watching to the rear. He grunted and then pushed the glasses tighter against his eyes.

"Oh yeah, I have running lights coming up on our port rear. Looks like he could be our baby."

"All quiet," Murdock said. "Engine at idle. Jaybird, how far off his course line are we?"

"Maybe three hundred yards."

"Let's stay out here and then come at him from his stern. Just the way we planned it."

They sat there, and soon all could see the running lights of the small boat. It looked even smaller now in the open sea. It came closer to them than they had figured, and Murdock told Jaybird to move them off another hundred yards.

Then the low growl of the diesel engines came through the water, and they saw the craft slipping along, riding high with no cargo. When it was past, Murdock waved at Jaybird, and he turned the small rubber boat and pushed up the throttle, and they fell into the wake of the larger craft and steadily gained on it.

When they came up to the stern, Van Dyke threw a line around a brace and tied the boat fast, then scrambled on board followed by the rest of the SEALs. Each man had his assignment. Murdock took the stairs to the small pilot house forward. He stopped at the door and looked through the glass: one man, leaning over the wheel, staring at the compass. Murdock jerked the door open and charged in, putting his KA-BAR against the man's throat before he knew he had company.

"You speak English?" Murdock asked.

The man shook his head and chattered in Arabic.

Murdock understood enough of it. He spoke back in Arabic, and the man's head jerked around in surprise.

"Move that way again and you're dead," Murdock said. He tied the wheel in position, left the throttle where it was, and secured the man with riot cuffs hands and feet, then put a gag around his mouth.

Murdock eased out the door and down the steps. A shadow came out from the lower cabin and lit a cigarette. He noticed Murdock and said in Arabic, "Why have you left the wheel?"

"So I could kill you," Murdock said in Arabic and triggered the MP-5, with three silenced shots hitting the man's chest. He wavered on the rail for a moment, then plunged overboard to add to the top feeders' menu on the food chain.

Below, Jaybird had opened the door marked "crew" and found one terrorist waiting for him. The Arab fired a pistol and Jaybird countered with six rounds from the MP-5. When the noise in the small room faded, Jaybird found a light in a ceiling fixture and turned it on. The terrorist lay against a bunk holding his belly where all six rounds must have entered.

"You killed me," he said in English, then his head rolled to one side and he was singing his petition to Allah.

"Jaybird, I have one down."

"Murdock, I have two down or tied."

"Bradford, I found the three hostages. They were tied up, but I figured out the knots and they are free and yelling and screaming. They want to go home."

"Vinnie here. Nobody in the galley or engine compartment. Sounds like the fun is all over."

"Lam here. Nothing in the rest of the hold or second crew quarters."

They assembled in the galley, where the three native Polynesians put out a spread of food from the stores and set out beers all around.

"How would you men like to own a boat?" Murdock asked the largest of the three, who it turned out could speak good English.

"One like this one? Never in my life I have enough money. Cash hard to come by on our atoll."

"With this boat you go could into business," Murdock said. "We have been instructed by the U.S. Navy that this boat is a prize of salvage. All you have to do to own it is to sail it back to your atoll and file the salvage papers. It's yours, the three of you."

One man squealed in delight. The third one had to be told what had happened, then he grabbed Murdock and kissed him on both cheeks.

"Maybe we should be calling back our chopper," Murdock said. He went to the deck and used the special Navy radio they had loaned him. The chopper responded on the first call.

"Hey, you said it wouldn't take long. How many to fly back to the carrier?"

"We have six. One Arab without papers, who Don Stroh is going to be crazy to talk to. Let me read you our

GPS coordinates." He did. "We have two crated jugs of plut for you."

Ten minutes later the chopper shone his spotlight on the small ship that had turned and was heading back toward the atoll. Murdock called the Navy to get a heading for the small boat to sail back to Rongrik. The Hawkeye came through and the three islanders cheered.

The Sixty came in on the stern. The boat had gone dead in the water. The SEALs stepped into the cold Pacific as the SH-60 edged up toward them. He was about twenty feet in the air and the rope ladder didn't reach the water. He went around and edged down lower until the rope trailed in the water. Jaybird swam to it and went up first, then Lam, and Vinnie Van Dyke. Bradford held the rope as Murdock went up, then came up himself. Murdock talked to the pilot, who came in so his rotors would miss the boat's antenna, then let down a rope to the rear deck. The new boat owners tied the rope securely around the still bound Arab, under his arms, and fastened it snugly. They gave two short jerks on the rope and the Arab was pulled upward into the SH-60, where the SEALs swung him in the door and dropped him on the floor.

"Oh, but Don Stroh is going to have a field day with you, my man," Bradford said.

Thirty minutes later they were on board the carrier, which had changed directions and was steaming at full speed toward the Wotje Atoll. There was still no word from Gardner and his crew about developments with the other plutonium-packing boat.

Don Stroh paced the narrow confines of the CIC. "Why in hell doesn't he call in?" Stroh asked no one. "He can't be more than two hundred miles away. What the hell is happening at Wotje?"

23

Wotje Atoll
Marshall Islands

Lieutenant (j.g.) Christopher Gardner with his five SEALs and his eight U.S. Marines grouped around the SH-60 Seahawk helicopter from the carrier. They waited. Lieutenant Gardner had just come back from a trip to the tiny general store next to the dock on the amazingly blue lagoon.

"They told me no boat had arrived here in the last two days," Gardner said. "So we wait for it. We'll scout out good firing positions and be ready to take him down when he docks."

"Doesn't feel right," Canzoneri said. "Just doesn't seem quite kosher to me somehow. I know the Hawkeye reported the boat had slowed, maybe from mechanical trouble, but how did we get here so much ahead of it?"

"The old laws of physics and the art of traveling through the air instead of on the water," Rafii said. "Hell, we're here, they aren't—we wait for them and zap the bastards before they know what hit them."

"Hopefully," Gardner said. "We saw some planes at that little airstrip when we came in. Two of them looked too large for pleasure craft. Canzoneri and Fernandez, grab two Marines and go check out the planes. See if you can find out how long they have been here and who owns them or who flew them in."

"Roger that," Canzoneri said. "We're moving." He pointed to the two closest Marines and they jogged away

from the softball field the chopper had landed on, toward
the airstrip a quarter of a mile away.

"Mahanani, you've got the con here. I'm taking Prescott and two Marines with me and contact the local law.
Let them know that we have governmental permission to
land and function on any of the atolls in the country."

The police station was half of a building. The other half
was the post office. The entire building was the size of a
twenty-man tent. Gardner cautioned his men to sling their
weapons muzzle-down as they went into the lawman's
office.

At first glance, Gardner thought it was a movie set. A
counter angled across the room a third of the way back.
One desk behind it held a lamp and some papers, but no
cop. In front of the counter stood a second desk where a
pretty, dark-haired girl in a print dress sat working on a
computer. She turned and smiled.

"Yes, the U.S. Navy is here. We heard on the net that
you were in the process of chasing some bad guys. Are
they heading for our atoll?"

Gardner stepped forward. "Miss, I'm Lieutenant (j.g.)
Gardner with the U.S. Navy SEALs. We're expecting an
outlaw boat to be coming into your lagoon shortly. Just
wanted to check in with the sheriff or police chief or whoever is in charge."

The girl stood. She was slender with long black hair
and an infectious smile.

"Well, that would be me. I'm Sheriff Ronsan, duly
elected by a majority of the voters on Wotje Atoll. As I
remember I won the election twenty-one to twelve. Not a
good turnout. Welcome aboard. It's good to have some
real firepower. Do you know about our visitors?"

"The ones who flew in the planes down at the airstrip?"

"Yes, those. Most visitors we've had here in years.
There are ten of them, all men, some Arabs, some Ori-
entals, and two I couldn't categorize."

"All men, I'd guess, and they aren't here on vacation.
Right?"

"True." She frowned. "I really need to know why

they're here. But this is a free country, and we don't re-
strict travel or anything like that. But I want to know why
these men are here. They all have money, more money
than most of us on the atoll have seen in some time."

"Where are they staying? I don't see a big motel or
resort."

"Oh no, not enough tourists. But we do have three bed
and breakfast houses on the net. They are staying there.
Been here for three days now and are getting irritable.
Last night two of them drank too much at our local bar
and I had to help them get home."

Prescott edged up to his squad leader. "Skipper, sounds
like they could be customers for the plut."

"Sounds about right." He turned to the girl. "Sheriff,
could you point out where those three bed and breakfast
houses are? We need to have a talk with your visitors."

She frowned, hooding her eyes for just a moment. "Be
careful. I know they are armed, handguns I'd suspect. But
I didn't have the firepower to challenge them."

"Now you do," Murdock said.

"Great." Her eyes sparkled. "Want me to come along?"

Gardner hesitated, then shook his head. "No, ma'am. It
will be better if you stay here. There my be some gunfire
there and when a boat comes in that's due anytime. Remember, we're the good guys."

Outside, Gardner sent one of the Marines back to the
chopper. "Tell the pilot to call the carrier and tell them
our situation. We landed here, the boat isn't in yet, there
are some large planes at the small airstrip and some suspicious visitors waiting around, probably for the boat to
come in."

Gardner angled past the small cafe to a house right next
door. It was wood frame but had Polynesian art on the
doors and window frames. He knocked on the door. A
round little woman answered. She was no more than four
and a half feet tall, and her face was a huge ball of a
smile.

"Oh, yes, the U.S. Navy. We saw your helicopter come
in and land. You want bed and breakfast?"

"Sorry, no. We're looking for your guests. I understand three or four strangers are staying with you."

"Yes, yes, no room for more. Others go to other places. Not as good as Mary's House. That's us, here. We Mary's House. Best bed and breakfast in all of Marshall Islands."

"Yes, I understand. And you must be Mary." She laughed and nodded.

"Me, Mary, yes, yes. No more room. So sorry."

"No, we don't want to stay here. We just need to talk to your other guests. You have four?"

"Four good men, yes. Pay good U.S. dollar right up front. Mary love these four guys."

Something moved behind the small woman. Then a figure came out of the low light in the house's front hall. He was tall, with heavy shoulders and a shaved black head. He was dressed in a black T-shirt and black pants and held his big hands loose at his sides like a boxer ready to pounce.

"Mon, you got the many questions. You ask me."

"Good, we're on a special U.S. Navy cooperative assignment with the Republic of the Marshall Islands, to interdict drug trafficking. We've had information that this atoll is to be used as a distribution point for twenty tons of heroin right out of the Golden Triangle. Would you know anything about that?"

"Drugs. We don't do that shit. No drugs. Get out of our face." The man turned and walked away.

Gardner nodded at the small, round woman. "Thank you for your time and good day."

They went back to the street of crushed coral, and Gardner used his Motorola. "Canzoneri, what do you find with the aircraft?"

"You were right, Skipper. Two of the four planes are big enough that they each could haul out of here one crate of plut the way it's packaged now. Probably what's coming on that boat, if it ever gets here. The other two planes are six-place passenger craft. Used like taxis for inter-atoll hopping. The guy who runs the airstrip said the twin engine planes came in three days ago, and the flyers gave

him a hundred dollars for each one for tie-down and refueling. He's delighted."

"Right. Well done. Now get back here so we can set
up around the dock. Boat should be coming in anytime
now."

"Roger that, Skipper. We're moving."

The SEALs and Marines went to the dock and checked
it out. Gardner picked out spots for four guns. He had two
sniper rifles and two Bull Pups. All four men were behind
protection and concealed from the dock. He'd use them
if he had to. He posted Rafii, Prescott, and two Marines
to cover the dock.

"Now we need some intel. Fernandez, see what you can
find out about heavy equipment on the atoll that could lift
the plut crates. Forklift, maybe a crawler tractor with a
front bucket. Anything that would do the job. Check out
the stores first, all three of them."

Fernandez nodded and jogged toward the first store,
which billed itself as "Hardware, House Wares and Everything Else."

Gardner was well aware of the effect of heavily armed
men walking up to a house and asking questions. He relied on the shock value and knocked on the next bed and
breakfast door. A man answered. He was a local, with
heavy black hair and broad features. He was five-eight
and overweight. His eyes were so dark they could have
been black, and Gardner caught a hint of irritation in the
man's stance.

"Good morning. We're with the U.S. Navy on your
atoll looking for some men who are imposters and here
to perform some highly illegal acts. We wonder if we
could talk with your visitors."

"No. Not your business. Our business. You go away."

"They paid you well to say that, didn't they?" Gardner
said, swinging the muzzle of his MP-5 submachine gun
upward so it centered on the man's chest. "Now, let me
ask you politely again to go bring out your visitors so we
can talk with them. If you don't, my men and I will have
to move inside your house and find them. My men are

clumsy and might break all sorts of things in your home. I'm sure you understand."

"Yeah, you sombitch, I understand. Wait a minute." He turned and left the door. Gardner pushed it open and kept his MP-5 pointing into the hallway. It was thirty long seconds before anyone came, then a man dressed in an expensive suit and carefully knotted tie, with a white handkerchief in his upper pocket, came to the door. He wore a small mustache and above it his blue eyes were pinched in a frown.

"Why this inquisition, and lower your weapon. We're here on business that is no concern of yours. Any more of your threats and I'll be forced to call the sheriff."

"Please do. We've already cleared our visit with you with her. We're looking for drug smugglers, and you and your friends seem like prime suspects."

The dapper man laughed. "Drugs. You must be insane. I would never touch drugs. Here it would be heroin from the Golden Triangle, I would guess. Wrong on all counts. I'm not in the drug smuggling business."

"Not when something is much more valuable, right?"

"Like what?"

"Like plutonium 239."

The words left the well-groomed man speechless for a moment, then he recovered.

"I don't know what you're talking about." Before Gardner could get his foot in the way, the man slammed the bed and breakfast's front door.

Gardner took his squad into the street and looked for the third bed and breakfast house. There weren't more than twenty houses in the whole village. Before he found it, the Motorola came on.

"Skipper, we've hit paydirt," Fernandez said. "There are two rigs on the atoll that could handle the size and weight of the plut crates. One is a large forklift, the other is a wheeled Massey-Harris tractor with a two-yard bucket on the front. The forklift can load the first crate into the bucket, then pick up the second one and choggie. Both these rigs are hired and paid for. Three hundred bucks to

do some work today. They are to come when they get a
phone call. Supposed to go at once to the boat dock."

"Copy that. Good work. Fernandez, see if you can rent
or borrow a pickup over there, and come to the street here
and grab Claymore and two Marines and go down to those
planes. I'd like to see the rudders on both of those large
transport planes blown all to hell. By this time they may
have some protection for their aircraft down there, so be
careful."

"Roger, that, Skipper. I'm on my way."

Five minutes later Fernandez rolled up in a six-year-
old Ford half-ton pickup, loaded on his Marines and Claymore, and drove toward the airstrip. Fernandez stopped a
hundred yards from the planes, and the four got out and
stood behind the pickup. Fernandez had his Bull Pup. He
had just gone prone behind the pickup and started to sight
in on the closest twin-engine transport, when rifle fire
slammed into the pickup. All four men darted behind the
protection of the Ford and waited. After a flurry of a
dozen rounds, the rifle fire stopped.

Fernandez dropped down again, this time just inside the
rear tire, sighted under the pickup at the tail assembly on
the two-engine aircraft, and fired one 20-mm round. It hit
the tail and exploded, shattering the rudder and one of the
stabilizers. The plane wouldn't fly for a long time.

Now dozens more rounds came pounding at the pickup.
The glass shattered, the windshield went out, both tires
nearest the shooters went flat.

"Out of here," Fernandez bellowed. He dropped down
and fired into the brush and vines at the far edge of the
airstrip, where he had seen some muzzle flashes. Then the
four picked up and ran straight away from the pickup,
using it for protection as long as they could. Thirty yards
over, they plunged into brush and enough large trees for
cover.

"Anybody hit?" Fernandez asked. He heard grunts and
voices saying no wounds. "Settle down behind some protection and I'll call the skipper." He had just made contact
on the personal radio when the JG cut him off.

"Hold there, Fernandez. We're going to be busy here. A boat just came through the channel and into the lagoon. It's heading for the dock. Can't be sure, but it looks like the one we've been waiting for. Soon we can see if it has three crates of plut tied down on its rear deck. If so, we're gonna be busy for a while."

24

Gardner had an early warning from one of his men at the dock when they first saw the boat outside the reef. "Looks like they're hunting the channel, which must mean they aren't natives," Rafii called on the radio. Gardner and his men rushed down toward the dock, finding hidden vantage points where they could bring fire on the ship once it tied up.

They watched as the sixty-footer edged through the lagoon, then idled up to the dock. Nobody showed on board the boat. The man on the engine worked the controls to keep the boat next to the dock. Then a shotgun blasted from somewhere on board the craft, followed by four more blasts.

Gardner heard the slugs hitting the small office, blowing out windows and shredding tarps and furniture. "That's double-ought buck they're using," Gardner said on the radio. "Keep your heads down. That stuff is murder."

Eight or ten more shotgun rounds came, then a bullhorn voice came across the space.

"U.S. Navy, we know that you're there waiting for us. We're waiting for you. Want the plutonium? Come and get it. Just try. We've got two hostages with us. You make any move at all to stop us and the hostages go down one at a time. Right now there are ten submachine guns at your backs. We can't see you from here, but our men behind you have you all spotted. Throw out your weapons or die on the spot."

Gardner angled his Bull Pup around the edge of the

building he had hidden behind and triggered an impact round on the small pilot house of the boat. It disintegrated, and the bullhorn gave off a shriek as it was blasted into rubble along with the navigation equipment. The shotguns blasted again.

Gardner turned and stared into the area behind the building. There was a patch of brush and vines, then the street, then the buildings of the village. There was no place where ten men could be hiding to threaten them. "Open fire at the boat," Gardner said, "but don't hit the two crates of plut on the deck. Shoot out the windows, shoot into doors. No more twenties. Let's wear them down. I can't see anyone behind us. He was bluffing."

The MP-5s and the Bull Pup 5.56 rounds slashed into the wooden boat. Then the shotguns fired again, maybe one less this time, Gardner figured. The shotguns trailed off and a bullhorn came on.

"Hold your fire," the voice shouted over the bullhorn. "I want to make a deal with you. I know that one of our planes has been destroyed on the airstrip. We can take away only one of the crates of plutonium. We have two hostages on board. They are the twin girls of the postmaster at Rongrik Atoll. They are eight years old. We will not kill the girls if you hold your fire and let us take one of the crates of plut to the airfield and load it on our plane and take off. Then we'll let the little girls go just before take off. I'm bringing the girls on deck now, so you can see I talk true."

"We're fucked," Canzoneri said on the net.

Gardner shouted at the boat. "How do we know you'll let the little girls go?"

"I give you my word of honor as a gentleman. I am from Persia. I do not give my word frivolously."

Gardner knew he didn't have time to talk to Murdock or to Don Stroh. It was a command decision. His command, his decision.

"You've got it, Iran. Cease fire. Hold your fire, SEALs and Marines. Hold your fire."

"Call off your four men at the airfield. If they damage the other aircraft, the deal is all off."

Gardner used the net. "You guys at the airfield heard what's going down. They have the upper hand for the moment. Don't interfere with the plane, or with the rig that brings the crate of plut out there and loads it. We'll have to figure something downstream."

"I've radioed the men at the airfield," Gardner bellowed at the men on the boat. "You're clear to move the plut."

"No tricks, Navy SEALs, or the little girls die."

"No tricks." Gardner turned to Canzoneri. "Can you get to the chopper without being seen?"

"Let me look around a little. I'm not far from the brush and the houses. Yeah, I can do it."

"Get over there and have the pilot radio the carrier what's going down here. Tell them we'll have a twin-engine transport in the air in fifteen to twenty minutes. They may want to shadow it with an F-18. Then you stay there so we can communicate through you to the carrier."

"Roger that, Skipper. I'm gone."

Gardner leaned against the building, then stood behind it, then sat down and crossed his legs. He hated waiting. What was taking the forklift so long? They had to use a forklift to get the plut crate off the boat. Then it would be a quick run out to the airstrip and the plane at the end of the runway. That was where they would let out the two small girls. Gardner checked his watch. It had been almost fifteen minutes since he gave the terrorists the advantage. Where was the forklift?

Then it came wheeling around the corner and stopped on the dock. It had a cable and winch it used to drag one plut crate to the very edge of the boat. Then it pulled it upright, and just before it tipped over, the operator lifted the twin lift bars and caught it and eased it backward against the rails. The forklift backed away from the pier slowly, then headed for the airport. A pickup truck came down next, and six men and the two small girls got into the truck, and it drove away.

"JG, this is Canzoneri."

"Go."

"Got through to the carrier. They have two F-18s in the sky this direction and will send them here. Take them about five more minutes to get here."

"Roger that, Canzoneri. Fernandez, keep me up to date what's happening out at the airstrip. The plut is coming your way."

"Damnit, JG. They going to get away with it?"

"So far, but the game isn't over."

The SEALs and Marines came out of their cover and checked the boat. The two crates of plut were intact. Gardner had Canzoneri have the chopper pilot radio that news to the carrier.

"JG, the carrier people say they have a chopper with radiation experts in it on the way. They will take over the plut."

"Forklift just rounded the corner and is moving over to the aircraft," Fernandez said on the net. "There are three men around it now opening a hatch. It looks big enough to get the crate inside. Yes, now I see, they have rollers on the floor of the plane to get the crate inside."

"What about the little girls?"

"Both are standing outside the plane. Oh, now they are being lifted into the front of the plane. The crate is inside. That was quick and easy. Side hatch door is closing. The plane's engines are starting."

"Let me know when they drop off the little girls. Canzoneri, the minute the little girls are out of there, you have the pilot tell the carrier. It might make a difference what they do."

"Roger that, JG," Canzoneri said.

Fernandez came back on. "Okay, they moved the plane. It's taxiing to the far end of the airstrip. Wonder if that strip is long enough. That plane has a big load. Yes, he's turning into the wind, checking his mags, or whatever they do when they run up the engines. So far the little girls are still on board. Now, now the side passenger door is opening. What the hell? No little girls. Looks like they threw the body of a man out the door, then closed it.

They're taking off. Little girls still on board."

"Canzoneri, tell the carrier. Where are those Eighteens?"

"She's struggling down the runway, almost at the end," Canzoneri said. "Damn, she made it into the air and missed some brush down there by not more than ten feet. She's up and gone. Coming toward you guys at the village."

JG Gardner could see the plane then, low and gaining altitude.

"We can shoot her down with our twenties," Prescott said.

"No, the little girls," Gardner said. Then he screamed. Two small figures, one after the other, tumbled out the side door of the plane and fell straight down. Both landed in the lagoon.

"The bastards," JG Gardner said. "Canzoneri, tell the carrier what they did. Ask him if he can give the Eighteens guns free to shoot the fucker right out of the sky."

They watched the plane turn and head east.

"What the hell is east of here?" Claymore asked.

"A lot of water and a few little islands," Gardner said. "They must have had a route all planned out when they put their planes here."

"East of here is Kwajalein," Mahanani said. "We've got a big missile base there, mostly for tracking I think. He sure as hell won't sit down there."

Canzoneri came on the net. "Oh, yeah, the Eighteens are within five miles of us and they have the small plane on their radar. They are tracking it. I can hear the pilots talking to the CAG on their radios. I've got a feeling they might have plans for the twin-engine transport with the baby killers."

"Plans?" JG asked.

"They were talking about how deep the water is around here, and how solid those lead bottles were. Somebody said deep ocean water would be a perfect insulator, keeping the plut way down there. Plut is heavier than water, so it would go to the lowest spot."

"If they shoot the fucker out of the sky," Mahanani said.

"Yeah, looks like a possible. The CAG said wait until they get about halfway to Kwajalein, that would be about eighty miles east of us here at Wotje."

"How deep is the water around there?" Gardner asked.

"I'll ask," Canzoneri said. He came back on a minute later. "The carrier folks say there are trenches along there that go down to twelve to fifteen thousand feet. That would put a cork on that bottle for a long, long time."

"How fast is the transport going?" Gardner asked.

"The Hawkeye puts it a little over a hundred and fifty miles an hour. So, along about a half hour we'll see what the brass has decided."

Prescott scowled. "So it's a choice whether you want to risk polluting a chunk of the ocean, or let the bad guys get away with plutonium 239 that could power up as many as forty nuclear bombs that could wipe out four hundred million people. Hey, I'll go for the ocean risk in a minute."

"Now we see if you've got the right stuff to be an admiral," Gardner said. "Let's give this boat a going over. They might have left something here that would indicate some more customers."

"What about the customers in the bed and breakfasts?" Claymore asked.

"Good idea. Fernandez, check with the guy who runs the airstrip to see if they said anything about how much gas they needed to get to their next stop, anything that we might use if the Eighteens don't do the job. The rest of you here check out the boat. I'll take two Marines with me and we'll go see the bed and breakfast people."

Mary answered the door at her house. Her smile was as big as ever. "Now we have room, do you want to stay over?"

"What happened to your other guests?"

"Oh, they didn't tell you. Most of them were going to fly out in the commuter planes that leave this afternoon for Majuro. Some of them were going in the transport aircraft that were out at the airstrip."

"They are all gone?"

"Far as we know. The commuter will be leaving in about five minutes, if you want to catch them."

"Not a problem." Gardner hurried back to the dock. The man who owned it and the office behind it was out counting up the damage. Gardner talked to him. "Lots of damage here. I know how to help. Put in a claim to the U.S. Navy. I'll make sure it gets paid."

The owner, about thirty, with buckteeth and angry eyes, softened a little. "No fooling, Sergeant? A thousand dollars would just about cover it."

"You have a boat and motor we could borrow? Want to see if we can find those two little girls."

Ten minutes later Mahanani and the JG were on the lagoon. They went to where they thought the girls had fallen into the water. They found the first one quickly. She had snagged on a coral head barely a foot under the water. They lifted her into the boat and kept looking.

"A body will sink when it's dead," Mahanani said. "Then after a few days the bacteria starts to work inside and bloats it and it rises to the surface. No sense looking here anymore."

Back at the dock they met the sheriff, who said she would take care of the body until the parents from Rongrik could come over.

"You guys leave a lot of bodies around. I hear there are two out at the airstrip, and three or four in the Jap caves. We'll get to them today, probably, and bury them this afternoon."

Canzoneri came on the net. "Skipper, it's been decided. The eighteens will try to shoot up one wing of the transport with their twenty-millimeter guns. Hopefully put the bird down with minimum damage, so it doesn't hit the water too hard and blow up the lead bottle. That's the idea. I'll see if I can get my mike up by the chopper's speaker. Moving it."

The pilot's voices came faintly over the Motorola net.

"Roger that, CAG. We use the twenties. She's about two miles ahead. We're starting our run now. Minimal damage, just enough to put her down. This is Transport Alert One going in on a strafing run."

25

"I have target acquisition, moving out to concentrate the twenties on the right wing," the F-18 pilot said high over the Pacific.

"Transport One, this is Two. After your run, I'll do a fly-by and see how our duck is quacking."

"Roger that, Two, I'm moving in."

The air was quiet for a few seconds.

"Oh yes. Should be five or six big holes in that sucker's right wing, enough to destabilize him, maybe kill out some controls."

"This is Transport Two, your little bird has a broken wing. He's in a shallow bank to the right and going down. He's at ten thousand feet, no way he can make any landfall. Angle of descent is increasing. He'll splash down in two minutes outside."

"Roger that, Two. I have him again. Oh yeah, he's not more than three thousand now and dropping in that banking dive to the right. Should hit fairly flat, right wing first, and cartwheel."

"He's close, One. There he goes, splashdown, the crate didn't break up, so the plut should be safe. He's floating for about ten to twenty seconds, then he's finished. Heads popping out of the doors. Five, six, seven of them."

"Roger that, Transport One. This is Home Base. I understand that the craft went down in mid-Pacific, and there were no survivors. I repeat, we understand that there were no survivors of the crash, so no S and R choppers will respond. Do you copy?"

"Aye, aye, Home Base. No survivors of the twin engine

transport out of Wotje Atoll. We copy that. No survivors. The craft is sinking. Another ten seconds. Yes, she's down—only blue Pacific swells down there. Request vectors to come home. Looks like our work here is finished."

Gardner looked at Claymore. "No survivors? The pilot said he saw seven heads on the wreck."

"My guess is that Don Stroh gave the order. He's had enough prisoners to interrogate. Besides, those bastards killed that woman and the two little girls."

Gardner nodded. "Yeah. Well, what else do we have to do to get cleaned up here?"

"What about the guy's pickup?" Fernandez asked on the net.

"Yeah, we owe him a new pickup. Fernandez, find the guy and get a statement from him about the worth of his rig. We'll figure out how to cover it somehow. We've got the dock man compensated, and the dead woman. We wait for the radiation chopper to come. Any more cleanup at the airport, Fernandez?"

"We'll go over the second plane, but doubt if they left anything in it. The operator of the airstrip says he's claiming it for damages to his office. He did lose a window."

"What about the boat?" Canzoneri asked.

"Probably rented out of Majuro," Gardner said. "We'll let the sheriff take care of it. If it's not a rental, she can claim it as salvage and sell it. Maybe some of the money could go to the family of the woman who was shot."

The big chopper came in a few minutes later. It was a heavy hauler. Two radiation-suited men checked out the plut crate and peeled off their suits. Only trace radiation found. They rigged cables and loading rings to the crate and waved the chopper in. It lowered a thick cable with a large hook and the cables were attached. Slowly the big bird inched upward. The crate slid one way, then the other, then eased off the boat deck and into the air.

Gardner watched the chopper fly to the west, then called in all of his men to meet at the softball diamond.

"Good work, men. We're out of here."

They buttoned up the SH-60 and took off, heading west to meet the carrier that steamed toward them.

Gardner, Murdock, Jaybird, Lam, and Canzoneri huddled with Don Stroh and the carrier's captain. Gardner's team had hit the deck of the big flattop only a half hour before.

"So we have a problem," Stroh said. "The CIA operatives have been following the aircraft that got away earlier and headed west. Yes, it did land in the Philippines, but not at the airports we thought it might. We had forty covered, and they found one we didn't. It refueled and took off at once. The flight plan filed was bogus. We know it headed on west. From there on, we're not sure of the route. They probably had contacts in India where they stopped, maybe twice for fuel and food. From India's west coast, it's a jump around Pakistan to Abbas in southern Iran."

"Any confirmation that the same plane landed in Abbas?" Murdock asked.

"As good as we can get. We have some people there. One of them said a similar twin-engine propeller aircraft landed at the Abbas airport within the right time frame and was at once taken to the far end of the field and guarded with fifty armed troops. That was a little over twenty-four hours ago. We've had no contact with our man in Abbas since his last transmission, and we hope that does not mean bad news for him."

"So they made it," Gardner said. "The four hundred pounds of weapons-grade plutonium 239 is in Iranian hands, and they will at once sell one or two bomb portions of it to the highest bidders. We're out of it."

Murdock chuckled. "Gardner is new to our fun and games, but he's a fast learner. If we we're out of it, JG, we wouldn't be having this high-level chat with the CIA and the captain."

"So we're going in after the plut?"

"Is the cardinal a Catholic?" Jaybird cracked.

"What we want to work out is how and when," Stroh said. "The office has sent some suggestions. We have some underground assets in Abbas that few people know about. When is as quick as we can get there. Your favorite business jet has been on its way from San Francisco for ten hours. It's due to drop down into Majuro Atoll soon. The captain tells me we're a little less than two hundred miles from that capital city. The twelve of you SEALs fit for duty will be boarding an SH-60 for a joy ride to Majuro. You leave in an hour. Now we get to work. The how is tougher. Do we go into the airport, or wherever they have taken the crates of plut, and get them back? Or do we find the plut and mix it with highly radioactive material, such as atomic-plant spent fuel, to render it unfit for boom boom?"

"How good is this undercover woman agent you have in Abbas?" Jaybird asked.

Stroh's head jerked up. "How did you know it was a woman?"

"Easier to keep a woman under wraps, especially in Iran with its strict dress code. Is she good?"

"She has good connections. She's an artist and has a certain amount of begrudged freedom."

"Where do we fly to nearby?" Murdock asked.

"We still have some friends in Oman, just across the Strait of Hormuz from Iran," Stroh said.

"Better to go in by boat to those marshes than try to drop in from the air," Lam said. "Boats are better for this job."

"Agree," Murdock and Gardner said.

"You'll be short four men," Stroh said. "Do you want to take four Marine Recon men with you?"

"No," Gardner said. "I worked with a squad on the atoll and we did well. But it was friendly country. We had no coordination and our weapons were different. In something this hot, we better stick with our twelve men and do the job."

Murdock grinned and nodded. "I'll second that motion."

Stroh looked at the carrier boss. "Anything to input here, Captain?"

The captain shook his head. "I'm still amazed the way your enlisted men step up and help in the planning. Remarkable. The Navy probably should learn something from that." He shook his head. "But we're in the black shoe navy. Things don't change much." He stood. The men around the small table jolted to attention.

"Thanks, SEALs. It's been good working with you and watching you operate. Good luck on your new assignment." The captain walked out and the men relaxed.

"No time for special chow, but they will have four big boxes of deli sandwiches and lots of coffee on the Seahawk," Stroh said. "Don't ask me your route. I have no idea. Now, who needs to clean some weapons and get ammo pouches loaded up? You'll be taking everything with you that you brought from the States. Oh, just as a change of pace, I'll be riding with you on this one. Let's roll."

"Move it," Murdock said and the men hurried out of the room toward their compartment to get ready to fly.

After the hour's flight in the noisy Seahawk, the SEALs settled down in the Gulfstream II business jet at the Majuro Atoll airport. The Coast Guard used the sleek plane for military VIP flights. The SEALs had ridden in the first-class seats before. A Coast Guard lieutenant welcomed them on board. He was sturdy, red-faced, and with corn-silk blond hair.

"I get first dibs on the steak dinner," he said. "No sweat, we've got plenty. I'm your bus driver for the tour. Don't ask me how long it will take to get where we're going. We're supposed to have diplomatic permission for some fly-overs, but some countries rethink these things as they come up. We'll play it by ear and get you to Oman as quickly as possible. Have a good ride."

He vanished into the cockpit, and two minutes later they taxied down the apron, hit the runway, and took off.

The steak dinner was fine, Murdock decided. It had come from the airport restaurant and was served on china. The flight steward had a time juggling the china, but he made it. When the dishes were cleared, Murdock took over.

"Rafii, front and center. We're going back to school. Arabic. We are going to have Arabic coming out of our ears before this flight is over. Start us out with greetings—how to ask where a street is, how to find the bathroom, where is a hotel, the usual tourist stuff. Then we'll move into the fun stuff, like put up your hands, or tell me the information I want to know or I'll shoot you." Murdock grinned and Rafii spoke rapidly to him in Arabic. Murdock held up his hands. He'd caught only half of what the Saudi native said.

Rafii laughed and then got into the job of refreshing and teaching as much Arabic language as he could in the few hours they had.

Al Fujayrah, Oman

Murdock was tired when they landed in Oman. Even though they had slept half the time, and studied Arabic the other half, he felt worn out and groggy. Once on the ground, the plane had been flagged down and signaled to follow a jeep with a large red flag. It led them to a transit hangar and they waited for the customs inspectors. Stroh met them at the door, mentioned two names, and the men simply looked inside, nodded at the heavily armed men, and left.

"Next step is to find the Oman Army colonel who is supposed to meet us here and let us use his barracks until we can make the needed arrangements to get across the Strait and start your trek into Abbas," Stroh said. A sleek black Mercedes pulled up shortly and an army officer hurried to the plane. He spoke to Stroh, who went to the car and talked to someone in the rear seat. Then the Mercedes sped away.

Stroh came back smiling. "Well, we have our barracks and a chow line, and a line on a boat. Beyond that, we'll have to play it by ear."

Jaybird had been scanning the maps that Stroh had brought with him. "If we can get somewhere near Jask, there's a road that leads up the coast right into Abbas. Wonder if they hitchhike in Iran."

"That's the end of the coast road," Stroh said. "Below that it's a wilderness. Might be a good spot to land." A twenty-man bus pulled up and the driver honked twice.

"Our limo is here," Stroh said.

Ten minutes later they had settled in the army barracks, all twelve of them, and now were checking maps, distances, and the exchange rate: roughly two rial to a dollar.

"How far to Abbas from that other town?" Gardner asked.

"Roughly a hundred and fifteen miles," Jaybird said. "Long damn hike."

"Does our artist lady friend have a car, or a van?" Murdock asked.

"She has a car, and can meet you at Jask," Stroh said. "She should be able to get another car to take you back up the road."

"Clothes, makeup, rials—we getting all that?" Mahanani asked.

Stroh checked his watch. "We're due there now. Looks a lot like a movie wardrobe department, but it's ours." He shook his head. "Damn, wish you guys weren't so tall. You'll have to slouch a lot. Wigs and hats and clothes and some face and hand makeup will help."

"You've got the boat big enough for twelve of us, but not big enough to attract attention?" Murdock asked.

"I have. An eighteen-footer with an outboard and a backup engine."

"How far across is it here?" Van Dyke asked.

Jaybird went back to his maps. "Just over a hundred miles. That far?"

"Too far in an open boat at night doing ten to twelve knots," Murdock said. "How can we cut down the time?"

Jaybird pointed on the map. "If we motor up north here in Oman to Diba al Hisn, and take off from there, it's only sixty miles across."

"Then we get a powerboat that can do twenty knots,

and we can do the trip in three hours," Gardner said.

"Bigger, faster boat," Stroh said. "Yeah, I can do that. Might take a little longer. Want to get you out of here with three hours of dark for your boat trip. If any of you have watches that aren't set yet, it's now just after oh-seven-thirty. We have lots of time until it's dark. We'll suit up here, get land transport up to Diba al Hisn, and launch you from there as soon after dark as we can. Then I contact our lady in Abbas and tell her where to find you."

"So we find her," Murdock said. "Does she know where the plut is?"

"She's working on it. There was a big push to get it out of town fast. They didn't want any accidents. Just where it was taken is not known yet. That may be a big part of your job. First find it, then take down whoever is protecting it, and then figure out some way to get it destroyed or mixed with material that will leave it highly radioactive, but render it unfit for powering nuclear weapons."

"Sounds like a piece of cake," Claymore said.

"Hell, we should be home by noon," Jaybird countered.

Three hours later the SEALs had been transformed into Arabs, with light-brown-dyed faces, hands, and arms. They had a big meal and soon were in an army truck heading up the highway toward Diba al Hisn, their port of embarkation.

"Hear we get an Oman Navy boat," Gardner said. "It should be able to do thirty knots, makes a hell of a lot of noise, and has two twenty-millimeter weapons for defense. Just in case we run into any Iranian gunboats."

"The Iranians have a navy?" Lam asked.

"Two destroyers in the three-hundred-seventy-five-foot class, with plenty of missiles and weapons," Jaybird said. "Also some frigates and a whole pot full of good-sized coastal patrol craft. Hope to hell we don't run into any of them."

The truck stopped just outside of Diba al Hisn and

Stroh set up his SATCOM antenna on the hood and positioned it. He made a call to the embassy in Oman and a moment later turned to Murdock, his face drawn and troubled.

"I just had word from our embassy here. Lila, the woman agent you were to meet in Kangan, was killed this morning in a shootout with Iranian Secret Police."

26

"Great timing," Murdock said.

"She must have been getting too close to the place they have the plut, or the Secret Police were on to her all the time," Stroh said. "We have a backup, but he doesn't have the connections she had. I'll get him, and tell him to find you just south of the town."

"Let's get to the dock and into that Oman Navy boat," Murdock said. "This trip is not starting out the best."

Twenty minutes later they attracted little attention as they boarded a sixty-foot patrol boat that was longer and narrower than most patrol boats. The design shrieked of speed. The SEALs wore their combat vests under the loose-fitting Iranian civilian-type shirts that were open at the bottom. Each man had a drag bag for two weapons, ammo, and other essential fighting gear.

They crowded below in a small cabin. An Oman naval officer came in and talked with Rafii a moment, then the boat moved out into the small bay and then into the strait. At once they could feel the power as the heavy engines drove the sleek craft through the water.

"Hell of a lot better than twelve hours in a sampan," Prescott said. Then the speed picked up and the boat began battering through the light chop of the unruly waters between the two continents.

They had been on the water for an hour when the boat powered down to a crawl.

"Must have company," Murdock said. He sent Rafii up

to the cockpit. The Saudi Arabian native returned a moment later.

"The lieutenant says there is an Iranian Corvette sweeping the area about half a mile ahead. He doesn't think the low profile of this boat will show on the big ship's radar. We're drifting with a slight current, and the lieutenant hopes we can avoid the ship with the big guns."

They settled in to wait.

Ten minutes dragged by, then the boat's engines picked up with a throaty roar and the craft moved ahead, then slammed into the swells and powered forward at close to its maximum speed of thirty knots.

"I guess we missed him," Jaybird said.

"Damn good thing," Gardner said. "That Corvette would outgun us a hundred to one."

Just under two hours later they nosed up to a rickety fishing boat dock five miles below Kangan on the southern Iranian coast.

"Move, move, move," Murdock whispered as the SEALs left the boat and raced across the rickety dock into some trees and brush just beyond a dirt road. The last SEAL hit the brush, and they watched as the blacked-out Oman Navy craft eased away from the dock and purred quietly west, headed back for Oman.

Murdock had surveyed the place as well as he could in the dark. He waved forward. "Up this road we'll find the coast highway in about fifty yards. We turn north, stay five yards apart, and keep it quiet. Lam out front two hundred. Moving."

Lam hiked along the track of a road that seemed to go only to the fishing dock. Then it met a blacktopped two-lane highway in good shape. He turned north. Lam saw no houses, no places that could be farmed in the hilly, swampy region. A mile up the road he used the radio. "Cap, I have something for you to take a look at. Not sure exactly what it is."

Murdock hurried up beside his scout and looked past a light cover of brush down the road.

"Sure as hell isn't a roadblock," Murdock said. "I don't see any men around it at all."

"Looks like a hayrack that my granddad used to work with on his farm in Nebraska. Only I don't see the horses that would pull it."

"Broken down?"

"Could be," Lam said. Murdock gave the hand signal for both of them to advance, and they worked their way quietly forward until they could almost touch the wooden frame. Inside was hay covering half of the rack. Murdock stopped and held his breath. Then he grinned. Someone snored up a storm inside the hayrack. They went to the front of the rig and found that one wheel had come off and the whole rig tilted toward the right.

Murdock and Lam went past fifty feet, then he called for the rest of the men to move up. "Just don't make any noise and wake up our snoring friend," Murdock said.

Four miles later up the road, they began to find houses and some small fields under cultivation. Although it was now past midnight, they still had to jolt off the road now and then for a stray car or light truck to go past. Most of the traffic was heading north.

Lam called Murdock again. "Check out the taillights up there," the scout said.

Murdock watched the twin red lights three hundred yards up the road. They stopped, then started again.

"Morse code," Lam said.

Murdock concentrated on the lights. Dot, dot, dot. That was an S. He watched the rest of the dots and dashes and grinned. "That taillight just spelled out SEALs in Morse code, little buddy. I think we've found our contact."

Lam moved up at the side of the road in some thin cover. As he approached, a man got out of the rig that Lam saw was a van. The guy leaned against the rear doors. He folded his arms and whistled a sad little tune.

Lam worked just past the van without a sound, came back to the road, and ghosted round until he was two feet from the man's elbow.

"Nice night out, isn't it?" Lam asked in English.

The man leaning against the van jolted straight up and spun around, his hand clawing for a pistol in his belt holster. Lam's MP-5's muzzle pressed against the watcher's chest.

"Easy, easy, we could be friends."

The watcher's eyes were still wide white beacons in the night. He gasped for breath, held up his hands, and his voice came through the gasping breath ragged and hard to understand.

"Hope to hell you're a U.S. Navy SEAL."

"Hope to hell you're a deep undercover CIA agent."

"Oh yeah. Tell Don Stroh I'll get even. Lila got caught in the middle. They proved to her they knew she was CIA and what she'd been doing, and tried to turn her into a double agent. She wouldn't turn, so they killed her. Bastards."

"Murdock, you can come in now, the water is friendly."

Murdock had been only ten yards out, now he jogged up to the van. He held out his hand. "Lieutenant Commander Murdock, Navy SEALs. Glad you know Morse code."

"From a long time ago. I almost went with an SOS. Oh, I'm Izzat Al-Jaafar. Yes, I'm Iranian. Grew up in the States from three to twenty-three. Went with the State Department and they shifted me into the CIA. I took my training and then came over here four years ago to be deep in the life of the city. You should call me Izzy."

"Good. Izzy it is. Hope Lam didn't shake you up too much with his elbow approach. He's going to give somebody a heart attack one of these days."

"How did he do that? I thought I was watching everywhere."

"You were. I was lucky."

"How many bodies?"

"Twelve, as advertised. How did you get here so fast?"

"I was halfway down the coast road when I got the message on my SATCOM. Had a lead where they might have taken the plutonium 239. Four hundred pounds of it." He shook his head in disbelief. "That's enough to build at least forty nukes."

"Not if we get there first. Where are we heading?"

"We don't have to go into Abbas. That's where they have a lot of hotshot secret police. About halfway between here and Abbas is a little town called Sirik. No roads show on the map, but I've heard that a new road was cut through to the other road coming north over east about twenty miles. Beyond that the new road continues into an arid region where there are no roads and probably no people as well. A few goat herders, maybe, but not much else. Baghdad will risk a few goat herders, but not anywhere that there is a city of any size. My information is that somewhere over in there is where they plan to break down the plutonium into ten-pound lead boxes and seal it up radiation-leak-proof and ready for sale."

"Can we get from here to there?"

"Not without a lot of persuasion. Yes, I stopped at the new road and checked it out on my way past. Looks like only military rigs on it. Which complicates matters some."

"So we grab an army truck and use it," Jaybird said.

"This is Jaybird; he has a lot of ideas," Lam said. "You'll get used to him."

"We should load up and get into a less obvious place to do our planning. I have a SATCOM that's wired to explode on command. We don't want the Iranians getting one."

"Inside, everyone," Murdock said. "Tight squeeze, but it's quicker than hiking for fifty miles." Murdock and Rafii rode up front. The two Arabs spoke in Arabic for a while, then switched to English.

"Are those weapons loaded?" Izzy asked.

"Not much good using them as clubs," Rafii said.

"Any roadblocks down this way?" Murdock asked.

"None when I came down, but they shift them around. You can't be sure. We'll use the soccer match ploy. There were four games down in Kangan yesterday. Several teams should be going home north on this road. Usually works."

"Your van?" Rafii asked.

"Not really. A company van. They paid for it. It's in the name of a man who died a few weeks ago. Records take a long time to get checked out here. Life isn't worth much in Iran today—unless it belongs to you, of course."

They followed the strait on their left as they worked north. Now and then they met a car or small truck. Twice cars passed them. They were big, heavy sedans.

"Government employees or police," Izzy said. "They are the only ones who can afford such cars. Petrol to go in them is amazingly expensive."

"We have plenty of cash, rials," Murdock said.

"Two to one, in case you do any bargaining or buying. Two rials equal about a buck."

They spotted a roadblock more than a mile ahead. It had been poorly placed in the flatness and with no turns in sight. "We try to run it with the soccer team ploy?" Murdock asked.

Izzy scowled, then slowly shook his head. "No, too big a risk. We might hit some angry officer or hotheaded enlisted man who would insist on talking to each man, asking where he was born, what he does for a living."

Izzy slowed the van but kept moving. "I'll go through with Rafii. He can fake it. The rest of you drop out of the van and move into the countryside a half mile. Then walk past the roadblock, and I'll pick you up on the other side about a mile, where I'll be having some engine trouble."

"Roger that," Murdock said. He went on the net. "Wake up, you guys, we're taking a hike. Roadblock ahead. Out and around, you know the drill. Open that side door and we drop out at five miles an hour. Remember, we're moving."

Lam was first out the door. He jogged directly away from the highway, then angled to the north to pick up the others. They all went on the same side. Lam didn't like the landscape at half a mile, and went another quarter, into some small mounds and hills, then turned north and started jogging.

When they were well past the lighted roadblock made

of three two-ton trucks angled across the road and ditches, Lam turned them back toward the highway. They spotted the van, and after Lam checked it out to be sure it was the same one, they climbed in and slid the door shut.

"Any problems back there?" Murdock asked.

"No. My usual cover is that I do surveying. Have an old transit and some chains in back. They insisted on talking with both of us, so it's a good thing we didn't try the other routine. Should be clear sailing now. They said about twenty miles on into town."

"We have any other assets in this area we can use?" Murdock asked.

"Not for this type of an operation. We didn't know it was coming until three days ago. Lila had something working, but she didn't tell me what it was. She knew about me, but we seldom met or talked. Quite a bit of army around this place from what I've seen on the road. We'll have to borrow some goods from the army guys."

"Might work at that," Rafii said. "But once we get the plut, what can we do with it? We don't have any radiation material to mix it with. We could pour it down a deep well, but the Iranians would figure that out and dig out a dozen wells if there are any out here."

"No oil out here," Izzy said.

"We'll get it, then figure out what to do with it," Murdock said. "We could always call in an air strike and scatter it over a hundred acres."

"Not too neat," Rafii said. "The environmentalists would shit their pants. Ours, too."

They started seeing houses, some fields. Soon there were more cars on the road. Streets branched off. The town came up suddenly around a corner.

"We have a safehouse here if your men need a break," Izzy said. "We could hang out the rest of the night and then tomorrow night make a try for an army truck."

"No, we need to get with it tonight," Murdock said. "We need to get as close as possible to the center where they're going to break down the plut into the smaller boxes. Any idea how far it is down this special road?"

"Twenty miles to the other north-south highway, then it's a guess how far into the desert. Ten, maybe twenty miles."

"How do we get an army truck?" Murdock asked.

"When I came through, I drove around some. Found the army's motor pool about a mile out of town. Looks possible."

"Drive past it and let's have a look," Murdock said. "Then we'll try to get in a back gate or under a fence and put some guards to sleep for a while. One good two-ton truck with a cover would be great."

They left town on the highway and a mile north saw the motor pool. It had floodlights on, a guard at the closed front gate, and only one interior guard that Murdock saw. They pulled off the road a mile past the army trucks. Murdock filled the men in on the operation. "We'll hike up to the fence, look for a spot to get over or under and take down the guards with silenced shots. Then we grab the truck we want and motor right out the front gate."

Izzy pulled an Ingram submachine gun from under the front seat and went with them. They found a breach in the wire and were all inside when a sentry with a guard dog leveled an automatic rifle at them.

"Stop, you thieves, or I'll blast every one of you into hell," the sentry shouted.

27

"Idiot, imbecile, asshole," Izzy screeched into the black Iranian night. "What the hell's the matter with you? Didn't you read the notice about a test exercise tonight? It was all over the motor pool. It's a test, you stupid dunderhead. A group of raiders were set to try to sneak in and take down the motor pool and burn down all of our vehicles. You and your guards were supposed to stop them. There are referees around you haven't seen yet. Officially our side has shot you down before you saw us, and now you're dead, so you sit down where you are, unload your weapon, and stay there until a referee comes and tells you that you can leave."

The soldier's rifle wavered. "A test? I didn't hear about a test."

"Did you read the bulletin board this morning or tonight before you came on duty? Hell no. Stupid goat herder," Izzy raged. "Now, sit down and shut up and don't even move a finger until a referee comes. They're wearing white helmets in case you don't know."

"But . . . but you have weapons."

"Don't you think anyone trying to break in here would have weapons? We have to make it realistic." Izzy had walked slowly forward and was now within arm's reach of the guard. The man had lowered his rifle until it pointed at the ground. "Now, sit down before I knock you down."

The man dropped to the ground. Lam came up behind him and pounded the side of his MP-5 down on the guard's head, knocking him out. Two other men jumped forward and bound his hands and feet with riot cuffs and carried him into some high weeds.

Murdock moved up with Izzy. "Good work. Good idea about setting the trucks on fire. That way they won't miss just one. Let's move up to that shed, then on to the parking lot. Didn't I see about a dozen vehicles lined up there?"

"Maybe twenty trucks and jeeps." They ran ahead to the shack, which proved to be a storage area for empty oil drums. Ahead they saw two guards walking near the trucks.

Jaybird squirmed up near Murdock. "I can take out one of them when he passes that last truck." Jaybird had out his razor-sharpened KA-BAR knife.

"Go. We'll get the other one with silenced rounds." They waited while Jaybird ghosted from one dark shadow to another as he worked his way thirty yards to the rear of the last truck in the yard. He crouched there until the walking guard made his turn to start back over to his post. Jaybird sprinted forward, caught the guard just as he turned, and drove the blade deep into his chest, slanting off a rib and daggering into his heart. The man slumped to the ground. Jaybird dragged him between two trucks and waved at Murdock.

The second guard came in sight again from around the front of the trucks. Two silenced shots whuffed from the SEALs' weapons, and the Iranian soldier went down without a sound. Izzy said he would pick the truck and drive it, while the SEALs set up timed C-5 bombs on the gas tanks of four of the trucks.

Now Izzy ran forward with the SEALs. He chose the second six-by-six covered truck in the line and found the keys in the ignition where they should be. He started it and drove it forward. The SEALs had been working on their small bombs—half a stick of C-5 and a timer detonator set for ten minutes.

"Charges ready?" Murdock asked over the net. All four chimed in as ready. "Set for ten minutes, activate." The four timers were pushed into the on position and the four

SEALs charged away from the trucks, toward the one that sat at the front of the group. They climbed on board and Izzy drove toward the front gate. A thin barrier barred the way. Two men stood at the gate. Izzy rolled down the window and scowled at the two soldiers.

"Didn't you get the word about a night exercise?" he asked in Arabic.

"Nothing on my schedule," a corporal said.

"Should be," Izzy said. He lifted the Ingram submachine gun from his lap and fired three rounds into the first guard's chest, then moved his aim and hit the second guard standing near the guard shack. Two of the three silenced rounds jolted into the soldier's neck, putting him down and bleeding severely.

Izzy put the truck into gear, hit the gas, smashed through the thin lift arm, and they were on the road heading back toward the small town of Sirik.

"We still have twelve SEALs?" Murdock asked.

"Ten back here," Mahanani said. "I'd say about three more minutes to the big bang-bang."

Izzy pulled to the side of the road and they looked back at the motor pool. One charge went off early, blasting a splash of light into the darkness and sending a rolling thunder of sound toward them. Then the other three exploded and the sound intensified. A rush of air went past them toward the explosion, then came racing back at them. They heard five or six secondary explosions.

"Fuel tanks going up," Prescott said.

Izzy put the truck into gear and drove on toward town.

"There's a turnoff from the main highway to the new road. It had a guard there when we came by. I'll pull into his spot and tell him we just saw a big explosion behind us. He might go for it."

Less than a mile later Izzy slowed and came to a stop on a turnoff that held a small shack and a soldier standing in front with a submachine gun.

"You came from the north," the guard said. "Did you see a big explosion up that way?"

"Damn big one. Looked like the motor pool went up.

Probably some asshole smoking around the fuel dump.
You got a phone, you should report it."

"No phone, no radio. You need a pass to get on this
road."

"Nobody told me that. Hell, where do I get one?"

"I give it to you." The guard held out a piece of blue
plastic about six inches square and thick. "Put that in your
windshield and you're covered."

Izzy put the plastic in the windshield near his side and
drove on through.

"Glad you came along," Murdock said once they were
past the checkpoint.

"Me, too," Izzy said. "I haven't been on a real operation
for three years. I was getting rusty and damn impatient."
He frowned. "We made one mistake. We shouldn't have
left that first guard alive back there in the tall weeds. He
can tell whoever will listen that a dozen civilians attacked
him, blew up the trucks, and—"

"We didn't make a mistake," Murdock said.

"You mean he won't talk?"

"Dead men never do," Rafii said. "SEALs don't take
prisoners, unless they are at least brigadier generals."

Izzy nodded, kicked up the truck to a higher gear, and
they raced down the road, which was surprisingly good,
well engineered and constructed, but without the blacktop
surface on it yet.

"I figure another fifteen minutes and we'll be to the
next north-south highway," Izzy said. "Then we'll have
to play it by ear and see what kind of security they have
and what the hell we do then."

Murdock used the net. "Listen up. We'll be coming to
the intersection up here. They may have heavy security
from there on east. We'll have to play it as it goes. Everybody get sharp. We don't know what we'll find or what
we'll do."

They saw the lights from a mile away.

"We've got the blue plastic pass," Murdock said. "You
can tell the guards we're bringing in more civilian workers for the plant."

"But, Skipper," Jaybird said, "if they challenge us, we're sitting ducks. It's for sure they have RPGs there, and plenty of automatic weapons."

"A quick recon couldn't hurt," Lam said. "We pull over, put up the hood, and if anybody stops to help, you're letting her cool off. Running too hot. I take a run up to the lights and see what I can find out, and call in on the net."

"I agree with Lam," Gardner said. "We're flying blind right now."

"Any more wild ideas?" Murdock asked. The radios were silent. "Okay, Izzy, pull it over and kick up the hood. Lam, take a hike."

"Yeah," Jaybird said. "And be careful out there."

Lam took off down the shoulder of the road. Not much vegetation along here. If a car or truck came along, he'd have to hit the dirt and play dead. Shouldn't be any cars, just army trucks. His civilian clothes wouldn't help him out here; in fact they could get him shot if this was a military-only area.

He jogged the first half mile. The lights were still well ahead. Another half mile and he was closer, maybe a thousand yards. He could spot army trucks around a flood of lights. No slipping through there. He could see the other highway, another two-lane blacktopped type. It was a grade crossing, so no overpass. He looked behind and saw headlights coming, still half a mile away. He walked into the desert at the side of the road and found a bush that he squatted behind. It didn't completely conceal him, but there would be no direct light on him from the headlamps. The truck pounded past, and he watched it as it came to the floodlighted area. It stopped. The driver and a front-seat person got out with hands up and stood for an inspection and a pat down. Then the two drivers marched away. The back of the truck was opened and three men with large lights stepped inside the truck. Soon they came out and a different guard got in the truck and drove it through the checkpoint and into the darkness beyond. The drivers were marched in that direction, but Lam never saw them get back in the truck.

Lam told the net what he had seen. "Not a chance we can sneak through, and my guess is they have plenty of arms on hand if we try to blast through."

"So we take a hike and pick up some transport on the far side," Murdock said. "Wait for us there, Lam. Get back off the road a quarter and we'll meet. Let's move it, SEALs. This is why you get paid the big bucks."

It took the SEALs fifteen minutes to find Lam, then another half hour to hike to the north-south highway and follow it south for a mile before they tried to cross it. There was almost no traffic, and they ran across on the first try, regrouping and heading north again a quarter mile out from the highway. When they came to the new and unfinished road heading into the eastern desert, they stopped and watched for traffic.

Nothing moved in either direction on the dirt roadway except six trucks in convoy heading to the east.

"If there was a single truck, I could play dead in the road," Jaybird said. "Did it once before and it worked."

"And you almost got yourself run over," Mahanani said. "I hate to try to patch a guy up who has been run over by a semi truck and eight wheels."

Murdock checked his glowing-dial wristwatch. "It's not quite twenty-four hundred. We'll do a five-mile hike and see what it produces. We need to get close to this plant where they break down the plut, but we'll also need a spot where we can hide out during the coming daylight. Let's choggie."

Murdock set the pace. It was a swift jog, moving them along at seven minutes to a mile. They took a break after the first three miles, then after ten minutes moved out again. They had seen two more trucks driving east during the run, and none going west.

"No suicide by truck, Jaybird," Murdock said. "Too dangerous with your dirt-brown clothes and the dirt-brown road. We hike again, see what we can find, and well before daylight find a nest we can crawl into until tomorrow night."

"Should be some way," Lam said. "Yeah," he said and grinned. "See that small hill just ahead. Can't see the road on the other side. We wait there for the first single truck to come along and we put out a red flare. Red means stop almost everywhere. The dumb-ass driver stops and we reduce him to a corpse, hope he doesn't have a load of soldiers, and utilize his transport for our own transportation eastward."

"Help if we had brought one of those army uniforms," Izzy said. "But I like the plan. It should work. Most of these trucks this time of night would be taking in supplies."

"Let's do it. Lam, double-time up to the spot and pick out where you want to throw the red flare. Pop it when you see a single truck's headlights coming about a quarter of a mile off."

"I'm gone." Lam moved down to the shoulder of the new road for better footing and ran his marathon pace toward the rise about half a mile away. The rest of them hiked in the desert near the road at their five-yard interval and regular pace. Murdock figured they might have an hour or two to wait.

Ahead, Lam picked his spot. There was a slight ditch here beside the road, as if they had thought of leveling out the hill then figured it was too much work. He pulled a red flare from his combat vest and watched down the road.

Ten minutes later he heard the rest of the platoon come up and flake out in the sparse vegetation near the road. He saw lights far down on the road and tensed, but there were three sets of headlamps. He relaxed and made sure he was out of sight of anyone on the road. Minutes later the trucks rumbled past, kicking up a storm of dust that covered Lam. He coughed and sputtered it out of his mouth, then pried his eyes open to check down the road. He hadn't yet dusted himself off when another set of headlights showed. Yes, just one pair. This was his meat. He picked up the red flare and decided where he would throw it, then waited.

If it was a normal-sized truck, the lights should be about a quarter of a mile away. He yanked the fuse and threw it into the roadway. It popped and burned a bright red in the dark sky. He heard the truck slowing down, then saw it in the red glow as it crawled up slowly toward the light. Lam had been somewhat behind the flare, and now he lifted up and ran to the side of the truck away from the driver and stepped up on the running board. The window was down. He fired three rounds from his MP-5 into the driver, who jolted against the far door, and the truck stalled.

SEALs raced up to the truck and pulled back the tarp over the high bows on the top. Murdock heard strange sounds from inside the truck. He brought up his flashlight and shone it inside the rig. He almost dropped the light. Smiling back at him were ten women, all in Western attire and half of them blondes. A voice came out of the truck in English.

"Well, what the hell you staring at? Just what the fuck do you guys want, as if I didn't already know."

28

Murdock's head snapped up at the words. "Well, ladies, this is a surprise. I expected some hairy chested Iranian soldiers."

"So were we," the voice said. One of the women stepped forward into Murdock's flashlight beam.

"Hi, sweetheart. I'm Molly, and me and my friends here had a date with some dumb-assed Iranian officers. They stink and talk funny but they pay damn well. What the fuck is your excuse for being in this stupid country?"

"We're trying to blow those same officers right off the face of the earth. We need to borrow your truck."

"Climb on board. You can't leave us stuck out here in the desert."

"True, so we'll share. Okay, guys, jump on board. Don't sit on any of the girls up there."

It was a tight fit and one of the girls giggled.

Murdock went to the front, where Izzy had the engine started and the lights back on. The red flare had long since burned out. Mahanani held up the cap, shirt, pants, and rifle from the dead driver. He waved and jumped in the rear of the truck. They drove down the road, watching closely for anything that might give them trouble.

Over ten miles later they saw lights ahead. Izzy cut the headlamps on the truck and they moved forward at ten miles an hour.

"Might be our target," Murdock said.

"Enough lights," Izzy said. "They must be protecting something." He shook his head. "What can we do with the women?"

"They must be expected. You suppose one of them can drive this rig?"

Izzy pulled to the side of the road and stopped. "Ask them," he said.

After Murdock asked the question over the tailgate, Molly spoke up.

"Hell yes. Is it a stick with a five-speed, or what? I used to drive a school bus, for God's sake. I can handle this."

Murdock helped her down and tried not to notice when the skirt she wore slid up to her waist. She pulled it down and went around to the driver's side.

"Single-range tranny with a five-speed box," Izzy told her.

"Piece of cake. You guys want to drop off before we get to the lights, right? Damn. I've never met a real live SEAL before. You guys do good work. I used to be with a Navy guy. What are you two grinning about?"

"You," Murdock said. "You came along at just the right time, with the ability to drive this truck."

"Yeah, and you and your guys don't even get one pop. What the hell, it's a tough life all over. You should hear how most of us girls got shanghaied into this hooker mess."

Izzy let her drive and sat in the middle. The lights were closer now. "How the fuck close you want to get to this place?" Molly asked.

"Slow down when we can see a gate or a guard post," Murdock said. "Our guys will drop off the back and charge off the road and into the boonies."

"You mean something that blocks the road like those two trucks parked end to end up there?" Molly asked.

"That would be it. Okay, SEALs, we're slowing to five miles an hour. Drop off the rear and move to the right-hand side of the road. Go now."

"I better turn the lights back on so I don't surprise them. The driver? I'll say he got sick and fell out of the truck and we couldn't get him back inside. No problem. These guys are so desperate for a hard-on they'll believe anything I tell them, as long as I show them a little tit."

The truck slowed but kept moving forward. The men at the roadblock wouldn't be able to tell how fast the truck was moving forward. Murdock and Izzy dropped off the front running board and jogged into the desert-scape to the right. It was mostly sand and rocks, with a few short bushes. Probably had wildflowers and cactus flowers after the few times it rained each year. The men bunched up, and Lam and Murdock got together.

"Half mile up to the lights," Lam said.

"Let's move out a half mile to the right and hike around the place to see what we can see," Murdock said. "One file, five yards apart by squads."

They hiked forward. Lam was out two hundred yards. This time Murdock went with him.

"Not a big outfit," Lam said. "Looks like maybe three prefab buildings, a couple of generators, and half a dozen trucks. Probably a barracks, a mess building, and one for working on the plut."

"Could be. No fence, no exterior guards that I can see."

"Let's move up closer," Lam suggested. "They could have some exterior fixed guard spots, maybe with machine-gun dugouts."

The line swung in toward the side of the small complex. At two hundred yards, they stopped and both Murdock and Lam used their field glasses to check the building.

"Oh yeah," Lam said. "The truck with the women just stopped at the farthest building." Murdock caught the movement and watched as the women slithered down from the truck into the arms of eager Iranians who led them into the building.

"That one we don't hit if and when we start shooting," Murdock said. "You spot any machine-gun emplacements?"

"No, but there could be some. What time is it?"

Murdock looked at his lighted-dial watch. "Just after oh-three-hundred."

"Not time enough to do good recon tonight and hit them," Lam said. "We need to know how many men they have, which building has the plut, and what kind of guards they have out."

"Get Izzy up here," Murdock said into his mike.

Three minutes later the Iranian CIA agent pushed down beside them in the weeds.

"We still have the uniform from that truck driver?" Murdock asked.

"Yo, I have it," Mahanani said. "Got some bad bullet holes in the chest, but it would fit Izzy."

"Get it up here," Murdock said. He turned to Izzy. "Your chance to do some close-up field work, buddy. You put on the uniform and drop in on your countrymen up there and find out everything you can: how many men, how many scientists, if they have broken down any of the plut yet. We need all the intel we can get. Can you do that?"

"Been waiting four years for a chance like this. Do I have to pack along the guy's AK-47?"

"Best. You have to blend in. Can you do it?"

"Hell yes. We're talking about saving the lives of twenty or thirty million people here. I've got to give it my best shot. I'll radio you back what I get, if I can use one of your Motorolas."

Lam took his set off and put it on Izzy, showing him how it worked in a no-hands operation.

"Go," Murdock said. The rest of the platoon heard the talk and settled down in resting spots ten yards apart.

"What can we do if they have a hundred armed troops in that barracks building?" Jaybird asked on the net.

"No chance," Rafii said. "This is a small operation. They won't risk that many troops when the scientists might goof and radiate everybody in the complex."

"Yeah," Fernandez said. "My guess is about twenty guards, five officers, and six scientists in the plut building. They probably are working around the clock."

"So when we get the word, we should hit them tonight," Jaybird said. "Fuck this waiting until tomorrow night. They could spot us out here in the daylight and then we'd be in big trouble."

"Possible to hit them tonight," Murdock said. "If Professor Fernandez's estimates hold up. We have only three twenties. That could be enough. Remember, when we start shooting, we take out the middle building. We don't touch the other two. One has to be where the women are, and the plut should be in the other one. We'll know as soon as Izzy gets back."

"Must be all the officers in the far building," Gardner said.

"Yeah, but with the first few shots the officers will grab their pants and run out with their sub guns," Prescott said.

"We hope," Jaybird said.

Then it was quiet for a while.

Izzy had been gone a half hour when the Motorola came on. "I wandered into the middle building trying to bum a cigarette. There were twenty men in there sleeping. It's a barracks all right and a kitchen in the far end. I can't get in the plut building. It's got a guard out front, and he says nobody, not even the officers, get in. He didn't have any smokes either. I asked if all five of the radiation guys were inside. He told me there were seven. Two more came up yesterday with a whole batch of lead blankets. That's about it. Three men on the roadblock front gate. I didn't see any interior guards, or any perimeter guards, so I'd say that's about the extent of their manpower."

"Get your CIA ass back here," Murdock said. "Good work. Let's have a net check. Gardner, count up your men."

The men of Bravo Squad sounded off. Then Murdock's men checked in.

"Okay, move up to us here in a line of skirmishers. Gardner. You have one twenty. Your job is to take out the roadblock and kill the two trucks there with the twenties, then do twenties on the barracks building. That's the middle building, Izzy told us. The plut building is the one closest to us. When Izzy gets back, we'll use our twenties on the barracks as Gardner hits the front gate. We move up to a hundred yards before we open fire. Then when the officers come out of their building, we pick them off with rifle and MP-5 fire. When we have reduced the guards, and taken care of the officers' building, we'll take down the plut lab. From there we'll play it by ear. We want at least two or three trucks that will run, so don't trash any more of the six-bys except those at the gate. Everybody on the same page?"

Lam nudged Murdock and pointed out front. Two men were coming toward them, both in Iranian soldier uniforms.

"Hold your fire, SEALs. Izzy here with the catch of the day." The two came into the line and Izzy pushed the other man down. He had captain's bars on his shoulders. "Gents, meet Captain Sasdi. He's the head of the guards. He tells me there are only four scientists inside the plut building and they are starting to break it down into the smaller packages. He told me he disagrees with the idea of Iran having nuclear weapons, or selling the plutonium to unstable nations here or in Africa or anywhere. That's why I let him live."

"Can you get anything else from him?"

"Not a lot."

"How many officers in with the women?"

Izzy asked the captain, using Arabic.

"He says there are seven. He's the Officer of the Day so he had to stay on duty outside."

Murdock grinned, remembering Fernandez's estimation. "Okay, guys, we're moving up to a hundred yards off the nearest building. Gardner, take out the guards at the gate, but save the trucks if you can. All the rest is as before. We don't fire into the plut building. We'll have to do that carefully by hand. Let's move up. Start shooting on my first twenty into the barracks."

Murdock led the line of skirmishers forward. When he figured they were a hundred yards from the closest building, he went to the ground and brought up the Bull Pup, switched it to 20mm and aimed at the middle building they knew now to be the barracks. He sighted in midway along the side of the wooden structure and fired. Almost at once four more weapons fired, then he saw his round hit the barracks, penetrate the thin wood sheeting, and explode inside. He put one more 20mm round into the barracks and then shifted to 5.56 and watched the first men come out of the far building. One man was trying to button his shirt. Another hopped on one foot working on pulling up his pants. Both met angry lead slugs from the SEAL guns and went down.

Murdock saw one of the trucks near the front gate blow up. Three soldiers there scattered but were soon hit by SEAL fire and dropped to the ground. He saw two more 20mm rounds go into the barracks. Half a dozen men staggered out a front door and were met by a barrage of small arms fire that cut them down quickly. Smoke poured out windows now as the barracks caught fire.

Two more officers came out the front door on the far structure, and Murdock's men shot them down and dead.

"Hold fire," Murdock said into his mike. "Watch for runners and nail them. Let's move up. Keep a straight line. Gardner, take your squad and check out the officers' building. Have Rafii yell into the door for the soldiers to come out or they will be hunted down and killed. Remember the women are still in there."

"That's a roger, Cap."

"Alpha, we'll concentrate on the plut building. Let's sprint for it, and watch for any live ones outside." They ran. Jaybird chopped a three-round burst at a soldier running for the front gate. He caught two of the three slugs, went down, sprawling in the powdery dirt, and never got up.

Alpha Squad hit the side of the building and held. Murdock and Lam edged around to the front. The guard who had been there before lay to the side moaning. Bradford put a round into the back of his head and Murdock checked the door. It was locked. He stepped back and fired three rounds of 5.56 into the area right beside the door handle. The door shuddered, then swung open an inch.

Murdock kicked the door open and held to the side of

the building, out of any line of fire. No shots came. He
and Jaybird pointed directions, then they dove into the
opening, Murdock to the right. He rolled and came up on
a concrete slab in a brightly lighted building with no windows and just the one door. The rest of the squad came
into the room right behind them. Ahead he could see the
remains of one plut crate. The other bottle, still crated,
stood to one side.

Izzy saw movement down the building and called out
in Arabic. "Everyone in this building is under arrest. Put
down any weapons you may have and stand and walk
forward with your hands in the air."

Two men in white labcoats came from behind a partial
partition and walked forward. Bradford and Lam put them
on the floor and bound their wrists and ankles with plastic
riot cuffs.

Izzy called again, but no more Arabs came to them.
Murdock checked the layout. The half wall was to the left
and ahead twenty feet. Between here and there he saw a
forklift, several four-wheel carts, but no sign of the large
plut bottle. Murdock signaled to Jaybird, and they covered
each other as they rushed down to the partition. Murdock
looked around it. He jerked his head back and a rifle
cracked ahead and the slug tore into the wooden wall
about where Murdock's head had been.

He dropped to the floor and fired six rounds from the
5.56. He looked around again and saw a man topple
slowly from where he had hidden behind a cardboard box.
Good concealment but no protection.

When the crashing sound of the six rounds died out,
Murdock heard a voice shouting in Arabic from ahead.
He caught most of it, but turned to Izzy, who was right
beside him.

"The man says he's a scientist, not a soldier, but if we
don't stop shooting and get out of his lab within two
minutes, he'll set off a charge of plastic explosives under
the plutonium and kill everyone within a half mile."

29

Izzy looked at Murdock and shook his head. Then he began to tremble. First his hands, then his arms and his torso. He wailed softly and crawled back from the stub wall.

"Rafii, get up here fast," Murdock said. The slender Saudi stepped forward and slid down beside Murdock.

"I heard what he said," Rafii growled. "Let me talk to the sonofabitch."

Murdock nodded.

Rafii's voice came out confident, sure, pleasant, not at all demanding. He spoke in Arabic.

"Look, we don't want to hurt you. Your two friends are here with us and not harmed. You're not soldiers. You're scientists. We respect that. There's no reason anyone must die here. Do you have a family?"

There was a period of silence, then the voice from down the room came softer, less angry. "Yes, yes, I have a wife and three boys. Two are smart, want to be scientists. I say okay, but you must study hard."

"What would happen to them if you die here in this forsaken place?"

"They would not be able to continue school. It is expensive. A private school for gifted children."

"What we're here to do is save lives. Yours and mine, and those of the hundreds of thousands who might be killed if this plutonium is sold to some unstable country which goes ahead and drops a nuclear bomb on its enemies. We don't want that to happen. It could start a domino effect that would produce a worldwide nuclear war. I don't want that. Do you want that?"

"No. But I have to do what I'm ordered to do."

"My name is Omar Rafii. I'm from Saudi Arabia. What's your name?"

A silence. Murdock looked at Rafii and frowned.

"I'm Amud Bardi. I'm a radiologist for a hospital in Tehran."

"The government sent you out here to deal with the radiation of the plutonium?"

"Yes. Then they said I had to break it down into the small lead boxes. I know what they will do with them."

"Sell them to the highest bidder, whether a country or a terrorist organization," Rafii said.

"Yes, but what can I do?"

"Are there any more men in there with you?"

"No, not now. One is dead; two left when you called."

"You could come out now and let us handle the plutonium. We promise that you will not be harmed. You and your colleagues will be free to go back to Tehran."

"I don't know. The government will be furious with me."

"You can stand that a lot better than leaving a widow and your boys, who won't get to go on to school."

Another silent spell. Then the voice came again, closer this time.

"All right. I'm coming out. Don't shoot. I can't stand guns. I'm coming out now."

Rafii told Murdock the man was coming out.

"No shooting," Murdock said on the net. "A man is coming out. Don't hurt him, don't tie him up."

A moment later a man came around the stub wall. He was in his fifties, with gray hair and a long face with a heavy black beard, and his eyes moved from side to side as if trying to assess his chances of staying alive.

"Good, you came," Rafii said. "We won't hurt you. Show us where the other bottle of plutonium is and how you have dealt with it."

Rafii told Murdock what he had said to the Iranian.

Murdock nodded, and the three of them stood while Rafii waved the Iranian back the way he had come.

Murdock, Rafii, and Jaybird followed the man around the stub wall and into a grouping of lead blankets hung from the ceiling and extending from the floor up seven feet. It turned out to be a kind of maze, with the final opening of the black heavy lead blankets leading into an area ten feet square. In the center stood the lead bottle held upright by foot-square chunks of lead. Six empty lead boxes like those they had seen before were on the concrete floor nearby.

"We tried to take the plutonium out of the big lead container," the Iranian scientist said. "In this state the plutonium is a solid that has been formed into balls of various sizes. The balls are what go into the nuclear device. They create the massive explosion. We couldn't roll them out. At last we decided that we need a safe room, heavily shielded with lead blankets and pierced with mechanical arms and hands to move the plutonium balls from the large container into the smaller ones. We've been trying to find such equipment, but it had to come from the West. We found a firm in Germany that would sell it to us, but it would take two weeks to get here. We are still waiting."

As the man talked, Rafii filled in Murdock and the rest of the SEALs with his comments.

"Is the plug still in the large lead container?" Rafii asked.

"Oh yes, we returned it and sealed it when we knew it would be some time. Too much radiation. We wore the radiation suits and had the lead shields, but one of our men got sick almost at once. Radiation poisoning. He died two days ago."

"Who has the Geiger counter?" Murdock asked on the net.

Fernandez said he did and that he'd bring it to the back of the building. "I've seen only trace elements of radiation out here," Fernandez said. "Almost none around the crated plut, so it's safe enough."

Murdock waved and the men moved back from the lead

blanket shields. When Fernandez brought up the Geiger counter, he gave it to Rafii, who hurried back to the lead blankets and began taking readings. He finished quickly and went out near the front of the building, where Murdock talked on the radio.

"Gardner, report in," Murdock said.

"Just about wrapped this up out here. We took down the barracks. Only two live ones inside, who didn't stay that way long. The officers and the girls were tougher. Three of the shitheads used the women as shields. We picked them off one by one. We have the front gate, three trucks, two jeeps, and two sedans. This place belongs to us. We have four prisoners who demanded that we capture them. What we gonna do with them?"

"Give them a water bottle and start them hiking back toward the highway," Murdock said. "We've got what we want. Now how the hell do we move it?"

"Got you on that one, Cap," Gardner said. "We found a forklift that works. Probably the same one they used to unload the trucks and move the goods inside. We're firing it up and moving it and three trucks over near that area. You can take your pick."

The SEALs looked at each other.

"Yeah, we've got it, now what the hell do we do with it?" Jaybird said.

"The man has a mind like a steel sponge," Lam said. "So what can we do with it?"

Murdock waved the men in around him. Men from Bravo straggled in and those driving rigs parked them and came over. "Let's get down to business here. What the hell can we do with this four hundred pounds of weapons-grade Plutonium 239?"

"We can't ruin it for weapons," Canzoneri said. "We don't have any radioactive waste products."

"We can't just scatter it around out here in the desert. It could kill a thousand people before anyone knew what the heavy black balls were," Murdock said.

"You know they're black?" Bradford asked.

"The scientist said they are," Jaybird said.

"What can we do?" Murdock asked.

"Dump it into a deep gully and blast down the sides to hide it good," Prescott said.

"Yeah, but the first good cloudburst would wash all the dirt away and expose the shit," Rafii said.

"No abandoned oil wells out here we could dump the plut down," Gardner said. "We can't truck the stuff very far, only deeper into the desert."

"We can't call in a couple of heavy lifter choppers to take the crates out of the country and stick them into an aircraft carrier's nuke rooms," Mahanani said. "Those big, slow guys would get shot down before they got halfway to the water."

Murdock tried to sum it up: "So we can't take it off-shore, we can't find a well, we can't leave it here or spread it around the landscape out there."

"Only thing left to do is bury it," Lam said. "No bull-dozer or front bucket here to work with, but we can dig a damn big hole with C-5. We find the side of a hill where there isn't a lot of runoff and we blast down about twenty feet and slide the crates in. Then we use the forklift with an eight-foot-wide wooden push frame on the front, so it works like a bulldozer. That way we can fill in the hole and normalize the area."

"I'll vote for that," Claymore said. "We know the Iranians will look for the shit, but chances of them finding it twenty feet down are damn near astronomical."

"Does anybody else have a plan?" Murdock asked. He looked around. "Okay, that's it. Claymore, pick three guys and get working on a push board for the forklift. Gardner, bring the forklift right up to the door. Let's tear down those lead blankets so we can get up to that uncrated plut. We won't bother crating it. Haul those lead blankets outside. We'll drape them over the goods once we put them in our hole. Move it. We don't know how much time we have."

An hour later they had the lead blankets all outside and draped over the bed of one of the two-ton trucks. Lam said he'd used a forklift before, and he maneuvered it into the building and picked up the still crated nuke. It took them ten minutes to work the big crate onto the forks and ease it out the door to the nearest truck. Lam lifted the package a foot at a time, then eased it into the truck and let it lean against the side. Then he went into the building again with the forklift.

Two SEALs had on radiation suits and stood beside the big lead bottle. The container was not long enough to reach across both of the forks. They hustled up four two-inch-thick planks and put them on the forks; then with ropes holding the top of the container, they tilted it over and let it down softly on the planks.

Lam took off his hat and wiped sweat off his forehead and out of his eyes. "Anybody else want to run this thing?" he asked. There were no takers.

He lifted the load a foot off the concrete pad and backed toward the door. Twice he had to move ahead a few feet and take a better angle around the stub wall and furniture. Once outside with the container, Lam relaxed a little. He moved the forklift to the next truck that they had backed right up to the door.

It took him three tries before he had the bottle safely inside the heavy truck. Then he realized he couldn't get the forks out from under the heavy lead container.

"I'm fucked," Lam said. "I can't move the forks."

Claymore laughed. "Man, I thought you said you'd used one of them things. No sweat. We start the truck engine, you put your rig into neutral, and the truck tows you right out to the dumping grounds."

"Might work," Lam said.

"For sure it'll work," Claymore said. "Done it a hundred times out in Iowa on the farm."

Murdock looked over the heavy plank form the men had built to front the forklift once they had the hole blasted. Prescott showed him how they would chain the form in place before using it.

Murdock checked his watch. It was after 0400.

"Two hours to daylight. We've got to move. Gardner,

you stay here with your squad and all the Bull Pups. We could have early morning company. Take out anyone who comes anywhere close to this place. We drive straight west. Oh, we'll need all the C-5 and TNAZ that you Bravo guys have."

They traded weapons, ammo, and explosives, then Alpha got in the trucks and they headed east over a track of a road that might have led somewhere once upon a time.

Three miles from the camp, Murdock stopped the trucks. They had come across two small hills and were out of sight of the men and the camp they had left. Murdock decided against the hill idea. He picked a flat spot without any drainage scars. He stopped the trucks and walked out into the area he wanted. "Right here," he said. "Let's do some blasting."

Murdock knew that digging a hole with explosives wasn't the easiest job. The blasts acted like a bomb going off, and the dirt and rocks flew in every direction. After four charges had been set in the new hole, they found they were only four feet below the surface. Both trucks had shovels on the sides. Murdock brought them over, and they dug holes in the bottom of the pit two feet deep, planted the C-5 in them, and filled up the hole before setting off the explosive. It blasted a lot more dirt out of the hole. The new method hurried the work. After an hour and two thirds of their explosives were used up, they had a bomb crater eight feet deep and twice that wide.

Murdock called a halt. It was starting to show streaks of light in the east. "Bring up the truck. The naked bottle first. Put the lead blankets down the side and on the bottom. Might cushion her a little."

They did, then stood back as Lam lifted the lead bottle off the truck and rolled up to the edge of the hole. The sides were sloping at about a forty-five-degree angle. He lowered the forks to the ground. The lead bottle remained lying on the planks across the blades. He backed up so the tips of the fork blades were on solid ground at the edge of the hole.

"Pry bars," Lam said.

They pulled two two-by-sixes off the pusher for the forklift and edged one end of each behind the bottle and pried it forward. Three tries later the big bottle tipped over, came to the end of the blades, and teetered for a moment, then rolled slowly down the incline and stopped on the bottom. The SEALs cheered.

The plut in the crate was easier. They edged it to the brink and pushed it with the blades until it slid down the side of the hole. It lay half on top of the other bottle but didn't look like it had ruptured it.

Lam went down with the Geiger counter and pronounced it safe. The makeshift bulldozer began to scrape the dirt and rocks back into the hole. Half of it was up to fifty yards away. Lam worked all around the edge of the hole, then attacked a small mound nearby with the points of the forks. He dug into the ground, then used the pusher to get the dirt and rocks and sand over to the hole.

They had the plut well covered, and the lead blankets that had been thrown on top of them, and now it was a matter of getting the land back to looking something like it had before. Lam found another soft spot nearby and pushed fresh sand and rocks and dirt across fifty feet and dropped it all into the hole. They were now only three feet below the surface of the rest of the desert. The depression couldn't stand. Lam kept working the soft areas and pushing the material.

The Motorolas came on. "Murdock, we've got company. Looks like a convoy of three two-ton trucks and a jeep out front. If you hear some shooting back here, it's probably us."

30

Lieutenant (j.g.) Gardner let the convoy get a thousand yards from the main gate, then he opened fire. The three Bull Pups jolted rounds into two of the trucks, stopping them and starting one on fire. The second salvo of 20mm rounds hit the jeep and the last truck in line, which was pinned behind the burning one.

Two dozen men tumbled out of the trucks and scurried into the desert land on both sides of the road. Gardner realized that at some point it had turned from night into day.

"Air bursts," Gardner said, and the three twenties lasered in on the scattered troops and pounded two rounds each that exploded in the air twenty feet over the cowering Iranian soldiers. Half of them never stood again. The men were advancing slowly on the camp, but then they stopped and turned and began to jog back the way they had come. They soon were out of range of the Bull Pups.

"Murdock, looks like we have no more problems up here. Maybe ten of them are still alive and heading for the highway."

"Okay, we're still working here. You have another truck?"

"Roger."

"Get it warmed up and put the women in it and the three scientists and get them driving for the highway. Molly can handle the driver duties. Now all we have to do is figure out how to get out of this clambake without getting a couple hundred bullet holes in our collective skins."

Murdock watched Lam on the forklift. He was getting good at it. They had to re-chain the push board twice, but they were within a foot or so of making the land level again. The forklift had also acted as a light but effective way to compact the dirt and rocks as they went.

"Bradford, you still have that SATCOM?"

"Glued to my back as my glorious leader specified."

"Good. Get its ass up here. We need to do some talking."

They set up the SATCOM satellite operating radio and angled it to the bird in the sky. Murdock got Stroh on the CIA man's personal frequency on the second try.

"We're about wrapped up here. We have a whole pot full of angry Iranian soldiers with guns between us and the wet. What would you suggest?"

"Your mission is successful?"

"The 239 is out of enemy hands and we hope lost forever."

"Good. I owe you two or three. Remember those times we left you inside enemy territory and couldn't get a chopper in to you? Well, now we're gonna bail you out. We're going hard and quick on this. We can get a chopper into your GPS coordinates. We'll run in four F-18s to fly cover for you. Get your GPS wound up and give me those coordinates. Take the most time to get the chopper in to you. We'll check the distance. We have a destroyer forty miles off Iran in the Strait of Hormuz. If you're no more than a hundred miles into Iran, we can grab you with a chopper with no sweat and get back to the destroyer's pad."

"Love the sound of that, Stroh. I may let you come fishing with us again as soon as the yellowtail come in. Now, here are our GPS coordinates. Be sure you take these down exactly."

He read off the series of numbers.

There was some dead air, then Stroh came back on. "Hell, you're only seventy-five miles from the water. Are you ready to move?"

"Been ready for twenty, thirty seconds."

"The bird will be off the destroyer in ten minutes. Then he has a hundred-and-fifteen-mile trip to find you. Show him your spots with a red flare. He should be there in about forty-four minutes from now. The eighteens will take care of any Iranian air that gets curious. See you later on today."

"Thanks, big buddy. You want us to bring out Izzy? He's probably blown here as an agent."

"Yes, bring him out. He's earned a rest."

Izzy heard the talk and came over.

"I'm going out?"

"Right on a wing and a prayer with us."

"Murdock, about inside there, all that plutonium. I mean . . ." Izzy shook his head. "I just freaked out. I know what that devil stuff can do. I lost a friend to radiation poisoning. It's no fun."

"Izzy, you got us here. You did your job. Nobody is saying a word to anybody about the time in the building. Forget it."

Murdock shook hands with the Iranian and then watched Lam do the last load of sand and gravel. He came off the fill and parked the forklift. Then he went back with some cut brush and began wiping out the tracks left by the forklift. Four or five more SEALs cut short brush and worked on the same project. Then they worked over the truck tracks until they couldn't be seen.

Ten minutes later they tied heavy brush bundles on ropes and dragged them on the tire tracks as the trucks and the forklift drove in a roundabout way back to the mostly destroyed camp.

Murdock found Gardner and looked at his stopwatch. "In exactly eighteen minutes we should be visited by a chopper from a destroyer just off the coast. Four F-18s will argue with any Iranian fighters who try to do any harm to us."

"It's a pleasure doing business with you, Murdock. I wondered how we were going to get out of here with those two highways bound to be filled with troops before long."

"The girls and the three radiation guys got off in their truck?"

"They did, and Molly says anytime you're in Tehran, you should look her up. She says she owes you a week of all-nighters."

"True, she does. Trouble is we just might not make it to Tehran for some time."

The SH-60 hugged the ground as it came toward them. It was no more than twenty-five feet off the brush and sand as it raced across the desert at 207mph, defying any radar trying to find it. The pilot must have seen the burned-out camp. He lifted up, checked the red flare Jaybird threw, and settled down in a blinding storm of dust and sand. The SEALs waited for most of it to blow away, then charged on board the bird. Murdock counted noses, including Izzy, and the chopper lifted off, heading back for the Strait of Hormuz but by a different route. When they hit the wet, they turned southwest, and less than an hour later they landed in Al Fujayrah, Oman, where the whole operation had begun less than twenty-four-hours before.

31

The men in Third Platoon, SEAL Team Seven, were restless. It had been a full week that they had been back from the South Pacific by way of Iran, and they didn't have a new assignment. They knew that always meant more and tougher training.

Murdock and Gardner sat in the tiny office of Third and went over a new training schedule.

"How are our cripples coming along?" Murdock asked.

Gardner looked at a clipboard he usually carried. He flipped over two sheets of paper and put his finger on the page.

"Yeah, Ching is back to active. He had an in-and-out in his thigh, but it missed the bone and he's recuperated well. He'll be hurting on a ten-mile, but he'll make it. He's tough.

"Jefferson took two rounds to his right shoulder and is still in Balboa Hospital. The doctors there said he should recover fully, but it will take two months before he's ready for SEAL workouts. Sadler is still in Balboa as well, and his situation is rougher. He took a round through his back and out his chest. Could have killed him. Missed vital organs by millimeters. They got all the lead out of him, but he's scheduled for another month at Balboa before he goes home. Then they say it will be two more months before he can tell if he's fit for SEAL work.

"Howard had two rounds, now we learn, in his right leg. Nothing serious. In-and-outs, and no bones touched.

He's back to active, but he'll be hurting on the O course and on anything in a swim of over five."

"Temp replacements or permanent?" Murdock asked.

Gardner twisted his mouth and rubbed his jaw. "Damn, hard call. Sadler is an important cog in our machine. But we stand the chance he won't make it back. In the meantime we have a three- or four-month gap. We've got to plug in a man. I'd say to go First Platoon of Seventh and grab their senior chief as a repo on a temp basis that could go permanent if we like him and if Senior Chief Sadler can't get back."

"Jefferson?"

"He's out for two months. Yes, we need a temp in there. We could get a call and I don't want to go out a man short."

"You know the senior chief at First. See if the master chief can request him. Then ask the Scotsman for three volunteers we can look at to plug up Jefferson's spot."

"Will do, Skipper." He turned to the phone. Murdock went back to his after-action report, which wasn't done yet. So much had happened in those few days.

When the last training hike was over, Ching limped over to his locker and got into his civvies. He had been thinking about what Kwan Tung had done to him less than three weeks ago. The police had found his burned car, and the insurance company had paid off while he was gone. Now he had a different car, not a new one but good enough. There was no arrest warrant out for him that he had been able to discover. Now it was time to pay back Kwan Tung for the beating he had taken and how they had tried to frame him for the murder of the girl who had been slashed and stabbed and thrown in the backseat of his car. Only the cleansing of fire had saved him from a murder charge.

Now for Kwan Tung and his entrenched tong. He ran the largest and only Chinese tong in San Diego. Others tried to start but were cut down ruthlessly by Tung. Ching had thought many times about how to punish Kwan Tung for what he had done—the humiliation, the beating, the try at framing him for murder. The retribution had to be just right, not too severe. He wouldn't burn down the restaurant. That would punish the people who worked there as well. It had to be pointed, humiliating if possible, painful, and costly to the old millionaire. But exactly what?

He drove his three-year-old Ford Expedition across the bridge and into downtown San Diego. One drive past Tung's place, the Friendly Dragon restaurant, didn't bring any ideas. He parked up the block, where he could see the place, and studied it.

Now with his aging problems, the old Chinese had moved into an apartment in back of the restaurant on the third floor. Ching had heard it was beautifully decorated in Old China style. A strike there would unnerve the old man. Yes. He drove on to his apartment, had a delivered pizza and a beer for his dinner and a short nap. At midnight he dressed in a black T-shirt with long sleeves, black pants, and black running shoes. He took only two weapons with him: a Colt .45 with a stub silencer in his waistband, for huge emergencies, and a slender knife in a scabbard on his left forearm, outside the T-shirt and easy to get.

His first probe might just be a recon. He'd play it by ear. The old Chinese was going to hurt; he was going to know that it was Ching who hurt him, and he was going to be so confused and worried that he would never try to harm Ching again. That was the plan.

He parked two blocks away and watched the night. Not much moved on this side street. It was just after 0100. He went up the alley behind the restaurant, keeping to the shadows. Partway up he found two men sleeping on cardboard next to a building, with cardboard folded over them. Their shoes were off and probably cradled in their arms so no one would steal them. A homeless person once told Ching that at night his biggest worry was losing his shoes.

The third story of the Friendly Dragon showed ahead. Ching went up an access ladder to the roof of a one-story building next to the restaurant, and then worked up a grating and a vent pipe to gain the roof of the two-story section of the Dragon. He went over the edge of the roof and lay absolutely still. Nothing moved in front of him. He saw the windows of the third floor. Two were lighted. Two were dark. He didn't know where the tong leader's rooms were. Ching lay there for five minutes, checking out the rooftop, the vents, the one door on the third floor that opened on a small patio built over the second-floor roof. A variety of plants and two small trees grew there.

Just before Ching moved, he saw a figure come away from the plants and begin a search of the rooftop. He figured Tung would have some security out. The man carried no obvious weapon, but Ching figured he had at least a pistol. Ching inched his way forward; then when the guard looked the other way, Ching rolled twice to the protection of a roof vent. It shielded him completely. Lights coming from the third-floor windows and from the downtown glow left the rooftop in half-light. The guard vanished across the forty-foot-wide roof, then came along the side of the closer area. Ching edged around the four-foot-square vent, keeping it between him and the guard.

Once the man came close enough, Ching would take him down. He wouldn't kill him. The man was doing his job. Ching waited.

It was another five minutes before the slow-moving guard came into the right position. Ching had the heavy .45 in his right hand, and when the guard turned to check to the side, Ching attacked. He took three running steps and dove at the man's waist, bringing him down with a good tackle. Ching swung up the .45 and slammed it into the guard's head as the two bodies fell to the black tar rooftop. The guard gave a sigh and passed out. Ching used plastic riot cuffs and tied his hands and ankles, then put a no-harm gag across his mouth and tied it in back of his head. He pulled the guard behind the vent and slipped across the roof without a sound, to the first lighted window.

Inside he could see half of a living room, with one long

couch, a small desk, a large-screen TV, and several other chairs. Kwan Tung, in a formal Chinese robe, sat in a recliner chair. In the next chair sat a young man of maybe twenty. They were snacking on a tray of food and each had a drink in a tall glass. Ching had not come with a plan. Now one started to form in his mind. It would be a blow that Kwan Tung could never recover from. He would have to sell his business here and move somewhere, change his name, try to avoid any tie with San Diego.

Ching smiled as he thought of it. Yes, it would work. The young man would recover. He wouldn't be identified. Yes. Ching looked at the window. It was multi-paned, with narrow strips of bamboo holding the panes together. He looked again and saw that the two men watched a movie on TV. He was about ready to make his move when a door down the side of the building opened on the patio and a man came out. He was older, moved slower than the first guard, but he carried a pistol.

"Chung, where are you?" the man called in a voice that carried across the rooftop. "If you're drunk on duty again, I'll have your ears and your father will disinherit you. Come on, come out from where you're hiding."

The second guard walked toward Ching, who edged against the building, past a small out-thrust that gave him cover. The guard kept talking as he came. At the last second, Ching leaped out from his hiding spot and hit the extended wrist of the guard's pistol arm with the butt of his .45. He heard the bones crack. The guard gave a startled cry of pain; then the .45 slashed across his forehead and he passed out. Ching caught him and put him on the roof. He tied his hands and ankles and put on a gag. Then he looked back inside. The two men were as they had been before.

Ching backed up and judged the distance. Then he ran, ducked his head, lowered his shoulder, and hit the multipanel window, smashing it inward, jolting many of the glass panels out of their holders, and breaking others. He hit the window shoulder-high, dove to the carpet inside, rolled, and came to his feet with the .45 up and pointed at the pair.

"Don't move, don't make a sound, or I'll kill both of you," Ching said.

Kwan Tung squinted. "Yes, I know you. The disloyal son of an old friend from San Francisco. Yes. Ching. I remember."

"Good, old man. I'm here to pay you back for trying to kill me, and for trying to frame me for one of your killings. She was probably just one of your prostitutes, but she was a human being."

The young man moved his arm, and Ching fired a silenced round into the chair beside him.

"I don't know who you are, kid, but one more move like that and you're dead meat, understand?

"Yes, yes." Sweat poured off the young Chinese man's forehead and ran into his eyes. He shivered.

"I want you to know who I am," Ching said. "When this is over, you'll never send any of your men near me, understand? You'll never again try to harm me, or I'll go to the police with what I know." Ching looked around the room. A vase sat on a coffee table. Nothing was in it. It was a delicate design, and Ching knew it must be one of the famous collection of Ming Dynasty vases the old man was so proud of.

Ching backed toward the table, keeping the men under his gun. He picked up the vase and threw it against the wall. It shattered into a hundred pieces.

Kwan Tung gasped, then his face turned red and he blurted out words that made little sense. He calmed slowly and glared at Ching.

"That vase was a Ming. It had been valued at more than a million and a half dollars. You are a beast."

"I'm just getting started. Right now I want you, old man, to strip naked. Now. Do it now or I'll put a bullet in each of your knees and you'll never walk again."

Slowly the old Chinese stripped off the robe. He wore little under it, an undershirt and boxer shorts. He pulled them off and sat back in the chair.

"Yes," Ching said. "Good. Now, young Chinese man, on your knees in front of him, then bury your face in his crotch."

"No," Tung bellowed. "I won't permit it." Ching shot him in the right arm and the old man screamed in pain and frustration. Ching pushed the young man down until his face was over the old man's genitals. Then he took out his pocket-sized digital camera and took five shots. He made the young man strip, and the men changed places so the old Chinese had his head in the young man's crotch. Ching took ten pictures this time, so the side of Tung's face would show but not that of the young man.

"You'll never get away with it," Tung shouted. "I have many contacts. I know people in high places."

"You also know how the Chinese community hates homosexuals. They don't foster the benefits of the family. They don't produce offspring to maintain a family line. They don't grow an extended family to create wealth. They are a festering boil on the backside of humanity." He watched Tung's face blanch white and sweat bead his wrinkled forehead.

"When I send copies of these pictures to the honorable men in the Chinese community, you'll be finished, Tung. The police won't care, but every Chinese in town will spit on you. No one will work for you. You'll have to sell your restaurant and other businesses at a fraction of what they are worth. You're finished, Tung—done, through, busted."

He saw three more vases, these in a protected glass case. He shot the door to the case and the glass shattered. Then he shot all three of the vases with the silenced rounds, blasting them into dozens of pieces.

Tung cried as he watched. Then he began sobbing. "You are a beast."

"Tell that to the next man you try to coerce into your foul tong. Try to make me believe that, when you tried to kill me and frame me when I wouldn't accept your offer. You're the outlaw here, Tung. You're the bastard grinding everyone down to fit into your plan and your scheme."

He looked at the young man, still on the big chair. Tung had collapsed on the thick carpet. "You can get your clothes on now, young one. You will never repeat a word about what happened here tonight. You'll be as surprised as everyone else when it turns out that Tung here is a pedophile and a homosexual. You will wait here for an hour before you leave. You will not let Tung use the phone or his cell phone or summon any help. Then you will leave and never think of this night again. Agreed?"

The man nodded and grabbed his shorts and pants. Ching looked around the room. There were some more Ming vases, he was sure, but the old man had paid his retribution. Ching held the pistol as he moved toward the broken window.

"There are two guards tied up out here. Young man, after your hour, go outside and untie them. Understood?"

The young Chinese's teeth had stopped chattering. The sweat had eased somewhat on his forehead. He slipped into his silk shirt and spoke softly. "Yes. I will do that. I'll do what you say."

Ching stepped through the broken window and hurried across the second-story roof and down the same way he had come up. Soon he was in the alley and jogging toward the end. The .45 with its long silencer was safely stowed in his waistband. He checked with caution at the street, saw only one car moving away, and turned and walked briskly toward his Ford Expedition. He was liking the utility rig more and more. Gas mileage was terrible, but he could stand that. He grinned as he thought of how he had taken down Kwan Tung. He wondered how long it would be before the old Chinese man moved out of town.

Ching hurried home to his apartment in Coronado, turned on his computer and color printer and printed out the digital pictures of Kwan Tung seemingly in the throes of a homosexual act. Yes, they would work. Before morning he would have a dozen posted on various telephone poles in Chinatown. Tomorrow six prominent Chinese community leaders would receive letters, each with four of the pictures inside. No note, no message, just the pictures that had been carefully handled with latex gloves, so they would show no fingerprints. He'd be up late, but should get to muster tomorrow morning on time. Yeah, Ching decided. A damn good night's work.

That same evening, after duty with the SEALs was over, Murdock turned his car over the bridge and toward the surfside community of Ocean Beach, halfway across town. He and Ardith had moved into the new condo on the very edge of La Jolla. Technically it was in La Jolla, but it had more of the flavor of the downscale Ocean Beach. In the condo, boxes were everywhere; some new furniture had arrived. They had pitched out some of the old stuff. Murdock got home just before Ardith did, from her job as a creative analyst in a computer-driven operation. She still wasn't quite sure what she was supposed to be doing.

Murdock slumped in a new recliner chair and stared at the spot where the TV would be. Second-floor condo. No yard work, no repairs or house maintenance, no yard either, or anywhere to plant a vegetable garden if he wanted one. Three hundred and twenty thousand dollars. He'd never dreamed he would buy anything that cost that much.

Ardith came in and sat on his lap. She nuzzled his neck a minute and then kissed him slow and long and hard.

"I think the lady is trying to tell me something," Murdock said.

"I don't know about the lady. But this woman is giving you a big, fat signal that I want your lean and mean body in the bedroom so we can test that new king-sized mattress. I mean, we have to initiate it. What if it doesn't work?"

Murdock grinned. "So far, sexy lady, everything we have tested, from the backseat of our car to the kitchen floor in the other apartment, has worked just dandy."

Ardith smiled, kissed him again, and reached for his

crotch. He caught her hand, lifted her away from him, and stood.

"Race you to the bedroom," Ardith said, unbuttoning her blouse.

"You'll win. I don't even remember where the bedroom is."

"Follow me, oh noble warrior. I'm going to have you jumping through the noodle before you know it."

Much, much later that night, or early morning, Murdock cupped one of Ardith's breasts with his hand and listened to her purr. He jolted his mind back to business. They had been beat up badly on the last mission. Four men wounded. At least no KIAs. They needed at least a month to get back into the swing, to get the coordination, to integrate two new men into the squads. Would they have that much time? There were so many hot spots around the globe right now, it was a crapshoot where they might end up next. In a strangely exciting way, Murdock couldn't wait for their next assignment.

Ardith purred again, then turned his face around and kissed him with all sorts of promises. "Hey, big guy, you just teasing me, or do you want to see if we can get sexy again?"

He rolled her over on top of him. "Hey, little one. Ready when you are, C.B."

SEAL TALK

MILITARY GLOSSARY

Aalvin: Small U.S. two-man submarine.

Admin: Short for administration.

Aegis: Advanced Naval air defense radar system.

AH-1W Super Cobra: Has M179 undernose turret with 20mm Gatling gun.

AK-47: 7.64-round Russian Kalashnikov automatic rifle. Most widely used assault rifle in the world.

AK-74: New, improved version of the Kalashnikov. Fires the 5.45mm round. Has 30-round magazine. Rate of fire: 600 rounds per minute. Many slight variations made for many different nations.

AN/PRC-117D: Radio, also called SATCOM. Works with Milstar satellite in 22,300-mile equatorial orbit for instant worldwide radio, voice, or video communications. Size: 15 inches high, 3 inches wide, 3 inches deep. Weighs 15 pounds. Microphone and voice output. Has encrypter, capable of burst transmissions of less than a second.

AN/PUS-7: Night-vision goggles. Weighs 1.5 pounds.

ANVIS-6: Night-vision goggles on air crewmen's helmets.

APC: Armored Personnel Carrier.

ASROC: Nuclear-tipped antisubmarine rocket torpedoes launched by Navy ships.

Assault Vest: Combat vest with full loadouts of ammo, gear.

ASW: Anti-Submarine Warfare.

Attack Board: Molded plastic with two handgrips with bubble compass on it. Also depth gauge and Cyalume chemical lights with twist knob to regulate amount of light. Used for underwater guidance on long swim.

Aurora: Air Force recon plane. Can circle at 90,000 feet. Can't be seen or heard from ground. Used for thermal imaging.

AWACS: Airborne Warning And Control System. Radar units in high-flying aircraft to scan for planes at any altitude out 200 miles. Controls air-to-air engagements with enemy forces. Planes have a mass of communication and electronic equipment.

Balaclavas: Headgear worn by some SEALs.

Bent Spear: Less serious nuclear violation of safety.

BKA, Bundeskriminant: Germany's federal investigation unit.

Black Talon: Lethal hollow-point ammunition made by Winchester. Outlawed some places.

Blivet: A collapsible fuel container. SEALs sometimes use it.

BLU-43B: Antipersonnel mine used by SEALs.

BLU-96: A fuel-air explosive bomb. It disperses a fuel oil into the air, then explodes the cloud. Many times more powerful than conventional bombs because it doesn't carry its own chemical oxidizers.

BMP-1: Soviet armored fighting vehicle (AFV), low, boxy, crew of 3 and 8 combat troops. Has tracks and a 73mm cannon. Also an AT-3 Sagger antitank missile and coaxial machine gun.

Body Armor: Far too heavy for SEAL use in the water.

Bogey: Pilots' word for an unidentified aircraft.

Boghammar Boat: Long, narrow, low dagger boat; high-speed patrol craft. Swedish make. Iran had 40 of them in 1993.

Boomer: A nuclear-powered missile submarine.

Bought It: A man has been killed. Also "bought the farm."

Bow Cat: The bow catapult on a carrier to launch jets.

Broken Arrow: Any accident with nuclear weapons, or any incident of nuclear material lost, shot down, crashed, stolen, hijacked.

Browning 9mm High Power: A Belgian 9mm pistol, 13 rounds in magazine. First made 1935.

Buddy Line: 6 feet long, ties 2 SEALs together in the water for control and help if needed.

BUD/S: Coronado, California, nickname for SEAL training facility for six months' course.

Bull Pup: Still in testing; new soldier's rifle. SEALs have a dozen of them for regular use. Army gets them in 2005. Has a 5.56 kinetic round, 30-shot clip. Also 20mm high-explosive round and 5-shot magazine. Twenties can be fused for proximity airbursts with use of video camera, laser range finder, and laser targeting. Fuses by number of turns the round needs to reach laser spot. Max range: 1200 yards. Twenty round can also detonate on contact, and has delay fuse. Weapon weighs 14 pounds. SEALs love it. Can in effect "shoot around corners" with the airburst feature.

BUPERS: BUreau of PERSonnel.

C-2A Greyhound: 2-engine turboprop cargo plane that lands on carriers. Also called COD, Carrier Onboard Delivery. Two pilots and engineer. Rear fuselage loading ramp. Cruise speed 300 mph, range 1,000 miles. Will hold 39 combat troops. Lands on CVN carriers at sea.

C-4: Plastic explosive. A claylike explosive that can be molded and shaped. It will burn. Fairly stable.

C-6 Plastique: Plastic explosive. Developed from C-4 and C-5. Is often used in bombs with radio detonator or digital timer.

C-9 Nightingale: Douglas DC-9 fitted as a medical-evacuation transport plane.

C-130 Hercules: Air Force transporter for long haul. 4 engines.

C-141 Starlifter: Airlift transport for cargo, paratroops, evac for long distances. Top speed 566 mph. Range with payload 2,935 miles. Ceiling 41,600 feet.

Caltrops: Small four-pointed spikes used to flatten tires. Used in the Crusades to disable horses.

Camel Back: Used with drinking tube for 70 ounces of water attached to vest.

Cammies: Working camouflaged wear for SEALs. Two different patterns and colors. Jungle and desert.

Cannon Fodder: Old term for soldiers in line of fire destined to die in the grand scheme of warfare.

CAP: Continuous Air Patrol.

Capped: Killed, shot, or otherwise snuffed.

CAR-15: The Colt M-4A1. Sliding-stock carbine with grenade launcher under barrel. Knight sound-suppressor. Can have AN/PAQ-4 laser aiming light under the carrying handle. .223 round. 20- or 30-round magazine. Rate of fire: 700 to 1,000 rounds per minute.

Cascade Radiation: U-235 triggers secondary radiation in other dense materials.

Castle Keep: The main tower in any castle.

Cast Off: Leave a dock, port, land. Get lost. Navy: long, then short signal of horn, whistle, or light.

Caving Ladder: Roll-up ladder that can be let down to climb.

CH-46E: Sea Knight chopper. Twin rotors, transport. Can carry 25 combat troops. Has a crew of 3. Cruise speed 154 mph. Range 420 miles.

CH-53D Sea Stallion: Big Chopper. Not used much anymore.

Chaff: A small cloud of thin pieces of metal, such as tinsel, that can be picked up by enemy radar and that can attract a radar-guided missile away from the plane to hit the chaff.

Charlie-Mike: Code words for continue the mission.

Chief to Chief: Bad conduct by EM handled by chiefs so no record shows or is passed up the chain of command.

Chocolate Mountains: Land training center for SEALs near these mountains in the California desert.

Christians In Action: SEAL talk for not-always-friendly CIA.

CIA: Central Intelligence Agency.

CIC: Combat Information Center. The place on a ship where communications and control areas are situated to open and control combat fire.

CINC: Commander IN Chief.

CINCLANT: Navy Commander-IN-Chief, atLANTtic.

CINCPAC: Navy Commander-IN-Chief, PACific.

Class of 1978: Not a single man finished BUD/S training in this class. All-time record.

Claymore: An antipersonnel mine carried by SEALs on many of their missions.

Cluster Bombs: A canister bomb that explodes and spreads small bomblets over a great area. Used against parked aircraft, massed troops, and unarmored vehicles.

CNO: Chief of Naval Operations.

CO: Commanding Officer.

CO-2 Poisoning: During deep dives. Abort dive at once and surface.

COD: Carrier Onboard Delivery plane.

Cold Pack Rations: Food carried by SEALs to use if needed.

Combat Harness: American Body Armor nylon-mesh special-operations vest. 6 2-magazine pouches for drum-fed belts, other pouches for other weapons, waterproof pouch for Motorola.

CONUS: The Continental United States.

Corfams: Dress shoes for SEALs.

Covert Action Staff: A CIA group that handles all covert action by the SEALs.

CP: Command Post.

CQB house: Close Quarters Battle house. Training facility near Nyland in the desert training area. Also called the Kill House.

CQB: Close Quarters Battle. A fight that's up close, hand-to-hand, whites-of-his-eyes, blood all over you.

CRRC Bundle: Roll it off plane, sub, boat. The assault boat for 8 SEALs. Also the IBS, Inflatable Boat Small.

Cutting Charge: Lead-sheathed explosive. Triangular strip of high-velocity explosive sheathed in metal. Point of the triangle focuses a shaped-charge effect. Cuts a pencil-line-wide hole to slice a steel girder in half.

CVN: A U.S. aircraft carrier with nuclear power. Largest that we have in fleet.

CYA: Cover Your Ass, protect yourself from friendlies or officers above you and JAG people.

Damfino: Damned if I know. SEAL talk.

DDS: Dry Dock Shelter. A clamshell unit on subs to deliver SEALs and SDVs to a mission.

DEFCON: DEFense CONdition. How serious is the threat?

Delta Forces: Army special forces, much like SEALs.

Desert Cammies: Three-color, desert tan and pale green with streaks of pink. For use on land.

DIA: Defense Intelligence Agency.

Dilos Class Patrol Boat: Greek, 29 feet long, 75 tons displacement.

Dirty Shirt Mess: Officers can eat there in flying suits on board a carrier.

DNS: Doppler Navigation System.

Draegr LAR V: Rebreather that SEALs use. No bubbles.

DREC: Digitally Reconnoiterable Electronic Component. Top-secret computer chip from NSA that lets it decipher any U.S. military electronic code.

E-2C Hawkeye: Navy, carrier-based, Airborne Early Warning craft for long-range early warning and threat-assessment and fighter-direction. Has a 24-foot saucer-like rotodome over the wing. Crew 5, max speed 326 knots, ceiling 30,800 feet, radius 175 nautical miles with 4 hours on station.

E-3A Skywarrior: Old electronic intelligence craft. Replaced by the newer ES-3A.

E-4B NEACP: Called Kneecap. National Emergency Airborne Command Post. A greatly modified Boeing 747 used as a communications base for the President of the United States and other high-ranking officials in an emergency and in wartime.

E & E: SEAL talk for escape and evasion.

EA-6B Prowler: Navy plane with electronic countermeasures. Crew of 4, max speed 566 knots, ceiling 41,200 feet, range with max load 955 nautical miles.

EAR: Enhanced Acoustic Rifle. Fires not bullets, but a high-impact blast of sound that puts the target down and unconscious for up to six hours. Leaves him with almost no aftereffects. Used as a non-lethal weapon. The sound blast will bounce around inside a building, vehicle, or ship and knock out anyone who is within range. Ten shots before the weapon must be electrically charged. Range: about 400 yards.

Easy: The only easy day was yesterday. SEAL talk.

Ejection seat: The seat is powered by a CAD, a shotgun-like shell that is activated when the pilot triggers the ejection. The shell is fired into a solid rocket, sets it off and propels the whole ejection seat and pilot into the air. No electronics are involved.

ELINT: ELectronic INTelligence. Often from satellite in orbit, picture-taker, or other electronic communications.

EMP: ElectroMagnetic Pulse: The result of an E-bomb detonation. One type E-bomb is the Flux Compression Generator or FCG. Can be built for $400 and is relatively simple to make. Emits a rampaging electromagnetic pulse that destroys anything electronic in a 100 mile diameter circle. Blows out and fries all computers, telephone systems, TV broadcasts, radio, streetlights, and sends the area back into the Stone Age with no communications whatsoever. Stops all cars with electronic ignitions, drops jet planes out of the air including airliners, fighters and bombers, and stalls ships with electronic guidance and steering systems. When such a bomb is detonated the explosion is small but sounds like a giant lightning strike.

EOD: Navy experts in nuclear material and radioactivity who do Explosive Ordnance Disposal.

Equatorial Satellite Pointing Guide: To aim antenna for radio to pick up satellite signals.

ES-3A: Electronic Intelligence (ELINT) intercept craft. The platform for the battle group Passive Horizon Extension System. Stays up for long patrol periods, has comprehensive set of sensors, lands and takes off from a carrier. Has 63 antennas.

ETA: Estimated Time of Arrival. The planned time that you will arrive at a given destination.

Executive Order 12333: By President Reagan authorizing Special Warfare units such as the SEALs.

Exfil: Exfiltrate, to get out of an area.

F/A-18 Hornet: Carrier-based interceptor that can change from air-to-air to air-to-ground attack mode while in flight.

Fitrep: Fitness Report.

Flashbang Grenade: Non-lethal grenade that gives off a series of piercing explosive sounds and a series of brilliant strobe-type lights to disable an enemy.

Flotation Bag: To hold equipment, ammo, gear on a wet operation.

FO: Forward Observer. A man or unit set in an advanced area near or past friendly lines to call in artillery or mortar fire. Also used simply as the eyes of the rear echelon planners.

Fort Fumble: SEALs' name for the Pentagon.

Forty-mm Rifle Grenade: The M576 multipurpose round, contains 20 large lead balls. SEALs use on Colt M-4A1.

Four-Striper: A Navy captain.

Fox Three: In air warfare, a code phrase showing that a Navy F-14 has launched a Phoenix air-to-air missile.

FUBAR: SEAL talk. Fucked Up Beyond All Repair.

Full Helmet Masks: For high-altitude jumps. Oxygen in mask.

G-3: German-made assault rifle.

GHQ: General Headquarters.

Gloves: SEALs wear sage-green, fire-resistant Nomex flight gloves.

GMT: Greenwich Mean Time. Where it's all measured from.

GPS: Global Positioning System. A program with satellites around Earth to pinpoint precisely aircraft, ships, vehicles, and ground troops. Position information is to plus or minus ten feet. Also can give speed of a plane or ship to one quarter of a mile per hour.

GPSL: A radio antenna with floating wire that pops to the surface. Antenna picks up positioning from the closest 4 global positioning satellites and gives an exact position within 10 feet.

Green Tape: Green sticky ordnance tape that has a hundred uses for a SEAL.

GSG-9: Flashbang grenade developed by Germans. A cardboard tube filled with 5 separate charges timed to burst in rapid succession. Blinding and giving concussion to enemy, leaving targets stunned, easy to kill or capture. Usually non-lethal.

GSG9: Grenzschutzgruppe Nine. Germany's best special warfare unit, counterterrorist group.

Gulfstream II (VCII): Large executive jet used by services for transport of small groups quickly. Crew of 3 and 18 passengers. Maximum cruise speed 581 mph. Maximum range 4,275 miles.

H & K 21A1: Machine gun with 7.62 NATO round. Replaces the older, more fragile M-60 E3. Fires 900 rounds per minute. Range 1,100 meters. All types of NATO rounds, ball, incendiary, tracer.

H & K G-11: Automatic rifle, new type. 4.7mm caseless ammunition. 50-round magazine. The bullet is in a sleeve of solid propellant with a special thin plastic coating around it. Fires 600 rounds per minute. Single-shot, three-round burst, or fully automatic.

H & K MP-5SD: 9mm submachine gun with integral silenced barrel, single-shot, three-shot, or fully automatic. Rate 800 rds/min.

H & K P9S: Heckler & Koch's 9mm Parabellum double-action semiauto pistol with 9-round magazine.

H & K PSG1: 7.62 NATO round. High-precision, bolt-action, sniping rifle. 5- to 20-round magazine. Roller lock delayed blowback breech system. Fully adjustable stock. 6 × 42 telescopic sights. Sound suppressor.

HAHO: High Altitude jump, High Opening. From 30,000 feet, open chute for glide up to 15 miles to ground. Up to 75 minutes in glide. To enter enemy territory or enemy position unheard.

Half-Track: Military vehicle with tracked rear drive and wheels in front, usually armed and armored.

HALO: High Altitude jump, Low Opening. From 30,000 feet. Free fall in 2 minutes to 2,000 feet and open chute. Little forward movement. Get to ground quickly, silently.

Hamburgers: Often called sliders on a Navy carrier.

Handie-Talkie: Small, handheld personal radio. Short range.

HE: High Explosives.

HELO: SEAL talk for helicopter.

Herky Bird: C-130 Hercules transport. Most-flown military transport in the world. For cargo or passengers, paratroops, aerial refueling, search and rescue, communications, and as a gunship. Has flown from a Navy carrier deck without use of catapult. Four turboprop engines, max speed 325 knots, range at max payload 2,356 miles.

Hezbollah: Lebanese Shiite Moslem militia. Party of God.

HMMWV: The Humvee, U.S. light utility truck, replaced the honored jeep. Multipurpose wheeled vehicle, 4 × 4, automatic transmission, power steering. Engine: Detroit Diesel 150-hp diesel V-8 air-cooled. Top speed 65 mph. Range 300 miles.

Hotels: SEAL talk for hostages.

HQ: Headquarters.

Humint: Human Intelligence. Acquired on the ground; a person as opposed to satellite or photo recon.

Hydra-Shock: Lethal hollow-point ammunition made by Federal Cartridge Company. Outlawed in some areas.

Hypothermia: Danger to SEALs. A drop in body temperature that can be fatal.

IBS: Inflatable Boat Small. 12 × 6 feet. Carries 8 men and 1,000 pounds of weapons and gear. Hard to sink. Quiet motor. Used for silent beach, bay, lake landings.

IP: Initial Point. This can be a gathering place for a unit or force prior to going to the PD on a mission.

IR Beacon: Infrared beacon. For silent nighttime signaling.

IR Goggles: "Sees" heat instead of light.

Islamic Jihad: Arab holy war.

Isothermal layer: A colder layer of ocean water that deflects sonar rays. Submarines can hide below it, but then are also blind to what's going on above them since their sonar will not penetrate the layer.

IV Pack: Intravenous fluid that you can drink if out of water.

JAG: Judge Advocate General. The Navy's legal investigating arm that is independent of any Navy command.

JNA: Yugoslav National Army.

JP-4: Normal military jet fuel.

JSOC: Joint Special Operations Command.

JSOCCOMCENT: Joint Special Operations Command Center in the Pentagon.

KA-BAR: SEALs' combat, fighting knife.

KATN: Kick Ass and Take Names. SEAL talk, get the mission in gear.

KH-11: Spy satellite, takes pictures of ground, IR photos, etc.

KIA: Killed In Action.

KISS: Keep It Simple, Stupid. SEAL talk for streamlined operations.

Klick: A kilometer of distance. Often used as a mile. From Vietnam era, but still widely used in military.

Krytrons: Complicated, intricate timers used in making nuclear explosive detonators.

KV-57: Encoder for messages, scrambles.

Laser Pistol: The SIW pinpoint of ruby light emitted on any pistol for aiming. Usually a silenced weapon.

Left Behind: In 30 years SEALs have seldom left behind a dead comrade, never a wounded one. Never been taken prisoner.

Let's Get the Hell out of Dodge: SEAL talk for leaving a place, bugging out, hauling ass.

Liaison: Close-connection, cooperating person from one unit or service to another. Military liaison.

Light Sticks: Chemical units that make light after twisting to release chemicals that phosphoresce.

Loot & Shoot: SEAL talk for getting into action on a mission.

LT: Short for lieutenant in SEAL talk.

LZ: Landing Zone.

M1-8: Russian Chopper.

M1A1 M-14: Match rifle upgraded for SEAL snipers.

M-3 Submachine Gun: WWII grease gun, .45-caliber. Cheap. Introduced in 1942.

M-16: Automatic U.S. rifle. 5.56 round. Magazine 20 or 30, rate of fire 700 to 950 rds/min. Can attach M203 40mm grenade launcher under barrel.

M-18 Claymore: Antipersonnel mine. A slab of C-4 with 200 small ball bearings. Set off electrically or by trip wire. Can be positioned and aimed. Sprays out a cloud of balls. Kill zone 50 meters.

M60 Machine Gun: Can use 100-round ammo box snapped onto the gun's receiver. Not used much now by SEALs.

M-60E3: Lightweight handheld machine gun. Not used now by the SEALs.

M61A1: The usual 20mm cannon used on many American fighter planes.

M61(j): Machine Pistol. Yugoslav make.

M662: A red flare for signaling.

M-86: Pursuit Deterrent Munitions. Various types of mines, grenades, trip-wire explosives, and other devices in antipersonnel use.

M-203: A 40mm grenade launcher fitted under an M-16 or the M-4A1 Commando. Can fire a variety of grenade types up to 200 yards.

MagSafe: Lethal ammunition that fragments in human body and does not exit. Favored by some police units to cut down on second kill from regular ammunition exiting a body.

Make a Peek: A quick look, usually out of the water, to check your position or tactical situation.

Mark 23 Mod O: Special operations offensive handgun system. Double-action, 12-round magazine. Ambidextrous safety and mag-release catches. Knight screw-on suppressor. Snap-on laser for sighting. .45-caliber. Weighs 4 pounds loaded. 9.5 inches long; with silencer, 16.5 inches long.

Mark II Knife: Navy-issue combat knife.

Mark VIII SDV: Swimmer Delivery Vehicle. A bus, SEAL talk. 21 feet long, beam and draft 4 feet, 6 knots for 6 hours.

Master-at-Arms: Military police commander on board a ship.

MAVRIC Lance: A nuclear alert for stolen nukes or radio-active goods.

MC-130 Combat Talon: A specially equipped Hercules for covert missions in enemy or unfriendly territory.

McMillan M87R: Bolt-action sniper rifle. .50-caliber. 53 inches long. Bipod, fixed 5- or 10-round magazine. Bulbous muzzle brake on end of barrel. Deadly up to a mile. All types .50-caliber ammo.

MGS: Modified Grooming Standards. So SEALs don't all look like military, to enable them to do undercover work in mufti.

MH-53J: Chopper, updated CH053 from Nam days. 200 mph, called the Pave Low III.

MH-60K Black Hawk: Navy chopper. Forward infrared system for low-level night flight. Radar for terra follow/avoidance. Crew of 3, takes 12 troops. Top speed 225 mph. Ceiling 4,000 feet. Range radius 230 miles. Arms: two 12.7mm machine guns.

MI-15: British domestic intelligence agency.

MI-16: British foreign intelligence and espionage.

MIDEASTFOR: Middle East Force.

MiG: Russian-built fighter, many versions, used in many nations around the world.

Mike Boat: Liberty boat off a large ship.

Mike-Mike: Short for mm, millimeter, as 9 mike-mike.

Milstar: Communications satellite for pickup and bouncing from SATCOM and other radio transmitters. Used by SEALs.

Minigun: In choppers. Can fire 2,000 rounds per minute. Gatling gun-type.

Mitrajez M80: Machine gun from Yugoslavia.

MLR: The Main Line of Resistance. That imaginary line in a battle where two forces face each other. Sometimes there are only a few yards or a few miles between them. Usually heavily fortified and manned.

Mocha: Food energy bar SEALs carry in vest pockets.

Mossberg: Pump-action, pistol-grip, 5-round magazine. SEALs use it for close-in work.

Motorola Radio: Personal radio, short range, lip mike, ear-piece, belt pack.

MRE: Meals Ready to Eat. Field rations used by most of U.S. Armed Forces and the SEALs as well. Long-lasting.

MSPF: Maritime Special Purpose Force.

Mugger: MUGR, Miniature Underwater Global locator device. Sends up antenna for pickup on positioning satellites. Works under water or above. Gives location within 10 feet.

Mujahideen: A soldier of Allah in Muslim nations.

NAVAIR: NAVy AIR command.

NAVSPECWARGRUP-ONE: Naval Special Warfare Group One based on Coronado, CA. SEALs are in this command.

NAVSPECWARGRUP-TWO: Naval Special Warfare Group Two based at Little Creek, VA.

NCIS: Naval Criminal Investigative Service. A civilian operation not reporting to any Navy authority to make it more responsible and responsive. Replaces the old NIS, Naval Investigation Service, that did report to the closest admiral.

NEST: Nuclear Energy Search Team. Non-military unit that reports at once to any spill, problem, or Broken Arrow to determine the extent of the radiation problem.

NEWBIE: A new man, officer, or commander of an established military unit.

NKSF: North Korean Special Forces.

NLA: Iranian National Liberation Army. About 4,500 men in South Iraq, helped by Iraq for possible use against Iran.

Nomex: The type of material used for flight suits and hoods.

NPIC: National Photographic Interpretation Center in D.C.

NRO: National Reconnaissance Office. To run and coordinate satellite development and operations for the intelligence community.

NSA: National Security Agency.

NSC: National Security Council. Meets in Situation Room, support facility in the Executive Office Building in D.C. Main security group in the nation.

NSVHURAWN: Iranian Marines.

NUCFLASH: An alert for any nuclear problem.

NVG One Eye: Litton single-eyepiece Night-Vision Goggles. Prevents NVG blindness in both eyes if a flare goes off.

NVGs: Night-Vision Goggles. One eye or two. Give good night vision in the dark with a greenish view.

OAS: Obstacle Avoidance Sonar. Used on many low-flying attack aircraft.

OD: Officer of the Day.

OIC: Officer In Charge.

Oil Tanker: One is: 885 feet long, 140 foot beam, 121,000 tons, 13 cargo tanks that hold 35.8 million gallons of fuel, oil, or gas. 24 in the crew. This is a regular-sized tanker. Not a supertanker.

OOD: Officer Of the Deck.

OP: Out Post. A spot near the front of friendly lines or even beyond them where a man or a unit watch the enemy's movements. Can be manned by an FO from artillery.

Orion P-3: Navy's long-range patrol and antisub aircraft. Some adapted to ELINT roles. Crew of 10. Max speed loaded 473 mph. Ceiling 28,300 feet. Arms: internal weapons bay and 10 external weapons stations for a mix of torpedoes, mines, rockets, and bombs.

Passive Sonar: Listening for engine noise of a ship or sub. It doesn't give away the hunter's presence as an active sonar would.

Pave Low III: A Navy chopper.

PBR: Patrol Boat River. U.S. has many shapes, sizes, and with various types of armament.

PC-170: Patrol Coastal-Class 170-foot SEAL delivery vehicle. Powered by four 3,350 hp diesel engines, beam of 25 feet and draft of 7.8 feet. Top speed 35 knots, range 2,000 nautical miles. Fixed swimmer platform on stern. Crew of 4 officers and 24 EM, carries 8 SEALs.

PD: Point of Departure. A given position on the ground from which a unit or patrol leaves for its mission.

Plank Owners: Original men in the start-up of a new military unit.

Polycarbonate material: Bullet-proof glass.

PRF: People's Revolutionary Front. Fictional group in *NUCFLASH*, a SEAL Team Seven book.

Prowl & Growl: SEAL talk for moving into a combat mission.

Quitting Bell: In BUD/S training. Ring it and you quit the SEAL unit. Helmets of men who quit the class are lined up below the bell in Coronado. (Recently they have stopped ringing the bell. Dropouts simply place their helmet below the bell and go.)

RAF: Red Army Faction. A once-powerful German terrorist group, not so active now.

Remington 200: Sniper Rifle. Not used by SEALs now.

Remington 700: Sniper rifle with Starlight Scope. Can extend night vision to 400 meters.

RIB: Rigid Inflatable Boat. 3 sizes, one 10 meters, 40 knots.

Ring Knocker: An Annapolis graduate with the ring.

RIO: Radar Intercept Officer. The officer who sits in the backseat of an F-14 Tomcat off a carrier. The job: find enemy targets in the air and on the sea.

Roger That: A yes, an affirmative, a go answer to a command or statement.

RPG: Rocket Propelled Grenade. Quick and easy, shoulder-fired. Favorite weapon of terrorists, insurgents.

S & R: Search and Rescue. Usually a helicopter.

SAS: British Special Air Service. Commandos. Special warfare men. Best that Britain has. Works with SEALs.

SATCOM: Satellite-based communications system for instant contact with anyone anywhere in the world. SEALs rely on it.

SAW: Squad's Automatic Weapon. Usually a machine gun or automatic rifle.

SBS: Special Boat Squadron. On-site Navy unit that transports SEALs to many of their missions. Located across the street from the SEALs' Coronado, California, headquarters.

SD3: Sound-suppression system on the H & K MP5 weapon.

SDV: Swimmer Delivery Vehicle. SEALs use a variety of them.

Seahawk SH-60: Navy chopper for ASW and SAR. Top speed 180 knots, ceiling 13,800 feet, range 503 miles, arms: 2 Mark 46 torpedoes.

SEAL Headgear: Boonie hat, wool balaclava, green scarf, watch cap, bandanna roll.

Second in Command: Also 2IC for short in SEAL talk.

SERE: Survival, Evasion, Resistance, and Escape training.

Shipped for Six: Enlisted for six more years in the Navy.

Shit City: Coronado SEALs' name for Norfolk.

Show Colors: In combat put U.S. flag or other identification on back for easy identification by friendly air or ground units.

Sierra Charlie: SEAL talk for everything on schedule.

Simunition: Canadian product for training that uses paint balls instead of lead for bullets.

Sixteen-Man Platoon: Basic SEAL combat force. Up from 14 men a few years ago.

Sked: SEAL talk for schedule.

Sonobuoy: Small underwater device that detects sounds and transmits them by radio to plane or ship.

Space Blanket: Green foil blanket to keep troops warm. Vacuum-packed and folded to a cigarette-sized package.

SPIE: Special Purpose Insertion and Extraction rig. Essentially a long rope dangled from a chopper with hardware on it that is attached to each SEAL's chest right on his lift harness. Set up to lift six or eight men out of harm's way quickly by a chopper.

Sprayers and Prayers: Not the SEAL way. These men spray bullets all over the place hoping for hits. SEALs do more aimed firing for sure kills.

SS-19: Russian ICBM missile.

STABO: Use harness and lines under chopper to get down to the ground.

STAR: Surface To Air Recovery operation.

Starflash Round: Shotgun round that shoots out sparkling fireballs that ricochet wildly around a room, confusing and terrifying the occupants. Non-lethal.

Stasi: Old-time East German secret police.

Stick: British terminology: 2 4-man SAS teams.

Stokes: A kind of Navy stretcher. Open coffin shaped of wire mesh and white canvas for emergency patient transport.

STOL: Short TakeOff and Landing. Aircraft with high-lift wings and vectored-thrust engines to produce extremely short takeoffs and landings.

Sub Gun: Submachine gun, often the suppressed H & K MP5.

Suits: Civilians, usually government officials wearing suits.

Sweat: The more SEALs sweat in peacetime, the less they bleed in war.

Sykes-Fairbairn: A commando fighting knife.

Syrette: Small syringe for field administration often filled with morphine. Can be self-administered.

Tango: SEAL talk for a terrorist.

TDY: Temporary duty assigned outside of normal job designation.

Terr: Another term for terrorist. Shorthand SEAL talk.

Tetrahedral reflectors: Show up on multi-mode radar like tiny suns.

Thermal Imager: Device to detect warmth, as a human body, at night or through light cover.

Thermal Tape: ID for night-vision-goggle user to see. Used on friendlies.

TNAZ: Trinittroaze Tidine. Explosive to replace C-4. 15% stronger than C-4 and 20% lighter.

TO&E: Table showing organization and equipment of a military unit.

Top SEAL Tribute: "You sweet motherfucker, don't you never die!"

Trailing Array: A group of antennas for sonar pickup trailed out of a submarine.

Train: For contact in smoke, no light, fog, etc. Men directly behind each other. Right hand on weapon, left hand on shoulder of man ahead. Squeeze shoulder to signal.

Trident: SEALs' emblem. An eagle with talons clutching a Revolutionary War pistol, and Neptune's trident superimposed on the Navy's traditional anchor.

TRW: A camera's digital record that is sent by SATCOM.

GLOSSARY

291

TT33: Tokarev, a Russian pistol.

UAZ: A Soviet 1-ton truck.

UBA Mark XV: Underwater life support with computer to regulate the rebreather's gas mixture.

UGS: Unmanned Ground Sensors. Can be used to explode booby traps and claymore mines.

UNODIR: Unless otherwise directed. The unit will start the operation unless they are told not to.

VBSS: Orders to "visit, board, search, and seize."

Wadi: A gully or ravine, usually in a desert.

White Shirt: Man responsible for safety on carrier deck as he leads around civilians and personnel unfamiliar with the flight deck.

WIA: Wounded In Action.

WP: White Phosphorus. Can be in a grenade, 40MM round or in a 20MM round. Used as smoke and to start fires.

Zodiac: Also called an IBS, Inflatable Boat Small. 15 × 6 feet, weighs 265 pounds. The "rubber duck" can carry 8 fully equipped SEALs. Can do 18 knots with a range of 65 nautical miles.

Zulu: Means Greenwich Mean Time, GMT. Used in all formal military communications.